"A searingly honest coming-of-age story with a heroine unlike any other I've met in a long time. I read this book through from start to finish in one sitting, simply unable and unwilling to put it down. Here's to another beautiful novel from Donna Everhart."
—Holly Chamberlin, author of *All Our Summers*

"Secrets, lies, peach cobbler, grits, a hot Alabama sun, and a girl named Dixie Dupree who shows courage in the face of betrayal, strength when all falls down around her, and shining hope in the darkness. This is a story you'll read well into the night."
—Cathy Lamb, author of *All About Evie*

"A poignant coming-of-age novel as gritty as red Alabama dirt. Dixie Dupree will stay with you long after you've turned the last page."
—Colleen Faulkner, author of *Our New Normal*

And praise for *The Forgiving Kind*

"Reminiscent of the novels of Kaye Gibbons, Lee Smith and Sandra Dallas, Everhart builds a firm sense of place, portraying the tiredness and hope of a dry Southern summer, and voicing strong Southern women."
—*Booklist*

"Donna Everhart has once again achieved the difficult task of expertly weaving light into a dark story."
—Eldonna Edwards, author of *Clover Blue*

"With a diverse cast and layered themes, *The Forgiving Kind* may be Everhart's best yet."
—*Historical Novels Reviews*

Books by Donna Everhart

THE EDUCATION OF DIXIE DUPREE

THE ROAD TO BITTERSWEET

THE FORGIVING KIND

THE MOONSHINER'S DAUGHTER

THE SAINTS OF SWALLOW HILL

Published by Kensington Publishing Corp.

THE
SAINTS
OF
SWALLOW
HILL

DONNA EVERHART

KENSINGTON
PUBLISHING CORP.

www.kensingtonbooks.com

KENSINGTON BOOKS are published by
Kensington Publishing Corp.
119 West 40th Street
New York, NY 10018

All Kensington titles, imprints, and distributed lines are available at special quantity discounts for bulk purchases for sales promotion, premiums, fund-raising, educational, or institutional use.

This book is a work of fiction. Names, characters, businesses, organizations, places, events, and incidents either are the product of the author's imagination or are used fictitiously. Any resemblance to actual persons, living or dead, events, or locales is entirely coincidental.

To the extent that the image or images on the cover of this book depict a person or persons, such person or persons are merely models, and are not intended to portray any character or characters featured in the book.

Special book excerpts or customized printings can also be created to fit specific needs. For details, write or phone the office of the Kensington Sales Manager: Kensington Publishing Corp., 119 West 40th Street, New York, NY 10018. Attn. Sales Department. Phone: 1-800-221-2647.

The K logo is a trademark of Kensington Publishing Corp.

ISBN-13: 978-1-4967-3333-7 (ebook)

ISBN-13: 978-1-4967-3332-0

First Kensington Trade Paperback Printing: February 2022

10 9 8 7 6 5 4 3 2 1

Printed in the United States of America

This story is dedicated to all the chippers, dippers, and tackers of tin

Acknowledgments

Whenever I sit down and think about my journey to become a writer, I am keenly aware I will never be able to thank every person who has in some way played a part for where I am today. Even while I'd love to do so, it's clear without these particular individuals, writing this recognition page wouldn't be possible at all. With that in mind:

To my editor, John Scognamiglio, I am sincerely grateful for your commitment to my writing, and your unwavering dedication in making sure I am doing my best work.

To my agent, John Talbot, you have always shown nothing but steadfast support, and your enthusiastic encouragement is infectious and sustaining.

To Vida, I can't thank you enough for all you do to promote my brand. You are meticulous in all you do, and I am forever grateful for your expertise.

To Kris, when I see the covers you create for my books, I always say, "*This* is her best yet." You stole the show on this one.

To Carly, your superior guidance through the copyediting process is reassuring, and tells me you care as much about my story as I do.

To the rest of the Kensington team, I value the hard work, dedication to excellence, and the attention to detail each of you exhibits as you manage your individual tasks which either directly or indirectly impact the success of each of my books.

To Lynne Hugo, thank you, thank you, for reading my earliest drafts when this manuscript was filled with what could only be called "ugly" writing. My word, not yours! Your positive encouragement works wonders—look, it's finished!

To my writer friends with NCWN and WFWA, your support means so much. Thank you for being there.

To booksellers and librarians, you stepped up during a very challenging time in our history. Not long after the release of my last book, my events were canceled one after the other due to the pandemic. Despite needing to rethink how to connect readers and writers, with ingenuity, creativity, and a whole lot of daring, new ways were forged to stay connected. I am in awe and want to thank you for blazing these new paths of individual sustainability.

To my readers, you are on the other side of the publishing spectrum. It's you who also enable me to continue to do what I love because of your passion for reading. A special mention to these devoted book advocates who cheer authors on as if their very lives depended on it. To Kristy Barrett, Susan Peterson, Susan Roberts, Dawnny, Denise, Linda Zagon, Nola Nash, and as always, too many others to name, thank you all once again for sharing your passion for reading.

To Jamie Adkins, of The Broad Street Deli & Market, thank you ever so much for your ongoing support, and for giving Dunn residents a convenient place to purchase my books.

And to my family: my son, Justin, who is always so helpful at my events; my daughter, Brooke, whose love of reading, while temporarily sidelined raising my grands (should she speak to Zibby Owens???), continues to be supportive by always listening. And most of all, to my ever supportive husband, who has definitely saved me from one of my plot holes more than once! I love all of you.

Here's to the land of the Long Leaf Pine,
The Summer Land where the sun doth shine;
Where the weak grow strong and the strong grow great—
Here's to "Down Home," the Old North State!

Here's to the land of the cotton blooms white,
Where the scuppernong perfumes the breeze at night,
Where the soft Southern moss and jessamine mate,
'Neath the murmuring pines of the Old North State!

Here's to the land where the galax grows,
Where the rhododendron roseate glows;
Where soars Mount Mitchell's summit great,
In the "Land of the Sky," in the Old North State!

Here's to the land where maidens are fair,
Where friends are the truest, and cold hearts are rarest;
The near land, the dear land, whatever our fate,
The blessed land, the best land, the Old North State!

—Leonora Monteiro Martin, "The Old North State: A Toast"

Part I

Flight

Chapter 1

Del

He'd been working on Moe Sutton's farm down in Clinch County, Georgia, a few weeks when he and three others finished the day's work and he'd let it slip it was his birthday. A newly minted twenty-eight, they started giving him a hard time about not having himself a wife yet. The joking went from questions about his manliness to maybe being a bit too clean. He bathed regular. Them? Only on Saturday nights. He made sure to wash and rinse out the extra shirt and pants he had so he had something clean to put on for the week. Despite themselves, they smelled like they'd not stuck their big toe in bathwater in months. Ripe, fruity scents floated about when they were near and only got worse as temperatures rose during the day. Their own clothes, despite the earnest effort of their wives scrubbing them, were slick with grease and dirt, and decorated with various stains from sweat and spills.

The loudest, Ned Baker, whose face remained bright red even when it was cool, said, "Ain't got no hair on his chest like this here, neither. Women? Shoot, they's partial to a hairy man."

He pulled his shirt aside to reveal a mat of black hair, thick as a boar bristle brush.

He dipped his head toward his house, winked, and said, "She's in there awaiting on me. I'd betcha ten to one."

Scraggly, pint-size Ollie Tuttle grunted in agreement, oily hair hanging in his face.

He said, "It ain't good for one's constitution, being that clean and such. You can give yourself the pneumony."

He sniffed his armpit, grimaced, and bobbed his head in affirmation the odor was as it should be as he bounced baby Jack on his knees and cooed at him.

He concluded, "Smell like a polecat, but I got me a wife, and she give me two sons." He nudged the colored man next to him, while gesturing at Del. "Our new man here, he's right purty, ain't he?"

The colored man, Juniper Jones, had no reaction, but that wasn't unusual. Del got the sense he didn't share his views on white folks and their business. He liked to kid around, and did sometimes, but turned back to serious pretty quick. He was most intent on making sure there was food on his table. Del learned him and his wife, Mercy, had been with Moe Sutton the longest and all told could outwork any of these "young whippersnappers."

Delwood Reese let them have their fun. Inwardly, he smiled at the fact he'd already become pleasantly acquainted with Baker's and Tuttle's wives. Del, as he liked to be called, considered how Juniper's wife, Mercy, kept mostly to herself, although he suspected she had to know there was some hanky-panky going on. He'd always wondered how it might be with a colored woman. Best as he could tell, she was a lot younger than ole Juniper. For all his luck with the opposite sex, he'd yet to have such an encounter, but he dreamed of it. Now, with them other two, it had started off innocent enough. He'd come here after the farm he'd worked at for a couple years failed and the family was forced to move in with relatives somewhere in Virginia. Since the big crash back in '29, farms were going bust all over the countryside with crop prices dropping so it was near about impossible for anyone to make a living, much less pay their bills.

Del had come to Sutton's farm with two dollars, the clothes on his back, a couple cans of Vienna sausages, his rifle, and Melody, the harmonica that had been his granddaddy's. He'd bundled all of it together using his extra pants and shirt, with a stick stuck through the tied knot, a real hobo-looking getup. He didn't need much nohow. He was a man of simple means, always had been. Besides, he was glad, considering the times, he didn't have a family to provide for. Moe Sutton grew acres upon acres of tobacco, alongside vast cornfields. Del had gazed across the fields, saw the sharecropper shacks and the share-cropper wives tending their small kitchen gardens, hanging out the Monday wash, caring for a passel of young'uns running around barefoot, and thought maybe he could stay here awhile. It was peaceful enough, the scenery not so bad. Moe Sutton seemed like he was doing all right despite the country's circumstances. Maybe it would work out fine.

It wasn't long after he'd been hired on, a day or two at the most, Baker's wife, Sarah, smiled kindly at him and invited him to eat after seeing him sitting in the doorway of his little abode, all by his lonesome, puffing a soft sweet tune on Melody. The Bakers were right beside him, each family taking one of the shanty houses set in a row facing the cornfields.

Sarah said, "Come have some supper."

It was the standard poor man's meal—fried potatoes, hot dogs, and biscuits—but they also had some fresh corn and tomatoes. She served the food on mismatched, chipped dishes, and when she set a plate in front of him, she turned it to hide the imperfection. She sure was easy on the eyes. Her fingertips brushed Del's as she passed what was meant to be butter, but they all knew was really lard tinted yellow with salt added. Sarah Baker had a pouty mouth and large breasts that jiggled without the benefit of an undergarment beneath the flour sack material of her homespun dress. He caught her staring at him several times, always dropping her eyes when he glanced her way. The two children, a boy of four, and another baby boy, gawked at him with big blue orbs clear as the summer sky. Del winked, and the older boy giggled.

Next day he'd seen Tuttle's wife, Bertice. She was fine-boned, quite timid in nature. A thin woman with a thin mouth. She carried a baby boy about on her hips while another child, a boy too, clung to her apron.

She poured Tuttle a cup of chicory coffee out on the porch, and as Del made his way by, Tuttle called out, "Come have you a cup, Del."

"Thankee kindly."

He climbed the steps and sat across from the man who constantly held a toothpick in the corner of his mouth and had a tendency to make odd *pt, pt, pt* sounds like he was trying to spit something out. Bertice generally kept her eyes averted, but her reserved nature didn't last long, not when Del began to work his charm, because if there was any woman anywhere within eyesight of him, it was as if he couldn't help himself. He had to know, what was *she* like?

Soon, she was inviting him over as often as Sarah, because, as she put it, "A man ought not have to eat alone."

It went on from there, insignificant, innocent conversations he'd have with one or the other that became more animated, more flirty, and then there came timid touching, progressing to brave banter and greedy grabbing. Del thought of it as a naturally occurring thing, that next step. If they were willing, well, so was he. He never went after them. He eased himself into their lives and let the chips fall where they may. If it happened, it happened. If not, it wasn't of any consequence. More often than not opportunistic moments came, and he snatched them up along with the faithfulness of their husbands. Swift couplings over kitchen tables while the man of the house went to use the privy. The shooing of older kids outside to play, babies nestled in a drawer bed with a sugar tit, chubby little hands waving freely while their mamas hastened to push aside the dishes. There among the scent of ham, biscuits, string beans simmering, sweaty effort lingered on in the crude, dusty shacks outside the cornfields.

Sometimes it would happen behind an outhouse, or by the side of a tobacco barn that faced dense pines, or way, way back in a field of tall, almost to the sky corn, the only witnesses, the sun overhead or the occasional squirrel sitting on a branch. Opportunities arose regular as night turning to day, and he had to be careful one didn't find out about the other. There was danger in it. Excitement. Close calls. They were addicted to him, tender toward him, most important of all, protective of him, swearing everlasting loyalties. They seemed needy for something only he could give, and he was willing.

Baker and Tuttle continued to poke and joke. To hint maybe he was, you know, funny in that kind of way. They'd sometimes seem suspicious when Sarah or Bertice stared at him a mite too long. Del didn't mind the trivial witticisms about his nature. He had it real good here, almost enjoying himself, though he was tired most of the time. Meanwhile, Juniper's wife, Mercy, remained aloof, undiscovered territory, like when he'd venture into a new county and everything was fresh and new to the eye.

One afternoon he was behind one of those tobacco barns with Sarah, and he spotted her, Mercy. There he was, red-faced and perspiring like he was hand-picking corn of a summer day, giving Sarah his all—again—for the third time this week. Sarah couldn't see a thing with her dress flung over her head. Mercy sat tucked away on her small porch, partially hidden under a pink crepe myrtle, looking like she wasn't looking, but maybe she was. She sat there, a bowl in her lap, shelling peas. He kept his gaze on her the entire time, fantasizing, and only paused a second when Sarah's head accidentally banged into the side of the tobacco barn, so wrapped up in the moment was he.

"Ow!" she said. "Slow down!"

Right after she spoke, Mercy went inside and firmly shut the door. Del tilted his head back, stared at the clouds floating by as he finished his mission. Damn, but he was curious about that one.

Then, he met Moe's wife, Myra. Myra was a large woman, almost as tall as Moe. She stood on the back porch of their house, a two-story, columned affair that could easily fit all of their tiny shacks inside of it and then some. Yes, Moe Sutton had done good for himself, considering not only the economic situation, but with respect to his wife. Moe was not a handsome man, but Myra? Myra's hair was the color of a brand-new penny, her skin pink and smooth. Del imagined her like a bowl of peaches and cream, and his typical curiosity went to an even higher peak with regard to her.

He'd come to the big house to work a different field and stood at the bottom of the first step waiting on Moe. Those steps led to the porch, where the fetching vision that was Myra stared down at him as he twirled his straw hat.

"Who're you?" She had a lace hanky and waved it in front of her face in a vain attempt to cool off.

"Name's Del, ma'am."

He caught the scent of her, lilacs and lust.

"You new, ain't you?"

"Yes, ma'am. Been here about a month."

"Doing what?"

"Whatever your husband tells me."

Moe came out, glared at her, and she scooted back inside

and slammed the door shut. Afterward, it seemed to Del she was all over the place. Strolling about the yard as he and the others walked by on their way to a tobacco or cornfield. Pointing out something to be done to one of the help. Glancing his way a little too often. One evening she showed up as he sat on the steps of his shanty and asked his advice about a poorly mule.

He said, "What makes you think I know anything about mules?"

His thinking went in another direction as she twirled a strand of brilliant hair, pondering if what lay under her skirt was the same color. Maybe she could interpret he'd had such thoughts, because he caught the change in her expression, a knowledge she was aware she had an effect on him.

She ignored his question and said, "He's in the barn. Been limping. Won't you look at him?"

He followed her swaying backside, and once in the barn, she bypassed niceties, pleasantries, or anything else considered respectable prior to such a coupling. Moe was off somewhere, she said. Hurry, she said. He had her in the stall beside the perfectly healthy mule. From that moment on, Del was a busy man juggling three women, but it was Myra who was most demanding. On a warm evening she ordered him to meet her in the woods near a distant cornfield. He'd been with her earlier, a hasty encounter by the tomato vines growing behind the ham shed. Wasn't that enough? Could be she was jealous. Maybe she'd seen him with Sarah, because she directed him to go to the same cornfield he'd been the day before with the other woman.

They started like always, quiet, surreptitious. He was about *there*, when out of nowhere Myra caterwauled, loud as a screech owl. Startled, he clapped a hand over her mouth when another, different noise came from behind him. He disengaged from Myra and quickly did up his pants. There was a hush all around, the woods unnaturally quiet, and now, he'd lost his nerve, among other things. Myra huffed and yanked her dress down.

"What's the matter?" she said.

Del moved away from her and saw the source of his unsettled feeling. Moe, that big lug of a man who could eat five chickens in one sitting, scowled at him from a few feet away. Stomping through a row of the corn, shotgun aimed at Del, he looked fit to be tied. Myra bent down to pick a wildflower, acting as if her husband's appearance was as common as a sudden rain shower.

Del raised both his hands, "I was out for a walk, and your missus here joined me, no harm intended, or done."

Myra held the wildflower to her nose, ignoring her husband. Moe abruptly stuck the end of the barrel under her dress and flipped it up, exposing her thighs.

She snatched the material down and yelled, "Moe!"

He yelled back, "Where's your doggone bloomers, Myra? What are you doing out here without no bloomers on?"

Myra said, "It's hot! I'm cooler this way!"

Moe grabbed her elbow and pushed her in the direction he'd come.

He said, "Git on back to the house! Git! I'll tend to you when I get there."

Myra flung the flower on the ground, grumbling as she made her way through the stalks. Moe turned to Del. He stared at him long and hard, and Del had the feeling he was contemplating his next move. He couldn't be certain of what Moe had seen or not, but the other man's countenance suggested it was more than Del wanted. Del started to speak, only Moe turned away and started after Myra.

Over his shoulder, Moe said, "Tomorrow, I want you working the grain bins."

Del rubbed his forehead and worried over the job. He could

set plants, sucker, and hand tobacco, pull corn, but working the grain bins? It was dangerous if you had to go inside them.

He couldn't refuse unless he wanted to lose this job, so he said, "Okay."

Back at his shanty, he filled his wash bowl, splashed his face, neck, and forearms. He rummaged around for what he might eat, only to settle for a can of beans, his appetite gone. He started to brew some coffee, but his last bit was running low and it was hard to come by. Rationing was happening all over, and stores couldn't hardly keep sugar, meat, fish, eggs, cheese, and real coffee on shelves. Nowadays it was the chicory kind. He went on the porch, spooned beans in his mouth, chewed slow, and thought. He could hear the murmur of his neighbors' voices, the clanging of pots, and he caught the smell of something frying. Out of the three women, he wished it had been one of the other husbands who'd caught him. Not Moe Sutton. After he'd eaten, he pulled out Melody and tried tooting out a tune. Even that didn't help his jangly nerves.

The next morning, Del joined a couple new men he'd not met before at the big house. Thomas Wooten, "Woot" for short, introduced himself as Moe Sutton's repairman. Any farm equipment broke down, he was the one to fix it. He bragged about how he kept everything repaired, wheels oiled, sheds restored like new, fences mended, anything to do with wood or engines, he was Moe's man. Hicky Albright rolled his eyes.

He said, "You got it easy. Try working them damn chicken houses. He got near about four hundred birds, and I can't get the smell off'n me."

They stood with Del in Moe's backyard, smoking, flicking ash, getting acquainted. Moe came out the door, biscuit filled with sausage in one hand, cigar in the other.

He pointed at them and said, "Let's go." To Woot and

Hicky, he said, "Y'all shovel." To Del, he said, "You, you get to walk down the grain."

His face, cunning and shrewd, made Del's innards shrivel. Everyone made their way to the bins, shovels and picks over shoulders, the early morning already warm as the rising sun broke over the horizon. Moe had three circular corrugated steel structures about twenty-four feet tall, with the name BUTLER painted in a faded blue near the top. They appeared harmless, but anybody who'd ever done farm work knew they could be a death trap. Del stared at them. Three bins, one for each woman he'd cheated with here. A door located at the bottom would be opened to allow grain to spill out once he'd loosened up the corn. Woot and Hicky went and stood by the door of the first one. A 1928 Chevy truck with a wood bed built on the back sat nearby to shovel corn into once it was free and flowing. Del's job was to go inside and as Moe said, walk it down, which sounded simple but wasn't.

Del picked up a shovel and went to the ladder attached on the side near the door and stared up. He'd farmed in some capacity the past several years. None of it was easy. Most of it was hard. All of it was dangerous, he reckoned, to some degree. This job, though. He'd known a feller who suffocated when he sank in the grain to his chest. It wouldn't necessarily happen to him, it was only a possibility. With this encouraging thought in mind, he gripped the shovel and began ascending the ladder. Moe followed on his heels.

Del said, "When's the last time corn got taken from this bin?"

"A while."

He worried over this. The corn was likely moldy, stuck together. When he got to the top, he had to yank a couple of times to pull the trap door open. He looked inside. The bin was more than half full. By Del's calculation, there was at least a fifteen-foot depth of hardened corn kernels.

Moe, several rungs below him, said, "Git on in there."

"You got a rope, or something I can tie off to the ladder?"

"Ain't got no rope."

"What if I step somewhere and sink, what am I to grab a hold of?"

Moe was direct. "Best start praying, I reckon. Now move."

Del stuck a foot into the hole, searching, and finding the top rung of the ladder inside. He lifted his other leg over and in, and then lowered himself so he stood on the last rung still above the corn. After letting his eyes adjust, he noted the grain around the perimeter was higher, with a gradual slope that dipped in the middle, shaping the corn like a cone. He eased one foot onto the surface, then the other, and sank to his ankles. He gripped the rung, afraid to let go.

Moe's head appeared in the opening above him. "Why're you standing there, get busy."

Del took his hand away from the ladder, carefully prodding at the grain with the tip of the shovel. Nothing drastic happened, so he hobbled to the side of the bin, and began stabbing the end of the shovel into the grain one-handed while keeping his other hand on the wall for balance. Despite the moldiness, it came loose easy enough, and he kept walking in a circle around the edge, poking here and there. Eventually, after nothing happened, he got brave enough to go to toward the middle, and after a while, he'd done all he could. He went back to the ladder, climbed it, and stuck his head through the opening like a gopher coming out of a hole, relishing the warm, fresh air.

He yelled to the other two. "Open the door!"

Hicky gave him a thumbs-up and swung the door open.

They took their pick axes and began chopping at the wall of grain, and Woot yelled, "Here it comes!"

Del descended the outside ladder, relieved. He'd been given a pass for the first woman. By the end of the day, they finished emptying the bin. Two to go. The second day went like the first. Del inside, loosening the grain before helping Woot and Hicky shovel for all they were worth, eager to be done. A second forgiveness for another wrongdoing. Moe hung around watching, smoking one of his fat cigars. Third day, Del climbed the ladder and stared inside like he'd done with the other two, gauging the depth. This bin had more in it, about three-quarters full.

"Last one," he said out loud to nobody.

Moe stalked to the base of the ladder and prodded him with a command: "Quit wasting time!"

Del entered the bin and began like usual, chipping away at moldy, compacted corn, until Moe shouted, "Open the door, let's get this show on the road," and Del froze, mouth open.

Hicky's voice raised in protest. "It ain't safe with him in there, is it?"

Alarmed, Del went to high-stepping it back to the inside ladder quick as he could. His sudden movements caused him to sink, and he fell, becoming more rattled when he couldn't get up right away. He scrambled to his feet somehow and began promising himself, when he got to the ladder, and got out of the bin, he'd tell Moe he'd do anything but this, and if Moe didn't like it, he'd quit. He'd find work, and if he didn't, he'd live off the land. He'd done it before. Ten more steps, and without any warning, what he'd feared happened. The corn suddenly began to collapse around him, and he slid toward the center of the bin, where he was quickly buried to his thighs. His legs felt as if they were encased in cement. He couldn't move them one bit, and he fell forward, grabbing at the grain, which did nothing but cause more to cascade down around him. He straightened up and it was to his waist.

He yelled as loud as he could, "Shut the door, shut the damn door!"

He stared up at the hole he'd climbed through. Empty. He

coughed, wheezed, and choked on the dust created by the moving grain.

He yelled, "Help!" as Moe yelled, "Shovel!"

He sank to his chest, his arms resting on top, futilely clawing at the kernels. It was like treading water; all he was doing was moving them around. The pressure and his descent increased with every exhalation. The corn acted like a vise, clamping down, squeezing tighter for every tiny move he made. The air gave off a distinct musty odor, and the scent made him sick. The corn was restless, relentless, like some freakish living mass that continued to build around him. It had happened so fast, if he became completely buried, how long would it take a six-foot-two-inch man to suffocate? Too long. It was to his neck now. Kernels touched his lips, slid inside his ears. He raised his chin, spit, and gasped. Seconds passed, the pressure on his chest was unyielding. He couldn't inhale deeply anymore and became so light-headed, he saw stars like he'd hit his head. With his face tipped up, his breathing grew shallow, and he focused on the opening, that small square of blue sky, willing someone, anyone, to appear. Sweat and tears blurred his sight.

He wasn't ready to die.

Chapter 2

Rae Lynn

Rae Lynn Cobb couldn't help but notice the first digit missing on the pointer finger of her right hand. She studied it as she waited for Billy Doyle to push a Blue Whistler filled with pine gum up the crudely made ramp and into the wagon. Warren, her husband of seven years, stood in the back, urging him to go slow and easy. At twenty-five, Rae Lynn was sure she had more scars and marks on her body than someone who lived to a hundred. At least Warren was decent and kind, if a bit clumsy and careless. At least he'd seen fit to keep a business going while others struggled during these hard economic times. When Billy showed up, Rae Lynn figured the Doyles must be pretty bad off.

It was April 1932, three years since the stock market crash, three years of nothing but bad news in the papers, yet they'd been able to make a bit of money selling pine gum. So what if she got hurt now and again? It wasn't like he did them things on purpose, not like when she'd been at the Magnolia Orphanage, where those in charge had a propensity for pinching the soft flesh of upper arms, leaving grape-size bruises if gum. Warren, he certainly was set in his ways. When a man died after a tree fell on him, the same tree Warren had been cutting a box into the day before, Rae Lynn suspected it was the final straw. The flow of workers dried up like an old pine that's done give out of sap.

She didn't want to think about how she'd lost part of her own finger, but her mind took her back to that day anyway. They'd been married only a week. She hadn't yet learned how treacherous it was working alongside Warren, but her first lesson was only seconds away. He had a propensity for not paying attention at the most critical times. Prone to being a bit too fast, a bit careless. That day, he'd said, "Hey, shug, come over here and take ahold a this here for me."

He handed her a sign with COBB TURPENTINE FARM painted on it. She'd been smiling and he'd been smiling, excited at the prospects of this new undertaking after he'd finagled a deal with someone who'd buy gum from him. Warren had flipped his box ax around to use the blunt end like a hammer. She held the sign so he could nail it to the pine tree, and next thing she knew, he'd whacked the end of her forefinger. She yelled, and he promptly dropped the ax, which landed on her foot. Both hurt, but it was the sight of her fingertip that made her shut her eyes, feel sick to her stomach. It had been hit hard enough, it spread out like a paddle. The entire end of her finger filled with blood, the nail bed turning purple. She sank to the ground, cradling her hand. Warren had paced around her, cussing himself for being a clumsy nitwit.

After a minute, when the sharpness of pain had dulled a bit, she said, "Warren, it ain't nothing, don't worry, it'll be fine."

She got up, went inside, used some of their endless supply of turpentine as a disinfectant, and wrapped it in a soft strip of cloth from an old apron. She worked the rest of the day, but by nightfall, it hurt in a way that deprived her of sleep. Every heartbeat came out through the end of her finger. It felt enormous. It was odd, she'd thought, how big the pain, for such a small injury. The end felt sort of mushy. She believed he'd crushed the bone. After two days, she hadn't been able to stand the throbbing anymore. The entire finger was an off color and swollen.

Warren said, "Look a here, I got just the fix for it."

She sat at the kitchen table watching as he took a coat hanger, straightened out the curved end, and held it over the wick of an oil lamp.

When the end glowed orange, he'd said, "Gimme your finger."

Dubious about his "fix," she'd been hesitant, but he'd promised her it would work.

He'd said, "I seen my own Daddy do this for hisself."

Reluctant, she gave him her hand, and he pressed the glowing tip onto the center of the blackened nail. A tiny puff of white smoke appeared and in seconds, a hole was burned through to the nail bed.

He'd squeezed it, and she'd yelled, "Ow!" as blood shot out, right across the table. To her amazement, the pressure was relieved, the throbbing less intense.

He'd said, "See?"

She had to agree, it did feel some better. She'd kept it wrapped and was sure it would heal now. But no, after a couple of weeks, it took to smelling bad. The pain came back, worse than before. The skin blackened, and she felt sickly with the fever.

Warren had sent for Doc Perdue, who took one look and said, "You got the gangrene."

Rae Lynn had said, "What can you do?"

"Got to take it off at the first joint, maybe a touch more."

Mouth open, she'd looked over to Warren, his hangdog expression hard to read. Doc Perdue had pulled a metal syringe

out of his black leather bag and injected her finger with something to numb it. From that moment on, she'd not been able
to watch, but she heard, smelled, felt what was happening because the numbing solution didn't work completely. Pressing
her lips together at the snipping sound, her stomach protested
again, especially after the few seconds of sawing. She felt the
tug and pull as he stitched her finger, and started to feel some
better. After it was over, her finger resembled the end of a pillow, and she hadn't been able to quit looking at it.

Like now.

Billy continued to shove and push, working hard, but the
barrel was winning due to gravity, and the fact it was so heavy.
Rae Lynn was certain she'd seen ten-year-old boys bigger than
him, and it was likely the barrel weighed more than he did.
Billy inched it along, rolling it up the two crudely made slats,
and the farther he went, the more they bent. The one slat on
the left especially looked like it was about to give. The boards
had been filled with termites, and she'd told Warren so.

"Them ain't gonna last, especially that one, it's riddled with
holes. Look a there."

Warren had considered the plank before waving his hands
through the air, swatting her words away. *Like they's gnats
bothering him,* she thought. Billy's shirt hung off his bony
frame, soaked through, and here it was, not yet going on nine
o'clock. He wore a straw hat shoved back on his head, and a
bit of white-blond hair stood out against his reddened face.
All of twenty, wiry and eager, he'd started off strong but appeared like he was already on the verge of petering out.

He gasped and swore, "Dammit all!"

Warren stood in the back of the wagon and encouraged
him. "Doing fine, son."

Billy hadn't made much progress. His feet pointed out-
ward, the tips of his shoes so worn they'd lost their stitching

and hung open. She could see holes in his socks, pink toes. Like a baby's. God bless him. He needed somebody to mend them. Maybe she could do that for him, if he stuck around.

Warren said, "Ain't but a couple a feet and you're home free."

Not quite, Rae Lynn thought. They had lots more barrels to load. The crack of splintering wood was quick, the sound sharp as gunfire. Billy attempted to keep the barrel from rolling back on him, a valiant effort, except he listed to one side, quivering against the weight. Warren's hopeful face collapsed in dismay. Billy, face purple with effort, gave a strangled groan. He was clearly disadvantaged. The barrel landed on his foot and his howl echoed through the tops of the pines and into the deepest part of the woods. A crow flew away, cawing "uh-uh, uh-uh" across a pewter-colored sky. Warren jumped off the back of the wagon, and Rae Lynn rushed forward.

Billy screamed, "Lordamighty!"

His body went one way, then the other in a twisty move like he wanted to yank free but didn't have the nerve.

Warren started to roll the barrel off, and Billy hollered, "No!"

Warren stopped, unsure of what to do.

Rae Lynn stood beside Billy and said, "We got to move it. Can't see what's happened, how bad it is and all."

Warren paced, and swore. "I will be damned."

Billy gasped, hands at his head, crushing his hat.

He said, "How bad? It's bad!"

Rae Lynn said, "Well. You wanting it to stay there?"

Billy panted, puffed. "I reckon not!"

The last word was like a screech. Rae Lynn left Billy's side and dashed into their house. The interior was dim after being out in the bright sun, but she knew what she was after, and she went right over to the huge cast-iron sink where they had a pump for water and got the bottle of whisky off the small shelf over it. She rushed back outside, screen door banging behind her, and gave the bottle to Billy. He snatched it, took a swig, then another. Warren motioned at her, and she went to his side to help. Billy had taken to moaning.

"Look here, son. Now. We're gonna move this off'n your foot."

Billy's face was pasty white.

Rae Lynn said, "Ready?"

Billy took another slurp, swallowed, and said, "Go."

Warren and Rae Lynn shoved quick and hard, and as the barrel rolled away, Rae Lynn winced as Billy let off another howl before staring bug-eyed at his foot, as if expecting to see a mangled mess.

Finally, he said, "It don't look so bad, but it hurts like a sonofabitch."

He started to untie his boot, but when he went to pull it off, he stopped. He straightened back up and looked to Rae Lynn.

"I cain't," he whispered.

Rae Lynn said, "Want me to?"

Billy swore again, then said, "I'm 'bout to puke."

Instead of trying to pull his boot off, Rae Lynn lifted the flap of leather at the toe. The once-pink toes were blue, and there was some blood. Like her finger, she was almost certain Billy's foot was crushed. She raised her eyes, her green meeting his blue.

She wrinkled her forehead, and said, "Them toes, maybe higher too, it's all been pinched but good."

Her calmness and choice of words didn't match the tragic expression on her face. Billy's awareness of his predicament sunk in.

He said, "How in hell am I gonna work with a busted-up foot? They said I ought not come here. Now look what's happened."

Warren got offended. "Didn't nobody twist your arm. And who said that anyway?"

Billy tried to test his foot to see if it could bear his weight.

Rae Lynn put her hand on his arm to help, but he pulled away and said, "Keep your damn hands off'n me." He turned to Warren, "Everyone says it."

Rae Lynn was offended now. "Fine. Go on then."

Billy limped about, searching until he found a stick nearby to help him balance and walk. He managed, hobbling badly, though, and there he went, back where he came from. She turned to Warren with a disbelieving look.

He threw up his hands. "He didn't know what he was doing anyway."

"We got to have help, Warren. We can't do this all on our own. Won't you send Eugene a letter, ask him to come?"

Incredulous, Warren reared his head back and said, "Eugene? Naw. He's busy running that law practice a his. If he ain't been home in all this time, why you think he'd come now?"

"Because he's your son?"

Warren gave a contemptuous snort. "He always was a mama's boy, and after she died, he said he won't never coming back, not unless there was something in it for him."

Within a month Warren's words would come back on him, ringing with truth.

Chapter 3

Del

Del didn't know Moe climbed the ladder and stared into the grain bin where nothing but corn could be seen. He couldn't have seen him if he wanted. The kernels covered him completely, pressing his flesh from all directions like he'd been locked down by some strange force. He tried to gulp air, but the rise and fall of his chest was shallow. He choked, strained futilely, exhaled, and finally was unable to draw in any air. His mind sent his body warnings, and his heart shuddered, in shock. He was vertically entrapped four feet below fifteen feet of grain.

Moe yelled to the other men. "Can't see nothing. He's gone under. Probly dead."

Del heard those words, and then he could see what was happening too. How Moe descended the ladder. How Hicky and Woot dug furiously, tossing corn by the shovelful over their shoulders. He no longer felt crushing pain in his chest. He watched a third man run across the field next to the bin and open a door on the other side. He grabbed a shovel and began stabbing at the wall of corn. Del didn't know how this was happening, how he was able to see all of this. He must be dreaming. Moe stood off a ways and lit a cigar. The compacted corn began to flow out of both doors freely, while the men worked furiously to keep the openings clear. Unexpectedly he watched himself tumble out on the side where Hicky and Woot worked, his body limp, inert, a crumbled form of humanity, coated in dust.

Hicky flipped him over and swiped out his mouth. He beat on his chest, yelling at him, "Hey! Hey!"

Moe said, "He's dead, ain't he."

The man sounded like he wanted it so. But wait. Dead? He wasn't dead, was he? He could see everything, yet he felt nothing. He heard the distant call of Pap's voice, years gone now, saying his name. How was this possible? Without warning, he was filled with a strong urge to separate himself from this experience, refusing to accept this outcome, his will so compelling it swept over him like the grain, and then it was corn all around him again. He felt himself moving, sliding, the sensation like falling backward. Crushing pain came, blossomed, and something akin to a lightning strike blinded his view of what he'd seen.

Del gagged, choked, and flopped onto his belly. He threw up. When he finally opened his eyes, he saw brilliant green stripes. He shut them, opened them again, and blades of grass came into focus. He rolled over and stared into the troubled faces of Woot and Hicky, gaping at him in openmouthed surprise. He felt like he'd been beaten, his body aching all over.

Hicky said, "Hey. Kin you hear me?"

Moe still puffing his cigar, said, "Thought sure you was a goner."

Del felt certain he was disappointed. He coughed some more, trying to rid himself of what he'd breathed in. He sat up, noticed his arms covered with the shapes of kernels dimpling the skin. He lifted his shirt, and his chest was worse, with bruising along his ribs. His legs felt numb, so he flexed them and rotated his feet on his ankles. They felt swollen, and looked it. He was wrung out, like he'd been working all day.

Woot said, "I ain't ever known nobody who come out of one a them after being buried and live to tell it."

Hicky said, "I ain't either. This here's one lucky son of a gun. God done laid His very hand on him."

Del hacked up phlegm, spit it out, and whispered, "Water."

Woot got a canvas bag from the truck and gave it to Del, who tipped it up, gulped it down.

Del wiped his mouth and said, "Where's the other guy?"

Woot and Hicky gave each other a look and said, "Who? Tyndall?"

Del said, "Don't know his name. There was a man shoveling. On the other side."

Moe said, "How you know that?"

"I seen him."

The three men digested this, then Hicky said, "When you come out a the bin, he went on back to work. But hell, that was ten minutes ago. You was still out."

Nobody spoke for a few seconds. Del was remembering what he'd seen. It was etched in his mind the way the grain pitted his skin. Those marks would fade, but he couldn't forget what happened. It was too bizarre. The other men watched him, their expressions wary.

Del stared at Moe and said, "You had'em open the door."

Moe said, "Hell, what do you know about any of it?"

"Hicky here, he was banging on my chest."

Woot said, "He's talking crazy now. How's he know that?"

Hicky said, "Hell if I know."

Even Moe got to acting a touch nervous. The other two men backed away, retrieved their shovels, appeared ready to get back to work again, or maybe they only wanted to get

away from him. Del continued to sit on the ground, thinking about what had transpired. Moe finished his cigar and
dropped it in the dirt.

He apparently had recovered from his initial surprise, and
said, "Well? You gonna sit there all day or what? I ain't paying
you for that."

Del stood, wobbly kneed, but he was upright, and he was
alive.

He said, "Well. Reckon I'll get back to it. Grain's loose
now."

He slapped his hat against his thighs to knock off the dust
and plopped it on his head. He winked at Woot and Hicky,
who were still spooked, their wide-eyed expressions following him as he limped over to the pile of corn, his feet still feeling half numb and swollen. He went in search of the shovel
he'd had. He found it buried in the middle, close to where the
bin spit him out. He began to shovel corn again, and when
Moe lumbered off, he stopped long enough to watch him go.
He'd bet a dollar the man would come up with something
else. Woot started asking him questions again.

Woot said, "Tell me again, what you seen exactly?"

Del leaned on his shovel and closed his eyes.

He said, "I saw the other man come running up, open the
door on the opposite side, and he started shoveling corn. He
had on a blue shirt."

Hicky chimed in and said, "And you seen us too?"

Del concentrated on the images in his head. The incident
had all the makings of a dream about to slip away.

"Yes."

Hicky said, "Don't see how it's possible. You was buried,
man!"

Woot said, "What else?"

Del said, "Moe didn't do nothing except puff on his cigar.

Hicky, you said, 'Hey! Hey, man!' just like what you said after I come to. And you was beating on my chest."

Woot said, "Huh."

Hicky said, "Dang. I ain't ever heard a such."

Woot said, "My granny said her uncle got sick, and he died. Then, law, she said he come to right 'fore they was ready to start laying him out. Told everybody he'd seen family members who'd passed years before standing right next to his bed."

The men shoveled a while without talking and when the silence broke again, it was about something new, not about Del.

Woot caught his interest when he said, "My brother wrote me, said there's work to be had in some a them turpentine camps. Mentioned one called Swallow Hill somewheres east of Valdosta."

Hicky said, "Them camps is all over here and Floridy. Hoowee. Now that's a rough life."

"Can't be no worse'n working for Moe, ain't it right, Del?"

Del said, "Wonder if they're hiring?"

Woot said, "Could be. You done turpentine work, have you?"

Del had. Actually, his family had been turpentiners starting with his granddaddy, then his pap.

He said, "Some," then he got quiet.

He felt dizzy, sort a strange, and his mind was on Moe. He didn't trust the man not to try again. By the end of the day, the last bin was emptied, and Moe had returned, gnawing on a fried pork chop.

He inspected what had been done, pointed at Del, and said, "Tomorrow, we're gonna bring in some field corn. I want you back inside these bins here, ever one of'em, and make sure they's ready. Clean'em out good, then we fill'em again. Maybe this'll be your reg'lar job. What'choo think about that?"

Del made a gesture like he didn't care.

Moe said, "All right. Quitting time."

Del went back to his shack and laid on the bed knowing he wouldn't ever go back inside a bin. He didn't like to hightail it and run. It made him look bad, like he was weak, scared, or plain worthless. These days, a man's name and his reputation were all one had, and the most one could hope to keep, but he determined the best thing for him to do would be to slip away in the dark. Who cared what Moe Sutton or any of the rest thought of him?

Night came, a black blanket pulled up and over the landscape, and that's when he gathered what little he had. The extra pants and shirt. He didn't have any more beans or Vienna sausages, but he had leftover corn bread. He wrapped it in some brown paper he had and tucked it in a tin bucket he'd saved from one of the farms he'd been on. He looped the handle of the bucket through his belt so he wouldn't have to carry it while wishing he had a water bag, like Woot's, but wishing got him nothing. He patted his shirt pocket, made sure he had Melody, grabbed his shotgun from over the door, and worked his arm through the leather sling.

He stepped outside, silent as the sundown, and eased the door shut. To his left was Baker's shack and beyond it, Tuttle's. Across the way was the Joneses. Nothing to hold him here, not really. These people had been nice and all, but he was ready to move on. He stood on his porch, letting his eyes adjust to a moonlit path, the pale, cream-colored sandy soil showing him the way, to what, he wasn't sure. He only knew if he stayed, there'd be a reckoning. He set off, eyes occasionally on the night sky speckled with stars, a honey-colored moon hung low.

A couple days into his wanderings he was hot, thirsty, and a bit hungry. He spotted a small store and went inside to find a young woman behind the counter, fanning her face with a section of the daily paper. He picked up a package of Nabs, and over at the vending machine in the corner, he put in a nickel and pulled out a cold RC Cola. After popping off the top, he went to the counter to pay for his crackers. She was a real looker. She leaned forward, her arms bolstering her breasts so they rose above the top of her flowered dress, eyes slowly roving over him. Confident too, he'd give her that.

She said, "Ain't seen you round here before."

"I'm only passing through."

Sweet talcum powder mixed with a hint of sweat wafted into his nose. Her attractiveness and her apparent interest failed to produce his usual reaction. She blinked and raised an eyebrow.

He dropped his gaze and said, "How much?"

She appeared offended. "Hey. I ain't that kind of girl."

He pointed at the Nabs. "For them."

Her cheeks flushed pink. Embarrassment and finally irritation made her face an open map for him to read.

Annoyed, she frowned and said, "Nickel."

He set the coin on the counter, spun on his heels, and headed for the door.

She called after him, "You ain't all that good looking."

He stopped and faced her again. "I ain't? Well, darn."

She relaxed, and a hint of a smile curved her mouth. "You're *real* good looking is what I mean."

Why not. He flipped the sign to CLOSED, strolled around the back of the counter, pulled her close, and slid his hand under her dress.

She gasped, groaned, and said, "I don't know. My daddy might come back any second now."

"Where is he?"

"At the house eating dinner."

He leaned into her, his hand still under her dress, but he was having trouble. What normally happened, wasn't.

He paused, and she said, "What'sa matter?"

He backed away and said, "I can't. Sorry."

Smoothing her dress down, she appeared as embarrassed over the failed encounter as he was. Neither looked at the other as he rushed out the door. Mystified, he cogitated on the incident the rest of the day. Come dusk, he set up camp for the night, and in the dim glow of his dying campfire, he played a couple of melancholy tunes on Melody. After a while, curiosity got the better of him, and he set the harmonica aside. He needed sleep, except he was still perturbed. Tentatively, almost embarrassed-like, he reached down to himself and let his mind wander to the times with Sarah, Bertice, and Myra, while trying to forget what happened with that pretty gal at the store. He concentrated on imagery, dresses flipped over heads, round backsides, moans and groans. He dwelled on Bertice's skills at taking him in her mouth. And, Myra. Wild, reckless Myra, the most enticing one of all. Despite his imaginings, the results were less than encouraging, and he stopped. What the hell was wrong with him? Had the wrongdoings of his past caught up to him by way of Moe Sutton and a god-forsaken grain bin?

He continued wandering about Clinch County, and oftentimes would recount his astounding story to various individuals he met, and they would listen, shake their heads, and agree on the dangers of working grain bins. All went along fine until he started describing how he'd *seen* himself lying on the ground. He tried to explain it, and the best he could do was to say he'd been floating in the air above himself watching everything as it unfolded. He'd tell how he'd seen a third feller helping out, and how the others confirmed him being there, though the man was gone long before Del came to. These individuals got a worried look in their eyes, a look that said they deemed him tetched in the head, maybe even downright crazy.

They would cut him short, and say things like, "Oh! You

was surely dreaming," or, "Was you drinking when it happened?"

With elbow jabs and dubious expressions, they'd change the subject. Finally, he quit talking about it. He continued to drift as if lost. He spent more time with birds, squirrels, rabbits, and frogs than he did with people. His beard grew out and so did his hair. He didn't have the extra pants or shirt anymore, because his others got wet one time too many and started to fall apart, so he had to put them on and burn the old. His constant and only companion was Melody, but even attempting to brighten his mood by playing soon fell flat. Del finally concluded there was nothing much forthcoming from the woods of South Georgia. He was going to make himself crazy, thinking and thinking on that wondrous, yet terrible incident. And he wasn't doing himself any favors as he was about out of money. It was time to try to put the past behind him and find a job again. He set out walking. After a while he came to a small town called Argyle.

At the General Mercantile, he splurged on crackers and hoop cheese while asking the man behind the counter, "Is there a train to Valdosta?"

The store owner, with three-day-old whiskers and strangely white teeth, said, "Sure. They got trains running over to Valdosta from Fargo. If you can get to the station down there, look for the GS&F symbol. That's the one you want, the Georgia Southern and Florida Railway. Also called the Suwannee River Route."

"Fargo, huh. That's a ways from here."

Another man came in to pay for gas and upon hearing the last part of the conversation, he pointed at his truck loaded with cantaloupe in the back, and said, "I'm heading to Fargo. You're welcome to ride with me."

Del stuck out his hand, and the man shook it.

"Sure do 'preciate it."

"T'ain't nothing."

After a month of sleeping on the ground, drinking out of creeks, and having little to eat, he'd made up his mind. He hadn't known he was heading that way until he got to thinking on what Woot said about that turpentine camp. He followed the stranger out, and when they got to the truck, the man cut open a cantaloupe and handed him a slice to eat while he rode.

Del said, "I'm obliged to you," and settled onto the front seat to enjoy both the ride and the fruit.

The sweet, fragrant scent filtered into the cab, reminiscent of summer days at home on the back porch, splitting open ripe melons with his sister and gorging themselves until they could eat no more.

His ride dropped him at the station, where he checked the schedule, then took himself a ways down the track. It was late in the day and there wouldn't be another train until morning. He rested against a large pine, too tired to coax any tunes out of Melody. Cricket frogs began to burp out their own evening song, and next thing he knew, he was waking up and surprised to see he'd slept through the night. He drank from a nearby stream, cupping his hand down into the coolness. He splashed water over his head and face, ate a few crackers with cheese, before making a few adjustments to what he carried. He moved closer to the tracks to wait. He was nervous about jumping the train, and his small breakfast rolled about in his stomach.

Midmorning came a low whistle and rumbling along the rails. He put his hand down on the metal and felt it vibrating beneath his palm. He lowered his hat on his forehead to shade his eyes, and a few minutes later, it appeared like some giant hulking monster, a funnel of smoke rolling over the top of it. His mouth went dry as he got himself ready, moving to a spot closer to the tracks, keeping low and out of sight. He believed it was going slow enough. The engine came and went. He remained hunkered down, hidden behind the scrub brush. There were a few cars loaded with coal, then the boxcars started rolling by. He picked one, hesitated, and it was too late.

He talked to himself. "Come on, fool. You ain't got but so many chances."

A green car caught his eye. He decided green was his lucky color and began running, his gear bumping and banging against his backside and hip. He found it harder than he thought, so he ran faster. As he reached for the handle to haul himself up, he locked eyes with a skinny man missing a few teeth who grinned down at him. He faltered, tripped, and tumbled over the rocks and into briars.

"Dammit!"

The toothless man's chortle blended in with the clacking along the metal rails. He stood, swiped the blood off his scratched arms, and spotted a blue car. Blue. Blue could be the lucky one. He'd learned on his first try and started running before it got to him, his sprint lively and quick. This time he grabbed the handle, and this time a pair of hands helped haul him in. His boots skimmed the rocks only for a split second, and then he was unceremoniously dropped like a fish in the bottom of a boat. He got to his feet, winded, but relieved. He adjusted his stance to the rocking motion as he looked at the men who helped him. One had to be in his sixties, silver haired, and the other was about his age.

"First-timer, I 'spect," said the older man before he shuffled off to a corner.

The younger one had an aloof way about him, only nodding once before he went to the opposite side and sat in the shadows.

Del said, "Thanks," and kept himself planted by the open door of the boxcar, swaying to the rhythm, edgy and ill at ease.

There were others aside from the two who helped him, but they were as withdrawn as the rest. This was the most humanity he'd been around in a while. One man glanced at him once too often and kept a hand in a pocket, maybe to send a message to Del he might have a pistol or some sort of weapon. About two hours later, the train slowed and everyone started moving toward the opening, ready to bail out. Del felt a bit hemmed in and didn't much like it.

The old man came forward again, and Del said, "This Valdosta?"

"Close enough."

Del saw his chance, right after a narrow creek where the wiregrass was thick and soft. He didn't bother with niceties. He simply jumped and let his legs collapse as soon as he hit the ground, and he went into a roll. Seconds later, one or two others did the same, took a leap and tumbled out. The train trundled around a curve, heads still hanging out of the openings, and then it was gone. Del stood, brushed off his clothes, adjusted his gear, and set off in the same direction as the train. He stayed mostly on the tracks but sometimes veered off for the coolness under the trees. He had no idea where the others went, and didn't care. After a while, the tracks crossed a dirt road, where he spotted a poorly looking sign, hung crooked. It said VALDOSTA, with an arrow pointing down the road. Encouraged, he walked toward it and began passing fallow fields, and occasionally a farm like Moe Sutton's, where maybe somebody had seen to save for hard times so they could keep going. He thought of stopping, asking for a job at one of the big ones, except he wanted to do something different, and turpentining was really what he knew.

He'd gone only a little ways when behind him came the

squeak of wagon wheels and the familiar *clop, clop* of an animal's hooves. He turned and laid eyes on a man and three kids, all tow-headed boys, riding in a dilapidated wagon pulled by what had to be the ugliest mule Del had ever seen.

The man said, "Need'n you a ride somewheres?"

Del said, "I'm heading for that turpentine camp called Swallow Hill. You heard of it?"

The man said, "Sure. Who ain't? I can take you to the store a couple miles or so down this a way. You won't have far to go after that. I'd take you all the way, but it's due west and I ain't going that direction."

Del nodded and hopped onto the back end of the wagon.

He said, "Fine by me."

The boys turned around to stare at him.

The man talked over his shoulder and said, "Name's Tom. These here are my boys, Tom Jr., Samuel, and the youngest one is Tucker, named after my maw's side of the family."

Del raised a hand in a half wave to the boys and got no reaction. They remained silent as clouds passing overhead. Probably taught to be seen, not heard, like him.

He said, "Name's Del Reese. Pleased to make y'all's acquaintance."

He turned back around and faced the direction from which he'd come, watching as the red dirt rolled by under his booted feet, thinking about how lucky a man was to have sons.

Chapter 4

Rae Lynn

It had been raining almost nonstop since the accident with Billy Doyle. The steady downpour from heavy-bottomed clouds to the west created a dreary view out the kitchen window. Rae Lynn and Warren sat holed up in the house, unable to work the crop of trees they'd started with Billy. Butch Crandall, a friend of Warren's, had stopped by and sat at their table drinking sweet tea, waiting on the rain to let up. He always broke the monotony when he came for a visit and today, what he had to say was particularly interesting, at least to Rae Lynn. He was going on and on about the turpentine work going on in Georgia.

Butch said, "They got several camps down there. S'what I heard 'cording to Lenny Crawford. Said he's going to go to work at one of'em. So many's done folded in on their farms and ain't hardly no mill jobs to be had. Said he can't make him a living, but he 'spects he can do something, despite the fact he's one handed."

Warren said nothing. Lenny had broken his arm real bad while working at Cobb Turpentine Farm and because he hadn't been able to afford the doctor, it hadn't healed properly.

Butch went on. "Heard tell they rent out fifty-cent, one-dollar, and two-dollar shacks. Wonder what the difference is?"

Warren said, "Not much, though some might have an extra room, or maybe they's a tad bigger inside."

Butch said, "Shoot. Got their own store, juke joint, schoolin' for the young'uns, churches, just about anything you need'n is right there, and get this. The whole entire shebang can pack up and move when they's done working a particular area."

Warren said, "I been in them camps before. It's some rough living now, mind you. Besides, we doing all right right here, ain't we, shug?"

He grabbed Rae Lynn's hand and squeezed. Rae Lynn didn't answer; she was listening to Butch, an idea forming.

Warren jiggled her hand, waiting on her to agree, but what she did was to turn to him and say, "What if we went there to work for a while, Warren?"

Warren dropped her hand and said, "Why would we want to leave here when we got this house? And we got enough work for everyone in the county who wants a job."

Exactly, Rae Lynn thought, *and only me and you to do it.* She pushed her hair back off her forehead, the damp air making it unruly. Butch sat back, ogling her.

He said, "Rae Lynn, I ever tell you what a purty sight you are?"

Rae Lynn said, "Every time you come over, Butch."

Butch turned to Warren, "Ain't she, though?"

Warren, still put off by her suggestion, picked at a thread on his shirt.

Rae Lynn said, "What you want'n, Butch? A piece of that pie I made?"

He said, "A piece'll do."

He sniggered at his little joke, and when Rae Lynn shot a look at Warren, he now became preoccupied with adjusting the straps to his overalls. She got up to serve Butch his pie.

Butch was all right, but he had ways that annoyed her, like staring at her a tad too long while Warren acted like a knot on a log over his obviously rude remarks.

Butch switched to a different subject, to her relief, turning his attention back to Warren.

"How's ole Eugene doing with that law practice a his in South Carliny?"

"All right, I reckon," and the conversation went on from there.

When Butch was done eating, he rose from the chair and told them he had to go see about some hogs. The rain came down harder after he left, and the wind picked up. The trees bent this way and that, catching Rae Lynn's eye as she stirred a pot of stewed okra, the steam flushing her face pink. She was checking on the biscuits in the oven when a loud bang and then part of a limb shot through the roof almost over her head, startling her. Water immediately began dripping inside, hitting the hot stove and making it sizzle.

"Warren!"

He was right behind her, and said, "I will be damned. I should a cut some a them branches over this house like I said. I was afraid this might happen one a these days, what with that piece a tin missing up there."

The hissing grew louder as the water continued to hit the stove. Rae Lynn grabbed a bucket filled with wood near the stove, dumped the wood out, and stuck it under the leak. Warren stared at the ceiling.

He said, "I got to get that limb off the roof, or it's gonna make it worse."

"You can't do nothing in this downpour, Warren. The food's done, anyway. Come on and eat. Wait till it stops raining at least."

"I got a canvas piece with some pitch on it; it'll hold till I can fix it proper. All I gotta do is move the limb and cover the hole."

"It ain't no sense in doing it this minute!" Rae Lynn's temper rose as he ignored her.

He said, "I need you to hold the ladder. Get your coat on. Won't take long."

She huffed in frustration, and she decided then and there to put her foot down. To say something.

"No, it's a bad idea. You might get hurt. Or me."

He stared at her in surprise. "You ain't gonna help me?"

She folded her arms. "It can *wait*, Warren."

He flapped a hand at her and went outside. She watched as he ran to the small barn behind the house, where they kept their john mule, Dewey. A few minutes later, he came out with a ladder, the pitch bucket covered with a cloth, and the canvas plopped over his head. She went onto the porch, saw him lean the ladder against the side of the house near the midsection where the chimney rose. He climbed one-handed, carrying the pitch bucket and was almost at the top rung when she yelled at him, her voice barely rising above the clap of thunder.

"I wished you'd wait!"

Warren yelled back, "I don't want the damn house full of water. Do you?"

Rae Lynn fumed at his stubbornness as the storm grew worse. The split rail fencing, pines, and outhouse were shrouded in mist as the temperature dropped from the heat earlier in the day, and Rae Lynn actually shivered. Back inside, she dumped the okra and tomatoes into a bowl, not caring she spilled some. She set the biscuits on the table while listening to Warren thumping about overhead. The limb remained partially through the roof, moving now and then like he was tugging on it. She tried not to envision his attempts to free it while standing on a slick roof.

She forced her attention back to setting the table, placing a crock of butter beside the biscuits. More scraping noises came and she grabbed a rag to mop up the puddle forming on the floorboards where rainwater drizzled in. The limb still poked through.

She was still on her hands and knees dabbing at another puddle when she heard, "Oh hell!" and an ominous skidding noise followed by a heavy thud.

She whispered, "Dear God," jumped to her feet, and ran outside.

Warren lay facedown, draped over the wooden flower box he'd built for her five summers ago. The ladder was on the ground. Before she could get to him, he rolled over onto his back. It was the way he looked, the sound coming from him that stopped her. Grimacing and clenching his teeth, a guttural sound rose from him, but he cut it short when he saw her. He raised his arm, and she went to his side, dropping to her knees in the mud. She lifted his head onto her lap.

Bent over him, she said, "Where you hurting?"

Warren dug at his left side, below his ribs. He tried moving, his fingers prodding the area, his pain obvious.

Rae Lynn said, "Can't you get up?"

Another crack of thunder came, followed by a flash of lightning. Warren looked around, appearing disoriented.

She repeated the question, "Warren, can't you get up?"

He rolled onto his knees and hands, letting out a deep moan as he did so.

"I done got stoved up but good!" he wheezed.

"Let me help you."

She grabbed his right arm, and between the two of them, he got to his feet. Hunched over, he continued to hold his side as she stumbled along with him through the muck and driving rain, both of them soaked now. When Warren got to the steps, he let go of her arm and grabbed the rail to haul himself up, one step at a time. He staggered through the front door and on to their bedroom. She followed, her hand on the small of his back.

Once there, she said, "Take off them wet clothes and get in the bed."

He pulled the straps on his overalls off his shoulders and let them drop to the floor in a blue sodden pile around his ankles. He sat, and she pulled his boots off. He kicked the overalls out of the way and twisted around so he could lie on the bed while Rae Lynn raised his undershirt to reveal a bruised, reddish area.

"It's god-awful," he gasped.

"You might've broken a rib or two."

"Wrap it good and tight."

Rae Lynn went into the kitchen for her supply of rags. She took an old bedsheet back to the room and got her scissors from her sewing basket. She began cutting it into long strips, fast as she could. Every time she looked at Warren, his face was contorted with pain.

In between panting, he said, "It hurts. Something fierce."

She could see the area had already discolored, and Warren had turned pale. She started to speak, but he cut her off, as if reading her mind.

"It'll heal," he insisted.

She exhaled sharply. "You ought to let me fetch the doctor."

Warren was obstinate. "No, just wrap me up like I said, and let me rest."

Concerned, Rae Lynn did as he wanted, him still panting as she wound the long strips round and round his torso, making them tight as she could. When she was done, she helped prop him against the pillows, and he made a show of acting like he felt better.

He grabbed her hand, kissed the back of it, and said, "Thank you, shug."

The deep lines in his brow, his face glistening with sweat told her it was as bad as it had been before she'd done the wrapping. She brushed his hair back, and he squeezed her hand.

He tried to sound reassuring when he said, "I'll be fine."

She couldn't think of what else to do, so she went into the kitchen and sat at the table, where the food waited to be eaten, but she'd long since lost her appetite. The sun was back out, the early-summer downpour having already moved off to the east. The irony. If he'd only waited like she said. If only she'd held the ladder for him. She heard the bed squeak, and rose from the chair to check on him. He hung halfway off the side of the bed like he couldn't hardly stand whatever was wrong inside of him. She frowned, concerned. She didn't want to be upset with him, not now, and especially not over some foolish argument about how he chose to do things.

He said, "My left shoulder hurts too. Must've jammed it somehow."

She tried again. "You sure you don't want me to fetch the doctor?"

He fell back onto the bed and said, "No, we ain't got the money for such."

Troubled, Rae Lynn watched as he closed his eyes, as if wanting to block her from his view. They had a whole fifteen dollars. More than most. Why couldn't he spare a dollar to see a doctor?

She waited a moment in the silence, then said, "I'll let you try to sleep."

He didn't respond, and she went out, closing the door behind her. Back in the kitchen, she took the food off the table and set it in a cupboard. With nothing else to do, she sat in a chair, watching the door to their room. She wanted to see Warren standing in the doorway, perfectly fine. She reckoned what happened to him shouldn't be all that shocking. Quite honestly, how something like this hadn't occurred already was a wonder. Rae Lynn could only hope he'd recover, and that it might somehow change him, make him think about outcomes. The afternoon turned to evening and every now and again, he would moan. Once he cried out so loud she thought sure he'd relent and allow her to get Doc Perdue.

When she went in to see what she might do to help, only wanting to ease his suffering, before she could speak a word, he barked at her, "It ain't a thing to be done but to let me be!"

This short temper wasn't like him. It was the pain speaking, so she said nothing and backed out of the room. Butch happened by, and she really wasn't in the mood for his wisecracks, but after going in to see Warren, he came back out, his face filled with concern.

He said, "You ain't got him no doctor yet?"

Rae Lynn shook her head. "He don't want one, Butch."

"Maybe you ought to get him anyway. Don't listen to Warren, he's always been like'at."

"He won't let him see him, even if I did."

Butch scratched his head. "I reckon that'd be like him too." He looked back toward the room, and Warren wheezed out, "I can hear you. No. Damn. Doctor!"

Rae Lynn raised an eyebrow, and Butch shrugged, then left.

Evening became nightfall, bringing a hint of relief from what had been a hot, humid day. The sun was below the trees, and the creaking of crickets and tiny blinking orbs of fireflies at the edge of the woods signaled day giving in to night. Under normal circumstances, they'd sit out on their porch, her shelling peas or maybe doing some mending by the dim light of a lantern. Warren would roll a cigarette, have him a smoke, and talk about the next day, what they might get done. She stepped outside now and took several deep breaths as a light breeze sifted through the pines, whistling soft and low. It stopped, then came again, as if Mother Nature breathed with her. She turned her face into it, and a tear or two slid off her chin. Aggravated, she rubbed her face dry. It would be all right. Tomorrow when the sun rose, Warren would be better, she told herself as she hugged her arms tight around her body. She had to believe this.

After a couple of sunrises and sunsets, Rae Lynn started losing track of how many days had come and gone. She'd had little sleep, so little in fact she almost dozed off while standing at the stove frying fatback one hot morning. Why cook? She was the only one able to eat, and she didn't feel much like it any more than Warren. He did nothing but stare out the bedroom window, maybe traveling in his mind on where he ought to be, or what he should be doing. Every once in a while, he glared at her, and she thought maybe he resented her refusal to help him the day it happened. It got to where when she entered the room, no longer would he turn his head toward her, speak to her. They had argued about the doctor once more. Sometimes he acted confused, fretful, and if he didn't act that way, he yelled at her. The day before, he'd even started crying. She'd never seen him cry before except over his old hound dog, Bessie, and it had scared her.

She'd rushed to the bedside, asked him, "You hurting, is it pain?"

He apparently wanted to drown her out, because he wailed louder, beating his fists against the sheet. She went to take his hand, and he pulled it away.

He gathered enough strength to say, "Leave. Leave me alone."

"But, Warren . . ."

"Out. Out!"

She didn't know what else to do but as he said. She left his side, certain the gloomy heaviness within the room was Death, watching patiently from a corner.

Chapter 5

Del

At the crossroads, Tom pointed to a sign tacked to a big oak tree, crudely painted with the words SWALLOW HILL WORK CAMP and an arrow pointing right. The sun was overhead, high noon. Del made his way to the front, and Tom reached out a hand.

Del shook it and said, "Thankee kindly."

Tom said, "Good luck."

He pulled away and Del stood for a moment, watching the three blond heads bobbing in the back. He gave another little wave, and the oldest boy returned it. The walk was easy, and Del's legs felt fresh, rested from the ride. He made his way along a narrow dirt road where mule-drawn wagons had destroyed anything growing in the hard-packed soil, except for the hardiest of weeds. He swung his arms, suddenly filled with anticipation at being in a different area. As he walked, the wildflowers occasionally offered a bright spot against a dry, sunburnt landscape. Everything had its moment in time. Maybe here he could start afresh, put the grain bin incident behind him, return to normal. Be his old self again.

He smelled the camp before it came into view, the pungent
odor of the turpentine still, the smoke of wood burning, and
the scent of pines. He came from North Carolina, the state
once a prime producer of naval stores. Eventually, the longleaf
pines were tapped out, and the industry migrated south to
Georgia and Florida like birds do. All too soon, the longleaf
version once so abundant in all the Southern states was deci-
mated, and a lot of the trees ended up on the ground. Wooden
corpses. Not from the scarification to create the signature
"catfaces," but from the old technique of chipping boxes to
hold gum at their base. When strong storms came through, it
would sometimes push them over. Ultimately the trees could
no longer be worked because the chevron patterns reached
as high as a worker could get, even when using a special tool
called a *puller*. At that point, some were harvested for timber,
while many remained, their ghostlike catfaces stamped on the
trunks, a symbol of bygone times.

His family history was in turpentining. His granddaddy
had worked as a woods rider in the camps, and so had his
pap. Del was always right by their sides and learned about
chipping, dipping, and tacking tin from a variety of teachers,
coloreds and whites alike. His granddaddy had planted trees
on the land where he'd grown up, alongside his own granddaddy, for a turpentine business one day, they said. Those
trees were coming into maturity now. It took at least fifty
years, and though Del had yet to return home to work them,
he thought about it often, knew one day he'd go back, when
the time was right.

Experience told him working at Swallow Hill might set
him back, not ahead. Camp commissaries were prone to high
pricing. As long as no one minded getting "tokens" or "scrips"
instead of real money, it was possible to avoid starvation,
barely. The system caused grumbling, but what else could be
done? This was a time when men needed to provide for their

families. Work camps offered shacks for living accommodations, though they might not be in the best shape; some believed it a step above Hoovervilles. The camps had churches, schools too, and there was always a juke joint somewhere in the midst for Saturday night rabble-rousing.

He'd been fourteen when they'd come to Georgia for the turpentine work the first time, so he'd been in a camp before. His grandpa and grandma, both too old and weak to tolerate the conditions, stayed behind. Mother had cried as she packed what would fit in the back of a wagon.

Pap hugged her shoulders, said, "Don't you worry none. We'll be back. I promise."

The morning they left the old farmhouse along the Cape Fear River, Del had lain on his back in bed, allowing the golden rays of the sun to touch his face in the same spot it had for years. He wanted the memory and had stayed there till Mother yelled for him to get up. They ate the ham biscuits she'd fixed, drank hot coffee, and then he and his sister, Sudie May, hugged their grandparents and climbed onto the back of a wagon loaded with all they had in the world. Mother followed, her cast-iron skillet tied in a bedsheet with her other cooking implements, and the parcel thumped against the side of the wagon periodically after the mule got started.

For him, it was an adventure, but Mother cried again. The last view they had was of their grandparents in the doorway, waving. As they got going, he and Sudie May swiveled their heads, taking it all in, and while it was only more pine trees lining a long, hot road, soon they crossed over into South Carolina, and it was the farthest either of them had ever been. They arrived at the camp days later, and the work began. After a couple of months, Grandma wrote and said their grandpa's heart had plumb give out, and he was gone.

"It was broke," Mother said.

They stayed gone three years until his parents returned

home to Bladen County, both having suffered typhoid and unable to work in such conditions anymore. They went back to take care of Grandma, and Sudie May went with them.

His father had said, "Come with us, son. See how them trees have fared. We might have a few we could work now."

He'd refused, wanted to be on his own for a bit, see something of the world. There'd been such disappointment in Pap's face as he'd turned away. The years passed, and it seemed before he knew it, Sudie May was the one writing, telling him Pap was gone. Another couple of years, and it was Mother. Sudie May had been the more practical presence in their lives, especially toward the end. Her last letter about Mother got forwarded several times before it made to his latest location, and in reading it, he felt a jolt of guilt, and an even deeper regret. Next came the thought, what was the point of going home now? Another letter arrived a couple years later when she wrote to say she'd married. As always, she extended the invitation to him to come home. She wrote, *I miss you. Amos and me, we doing all right here, keeping it up, but it's not the same no more without Mother, Pap, and you.*

Del took a moment beneath the swaying statuesque pines capped with the deep-green needles, inhaling the pungent aroma of smoke, the sharp odor of turpentine, pitch and tar, all mingled in with the warm evergreen-scented wind. The cicadas sang, starting as a low buzz that worked to a feverish, high-pitched hum. The turpentine camp that was Swallow Hill came into view. There was a commissary, a house beside it, a cooper's shed, and a distillery. Workers' shacks were set some ways off, row after row of them. A couple of white women hung out the wash in one section. Another path led toward rows of smaller shanties farther down and on the opposite side. A colored woman came out of one those and tossed out a bucket of dirty water onto some plants in a small garden. For some, there was fencing to square off a tiny spot of land where chickens were kept, and most had little plots staked out for vegetables.

Del came upon a man sitting outside the commissary. He peeled an apple and ate the slices off the end of the knife. He didn't look friendly, but he didn't look unfriendly neither. He had dark brown hair, deep creases around his mouth, eyes the same color as his hair, set close together, one going inward a little more than the other. Beside him was a hat with a crow feather stuck in the band.

Del approached him and said, "Hidy. Who would I see about working here?"

The man's gaze, while uneven, was steady. He pointed with his knife toward a small building with a sign hanging by the door that said OFFICE.

He said, "Feller named Pritchard Taylor. Over yonder."

Del thanked him and walked away, the hairs pricking on the back of his neck. Inside the office, he found himself face-to-face with a short man and a wild, unruly head of hair. The man extended his hand, and Del shook it and started to speak, except he was cut off.

"Pritchard Taylor, call me Peewee, if you want. You here about a job? I assume you is 'cause you wouldn't be standing there. We got work a plenty, but I ain't got no need a no more boss men round here. Not right now, least ways. Could use a wagon driver, or someone to watch over that goofball, Weasel, in the distillery maybe, see to it he don't blow us all to Kingdom Come."

Del was about to tell him he didn't necessarily want to be a boss man, only Peewee went on. "Got about two hundred men or so, lots with family, a few without, but what I really need me is some good nigras. If you know any, send'em my way, but it's all I got. Nigra work."

Del said, "Well, I actually wouldn't mind working the trees, if it's all right."

"That's nigra work."

Del said, "I've done it all, but I like working the trees best. Grew up doing it."

Peewee rubbed his chin and seemed to think on it. "I don't know."

He twiddled with his pencil some.

Finally, he said, "Look, it's fine by me. We need more doing that sort a work, but I ain't wanting no trouble around here."

Del said, "Won't be no trouble from me."

"Maybe not, but I got this woods rider who's got his own ways of thinking. We generally start early, go until dusk. You can work some today if you want, they's plenty to do. Pay's seventy-five cents a day. I see you got your own syrup bucket. If you want'n supplies and such and if you're short on cash, tell Otis over to the commissary to put it on an account under your name. It'll get taken out of your pay. We use scrips instead of cash. You married?"

All this in one breath.

Del said, "Ain't nobody but me, and I don't require nothing fancy."

"Right. All jobs right now is under Elijah Sweeney, goes by name of Crow. He ain't particular to whites and coloreds mixing, but you tell him I said it's all right."

"Crow? I think I seen him. Got a hat with a crow feather in it?"

"That would be him. And listen, he's real peculiar about them trees. Be sure you're careful about your work. Anyway, you got number forty-two. That's in the section for unmarried men. Plus, everything is fixed to accommodate accordingly. Nigras there, whites there. See? Go that way. Numbers are on wood blocks above the door. If you get lost, ask."

Peewee waved him out. As he made his way toward the commissary, he looked for the man called Crow, but he'd disappeared. From the cooper's shed, Del detected the powerful odor of cut wood, along with the sound of rapid hammering. He noticed the man doing the pounding was working to fasten a stave around a row of curved lumber, the slats forming a barrel. Inside the commissary, the proprietor stood behind the counter hunched over a ledger, while a woman dusted off long wooden shelves at the back. She ducked behind a curtain concealing the backside of the store as soon as he made his way toward the counter.

He said, "I'm just hired on and need'n to get a few things."

The man quit scribbling, and said, "Otis Riddle."

"Del Reese."

Otis jotted Del's name down and gestured at the stocked shelves.

"Get what you need and my wife, Cornelia, she'll gather it up for you."

Del walked around selecting a few items—cornmeal, lard, beans, and grits—and carried everything back to the counter.

Once there, he said, "Kin I get some salt pork?"

Otis hollered, "Cornelia! Where the hell you at?" before he made a motion of frustration at Del and said, "Damn woman. She ain't never round when I need her."

He disappeared behind the curtain while Del continued perusing the store. He added a bar of soap to his pile of items. Otis came back to the counter, followed by the woman he'd seen earlier.

"Hurry it up," he said, and swatted her on the backside.

Embarrassed for the woman, Del dropped his eyes while Otis scratched his armpit. Cornelia first sliced some salt pork, then set his items in a wooden crate, her blazing-red face averted. When she finished, she ducked behind the curtain again, never having once spoken to Del. She sure was fine looking, with a tangle of dark, almost black hair falling loose from where she'd pulled it back. Meanwhile, Otis licked the end of a pencil, scribbled a bit before gesturing toward the curtain where Cornelia had disappeared.

He said, "She and I, we ain't been married but about a year. I'm still learning her on how I like things, if you know what I mean." He leered at Del like Del knew what he meant, then said, "Alrighty, that's gonna put you in arrears about six dollars."

Del quickly calculated what he'd make, and concluded by the end of a full workweek, he'd already be short a few days wages. He hadn't started yet, and he was going into this thing indebted. It was common in these camps and while he didn't like owing nobody, he had no choice; hardly anyone ever did when they come to work at a turpentine camp. He nodded at Otis in agreement, grabbed the crate, and went back out into the blazing heat to walk to his new home.

He found number forty-two quick enough. Inside it was a mess. He saw one of the previous occupants had patched the leaky roof, but he was certain the entire population of flies and chiggers in the county had taken up residence. He put the shotgun over the door, propped behind the nails hammered on each end. While he was unloading what he'd bought, he heard a raspy, slithering noise overhead. He suspected a king snake, or at least he hoped that's what it was. The interior stunk to high heaven, and he tried to find the source of the smell. He pulled open the door on the wood-burning stove and drew back when he looked in. There was the carcass of a possum in the oven, half cooked, now rotted. He held his nose, surveyed the tiny room, noted a stained mattress filled with a less-than-adequate amount of Spanish moss upon which he was supposed to sleep. The walls had gaps in the wood wide enough he could stick a finger through them, and daylight spilled into the dank interior, creating vertical gold streaks across the dirt floor. At least the gaps allowed the air to stir, but come winter, he'd have to chink them somehow, or fill them with newspapers. Hard to believe this was one of the nicer spots intended for the whites. At least he had a roof over his head, crude though it was.

He found a bucket, pulled the possum out of the stove, and dumped it in that. He shut the door to the shack, hurried down on the steps, noticing the turpentine work was starting back up. He tossed the possum into the woods, set the bucket inside his fence, and headed toward the voices echoing in a singsong like chant off in the distance. It was an old familiar rhythm he recollected from earlier times and as he came closer, call names like Sweet Thang, Big Time, and Dew Drop almost made him smile. There was usually meaning behind the names, nonsensical to anyone who didn't do the work, but they delivered a hint of the owner's personality, their dreams, their special loves, or whatever struck them. For the woods riders, or tally men, it was how they kept up with what was being done by each man. In between were snatches of songs. Near to the woods, he took note of a vacant section already worked and the timber cut. In the cleared area, in a remote spot away from the camp, was something he'd never seen. A wooden box sat in the hot sun, an oddity against the backdrop of nature. About the same length as a coffin, that's exactly what it resembled. He'd heard of something like this being used as a disciplinary measure. It was called a sweatbox and for good reason.

Curious, Del looked around, then trotted over to it. He noted how the weather had allowed cracks in the wood. He squatted down and peered through them only to stand back up quick, startled by bloodshot, wild-looking eyes blinking at him. He backed away, then heard a scrape, and a soft whisper.

He said, "Hey. You all right?"

It came again, a whispered request. "Water."

Who did they have in there, and what had he done? The nearest well was back the way he'd come, but he had to try to do something.

He said, "Hang on."

Whoever was inside moaned. Del hustled along the path and slowed down at the sight of his new boss ahead.

Crow called out, "Hey! What're you doing?"

Del pointed back at the box. "Thought I heard something."

"That ain't none of your business."

Del didn't want to get off on the wrong foot, and changed the subject.

He said, "I just got hired, working for you, actually. I'm ready to start if you got something for me. I'll chip, tack tin, dip gum, it don't matter much to me."

Crow raised his eyebrows and said, "What? That's nigra work."

Del felt compelled to explain. "Mr. Taylor, Peewee, said he ain't looking for no boss men, and he said I could do what I wanted."

He and Del assessed each other for a second or two, then Crow said, "Follow me."

He took off, and Del fell in behind him, giving one last apologetic look over his shoulder. Neither of them spoke the entire time it took to get to the crop of longleaf. Once there, Del noticed the cleared bases and slashes on trunks to identify where to work. Crow retrieved a tool from a burlap bag near a tree and handed it to him.

He said, "What's your call name gonna be?"

Del considered the question for a second, then said, "Butler."

Crow scribbled it on a pad and said, "Show me."

Del walked over to stand near the trunk of a longleaf pine, the strips of bark taken out previously beginning to reveal the telltale catface. It had been a while since he'd wielded a bark hack. He turned it so the sharp edge would hit the tree, and struck once above an old streak. The method came back to him quick. He swiped to the right. This created a new slash above the last. He moved it to the other side and did the same, the two streaks now meeting in that distinctive chevron. The newly made marks allowed gum to run toward the tin gutters positioned to guide the thick, syrupy runoff into a clay cup. He recognized the clay cups and gutters as a new technique invented by a man with the last name of Herty, known as the Herty system.

He pointed at a clay cup and said, "I've heard of this, but ain't never seen no one using it. Some's still using the box method."

Crow lifted his gaze from his tally book and for the first time seemed interested in conversing. "I recommended it. I don't like cutting boxes at the base of a tree. It tends to make'em go weak, makes'em susceptible to falling over during storms. Bad enough when a lumber company comes in to tear'em down, but ain't no need in not giving the tree a chance, especially if there's a better way."

Del nodded. It made perfect sense to him. He moved to the next tree, working at waist level, where it was easy to leverage the tool so it wouldn't go too deep. By the time he'd chipped his fifth tree, Crow left him to work alone, moving to a central vantage point so he could track Del and the others as they called out. Del saw this as a good sign. He timed how long it took him to complete chipping a catface, including walking to the next tree. Twenty seconds. That was three every minute. He'd have 720 by the end of the four hours. It might be good enough, but he could go faster, get 800 maybe.

He shouted, "Butler!" over and over, his voice blending with the others he couldn't see, though he knew they were spread out in the other wooded areas.

After an hour, his clothes were soaked. He hadn't seen any water carriers yet. They were often colored women or boys who went around with a bucket and a ladle. He kept working while thinking about that feller trapped in the box. It had to be like being buried alive. Hell, like being in the grain bin. An occasional puff of wind brought a few seconds of respite, and he hoped the man could at least feel it too, but most of the time, the air was perfectly still, not even a pine needle moving. Water finally came by way of a reticent, dark-skinned boy who refused to look at Del. He had thin scars running across the backs of his legs.

Del tried to engage him in a bit of talk, but Crow, as if sensing a moment's pause, appeared from out of nowhere, and said, "Boy, do I need to take my whip after your hide again?"

Del dropped the ladle into the bucket and wiped his mouth on his shirt sleeve. The kid took off down the path silent as a moth in the night.

Crow stared after the water boy and said, "Shiftless, like his damn daddy."

Del made no remark. The only sound from him was his tool striking marks into the next tree. Toward dusk and quitting time, the regularity of call names was unexpectedly disrupted by shouting and followed by a hoarse scream. Del straightened up and squinted toward a section of the woods. It could be all manner of things to cause a body to carry on like that. Snake bite. Accident with a tool. Patches of grays, blues, and tans began to appear in between the thick tree trunks, the colors of clothing from the other men riding in a wagon pulled by an enormous mule. Surefooted, it wound its way around the trees expertly. Another shriek, more yelling, and the men in the back of the wagon grew restless. They kept their eyes downcast as Del hopped on the back. The wagon's wheels squeaked and again, a distinct crack, and another scream reached their ears.

The men ignored what happened a couple hundred feet

behind them, like it was an everyday occurrence. Del could not. Crow rode behind a colored man who stumbled along while Crow's horse shimmied sideways, head bobbing, disturbed. Crow raised a whip and brought it across the man's back. The workhand fell to his knees, then his belly, silent now. Crow left him there, nudged his heels against his horse's sides and caught up to the wagon.

He spoke to no one in general. "See what happens when you chip too deep and ruin trees? Keep doing it, and it's the box. Same goes for any one of you. Skip or miss trees? Right to the box. Sometimes, it's the stupidity of your actions, sometimes, it's the kind a mood I'm in what might put you there. Don't none of you forget it."

Crow scanned the group, and Del, like the others, averted his eyes until Crow rode on. The wagon stopped.

The one-eyed driver said, "Go help him."

Del and another worker took hold of the beaten man under his arms. His shirt, if it could be called such, was a burlap sack, holes cut out for his arms. Burgundy streaks marked the back in a crisscross pattern. The man wobbled between them, his bare feet grimy and stained black on the bottom with pine gum. Del thought, *That kind of camp.* Maybe this had been a mistake, but, he was already indebted. Leaving when one owed meant the boss men could do what they wanted. They were law unto themselves—would, and could, do as they pleased.

They might find you, but they'd make sure nobody else did. *Oh, he done run off,* is what they'd say, *we're still looking him.*

If a law man got involved, the boss would say, *You catch him, haul him back here, he owes me.*

They helped the man into the wagon and moved on. As they arrived to the outskirts of the camp, Del saw the lid to the sweat box was propped open and there was no sign of the earlier occupant. Crow was already on his porch, sharpening his ever-present knife. He didn't lift his head, or acknowledge the wagonload of hands as they passed him by. It was as if they didn't exist to him now the workday was done. Del looked at the beaten man in the bottom of the wagon, trying to determine which would be worse, that box, or a whip.

The next morning, Del arose before the cowbell, having had a troublesome sleep. He took a moment to walk among some older catfaced pines nearby, eyeing the scarified trunks, the marks obvious against the bark in the moonlight. He felt along the bone-hard wood beneath the old scrapes and took notice of the fresh, virgin timber beyond yet to be tapped. He figured he'd give it some time, see how it went, see if what he'd seen so far was typical or not. He only wanted to blend in, get his work done. Find the rhythm to his days here. Five thirty found him waiting for the wagon by the fence and when it came, he got in, sat on the tailboard, his back to the rest of the hands. Crow smirked at him. At the hang-up ground, he fell in with the group as they made their way to the large shade tree. He hung his dinner bucket over a branch, noticing how no one talked. They quickly hopped back into the wagon and as it pulled them through the woods, Crow called out their woods name, and one by one they jumped off the back and disappeared.

Crow said, "Butler!" and Del moved with purpose.

He walked into pine-laden forest and examined the chip marks. They were deep, deeper than he'd make, and he hoped the trees weren't ruined. The area was marked well, the bases of the pines having been raked back during the cold months. He got started. Two thousand trees meant no time to ponder on much other than chipping and calling out his name, over and over. As he worked, he got to thinking about the longleaf they'd planted back home, wondering how it looked now. Maybe he'd plant more there some day, and no matter it might take fifty years for'em to grow, they'd outlive him and his sons, if he ever had any.

His pap once explained the trees could survive five hundred years. Del's dream continued with him imagining himself teaching his own boys about how land and trees like the longleaf were richer than any money they might earn. How, if they weren't careful, it could all disappear. He'd seen it. Like Crow alluded to, entire forests were wiped out after tapping the trees to the point of being dried up. Then, lumber companies came to clear-cut the wood. Shoot, someone once said a squirrel could start from treetops in Virginia and get to Texas without ever touching the ground. He'd bet this was no longer the case.

Though he had his doubts about Swallow Hill considering what he'd seen so far, he was here now, so he'd make the best of it. He didn't stop all afternoon, though he'd not had much to eat since he'd taken to the woods and wasn't as strong as he'd been at the Sutton farm. The work was hot and difficult, but he chipped fast and accurate, gaining confidence. He'd estimated doing 167 trees per hour sunrise to sunset. He'd make his numbers, and as long as he kept up, he'd do all right, at least this was what he chose to believe.

Chapter 6

Rae Lynn

Pain riddled, agitated and morose, Warren kept moving around in the bed to the point neither one of them slept much. It had been four days since the accident, and Rae Lynn's head throbbed from lack of sleep and worry. She rose and went into the kitchen for some aspirin, and when she returned to the bedroom, she stopped to watch Warren swing his feet over the side of the bed and make an attempt to stand. He stayed bent over, his arm over his midsection. Rae Lynn was transfixed, holding her breath. Some part of her willed him on, willed him to move without pain, to put things back to normal for them. Gripping his side, he slowly straightened, but before he'd unfolded himself, he doubled over again, gasping in distress. Her shoulders sagged with disappointment. She went to the bedside and stood by him. Warren's head hung down and he didn't bother to lift it.

"You shouldn't have tried. It's too soon."

He whispered, "Where's my horse?"

She'd been about to put her hand on his shoulder, but what he'd said was so strange, her hand fell away.

Bewildered, she said, "We ain't got no horse."

"Huh?"

Rae Lynn put her hand on his forehead. It felt clammy.

She said, "Lie back down and try not to move. You're making it worse."

"Worse? What could be worser'n this? Dammit, Rae Lynn."

He'd cussed in the past, but never at her.

She said, "You could've broke your neck and be six feet under, that's what could be worse."

Tentative, her fingers probed his belly. It was hard, hot, and distended. Something was horribly wrong inside him, she was sure of it. He put his hand on top of hers and stared at her so pitiful-like, she couldn't think of a thing to say.

He whispered a word: "Will . . ."

She didn't understand and she attempted to help.

"You need something? Will I . . . ?"

Warren shut his eyes. He didn't go on, so she stroked his arm until his breathing eased. For the rest of the day, she tried to keep busy, checking on Warren in between her chores, setting cool cloths on his forehead, and giving him sips of sweet tea. When it was time to finally begin her nightly ritual, she only wanted sleep to come for the both of them. She filled the wash basin and took it to their room. After undressing, she washed and pulled on her nightgown before removing the pins that held her hair up. Her head still hurt but brushing her hair helped. She caught Warren's eyes on her from the mirror, and turned to him as he spoke, his voice was weaker than it had been earlier that day.

He whispered, "Your hair. It's so purty."

She set the brush aside, picked up the cloth, dipped it in the water, and went to his side. She wiped his face while sitting on the bed beside him.

He gazed at her and said, "Who're you?"

She drew back a bit and frowned. "It's me. Rae Lynn. Your wife."

He blinked. "Rae Lynn?"

Unnerved, she said, "You thirsty? Can you drink some water?"

He nodded, and when she brought him some, his hands trembled as he reached for the glass. He clutched it tight and drank till it was empty. She set it on the nightstand and got in the bed beside him, trying not to jostle him. Somehow, she slept and didn't waken until she heard a mockingbird singing outside their window the next morning. She turned to Warren and saw he was awake too, but the man staring back at her didn't resemble her husband. Gray-skinned, purplish half-moons staining the area beneath his eyes, he was nothing like the old Warren, yet there was a clarity in his gaze she'd not seen for the past few days.

Trying to inject a bright tone, she said, "You feeling some better?"

He didn't respond, as if her question tired him.

She went out to empty the chamber pot, and when she came back to the room, his gaze sharpened, and he gasped, "Need. Something."

She went to him and said, "Anything."

His pointed at the dresser.

She felt the beginnings of dread. "Can you tell me?"

She didn't mention the doctor again, not wanting to agitate him.

"Like I done. For Bessie."

Bessie had been Warren's redbone hound, a dog Rae Lynn had grown attached to after she'd moved in. Bessie had been a good old girl who slept under the porch in the summer and under their bed during the winter. She got to where she couldn't hardly walk, couldn't control her bowels or bladder, and then stopped eating. She watched them with mournful eyes, her tail no longer thumping.

He'd put his big hand on the dog's head and said, "She wants to go."

He rubbed on her for a while, got his .22 revolver, gathered the old girl up, and disappeared deep into the woods with her. Rae Lynn had paced the kitchen, bracing for the gunshot, and when it came, and she knew it would, still she'd jumped, and felt her heart break. It took them a long time to get over Bessie. She'd filled a space in their hearts and took that piece with her when she went.

Rae Lynn was on the verge of tears.

"Warren. You can't mean that."

"I do."

Sickened, she exclaimed, "I can't. You shouldn't ask me."

"It's. Unbearable."

His hands shook as he laid them on his left side. She left the room, alarmed, afraid of what he asked, and his plea followed her through the house.

"Please."

She tried to distract herself by cooking breakfast as if nothing was wrong. She brought it to him, but he'd turned his head so he faced the wall. She sat down, preparing to do like she'd been trying to do each and every morning, offer him some soft-cooked eggs, except he turned his head to the wall.

"Won't you eat?"

Silence. She set the plate down, angry.

"That ain't the answer. I wouldn't ask you, if it was me."

"Ain't asking. I'll do it."

The words blew through her like a cold wind in the dead of winter. She pictured him doing what he wanted, and her standing there, letting it happen. My God. Just thinking about it gave her such an emotional jolt, she felt dizzy, nauseous.

She said, "I don't understand this thinking. Let me bring the doctor, Warren!"

"Too. Late."

Arguing with her cost him because he began panting. Rae Lynn went to him, reached out, and he pulled away. Hurt, she left the room and paced the kitchen floor. She tried to see it his way. Would it be an act of kindness? She was torn by his suffering, but this idea of his, it was barbaric.

She marched back into the room and said, "I'm getting Doctor Perdue."

His eyes widened, and she thought it was because of what she said, but instead he heaved onto his side and threw up in the basin, filling it with thick black matter. Frightened, she went to him, rested her hand on his back as he continued to expel what was in him. He collapsed back on the bed, his mouth rimmed with what had come out of him. The smell in the room had changed, coming from what he'd left in the basin, as if he was dying from the inside out. For a second, she thought he had, until his chest rose and lowered. He still breathed, only barely.

Backing out of the room, she went outside onto her porch and took a deep, cleansing breath. At the end of the property line was a sagging, old tobacco barn, and she walked to it. Once there, she tugged the door open, the rusty hinges squealing. Stooping to enter, a memory came of her and Warren running inside it because of one of those typical, pop-up thunderstorms suddenly appearing on what had been a hot, sunny day. She turned her attention to where they'd lain as the pungent odor of tobacco greeted her, and those long-ago moments, a gift from her past, came rushing forward. She remembered taking off her wet dress, and Warren, usually shy about relations, shrugging out of his overalls and having her right there.

Afterward, she was sure she'd get pregnant because the impromptu act was as passionate a moment as either ever had. With Warren, it had always been lights out, under the sheets, hidden away. But, two weeks later, her blood came, and as was their way, neither of them said a word about how they'd been married several years and had yet to have a child. Rae Lynn didn't know why. Didn't know, was it her fault or his, and had long ago concluded it must be her. There was Eugene, after all. Her thoughts were chased off by what was going on at the house, as if she still stood beside their bed, the only witness to his suffering.

"Lord, please, please have mercy on him. Take him. Give him peace. Free him of this awful pain. Don't let him have to do this," she whispered.

She put her memories and prayers away, and left the barn. Halfway to the house she heard it, exactly the same as with sweet Bessie. The gunshot echoed through the woods and she almost screamed, *No.* Instead, she ran, her mouth set, her shoes thudding against hard-packed soil, slipping in the low-lying area that always held water, where mud slick as oil caused Warren's truck to get stuck time and again. The house came into view, and she slowed to a walk, hoping she was wrong. Her legs trembled, and the tremors traveled upward until she shook all over. She was petrified as she climbed the steps. At the threshold of the front door, the old clock on the mantel clicked away time, a sound she usually barely noticed, but it now filled her ears. From where she stood, it was easy to see Warren was no longer in the bed. He'd slid off it and onto the floor, his legs twitching with an unnatural movement, like he was having some sort of fit.

She put a hand over her mouth to quell the sound welling up inside of her as she willed herself forward. Warren's midsection was covered in blood. Her gaze traveled to his face to discover him staring at her, mouth opening and closing, as if trying to speak. With his eyebrows raised, he seemed to inquire, *Would she?* She quickly knelt beside him, brushed his hair back.

She whispered, "Dear God, Warren, what have you gone and done?"

His mouth moved, and she made out the words, just barely. "Messed . . . up. Finish. It. Please."

He'd managed to get out of the bed and over to the dresser, and she couldn't help but think, even in this, Warren had somehow bungled. The gun lay on the floor by his hand. She knelt by his side and picked it up. He nodded, reassuring her. *Like Bessie,* she reasoned. *Merciful at this point,* she rationalized. She laid a trembling hand on his forehead, moved his head so he faced away from her, and saw his gaze turn to the blue sky visible through the open window. Lord, dear God, how it could be such a pretty day when such was happening. She took a breath, gripped the handle with both hands, her amputated finger making the hideous task more difficult. She aimed close to his temple, doing her best to not to touch his skin. She didn't want that to be the last thing he felt. He lay with eyes wide, waiting, and she spoke the final words he'd ever hear.

She murmured, "I love you with all my heart, Warren Eugene Cobb. You was such a good husband to me," and squeezed the trigger.

The sound was deafening, and the high ringing that followed quickly became muffled, like she'd stuffed her head with cotton. She let out one loud sob, then heard a noise behind her. She twisted around to find Butch Crandall in the bedroom doorway, looking at her in disbelief.

"Rae Lynn? What in tarnation is going on here?"

Chapter 7

Del

The shack rouser shouted and rang a cowbell at 4:30 a.m. Del groaned and swore to himself and he heard other work hands doing the same, their bone-deep fatigue echoing around the camp. He rolled off the mattress, the one he'd yet to fix, and went outside in the dark to relieve himself. Nearby pump handles squeaked, and the scrape of a log pulled from a wood stack blended with the mild odor from morning cook stoves and the fresh-scented pines above him. He was reminded of home, and of his mother in the kitchen in the early-morning hours cooking breakfast. He stretched, reaching his arms over his head. Her and Pap had been close, hardly ever apart their entire lives. Their dedication to one another was something, and he wondered why it came to him so clearly this morning. Since he'd come of the age where women interested him, that sort of commitment generally never crossed his mind.

He pumped his own water and splashed it over his face and neck. After he dried off, he brushed his hands through his hair, which still hung long, as did his beard, and realized he could smell himself. He'd not washed proper since he took

to living in the woods, and his clothes reminded him of Ned
Baker's and Ollie Tuttle's, stiff with grime. He had a tang he
normally couldn't abide, but it wouldn't do him any good to
stand out, particularly now. Inside, he fixed a pot of chicory
coffee and drank every last bit of it laced heavy with molasses.
He set some beans inside his syrup bucket with an opener he
found hanging on a nail by the cook stove. It had to be good
enough because it was all he had time to do. He stood by his
fence, and to his left came the sound of creaking wheels. The
sky offered a pale-auburn light from the east as the wagon
broke through the early-morning haze. It came slow enough
for him to hop into the back as it rolled by. The same workers
he'd ridden with the day before sat hunched over, elbows on
knees, heads down, whereas others sat sideways, staring into
the woods. Everyone appeared intent on mustering enough
strength to face a new day. Del caught a whiff like a few had
been into something a little heavier than coffee. It wafted off
their bodies, powerful and sharp.

The one-eyed driver looked back at him, the deep scars
near his brow on the left side giving him a bit of a lopsided
appearance. He turned back around but kept his head tilted
in a way so he could listen to whatever might be said. Del got
the sense the workers in the back weren't used to a white man
riding along.

He broke the silence and said, "Name's Del Reese, woods
name, Butler. My family, we used to work the camps. Grew
up doing this sort of thing."

The man who sat closest spoke in a low voice like he didn't
want to be heard.

He said, "Yeah? Well, what you think you doing now?"

Del hesitated. "What do you mean?

He snorted, looking around at his companions.

"I mean, what you doing, with *us*?"

Del kept his tone level.

"I'm doing like everybody else. Working."

The man jerked his thumb at Del, gesturing to the others. "Like everybody else. How about that?"

The rest of the men said nothing, although a few sent a cynical look his way. Del figured he was the odd man out with whites and the coloreds, apparently.

After a while, the man said, "Nolan Brown, woods name Long Gone, 'cause one of these days, you watch, I'm long gone from here." He assessed Del, still wary. "We ain't never had no white man do the kind a work we do, not in *this* camp."

Del said, "Ain't no big deal, not to me. Work's work."

Nolan said, "Cause ain't nobody gone do you like they do us."

Nolan made a circular motion toward the others. Del's experience in a labor camp had been with his parents when he was younger. He knew of what Nolan hinted about, but he'd stopped working camps after his pap and mother returned home, and had never experienced or seen what the other man suggested.

Nolan said, "What's Butler stand for?"

Del gave a small laugh. "It was painted on the outside of a grain bin I worked in once. Swallow Hill's an interesting name."

Nolan said, "S'posed to be 'cause a them barn swallers nesting in some of the buildings, but I say it's 'cause what goes on round here is hard to swaller."

The others grunted in agreement, and then, one by one, they slowly introduced themselves to Del.

"Earl Dillon, or Big Time."

"Leroy Ratliff, or Dewdrop."

Nolan leaned in toward Del and said, "Dewdrop's also the name a the juke joint in the middle of the camp. It's the only way round here to have any kind a fun."

Del didn't drink, but he reckoned he could understand it might help after a long day.

The next man said, "Jonesy Jones, or Steady Now."

Nolan cut in again and said, "Steady Now, my foot. Every time I turn around, you gone missing. Best not let boss man see it happening."

Jonesy rubbed the back of his neck and said, "I got something wrong with my innards. Can't keep nothing down."

Nolan said, "You right. Pecker a yours is always aiming for the sky seems like."

The others snorted quietly against the palms of their hands, smothering their laughter.

The last man said, "Charlie Burns, or Burning Up."

Charlie made a bizarre braying sound, not much different than a donkey, and Del believed it was the goofiest laugh he'd ever heard. It made the others snicker again, while their eyes switched here and there as if on the lookout for danger. The only other white man aside from Del was the driver.

He tossed his name over his shoulder. "Gus Strickland. Mule's name is Dandy Boy."

The men obviously trusted Gus or they wouldn't have talked about the things they had.

Del scrutinized the mule. He was huge, at least seventeen hands. He'd seen ones similar when his family worked in turpentine. He was a draft mule and those could weigh as much as fifteen hundred pounds or more, a breed bigger than mining, cotton, or farm mules. Turpentine camp mules were surefooted and knew how to get through the tightest of spots between trees. Gus didn't guide Dandy Boy. The reins were tossed over his knee, and he didn't bother looking where they were going until Crow emerged from some section of the woods to ride alongside them. They reached the hang-up ground, where some had already arrived and were unloading.

Another woods rider sat on his horse in the middle of a large group of workers, calling out to the men as they climbed out of the wagons. Upon first glance one might peg him as dangerous. He had squinty eyes, which darted about, never landing on anyone for too long, and a headful of dirty blond hair that hung over his ears, giving him the appearance of an outlaw.

In a gravelly voice, he yelled, "Go on and get them buckets hung up. Let's go, let's go!"

Looks aside, when he spoke to a worker here and there, he made them grin. Meanwhile, Crow and a couple other woods riders watched the ones in their charge as they left the wagons to hang dinner buckets on lower branches, and there was no grinning or cutting up.

Crow said, "Better be no mistakes today. Understood?"

The chippers and dippers mumbled varying degrees of assent, "Yassah," and "Sho thing, boss man." All maintained neutral expressions, eyes to the ground.

Satisfied, Crow prodded his horse and made his way over to the woods rider with the dirty blond hair.

Nolan grumbled as he returned from the hang-up ground.

"Got to say the same crap every mornin'."

He seemed to be the leader when it came to the others' thoughts and beliefs, because they again grumbled in agreement. Everyone clambered into the back of the wagon once more, and Dandy Boy leaned into his harness.

Del said, "He got any family?" gesturing toward Crow, who still talked with the rough looking woods rider.

Gus spoke up.

"He ain't married, that I know of. Some old woman comes to stay with him now and again. His mama, I reckon."

Earl said, "Alls I know, he loves a tree more'n he loves hisself. Jim Ballard, now, he's all right." He pointed at the blond woods rider. "He don't go crazy if you got a problem with a tool or need to take you a little break long as you get the work done."

Nolan said, "They's lots of ways to meet your Maker round here. Could get the trots drinkin' swamp water. I seen people get so bad, they like a dried-up turnip when they pass. Might get the fever, turpentine still could blow us all into the sky, or get killed over to that juke joint over a coin or two. But get on the wrong side a Crow? You get the livin' daylights beat outta you or land in the sweat box, or both. I been in that thing once, and I ain't gone back, naw suh. I know this too," and his voice went lower, "he gone hide a body if sumpin' happens. He's law unto himself."

Earl said, "'Member when Henry Goodall say he couldn't work with them dippers 'cause a his back? He was hurtin' something fierce. I mean, it ain't easy rolling barrels when they's full, even if you is feeling fine."

Nolan said, "I 'member," and he turned to Del. "He put Henry onto chippin', and everybody a workin', and me, I'm keepin' an eye on Henry, and so's Crow, like he hopin' he gone mess up. Henry's tool, it ain't doin' right. He keep on tryin', but he know somethin's wrong with it. He finally go on and take it to Crow to show him, and damned if Crow don't act like he makin' it up. Say for him to get on back to work. Henry, he say he can't work with it, and Crow grabs it, takes one good swipe. Slit his neck open. Henry, he lay chokin' on his own blood, and Crow says, "pears to work just fine to me.' Couldn't nothin' be done. He bled out like a stuck pig, right there. Henry's family, they come lookin' him and got told he run off. Everybody too scared to say or do nothin'."

Del said, "Don't Peewee do nothing?"

Charlie shook his head. "He and Crow go at it now and again, but that Crow, he sneaky now."

Del said, "Why's he called that?"

Nolan leaned in and said, "He say it's 'cause crows is smart."
Gus said, "It's 'cause he brags. You wait. You'll hear him."

The subject of their conversation rode up and the men quit talking. As Crow called out names near various drifts to be worked, each hand hopped off the back and disappeared into the woods, until only Del, Gus, and Crow were left. Dandy Boy swung a wide circle to turn around, and Crow pointed to the area where Del would begin. He slid off the back, and as the wagon went by, Gus shot him a look he couldn't interpret before disappearing down the path where he would haul gum to the distillery for the rest of the day. Crow followed Del into the woods, his gaze on the treetops, and his voice took on a different tone. Softer. Thoughtful.

"I read not too long ago how some trees don't touch one another at the top, and if you look up, you can see a blue sky river cutting through the green."

Del looked up, but the waving tops of pines revealed no sky river.

Crow said, "It's a new finding. They got a name for it. Crown shyness."

Del started to repeat the words, but Crow cut him off, still reflecting on what he'd learned.

"Trees of the same age and type don't touch the branches of other trees at the top. It's the order of nature, see. They think it's 'cause healthy trees are trying to avoid the spread of disease that might damage them. Ain't it something?"

Del said, "I guess."

Del didn't know what he was after, so he kept his answer vague. Crow snorted, giving his opinion of Del's response.

"Every living creature knows to protect its species. Even the damn trees. I ain't into muddying the waters. The white race needs to remain strong."

Del said nothing.

Crow said, "Where'd you do work before here?"

Del said, "Clinch County."

Crow said, "You work with the nigras there?"

"No."

Crow leaned back in his saddle and spit a stream of brown tobacco juice on the ground, while he contemplated Del, who only wanted to get to work.

He said, "What you reckon about them nowadays?"

Del shrugged. "Who?"

"The nigras, what's your opinion of them?"

"Just trying to get along like everybody else, I reckon."

Crow folded his hands across the pommel and stared off into the woods.

He said, "Some seventy years ago when Lincoln wrote that emancipation shit, boy, that done it. It ain't been the same since. One thing's certain. It don't count for nothing, not in these woods. I like keeping things as nature intended. We got to remain elevated, see. Stay clean, and pure."

Crow leaned forward all of a sudden and whispered, "You ain't one a them lowly nigra lovers, are you?"

Del started to back away, looking over his shoulder.

He raised his hands and said, "I won't looking for nothing but a job. I ought to get started."

"Yeah, you do that. Wouldn't want you to fall behind or make no mistake or nothing. Trouble likes to visit when that happens."

He gave Del a humorless smile before moving on.

Del chipped quickly, then called out "Butler!" and hurried to the next longleaf, thinking Crow a troublesome, odd man.

Several days passed without incident. Occasionally he'd catch the boss man out of the corner of his eye watching him. Del was efficient and fast, made his numbers, and he wasn't worried. Knowing how Crow thought didn't keep him from trying to make friends at Swallow Hill, either. To hell with him. He'd speak to who he wanted, when he wanted. The

coloreds were cautious, filled with distrust whenever he tried
to strike up a conversation. Del noted Crow had a tendency
to appear out of nowhere, overly interested in Del's attempts
at being friendly.

At one point, Crow said, "Who taught you this work?"

Del looked him in the eye and said, "Colored man by the
name of Mr. Leroy."

Nobody had minded nine-year-old Del tagging along, asking questions about whatever came to mind. Not Pap, nor his
granddaddy. They were busy overseeing the crops of trees as-
signed to them. Some said Mr. Leroy had been close to a hundred years old when he'd taught young Del about chipping a
tree too deep, explaining how it could ruin it for future gum
collection. He'd demonstrated how making a scrape too wide
affected the running sap. About having to get the "scrape," a
job nobody really liked, when after some period of time the
sap would dry, and workers had to, as implied, scrape it off. It
was Mr. Leroy's wife who gave Del his first taste of "dooby,"
a meal made of wild meat, like squirrel or raccoon, onions
and cornbread.

Crow said, "Your daddy didn't teach you."

Del said, "No."

Crow said, "Maybe that's your problem."

It worried Del, but he tried not to let it. One afternoon
Crow started looking at the crop Del was working. Del was
confident he was doing a good job, so he kept chipping, calling out, and moving on as he finished.

Crow approached him and said, "Stop."

Del shielded his eyes from the sun as he looked up at the
man astride his horse. Crow stuck his thumb over his shoulder.

"You missed some back there."

"Huh? I ain't missed none."

"Yeah, you did."

"Where?"

Del backtracked to check the longleaf, and he'd not missed a one. Crow followed, his expression conniving.

Del said, "Ain't nothing been missed."

Crow swung a leg around and dropped to the ground. He went to a cluster of loblolly pines.

"Them two, and all them over there."

Del said, "They ain't marked. They ain't turpentine trees."

Crow said, "Says who?"

"You can't chip much off'n them. They ain't big enough, and they ain't been marked."

"Reckon you think you're smarter'n me. Reckon you know it all. You forget yourself."

Del said, "I ain't forgetting nothing."

"You questioning me? I said them trees is part a this drift; they's fine to work, and you missed'em. Now you wantin' to argue."

Crow climbed back into the saddle and brought his horse around so he was behind Del.

Crow said, "Head on back to the camp."

"What for? It ain't . . ."

Crow unhooked the whip from the saddle horn, let it unravel so the tip rested on the ground. Del shoved the bark hack in his pocket and did as he was told. If the man was itching to have Peewee fire him, so be it. Distant calls from the other workers stopped as he and Crow made their way back the way they'd come. They passed by Nolan, who also stopped working when he saw them.

Crow said, "Long Gone, what're you looking at?"

Nolan shook his head. "Nothing, boss man."

Crow tossed his tally book to Long Gone, and said, "Keep up with their counts," and to Del, "Keep going, Butler."

Del was surprised Crow entrusted Long Gone with the tally book. This was more like it had been in the other camps, but he couldn't think about that now. They passed by more workers, and one by one, each paused in astonishment before they quickly turned back to their trees.

Jim Ballard rode up and said, "What's going on here?"

Crow said, "Mind your business, Ballard. I got this."

Ballard said, "Ain't getting involved, just asking."

"He's doing nigra work, it's only fair he gets the same thing if he screws up."

Del said, "I ain't screwed up."

Ballard gave a short laugh and said, "Since when you ever been fair? Where you taking him?"

Crow said, "Where you think? Move, Butler."

Ballard said, "Peewee only said this morning every hand is needed."

"He ain't gonna be missed."

Del said, "Hang on. I ain't getting in that box."

Crow said, "You got two choices. This"—and he snapped the whip—"or that."

Ballard said, "Peewee needs to hear about this."

Crow slowly turned to Ballard.

"Is that so? While we're at it, maybe we'll let him hear how you're taking a nip here and there while on the job."

Ballard rubbed at a lump on his neck and fell silent.

Crow said, "That's right. I know 'bout that."

Del had to hand it to Ballard. Least he tried. Del won't about to be whipped, nosirree, only the idea of getting in that tight space made him think maybe he ought to take the first choice.

They passed a section of shanties where colored women hung clothes, sat on porches snapping beans with bowls in their laps, watching the young'uns playing with chickens in grassless, sandy yards. Nearby, voices rang out from the open door of a tumbled-down shack evidently used as the schoolhouse where children shouted their ABCs. All was normal until he and Crow appeared, and again, everything came to a standstill. What an unusual sight to behold, a white man on a horse, his whip taunting another white man. Del didn't see the open mouths, he could only sense their amazement in the utter stillness that fell over the camp.

He couldn't quite believe it was happening himself. He could run into the woods off to his left, except it would only give Crow reason to shoot him. They passed through the middle of the camp, while Del tried to think of how to stop what was happening, and then, before he knew it, they'd arrived. Crow got off his horse.

He said, "My old man once told me, lie down with dogs, get up with fleas. Go on. Get in, and get comfy."

Del wished he had more fight in him, but suddenly he felt as ancient as one of them five-hundred-year-old longleaf pines. He did as he was instructed, and as soon as he sat, he was instantly surrounded by what he was certain was the smell of death. Crow took out his knife and got to cleaning his nails, mumbling to himself about the nature of things. Finally, he snapped it shut and stood over Del like a mourner at a funeral observing a deceased individual.

He said, "Don't many last long in here. You be thinking on the error of your ways. Who knows. Maybe you'll come out a changed man."

He slammed the lid, clicked the padlock, and Del was entombed.

Chapter 8

Rae Lynn

Butch turned a skeptical eye on her and said, "It's your word against mine."

Rae Lynn, despondent and exhausted, repeated what she'd said one too many times already. "I done what I had to. He was in terrible pain. He was dying."

Butch said, "Uh-huh. For all I know, you shot him both times."

"Why in God's name would I do that?"

Butch shrugged. "Can't say. Could be all manner of reasons."

"You ain't been by here in over a week, so what could you know about any of it?"

"I know what I seen, that's what I know."

Rae Lynn found herself doing what Warren used to do, waving her hands, swatting at his words. Butch had parked himself at the kitchen table after he'd come in on her kneeling at Warren's side, and hadn't left. She thought at first he'd be helpful to her, in her grief. But no. He'd listened to her and deduced she was covering up something. Now, she was simply exhausted, and overwhelmed. She sat slumped over, occasionally resting her forehead on her arms. She felt like she'd been turned inside out. Butch reclined in a chair, in no hurry, hands behind his head, eyelids drooping enough she couldn't read what was in them.

Eventually, he said, "I got me an idea on how to fix this."

Rae Lynn sat up straight and crossed her arms.

"Ain't nothing needs fixing. Him lying in there, it ain't fitting me not tending to him as I should."

"You gonna get word to Eugene?"

She expelled her breath and said, "Of course."

"What're you gonna tell him?"

Truth was, she wasn't sure. She felt guilty, but not for the reasons Butch thought. She should've held the ladder as Warren had asked and maybe he wouldn't have fallen. She should've gone for the doctor despite him telling her not to. The situation was difficult, if not impossible, to understand beyond anyone but herself and Warren. She could contact Eugene, tell him he fell off the ladder and died from his injury. It *was* the truth. There didn't need to be nothing more said. Butch's expression had turned sly when Rae Lynn hesitated.

"Tell you what. Just so we're square on the matter; it ain't nothing hard, it's simple. You be with me, you know, in that way, like husband and wife, and I won't say nothing to nobody. Not to Eugene, not to nobody. It'll be our little secret."

Rae Lynn could not believe her ears, and she gaped at Butch, appalled. At least he had the decency to flush a brilliant red after he spoke. *This is his way of fixing things? God forbid.* Speechless, she stood up and pointed at the door.

Butch stood too, and with a hint of anger, he said, "You think on it. You think on it good. There ought to be something to come out of what you done."

He left, and she slammed the door and locked it. It was then, and only then, she broke down, allowed her grief to consume her.

Butch came a day later with a crudely made coffin. She was grateful, but it was quickly apparent he'd helped only on account of his idea of restitution for keeping his mouth shut. He'd even joked about it. This, as they went about digging poor Warren's grave, near to his first wife, Ida Neill Cobb. Sakes alive, it was nothing but out-and-out blackmail. Who knew he'd turn out like this? When he made suggestions again as they were tamping down the last shovelful, she went inside, shut the door, and locked it again until he left.

A hellish week later, she stood at Warren's grave, shooing away flies, trying to have a prayerful moment. The flies didn't care about layers of dirt because they knew what was beneath the soil. The things of nightmarish dreams, of which she'd had plenty. It was why she was so tired. She kept seeing Warren, what he'd done, and the pitiful look he'd turned on her after she'd come back to the house. She'd cried tears of anger and remorse, but crying got her nowhere. She had to figure out what to do, how to handle Butch, especially after what he'd gone and done.

Just this morning, she'd gone to the post office to check the mail and was shocked to have a letter from Eugene. Back home, she ripped it open, and read:

> Received a letter regarding my father's passing from Mr. Butch Crandall, on your behalf, I presume. Arriving June 14th at 2:00 p.m. and expect full cooperation as I resolve the matters of my father's estate as per his will. Mr. Crandall has indicated there are matters of importance that need discussion. Please make sure he is present. Sincerely, Eugene Cobb, Esquire.

She tucked it back into her apron pocket, but throughout the morning, she kept pulling it out and rereading his terse, short sentences. Its very presence made her feel like she was inside a pressure cooker about to explode. Thanks to Butch, Eugene would arrive in three days, and he expected Butch to be around as well.

Speak of the devil. Here he was in that old truck, heaving along the path and making her grit her teeth. Without Warren around, Butch had become more emboldened, showing up when he pleased, talking dirty. She always made sure she was outside when she heard him coming, but he still followed her around the yard like a puppy dog, talking about all manner of nasty things he'd like to do to her. He apparently thought this was enthralling to hear. It *was* to him, because she'd caught him messing with himself through his britches when she'd stepped out from behind the sheets she was hanging. He had the nerve to flick his tongue at her and laugh when she cussed him.

Rae Lynn grabbed a rusted pail filled with cracked corn and began throwing out kernels, murmuring to the hens as they clucked and pecked about her feet. She seethed while glancing at the sky. The sun only just up good enough to clear out the morning mist, and here he was already. He approached her and looked at the sky too, maybe recognizing it might be a tad early. It didn't stop him from starting in on his sorry idea.

"What you reckon? Is today the day? It ought to be. All nice and sunny outside."

Rae Lynn tossed corn. She shivered, though it was already hot. He came over and watched, shifting from foot to foot, maybe waiting for her to invite him inside.

Finally, he said, "You heard from Eugene?"

The lie skipped out of her mouth easy as spitting on the ground. "I ain't heard from him."

Butch rubbed his hands together. "Is that right? Huh."

Rae Lynn took the bucket back to the shed and came out

with the hoe. She showed no reaction to Butch being right by the door, though he'd startled her. She went to go by him and he grabbed her arm.

She yelled, "Let me go!"

He said, "Not till you hear what I got to say."

Rae Lynn stopped pulling and stared at the ground.

"Like I done told you, you want me to keep my mouth shut about what I seen, you got to pay up. Here you went and shot your husband, my one and only friend, and now he's dead. It ain't no small thing. Fact of the matter is, I wrote ole Eugene myself. Told him his daddy has passed on and I had things to discuss with him."

She tried to jam the hoe handle down on his foot, but Butch had worked outside all his life, and his strength came from lifting heavy bales of hay, chopping wood, and running his hog farm, and to that end, she thought he smelled exactly like a hog pen. He yanked the tool out of her hand and threw it off to the side. He wrapped his arms around her while she pushed against his shoulders, but he remained unperturbed.

"Something tells me none of it won't set right with him if he was to know."

She averted her face and said, "You've shown your real side here, Butch."

"What I want, it ain't unreasonable, not if you think about it."

"Some friend you turned out to be!"

She reached up to grab hold of his hair, aiming to pull as hard as she could, when he unexpectedly let her go. She was set to give him a tongue-lashing until she saw the reason he'd released her. The letter had fluttered to the ground and lay between them.

Butch said, "Well now. What do we got here?"

She tried to grab it, but Butch was quicker. He snatched it up and twisted around, presenting his back to her. She tried

to reach around him, but he kept turning away. In the mean-
time, he'd flipped the single sheet open. She knew what it said
by heart.

He cocked his head. "Dang. Appears ole Warren might
could've forgot something real important with that will a his.
Oops. Looks like Eugene needs me here too."

Oh, but he infuriated her. This was none of his business.
He handed the letter back, and she crammed it back into
her apron pocket. Butch tipped back on his heels and looked
down his nose at her.

He said, "Appears we're gonna have to hurry."

Rae Lynn said, "You're crazy if you think that's *ever* going
to happen."

Butch said, "It ain't crazy. Only thing crazy is how I feel
about you, Rae Lynn. Always have, but out of respect for
Warren, I kept it to myself. Well. I might've let it slip now
and then. But, look a here, all I'm saying is you do it the once,
and I'll keep my promise. I won't say a word. Come on, now,
honey. I'll be gentle. I won't harm you atall. I'll take a hold of
you real soft-like and . . ."

Rae Lynn headed for the house.

Butch called out and said, "All right. All right. I'll give you
a bit more time to think on it. I can be generous. You'll come
to your senses. It don't matter where it happens. We can do
it right here in the yard, for all I care. Either I get what I'm
wanting, or I'm telling him what happened out here. Him
being a lawyer and all, well, can't imagine jail life would suit
you none."

She glanced over her shoulder at him in the hopes he was
leaving, and when she did, he got the wrong message.

He grinned, and he said, "Now that's more like it."

She ran inside and rushed to the bedroom. The front screen
door banged. He was inside.

He called out, "Yoo-hoo! Where are you? I bet I know.

You're in that bedroom already perched on the bed. Go on and take that dress off, 'cause here I come!"

She turned and faced the doorway. Butch appeared and at the sight of the pistol clenched in her hands, his face sagged in the same sad manner as an old bloodhound.

He said, "Well, darn, Rae Lynn. Being with me, is it that bad?"

She raised the weapon level to his chest. He backed up, and she followed him.

"Woman, you gone plumb nutty."

She said, "Get outta my house."

He said, "Ain't gonna be yours for long. I'll surely let him know what you done now! And here I was thinking of offering you somewheres to stay!" Rae Lynn cocked it, and he reversed course, yelling, "You gone off your rocker!"

He bolted for his truck and took off down the path, leaving a trail of dust and a bad taste in her mouth. She went out into the yard and waited, thinking he might come back. When some time had passed, and she was sure he was gone for good, she dragged the mattress from the bedroom into the yard. It had a horrible stain down the side of it when Warren had done what he'd done, and so she'd been sleeping on the couch. She soaked it with turpentine and tossed a match on it, then monitored the flames, raking back debris so nothing was around it to catch fire. She watched the flames dance over the darkened patches of dried blood, consuming it. Burning their marriage bed was purifying in a way she couldn't describe, as if by doing this, she was also burning the memories of what happened.

That night as she laid on the couch, clutching the pistol and the pillow Warren had used, and she'd thought to keep because it still smelled of him, she talked as if he was there instead of saying her prayers.

"I miss you. You took good care of me all these years. It was only 'cause of you I finally had me a real home, first one in my life. Now, I don't know what all's gonna happen. Oh, Warren. I only wish you'd listened to me, because it shouldn't've been this way."

Even while she talked, her mind was on Butch. What if she let him, just the once, like he'd said? No. To consider it was absurd. Not only would it sully the memory of what she'd had with her husband, she'd have to reconcile those actions for as long as she lived. No doubt she would regret it. As to Eugene, she knew nothing about him other than what Warren had told her, but one thing was certain, he'd not seen fit to come home all these years. He'd barely ever written, never addressed her in the times he did. When it came down to it, she believed his distancing had been because Warren married her, though he'd blamed it on Eugene not caring about the land. Probably to protect her. If she refused to go along with Butch's blackmail, and stayed, what might Eugene do once he heard what Butch had to say? All she knew was, she wasn't about to leave her future in the hands of these two men; neither was trustworthy.

She tossed and turned until finally, she heard the clock chime five times, and got up. Sitting there at the kitchen table in the predawn hour, she stared at the chair Warren always sat in, noticing how the wooden rung at the top had a deeper finish from where he'd put his hand many times. She'd never noticed this before, and tears came, as they did so often now. After a few minutes, she wiped her face on her apron. She stared at her kitchen, at all the little things she'd done to make it hers, realizing it really never had been, when it came right down to it. The tone of that letter said it was Eugene's. At least Warren had a little bit of money set aside, but once gone, that was it. They had some gum stores she could sell, but not much, and there was the question of time.

Rae Lynn poured herself some tea and as she was sipping

on it, seemingly from nowhere, she remembered something Butch said and her pulse quickened. She'd been focused only on what she and Warren had planned together, confining herself to those ideas and not thinking beyond. With the sun barely peeking into the kitchen window she began to formulate what she needed to do. The most important part was she had to hurry. She had to be gone before Butch came again, and her intention was to disappear. She grabbed the truck key and drove into town. Luckily, Dinky Dobbins, who ran the General Mercantile, was always open early. She went in and asked for the smallest sized men's boots.

Dinky said, "Warren, he wears a size eleven not a seven."

"Ain't for him."

He stared at her long and hard.

"You wanting this money or not?" she said.

He took it. On her way home she recollected how the orphanage pinched every single penny to make do, yet even by those standards, Warren Cobb had been tighter than a tick. Once, the soles of his shoes had got so thin he'd cut his foot when he'd crossed over the railroad tracks and stepped on some random piece of metal. He'd come home bleeding while waving two thin strips of rubber at her.

He'd said, "Got these off'n them tires from that no-good piece of junk truck sitting abandoned on the side of the road. This'll work better than 'Hoover leather,' don't ya think? They'll be good as new."

She was glad he'd been that way, at least now, as she thought about the money still left after this purchase. Sitting in the truck, she glanced down at her feet and felt a twinge of guilt remembering what he'd been buried in. She stared at the smooth, unmarred leather, wiggled her toes, guilt surging, retreating. Well, he wouldn't know the difference, and what was done was done, wasn't that the way of it?

Back home she confiscated his extra pair of overalls, cut

the hem so they didn't drag the ground. Next, she set aside a couple of his shirts. She was grateful he'd not been much bigger than her, a couple inches taller with more muscle. What she did next hurt, but only because of vanity. She moved with purpose onto the front porch, scissors in one hand as she pulled the pins out of her hair with the other. Grasping handfuls at a time, she began cutting section by section, then went back around again, and again, until it reached midway to her ears. She did the best she could and when she felt it was short enough, she stood in front of the mirror where Warren used to shave every morning. She had to stand on tiptoe to give herself a decent view of her face. It would have to do. With shorter hair, she could feel a draft against her neck and it was as if someone breathed on her. She thought of Warren sleeping beside her at night, his breath soft and steady against her skin.

She gathered the shorn hair where it lay around her feet, like some sort of boneless, skinless animal, and took it to the fresh mound near the line of old catfaced trees. She tossed it softly across the fresh dirt of his grave, as if scattering seed, leaving him this one last thing, a small token of her love. She stayed another minute, ruminating on the direction her life was about to take. She tried not to think too much on Warren, how she'd last seen him. It was not easy. Images came anyway, and in nightmarish color. She left the graveside and went back into the house. She'd already packed the truck with a few necessities. Her skillet, coffeepot, sheets she'd embroidered, the extra shirt of Warren's, some food for the trip, and some of the dry goods. What was left of the cash was in the bib section of the overalls she would wear in the morning when she left. She spent one last, tense night on the couch, holding on to the pistol. Come dawn she was up, and out the door for the last time.

Butch would come today, she was certain of it. By the time

he figured it out, she'd be well on her way. She went across the yard toward the chicken coop, a scrap of paper in hand, a cryptic note scribbled in pencil: *The chickens and mule are all you get from me.* She tacked it in plain sight, near the coop. She didn't want anything to influence her, make her change her mind, like worrying about her laying hens. She scattered corn, made sure they had water, and let the mule out into the pasture. Finally, she got in the truck, once again grateful to Warren for having shown her how to crank it and how to drive. She took his hat off the dash and slapped it on her head. She refused to linger or to look back.

She put the truck in gear, and drove away from the only home she'd ever known, grateful for him rescuing her from the likelihood of a life as bland as a bowl of plain grits had she gone the route the Magnolia House encouraged. She silently thanked him once more, for not only giving her love and a home, but for also teaching her new skills. The tobacco barn came into view and she stared at the structure, knowing the gap in her soul that belonged to Warren was there, caught up inside, and it would remain there, as well as in the little house under the fragrant pines. She lifted her arm and sniffed the sleeve of his shirt, caught a hint of him and their world in it. With tear-filled eyes, she came to the main road and headed south. She wouldn't stop until she reached Valdosta, Georgia, and the Swallow Hill turpentine camp Butch told them about, praying she could pull off her new identity as Ray Cobb, at least until she felt safe.

Chapter 9

Del

The box was like a vault, its interior murky except for slivers of sunlight leaking through the cracks and the air holes drilled near the top of his head. It reeked, a combination of human waste and death, traces from those before, of the hell they'd endured. Flies, persistent and droning, were all he could hear at the moment. Del lay seething, knowing this idiotic maneuver had nothing to do with missed trees. He was sure of it. It had to do with Crow trying to make a point. He didn't like the idea of Del working with the coloreds. He began to assess the cramped interior. He tested the width by touching the sides, and the length by pointing his feet so the tips of his boots reached the end. Realizing just how small the enclosure was, he went straight back to the grain bin and the suffocating experience of the corn collapsing around him. That had been the most horrific moment of his life until now. It wasn't only fresh air he was craving, it was moving without restriction.

Eyes clenched, he willed himself to stay calm, but his mind kept measuring the box, comparing his situation to the corn, until fear gathered in the center of his chest and made his heart pump wildly. Out came animal-like grunts of alarm. He couldn't stop thinking of the moment the grain covered him, of when he could no longer breathe. Abruptly, he hit his fist against the side, once, twice, and then his control disappeared, and his fear became fire on dry timber. He began pounding against the top, kicking the sides. He no longer cared who heard, if anyone. He paused, gasping, a hoarse, ragged wheezing unrecognizable to his ears filled the small space.

He said to himself, "It ain't the bin, you ain't in the bin."

He regained control and tried something else. He thought of Mercy, Juniper's wife, but not for the usual reason. One of the things he'd liked about her was her calm demeanor. He recollected her sitting among the crepe myrtles, the colorful flowers surrounding her like a picture frame, and her in a pale-green dress sprinkled with similar pink flowers, slow rocking and shelling peas. He thought of the tip of her nose, the curve of her shoulder, her soft humming as she worked. He stayed there, in his mind, with her, and he relaxed. What he'd been doing wouldn't do any good, and if Crow heard him, he could keep him there longer out of spite. Later he tuned in to the sounds of the camp, the thud of someone chopping wood, voices calling out, and snatches of birdsong. He listened to see if anyone came close. Eventually, he drifted in and out of sleep.

Hours passed, and as the sun rose higher, heat built inside the little box too. He needed to relieve himself and as he rubbed sweat from his face, he vowed, somehow Crow would pay. His head pounded in rhythm with his heart as he watched the streaks of sunlight coming through the cracks, slanting across him as time passed. He closed his eyes again, imagined pine branches waving in the evening's hot breeze, the horizon smeared with a melting orange sun. After a while, he roused and became aware of someone laughing directly above him, and thought he might be dreaming. He frowned, listening intently. The laugh came again and he recognized it. He didn't react, refusing to give Crow the satisfaction of begging to be let out. Something told him if he did, he'd never let him forget.

The snickering stopped abruptly and next came a loud knock, near his right ear. He looked through the narrow gap in the wood, remembering how the other man who laid here before him, who'd likely died in this very spot, had stared up at him, desperate and scared. He saw nothing. A heavier, steady thumping started on the lid, like someone dancing a jig, and dust from the top fell, and he had to shut his eyes.

Then, the voice he was beginning to despise said, "Yoohoo, anybody home?" Crow stamped his feet some more. "Hello?"

Crow hammered his fists against the wood. "Golly, I sure do smell something worser'n a skunk! What y'all reckon that is? I know. It's the smell of chicken shit!"

Ballard's oddly pitched voice came through, above the din of Crow cavorting about, enjoying himself.

He said, "Peewee told me directly we can't be losing no more men, got too much work to do."

Del heard the annoyance in Crow's voice as he replied to the other woods rider.

"I'm only showing this one he can't be skipping work, and if he does, he ain't getting off no different than nobody else."

"Yeah, well, since when have loblollys been part of a crop? Besides, we got business to discuss, so when you're done entertaining yourself, Peewee needs you in his office."

There was some mumbling, a click, and the squeal of rusty hinges. Del lay straight-legged, arms at his sides, squinting up at the man standing over him. Crow chortled at him, then pressed a hand over his heart and began play-acting.

"Dearly beloved, who are gathered here today . . ."

He thought this hilarious and laughed hard enough to start wheezing. Overcome, he squatted, while Ballard, stoic and serious, stood nearby. The other work hands rubbed their jaws in nervousness, and some allowed a few random chuckles here and there, wary and forced. Crow wiped his eyes, leaned toward the box, and peeked in at Del, who'd not moved.

He said, "Boo!" and fell onto the ground howling again.

Del sat up. His entire body shook, and he thought he might get sick. He would've liked to have punched Crow if he'd had the strength, but he'd never been the fighting type, and what good would it do nohow? He stood, and ignoring the other man, he stepped over the side and began walking away, intent on getting water, but mostly wanting to get away from crazy Crow.

Crow's laughter subsided, and he called out, "Hey. You."

Del stopped but didn't turn around.

Crow called out, "You understand, right? How things is? You chose how it's gonna be. Can't blame nobody but yourself, is how I see it."

Del paused, then faced him, and Ballard suddenly came forward, as if anticipating a fight of some sort. Del would only have told the man his choices ought not matter so much. The work got done, didn't it?

Ballard said, "Okay, everyone, let's all get a good night's rest. Tomorrow we go at it again, bright and early. Come on, Sweeney. We got to meet Peewee."

Crow kept his gaze on Del and said, "That's right. Tomorrow's another day for you poor suckers."

Del let it go. He really didn't care to explain himself. He started walking again while the spot between his shoulder blades remained tense, aware Crow watched him. Once again he'd somehow managed to get on the wrong side of a boss man, but this time, he surely wasn't to blame. As soon as he was at the shack, he went directly to the well. He pumped the handle and when the water gushed from the spout, he stuck his face under it and drank, and drank. Eventually he stuck his whole head under, blindly reaching over so he could keep pumping. He straightened up, and feeling better, he sank into a chair on the porch. He mulled over the idea of leaving, only he'd already run from Sutton's. Is that the kind of man he'd become? Somebody who ran away when in a tough spot? If all he had was his name, and his reputation, then he had to prove both meant something, at least to himself.

His clothes reeked from being in the box, but he was too worn-out to do anything about them. Instead, he went inside and came out, tugging the mattress. He let it drop on the porch, went around to the back and over to the edge of the woods, and began to gather Spanish moss off of the low-lying limbs of one of the few hardwoods in the area. Stuffing the mattress was low on his list, but he had to do something. Back on the porch, he began packing handfuls inside the dingy covering. Not long into it, Nolan wandered by, propped himself on the fence. He kept looking over his shoulder, while Del stuffed in moss, shook it down, and added more.

Nolan said, "French hair."

"Huh?"

Nolan pointed at the wispy gray strands hanging from Del's hand.

Del said, "Oh."

Nolan watched another minute or two, then said, "It makes it feel cooler."

Del said, "It does?"

Nolan said, "Um-hmm." He rubbed at his head and appeared troubled. "Gotta say, sure was surprised when boss man done what he done."

Del was in no mood to talk about it, so his reply was cryptic.

"No more'n me."

"Reckon he got it in for you, somehow."

Del stopped packing the mattress and considered telling Nolan it had to do with the fact he was working amongst coloreds, but he didn't have to.

Nolan said, "It's 'cause you working with us. I know how he is. Ain't gone do nothing but cause trouble."

Del stopped working and said, "Yeah. Well. I can't see why it matters so much."

"In this camp, it do. To some. He gone come down on anyone trying to change how it is."

"I ain't trying to change nothing. I needed work, somewhere to stay. I hoped to make a little money, too, but I should've known better."

"'S all any of us wanted, but it don't do no good getting him stirred up."

Del went back to stuffing the mattress, and Nolan was quiet. Music came from somewhere in the middle of the camp.

Nolan tipped his head and said, "Juke joint's kicking in."

Del turned his head a little and heard a bluesy wail coming from the colored part of camp.

He said, "I ain't ever been in one."

"You ain't never been jukin'? Well, after today, you could stand some music, and a little somethin' special. Come on. I ain't supposed to be over here as it is, but I got somethin' needs saying, and best way to do it is with a little liquor in me."

Del was tired and didn't feel like going anywhere, but he got to his feet and said, "Well, all right."

He pulled his mattress back inside and as a last thought, he pocketed Melody and the two men started off. They came to a grouping of shacks in a section backed against the woods with only one way in and out, the path they were on. This was the colored's section. As they passed by, most went about their business, but some glanced at him and Nolan strangely. Del was cautious, glancing over his shoulder and side to side, nervous that Crow might see him and decide he needed more learning.

They went by several shanties and a few of the men called out to Nolan, "Hey, Long Gone, you jukin' tonight?" and "Hey! Last time you went where I think you're headed, took you two days to get over it."

Del saw a different side of Nolan than when they'd first met. The man went along with an easy, big smile, walking loose, relaxed, and at one point, he even performed a little jig.

Someone hollered out, "Why you bringing *him*?"

They approached a tar-paper-covered shack decorated with hundreds of bottle caps and a couple of advertisements, one for Red Man chewing tobacco, the other for Coca-Cola. A few men sat outside in rocking chairs, easing them back and forth slowly, while others were perched on stools. All had some form of alcohol close by. He noticed jugs with the corks popped off, jars with varying amounts of clear liquid, set within arm's reach. Here faces were friendlier, their consumption of what they called "buck," which was corn liquor, had eased their aches and pains, and washed away the troubles of the day. A handful of them had instruments and were in the middle of a song. One strummed a banjo, one pulled a tune from a fiddle, another held spoons clacking out a rhythm, while yet another stroked his thumb rhythmically up and down an old washboard. The song wasn't familiar to Del, but he still wished he could join in on Melody. He would have liked to have played along with them, but Nolan was inside now, so Del went in too.

Off in one corner was a small table where four men sat, the blue haze of cigarette smoke hovering over their heads, faces illuminated by the oil lamp set in the center. They were playing cards but stopped long enough to raise their jars toward Nolan.

Nolan pointed at a small table and said, "Sit there, and I'll get us some hooch."

Del said, "I'm okay with a RC or orangeade."

Nolan shook his head, and Del raised his shoulders. He went and sat, continuing to take in the atmosphere, one that held an air of tension, a suggestion of something about to happen. A pool table sat in the center of the room, and two men played a boisterous game, calling each other derogatory names when one made a poor shot. He glimpsed a couple seated in a rustic booth, holding hands across the table, aware of no one but each other. He put his attention back on Nolan and the woman who served him. Nolan took some time to flirt a little before he came back over to Del and offered him a choice.

He said, "This one's straight, this one, it's got some lemonade added to it. Since you ain't a drinker, you might like it best."

Del took it, sipped, and raised his eyebrows in surprise. "It ain't bad."

Nolan grinned and said, "Still potent, 'specially if you ain't used to drinking."

They relaxed and watched the comings and goings frequently punctuated by the twang and creak of the spring-loaded screen door. The liquor begin to unwind the knotty spot between Del's shoulders as it warmed him from the inside out. After a few minutes, and a few more sips, Nolan sat forward, leaned across the table to stare directly into Del's eyes.

"What brung you here?"

Del rolled the glass between his hands. He wanted to tell him about the grain bin, felt he could for some odd reason. He started off with what most said nowadays.

"I needed work."

Nolan waited for him to go on while Del stared into his glass. The silence grew. He shifted on his chair, glanced again at Nolan, who'd not dropped his calm gaze.

"Something peculiar happened, and I've yet to figure it out, so I thought work might do me some good. I'd been living in the woods awhile."

Nolan sat back, took a sip of his drink, and said, "What's peculiar for some, ain't for others."

"You might change your mind after hearing this. Boss man I had before I come here, he didn't care much for me either. In his case, he had good reason. He told me to work in the grain bin one day, and while I was in it, he had a couple other workers open the door. The grain swallered me whole. I couldn't move, nothing. Then, I couldn't breathe. It was the worst pain I ever felt, until suddenly, I was outside the grain bin. I could see them trying to save me."

He stopped talking, watched Nolan for his reaction. Nolan only sipped some more, still listening.

Del emphasized what he'd said. "You understand. I was *outside,* looking down. I could see *everything.*"

Nolan leaned back in his chair, and he said, "My granny used to tell me stories like'at all a time. Said some souls trying to leave this earth get trapped 'tween places. Sometimes you end up roamin' the earth, looking a door to Heaven. You ask me, you was lucky."

Del felt a bit of relief. "You heard a such as this happening?"

Nolan said, "From my granny. Like I said. You was lucky. Least you didn't get stuck like some do."

"Well, I don't know about lucky. Ever since . . ." And he stopped.

His face grew warm and not from the drink.

Nolan was curious. "Ever since . . . ?"

Del leaned back. Crossed his arms.

He said, "I'm . . . broke. I can't, you know, be with a woman. It don't seem natural."

Nolan gave a dismissive wave. "Only takes the right woman. You ask me, this"—and he held up his glass—"and hard work helps. Reason I drink is to forget. Me and my Dottie, we was together over forty years. She been gone about five, but it seem like forever now."

They sat in silence for a bit, taking a swallow now and then, and Del reflected on how it might be to have someone like Nolan had. He finished his drink and said something he thought he'd never say.

"I'll get the next round."

Nolan dipped his head in agreement, and Del got up and approached the bar.

In his usual friendly manner, he said, "Hey, miss. How're you tonight?"

She didn't respond. Leaning against the counter, a cigarette pinched between her thumb and forefinger, looking bored, she pushed off the bar with her hip, blew smoke from the side of her mouth, and in a no-nonsense tone said, "What you want?"

He put a thumb over his shoulder toward Nolan and said, "Same as what he got before."

She said, "You know how this works, right? Like over to the commissary. Otis supplies the liquor."

Del said, "Figures."

She rolled her eyes and said, "Name, number where yer stayin'?"

He gave her the information, and she fixed the drinks, set them in front of him. She made some marks in a ledger, then ignored him and began moving jars and bottles around on the shelves. Del watched the movement of her backside under the snug material of her dress. Nothing. He sighed and made his way back to Nolan, almost spilling what he had when two men stumbled into him, jabbing at each other playfully, full of drink and good times. From across the room came a round of cussing.

"Dammit all, had me a full hand, now you tryin' to gyp me. You got my money!"

"Hell if it is! You a cheatin' sonofabitch and everybody knows it!"

There was a scuffle and the crash of a glass breaking. Two of the card players had jumped up and were leaning across the table, holding crude knives and jabbing at each other.

Another card player, an older man with gray hair sprouting from his scalp in a patchy manner and missing most of his teeth, said, "Y'all sit'cher asses down. Act like you got some sense, or you can leave this table. Me and Lanky don't need y'all to play us a decent game. That right, Lanky?"

The fourth man, Lanky, said, "You right."

The two men continued facing each other as if they would start fighting, and Del expected someone to get hurt. The older man stood up, knocking his chair over.

He pointed at them, the other hand in his pocket signaling he too had some sort of weapon. "I ain't messin'. I kin clear it up right now."

The other men eased back down in their seats, pocketing their weapons, but neither lowered their eyes. Nolan watched the men carefully as well, but it appeared the moment was over, and he turned back to Del.

He said, "Ain't easy workin' in a place like this, so they get liquored up." He took a few more sips and leaned back in his chair. "I ain't said my piece yet, and I best get on with it so we can get out of here before it gets rough."

Del detected a change in the tone of his voice, distant, less friendly.

Nolan said, "This here's the first and last time you and me do this. I can't be gettin' into no trouble. I know how *he* is.

We got our place in this camp, and it's best we act like we know it. It don't include minglin' with white folk. He see me with you, doin' whatever, even talkin', he gone think I went and got uppity, and he gone teach me a lesson. Put me in my place. That's just the way of it with him."

Nothing Nolan said surprised Del at this point. Sure, Nolan had to look out for himself, given what it might mean to any one of them, a death sentence essentially, and he couldn't blame him.

Del said, "Can't say as I disagree. It gives him the upper hand, though. If we stuck together, all of us, things might change. Ain't but the one box. He can't put all of us in it."

Nolan gave a derogatory grunt.

He said, "No. But whoever gets put in there, could be you, could be me. I ain't ready to die. You ready to die? It sounds to me like you meant to be here a bit longer."

Del said, "No, I ain't ready to die."

He thought the grain bin had been horrific, but it was quicker than a slow death in the box.

Nolan said, "You had you a few hours in it, but when it comes to what goes on round here, you got off easy. Won't be the same next time, for you or me, if he gets any reason to put one of us in it."

The next few minutes passed in silence, with Nolan appearing broody. Del, wiped out from the hours confined, was hungry, and the liquor was starting to make the headache he'd had earlier come back.

He said, "I hear you, Nolan. I 'preciate the time, and you clearing things up. I also 'preciate you listening to my other story. Good to know I ain't crazy."

Del stood, and Nolan gave him a bleary stare along with a final warning.

"Hmm. We all got a little crazy in us, main thing is, watch your back."

Del nodded, and crossed the small space, while suspicious eyes tracked him until he was out the door. The music coming from those on the porch didn't stop as he passed by them, although he was aware they watched him leaving too. On the path that wound its way around the little shanties, he was alone, most everyone gone inside for the day, except those at the juke joint. Wood smoke drifted from the cook fires, and the smell of suppers being cooked throughout the camp made Del hurry along, ready to eat and get to bed.

Near the single men's area, he saw an old beat-up truck rattling along down the path through the middle of the camp. He watched as it parked in front of the office building. The door opened, and a short, skinny man climbed out, overalls hanging off him, hat sitting low on his head. The stranger stretched with his hands on his hips as he bent backward, then forward, like he'd come a long way. The man caught Del staring, mashed his hat farther on his head, then sort of scuttled inside the office building. Del continued on his way, thinking if it was someone wanting to work, he was already doing better than most. He had him a truck, an uncommon piece of property. Most around here still got around on mules, horses, and wagons. Del was inclined to think if it was him, and if he had *him* a truck, he'd sell it, make some money rather than work here.

The sunset glowed like a long thread of orange laced through the pines, transforming the woods, and making them appear as if they were on fire. The sight gave him a shiver, like he was actually seeing trees burning, and he had a sense of impending doom. It was a feeling he couldn't shake, so much so his sleep was fitful, and before he knew it, dawn came again.

Chapter 10

Rae Lynn

She was going along at forty-five miles per hour when she swerved to avoid a pothole and something hit the front end. Immediately white steam came from the front under the hood and the truck's engine began to stall. She pulled over to the side of the road and stared in disbelief as the vapors rose in the air. A farmer tending his fields nearby saw her predicament and came over, looking from her to the ailing truck.

He said, "What you reckon you gonna do?"

Aggravated and feeling as hot as the overheated engine, Rae Lynn got out and stared at puffs of steam coming out from under the hood. The sun was a white-hot disk straight overhead, while cicadas rattled relentlessly in the distant trees. Rae Lynn, uncertain how she was going to fix the problem, didn't find his question one bit helpful. Plus, she was worried over how she appeared to him. She squared her shoulders. Stared him in the eye.

She snapped out a reply. "How would I know? It just happened."

"Well."

She didn't say anything else and he didn't either, both of them standing with hands shoved in pockets like they were having an impromptu social visit. As the silence expanded to the point of being uncomfortable, she realized, since she was a "man," it was expected she ought to be investigating what was wrong. Assuming fake confidence, she bent over and fiddled with the latches, lifted one side of the hood, and exposed the engine. She stared at the workings, which made about as much sense to her as the innards of a dissected frog, something she'd had to do in a biology class at the orphanage. She couldn't make sense of what was what in this truck, not without something to tell her. Besides, Warren had always been the one to work on it. She went back to the driver's side and dug around under the seat for a manual, a schematic, or anything that might help, and found only an old oily rag.

Sensing the farmer's watchful eye, she went back to the engine and proceeded to touch this and that, his presence putting her on edge. At least she was sweating like a man. She stopped tugging and adjusting the whatnots under the hood when he cleared his throat loudly. He was at the front of the vehicle.

With a dry tone, he said, "This here's your problem."

Rae Lynn straightened up and went to where he stood. He pointed at a hole in the radiator, which definitely had not been there when she started out.

He said, "I 'spect it ain't got no water left in it at this point."

She said, "No, I reckon not."

He said, "How far you going?"

She said, "Valdosta."

He said, "Well. You got a ways to go yet, but I reckon some brown soap would hold till you can get it fixed. Wait here."

She leaned against the truck, chewing a nail before dropping her hand. Would a man bite his nails with worry? She didn't think so, plus she'd been rude. And, to top it off, she was embarrassed by not knowing what ought to have been obvious, what with steam pouring from the front.

He was back a few minutes later with a bar of Fels-Naptha soap and a somewhat full bucket, part of the water having sloshed over the sides as he'd made his way back.

He handed her the soap, and she took it and said, "Thank you."

She held it, not sure if she was supposed to stick a piece directly into the hole or what. He frowned at her, and since she couldn't see what else would be done, she dug around in Warren's overalls, remembering he'd always carried around a pocketknife. Her fingers encountered the small tool, and she quickly cut a plug out and the farmer came to life, confirming she was on the right track and involuntarily guiding her by telling her a story.

"Had to do this myself about a week ago. Mashed a piece of soap into the radiator of yonder truck. It's got the rust, getting' on old, like me. Reckon I'll have to do something to fix it proper and all, sooner or later."

Rae Lynn barely paid attention to the rest of his prattling after he'd more or less told her what she needed to do. His hawkish observation made her nervous, and her sweaty fingers turned the soap slick. She didn't quite get it in, and it fell onto the ground. She retrieved it, brushed the grass off, and mashed it back into the hole, and that's when he noticed her finger.

"You must've lopped that off chopping wood or something like'at. Wouldn't be real smart, but things happen."

She glanced over her shoulder and glared at him. The soap stayed, thank the Lord. He unscrewed the radiator cap and tipped the bucket to refill it. He didn't look at her as he kept on talking.

"I tell you what. They's a lot to be said about depending on one's own self. As head of the household, we supposed to know everything. I ain't ever figgered out how some don't know doodly squat. Reckon it was their raising."

He side-eyed her and Rae Lynn resigned herself to having to listen. She was indebted to him, after all. He went on, freely speaking his mind.

"Seems to me somebody ought not take off knowing they's going so far without being prepared. Seems to me somebody would have them some extra water on hand, just in case. Hell, even in this day and age, having some soap ain't nothing, no matter how bad off things is. Nope. I mean, one's free, and the other, it don't cost much. Any growed man knows that. Least I reckon you's a growed man. And you, coming all this a way without none of them things. Least you did bring you some gas, right there in the back. Least you done that."

Her face flushed with a mixture of anger and humiliation. She fingered the money she had in her pocket. That twelve remaining dollars was a lifeline in case things didn't work out in Valdosta. Well, she'd at least give him a dollar for his trouble, and maybe two cents more. He finished in silence and after he'd put the cap on, and before he could say another word, she thrust the bill out. He stared at it, at her, and reached out to take it.

She said, "For your few minutes of trouble and the high-and-mighty sermon."

She smacked her hands together like she was ridding them of dirt, went to the driver's side, and got in. Because the engine was still warm, she could eliminate the choke steps for getting it started. As she pulled away, she looked back at him and saw he at least had the decency to give her a contrite little wave. Rae Lynn scolded herself: *If you aim to pull this off, you got to do better.* She faced forward, still fuming a bit over the things he'd said, while feeling aggravated with herself. She drove on, counting it as a much-needed lesson on remembering how she was supposed to act.

She'd estimated the entire trip to take fourteen hours, but with the radiator problem, and the fact she slowed down on account she was afraid she'd have trouble again, she ended up having to spend the night under a grove of old oaks. She could see the dim lights from a small farmhouse across a cotton field, the glow from the windows offering her a bit of comfort, knowing she wasn't completely alone. She ate some of the food she brought, a leftover biscuit filled with fatback, a few slices of her bread and butter pickles she'd put up the year before, and she drank water from a jar. She missed Warren terribly. The weight of the pistol in one of the pockets of the overalls was a constant reminder. She shifted on the truck seat, felt it against her hip bone, and considered maybe she ought to toss it into the ditch, but it was necessary, given her circumstances. Because she wasn't concentrating on driving, she had time to think, maybe too much.

Again, her eyes filled, and she spoke out loud. "Got to quit your squalling, Rae Lynn. Can't be bawling like a baby as Ray Cobb."

She tried to sleep, but that was nigh on impossible. Scuffling noises had her wondering what moved about she couldn't see. Warren had said the nighttime made noises louder, and she hoped he was right. Probably a possum, but sounded like a bear. She eventually did find sleep, but, at dawn when she sat up and gazed about, she felt bleary-eyed and exhausted. She wished for a cup of coffee, real coffee, not the chicory kind. Would it be so bad to go to the farmhouse and beg for a cup, the way some had come to her own back door now and again, those who'd found themselves off the beaten path and worse off than most? She thought about it only a second. As Ray Cobb, it would be safer to simply drink some water.

Now the sun was up, the landscape was once again friendly, inviting, and her unease over what she heard the night before seemed ridiculous. Opening the door of the truck, she got out and groaned as she started moving about. For all the convenience of these newfangled vehicles, the bumps and jolts on the hard seat for hours had her stiff and sore. She checked on the soap plug, which aside from having caught its share of bugs, remained in place. After taking care of her needs, she went through the tedious steps to crank the engine, grateful when it caught. She pulled away, the only sign she'd been there was the depression of the truck's tires crushing the clover and chickweed. She drove until late afternoon and reached the outskirts of Valdosta. Thirsty, she decided to stop for a cold drink and to find out where the Swallow Hill camp was exactly. After her little to-do with the farmer, she was more clearheaded about her role as Ray Cobb. She spotted a small roadside store, pulled in, and parked, then sat for a minute or two, staring at the door. Maybe walking with more confidence would make a difference. She went inside, making sure to clomp heavy footed across the planked floor as she went to get a cold Pepsi out of the cooler. She kept her hands crammed into her pockets in a manner she thought befitted a man. At the counter a broad-hipped woman, hair wrapped in a scarf, heavy breasts resting on the counter, frowned at her.

The woman pointed at her feet and said, "If them boots is dirty, you need to do all that stomping outside. I only just swept this floor."

Rae Lynn winced, and without thinking, said in her regular voice, "Oh, sorry," which earned her a questioning look from the woman. Red-faced, she popped the top off the drink and carefully approached the counter. She handed the woman a nickel and avoided too much eye contact.

In a low tone, she said, "I'm looking for Swallow Hill."

The woman took the nickel, opened the cash register, and said, "Ain't far."

Studying Rae Lynn with steady eyes, she gave her direc-

tions, mainly to go "that a way" and look for a small sign saying SWALLOW HILL.

"A couple miles or so, and you're there."

Rae Lynn said, "Thankee kindly."

The woman said, "You traveling alone? Where's your
family?"

Now it was Rae Lynn frowning at her. "Ain't none a your
business."

The woman said, "Huh. Reckon your mama ain't never
taught you no manners neither. Young men nowadays ain't
respectful atall."

Rae Lynn rushed out, screen slamming behind her. In the
truck, she wiped sweat off her forehead and felt a headache
coming on. She would get better at this, she had to. After a
few miles she spotted a decrepit hand-painted marker that said
SWALLOW HILL, fastened to a slash pine with an arrow pointing up. Next, she came to a long and narrow sandy dirt road,
not unlike the path to the house back home. With nothing
but big clumps of wiregrass and stately pine trees scattered
about, the area was isolated and lonely seeming. Rae Lynn
drove the last leg of her trip, and out of nowhere came the
distinct odor of a turpentine still, long before she came to it.

Minutes later, a cooper's shed came into view, and beside
that, the turpentine distillery. There was another building
with OFFICE over the door. She pulled in front of it and got
out of the truck, taking a moment to stretch. As she bent
backward, then forward, she noticed a man watching her
from a distance. She clamped her hat more firmly on her
head, shoved her hands in her pockets, and swaggered inside.
A heavyset man, busy with paperwork behind a messy desk,
puffed heavily on a cigar as if his very life depended on it.

Using her new voice, she said, "Heard there's work here."

He lifted his eyes, gave her a once-over and to her mind, it took him a tad too long. His brow cinched like he found her statement strange. Or maybe it was her appearance. She held her ground, didn't blink, didn't move. Didn't breathe.

He spoke finally. "We got plenty of work, too much. Name's Pritchard Taylor. Peewee to some, although there's a name suits you, not me so much."

She didn't know what to say to that. He jumped up with a boisterous laugh.

"I'm only kidding."

He put out his hand, and with relief, she stuck hers into his grip. He proceeded to grind her knuckle bones together as he pumped her hand. She managed not to flinch, and returned the handshake as firmly as she could, fighting the urge to rub her knuckles soon as he released her hand. He plopped back into his chair and commented on her size again.

"Sheeyoot. You look like a good wind could blow you away. You sure you up to this kind a work?"

Rae Lynn growled out an answer. "Always been a mite small for my age, but I'm strong as they come."

The new deep voice she used had an unfortunate crack at the end.

He gave her a doubtful glance and said, "How old are you, kid?"

She said, "Twenty-six."

"What? You ain't even got no whiskers. Fine, fine. You say you're twenty-six, I reckon I'm Methuselah." Peewee chuckled at his little joke and went on. "What's the name?"

"Ray Cobb."

"Family?"

"Sir?"

"Family. You got family?"

She said, "I was married, but . . ."

Peewee had been scribbling, and he stopped.

Rae Lynn was quick to reply. "He . . . I mean, *she* passed on. Tragic accident."

"Hmm. Sorry to hear that."

Rae Lynn cringed at her mistake, but Peewee apparently didn't notice her misstep. He tapped his fingers in a thoughtful manner.

Finally, he leaned forward and said, "I ain't looking no woods riders. You come expecting to do that, by chance?"

"No, sir. I ain't got a horse for one."

"Thought I heard a truck right 'fore you walked in."

"Yes, sir. I come in a truck."

"Ain't got many vehicles round here. Might could use you to haul turpentine to my buyers. We always needing ways a doing that."

"It's got a radiator problem."

"Oh. Well. Where you hail from?"

"South Carolina."

"All righty, then, so you can't be a woods rider, but always got the need for chippers, dippers, and tackers. Thing is, we typically only let the darkies do that sort a work, or making the gum barrels."

"I don't care what I do. I'm good at any of it."

"Some boss men don't take kindly to mixing things up, if you know what I mean?"

Rae Lynn didn't get a chance to respond because he kept on talking.

"I ain't in the mood to hear complaints. Tell you what. I'm gonna put you under Jim Ballard, let him figure out where you fit in. He'll use you where he needs you, and he don't care who's doing what long as the work gets done. The work wagon will come get you at five thirty sharp. Driver's name is Clyde. I'll let Ballard know you're to join his work crew."

She said, "Sounds fine to me."

"We got living quarters for men who ain't married that way. I got fifty-cent or dollar spots."

"I'll take a fifty-cent one. I ain't choosy."

He said, "Get what all you need from the commissary. We pay in scrips."

Rae Lynn didn't say anything about not needing scrips. Best to not let on she had some money.

He said, "You can stay at number forty-four. If it ain't to your liking and you want you a dollar spot, let me know."

She said, "Okay."

"Listen. We're setting dead center of thousands of acres. Make sure you don't get yourself lost out there in them woods. People been known to get gone in the swamp. Gators, water moccasin, wild boar can all be trouble to you. Pay's seventy-five cents a day. That good?"

She nodded. "Sure."

He shoved a piece of paper across the desk and said, "Sign here. This says you agree to that, where you're staying, and who's your boss man. You can park your truck under the lean-to over yonder. Tell Weasel over to the distillery I said it's all right."

She printed her name where he'd put an X, knowing her cursive was too nice for a man's writing. She was careful to put a *y* instead of the *e*, becoming Ray Cobb to him. He took it back, and she allowed him to mangle her hand again. She went out and pulled the truck under the lean-to like he directed, then gathered her things and began making her way to number forty-four. It felt good to stretch her legs some. After a while, right when she believed she might be lost, she passed by the man she'd seen earlier. He sat on his porch cramming Spanish moss into a mattress. Keeping her eyes straight ahead, she was intent on minding her own business. Spot number forty-four ended up beside him, and too close, in her opinion. No privacy whatsoever.

Climbing the short set of steps, she wasn't done in by the terrible condition of the dwelling, but more about what she and Warren would be doing right now if all was as it should be. She felt tears coming on, and held them in. She swiped at her eyes, before scrutinizing the tiny porch, which was covered with dirt. There was an old, worn chair for sitting outside, a dusty, empty bottle by one leg, and not much else. She set her things down and pushed against the door. It seemed stuck. She bumped her shoulder against it and it popped open. She went inside and immediately backed out.

With her hand over the lower half of her face to mask the smell, she scrutinized the small, single room, her new home. The sun had set and a weak light spilling in from two tiny windows made things hard to see, but one thing was certain, it sure smelled bad. Her home with Warren had been old, and showed signs of wear and tear, but it had been clean. This place, though, built to accommodate workers of the camp, had the appearance and stench of having been put here at the beginning of time. There were stains on the walls of questionable origins. The floor was planked but covered with dirt, like the porch. The unidentifiable fusty scent could have come from it being closed up for a while, plus the heat of the day, but she detected overlying odors of rancid grease and the unwashed left-behind dishes stacked on a rustic wooden shelf, encrusted with a mysterious black mold. A dull, dingy mattress was situated on what appeared to be a bedframe built into the wall of one corner.

Disheartened at the awful condition, it took her a moment to realize she was itching on her calves. She yanked a coverall leg up and saw black dots. She stomped her feet and began smacking her hands over her legs. Fleas, and no telling what else. She was still preoccupied with this when she heard a voice.

"Almost slept in the woods my first night. Would've been better maybe, 'cept there's chiggers, skeeters, and snakes out there too. Reckon it wouldn't have mattered much, in hindsight."

Rae Lynn spun around and saw the mattress stuffer. He was at her fence, leaning on it, hat tipped back to reveal a pale forehead in comparison to the rest of his face, hair longish, cheeks and chin bearded. To her mind's eye he was the saddest-looking feller she'd ever laid eyes on, but she didn't know him, so maybe this was his natural expression. He was an odd-looking one. No, not odd. Interesting. His eyes were so pale blue she almost couldn't hardly make out the difference between the irises and the whites. Aware she'd been staring too long, she turned to consider the grimy porch.

He said, "It took some getting used to."

Rae Lynn nodded, but that was it. She wasn't inclined toward being friendly. She'd only come up with this idea a couple days ago, had already seen how being Ray Cobb was rather exhausting, always having to watch what she said and how she said it. Having to watch how she walked. Not mess with her hair. Not forget the voice she was supposed to speak in. He stuck his hand out despite her lack of response.

He said, "Name's Delwood Reese. Folks call me Del."

She stayed where she was and jammed her hands into her pockets.

She tipped her chin up and grumbled her name, "Ray Cobb."

He put his arm down, and he said, "Where you from?"

"South Carolina."

"Which job did you take on?"

"Don't know yet."

She wished he'd leave her alone. She should've gone inside, no matter how bad it was.

He said, "Who you working for?"

Speaking in the unnatural tone she didn't trust, she said, "Ballard."

He stuck his own hands in his pockets and gave the fence post a kick.

He said, "Damn. That's a stroke of luck."

He leaned in conspiratorially, like he believed someone might be listening.

His voice lowered, he said, "I'm under a man goes by the name a Crow. We ain't getting along, but it's his problem more'n mine. Watch yourself around him, that's my advice to you."

Again, she stayed quiet, thinking the less she talked the better. He stared at the sky, then at her.

"Well, figured I'd introduce myself since we're neighbors. Salt works on them fleas."

Rae Lynn gave a nod and a terse response. "I know."

He pushed off the fence and walked back the way he'd come. In seconds, she caught the throaty quaver of a harmonica. The music he made with it lingered in the tepid air, a solitary tune Rae Lynn thought matched his overall disposition. She reentered the shack and began to make do the best she knew how.

Part II

Swallow Hill

Chapter 11

Del

One hot afternoon, he got a chance to watch the new man who'd arrived a few days before. He allowed that he was an okay chipper, kind of slow from what he could tell, but something else about him didn't seem right. The new man was working a drift nearby to his own, so he had a bit of time here and there to study him from a distance. Del pondered on what his situation might be. For one thing, aside from owning a truck, he had on new boots. Everyone here was either barefoot or they might as well have been, because they'd all patched what they had with some variation of Hoover leather. Del had made do recently using newspaper in his own boots since he'd near about worn out the soles. Everyone had a story as to why they were here, he supposed. As the day wore on, their individual drifts led them in separate ways, and now, there was nothing but the bark in front of him and the endless trees.

At quitting time, the wagon came and took everyone back into camp. Del hopped off at the commissary, thinking he'd just as soon settle for opening a couple cans of something. He was too tired to cook. As he entered the store, he blundered into a situation between Otis, his wife, and the new man, Cobb, who looked as hot and sweaty as Del felt. Otis and Cornelia were behind the counter, which wasn't unusual, but Cobb was back there too, facing Otis, pistol in hand. Cornelia was behind him.

Del stood by the door contemplating walking out, and heard Cobb say, "You best leave her be."

Cobb glanced at him, then back to Otis. Seeing as how he'd been spotted, he stayed.

Otis, cigarette dangling from the corner of his lips, said to Cobb, "This ain't none a your concern. She's my wife. She'll do as I say. You getting off on the wrong foot, and I don't take kindly to meddling."

Cobb said, "She was getting what I needed, you didn't have to shove her." He looked back at Cornelia. "You all right?"

Cornelia gave her husband a terrified look before she shifted her attention to the smaller man. Her features smoothed out, hardening like the compacted soil of the much-trampled-on paths between the shacks.

She said, "I ain't needing you to speak on my behalf with regard to my husband."

She faltered on the last part of the sentence, raised her chin, and stared down her nose at Cobb. To Del, she looked like she was trying to convince herself she believed what she said.

Cobb said, "Well, he ain't much of a husband treating you like that. Nobody deserves such."

Otis moved closer and Cobb stepped back, forcing Cornelia to do the same. Otis pointed his finger close to Cobb's nose.

He said, "This here's my store, and how I handle what goes on in here is my business. Ain't nobody got a damn say in it but us, mainly me. She's to obey *me*. Bible says as much. And put that damn gun down."

Cobb cocked his head as he listened to Otis's tirade, but he didn't lower the pistol.

He responded in kind. "Where in the Bible does it say anything about what you done?" He said to Cornelia, "It don't."

Cornelia's face was ashen, and she hesitated before speaking, but when she did, it was to quote Scripture.

"Bible says *obey* your husband. Says, 'Wives, be subject to your husbands as you are to the Lord.'"

Cobb's voice went oddly high. "'Husbands love your wives just as Christ loved the church and gave himself up for her.' Ephesians."

Otis stammered a few weak excuses.

"I take care a her . . . she can't say different . . . hell, she knows it. And she done cost me a purty penny. Done gone off and ordered herself that cloth to make a new dress without my say-so."

Cornelia stepped around Cobb and tried a different tactic. She started sweet-talking, while gesturing at a folded section of material.

"Otis, honey, I ain't had me a new dress since 'fore we met. This one's about to fall to pieces, and so is the other. They're nigh on indecent. You don't want me going round looking so poorly, do you? It ain't good for everybody to see your wife in shabby dresses."

Otis's answer was to pull the cigarette out of his mouth and grab her arm.

Del and Cobb both yelled, "Hey!"

Cornelia tugged against his hand, then froze as he hovered the hot end of the cigarette close to her skin. Otis stared at Cobb and Del, as if daring them to speak as he lowered the cigarette until it was within an inch of Cornelia's skin. Her arm was covered with past puckered, pink scars. This wasn't the first time the bastard had done this. Otis suddenly stuck the hot, ashy end to the material and ground it out. A tiny wisp of smoke curled up, and Otis let go of her arm and pushed her away.

Cobb, voice tight, pointed to the material and said, "How much?"

Otis said, "Huh?"

Cobb repeated himself. "How much did that dress material cost?"

"More'n you got, I can assure you!"

The kid pulled some cash from his overalls and waited. Otis's eyes grew big at the site of a fistful of paper money, and so did Del's.

Deceitful, calculating, Otis said, "Three dollars."

Cobb thumbed through the bills. Del couldn't believe it as he counted out three one-dollar bills and laid them in a row on the counter in front of Otis. Three whole dollars and then some riding around in his pocket. How did anybody come to have that kind a money when nobody around here hardly had two nickels to rub together? Cobb pocketed the gun along with the rest of the money.

He said, "She can make her dress now, if she's able to after you done gone and ruined perfectly good material. It sure don't seem real smart since it was costing you. We got a witness you been paid."

Del said, "That's right."

He sure was impressed with the kid, curious too. Cornelia eyed Cobb with distrust. Cobb's own back was rigid, eyes narrowed at Otis, not paying her any mind, waiting to see what Otis aimed to do.

Otis said, "Well, ain't you Mr. High-and-Mighty?"

Even as he said it, he scraped the bills off the counter faster than a robber holding up a bank.

He stuffed them into his front pocket and said, "Now, get the hell out of my store." To Cornelia, "And you. You get on to the house and you best be getting me my supper, and be quick about it, or else."

Cornelia moved toward the material, and Otis snatched her arm when she was close enough.

Cobb said, "Hey!"

Otis ignored him and said, "And don't you go getting all highfalutin 'cause a this."

He let her go, and Cornelia carefully gathered the cloth and held on to it, shivering like she had a small earthquake going on from within. It was so pronounced, her teeth chattered. Clutching the material, she carefully made her way out of the store.

Cobb followed her out, and while Del needed to get what he came for, he didn't feel like hearing Otis run his mouth. He left too, Otis's taunt trailing after them all.

"Yeah, y'all go on and get the hell out."

Outside, the day was ending at Swallow Hill. Greetings were shouted, and there was even laughter. Mixed in came the thunk of wood being chopped, the scent of supper pots simmering where maybe a bit of meat had been tossed in, if one was lucky. Someone sang a song. Soon the juke joint would get to going. To Del, the sights and sound of the camp appeared innocuous, nonthreatening, but he was becoming aware of an undercurrent, more apparent the longer he was there. It was all a smokescreen, like stepping in quicksand. That was what the camp was, quicksand. The more you struggled to free yourself, the deeper you went. Like the grain bin.

Disconcerted by his thoughts, Del turned his attention to Cobb and Cornelia, who'd crossed her arms and was in the process of confronting the small man.

She said, "I reckon you think I owe *you* now. If you think that's the case, you can forget it."

Cobb said, "What? No!"

Del frowned. Cobb's voice had changed again. He'd bet he wasn't more than sixteen, could be younger. He didn't even have any whiskers yet; his face was smooth as warm butter.

Cornelia said, "I'm paying you back. I take in some outside work now and again, sewing and whatnot, so it might take a while, but I ain't looking to be indebted to nobody else. Just don't be getting no ideas my debt will be paid off in some other form."

Cobb said, "You ain't got to pay me back. You don't owe me nothing."

Cornelia sniffed, disbelief showing in how she rolled her eyes, and with her arms still filled with the pretty dress material, she made her way toward her small house.

Del stared after her, before turning to Cobb. "Where'd you say you're from?"

Cobb mumbled, "South Carolina."

"What did you do before here?"

"Turpentining."

"In a camp?"

Cobb stared off into the distance as if he didn't want to answer.

Finally, he said, "It was a small operation."

"But ain't you using the call name Tar Heel? That ain't South Carolina. That's the Old North State. It's where I'm from."

One of Cobb's eyes twitched, and he offered no explanation. He sure was suspicious acting. Could be he was a runaway. Might have stolen that money he had, them boots too. For all Del knew, Cobb could be wearing the very clothes of a dead man, one he'd killed and took his money.

Cobb said, "If you don't mind, I got things to do."

Del raised a hand and let it drop in a dismissive fashion. "Yeah, me too. Although I'd come to get me a few supplies, and now I reckon if I go back in there, Otis ain't gonna be inclined to sell me nothing tonight."

Cobb inspected the ground, before lifting his gaze to Del, eyes wary. Del hadn't intended to put him on the spot. When

Cobb sighed, Del decided he wasn't *that* hungry. He might have a biscuit or two in the cupboard somewhere.

He said, "I'll make do," and walked away.

Cobb called out. "Wait!"

Del kept going. The entire exchange made him uncomfortable.

Cobb yelled again, "Hey, wait!"

Del stopped and turned around.

Cobb, a little friendlier seeming, said, "I got beans and leftover cornmeal, some chicory coffee. You're welcome to it."

Del approached him and said, "I don't want to put you out none."

Cobb said, "It ain't putting me out."

They fell into step side by side. Cobb didn't speak and Del felt the need to fill in the silence, but all he could think of were questions. For some reason, the smaller man's presence put him off of what he'd always believed was his natural ability to conversate. He reached for Melody and began puffing as they walked along. Del let his music dribble to silence when Crow came from out of the cooper's shed.

Crow said, "Well now, how about this. The two newest members making friendly with one another. Hey, what you got there, Butler. Lemme see it."

Del didn't want to hand Melody over to Crow, but Crow thrust his hand out, jiggling it impatiently. Reluctantly, Del laid Melody into his hand. Crow wiped the mouth piece off on his sleeve and put his own to it, blasting out a shrill note and to Del's ears, it sounded like a wounded bird. Crow stopped, then did it again, zipping his mouth up and down while blowing hard. Melody emitted a shriek at the abuse, and Del grew more uneasy. Crow pulled the instrument from his mouth, stared at it with disgust, and tossed it on the ground.

He said, "Useless."

When he lifted his boot to stomp it flat, Del reacted without thinking, driving both hands into the man's shoulders and shoving him backward. He grabbed Melody, but underestimated Crow's speed. Crow managed to catch himself and delivered a well-placed kick to Del's ribs. The air popped out of Del like a balloon bursting, and he collapsed to the ground. He kept hold of the mouth harp as he covered his head with his other hand. Crow kicked him again, and he rolled to his side balled up, waiting for more to come.

Cobb shouted, "Stop!"

From his left, Del heard Peewee yelling, "Sweeney! What the hell's going on? We got too much work for him to be laid out nursing his damn ribs!"

Crow said, "Good timing. This sonofabitch tried to pick a fight."

Del tucked Melody safely in his pocket before he worked his way to his feet. His midsection hurt, so he took his time and brushed off his pants until he could straighten up. He waited on what Peewee would say, his head filled with images of a square wooden hell.

"Is what he's saying the truth?"

Del said, "Hell no."

Crow said, "Well, golly gee. Wonder who laid hands on who first?" Crow turned to Cobb. "You saw it. Did he shove me first or not?"

Cobb shifted his weight one foot to the other, and Del noted how his new boots still held an appealing gleam. Cobb was in a real pickle with that question, and Del braced himself for him to side with the boss man.

Cobb, his voice a little gravelly, said, "He had cause."

Del shut his eyes. The little guy had just put himself in Crow's crosshairs, while Crow acted as if he was astounded.

"Cause? Hell, all I did was drop it by accident, and when I went to pick it up, *he* shoved *me*. Shit. You blind?"

Cobb's response came just as quick. "What's it matter? Arguing over something small as a stick that makes noise. It's dumb, ain't it?"

To Del's amazement and disbelief, Cobb walked off, leaving all of them slack-jawed.

Crow said, "That little sonofabitch."

Peewee said, "He's got a point. We got enough going on as it is."

Crow flushed bright red, and as he stalked off, he yelled at Cobb, "Hey!"

When Cobb turned, Crow made a gesture, forefinger pointing, thumb up. A threat.

Peewee exhaled forcefully and said to Del, "Y'all got to quit lighting his fuse."

"Hell, I think it was lit long 'fore I got here."

Del's side was already mighty tender, and he was sure to have a nice bruise from Crow's boot. He did a sort of hobbling, half run until he caught up to Cobb. Neither of them spoke as they made their way to their side of the camp.

After they'd arrived at number forty-four, Cobb said, "I reckon I see what you meant by watch your back."

"Yep. You just had your first run-in. I ain't sure I'm ever gonna understand how somebody can want for nothing but trouble."

Cobb said, "He ain't trustworthy, that's for sure."

"Naw, he ain't."

Cobb said, "Well, let me get them things together."

He opened his door, and Del stood on the threshold, waiting, and while he did, he noticed the inside was in worse shape than his, but Cobb had done something different most men wouldn't ever think to do. He'd stuck a bunch of wildflowers in a mug and set them in the center of his small, broken-down table.

Chapter 12

Rae Lynn

After almost two weeks in the camp, she'd yet to make her daily quota.

Ballard had been kind, but on her thirteenth day there, he told her, "Got to pick it up."

Crow, somehow conveniently close by, nagged Ballard, not only about whites working with nigras, lowering themselves, but also about her slowness. Ballard stuck up for her and while it made her uncomfortable, she was grateful.

"None a that ain't nobody's concern but mine and Peewee's."

Crow couldn't let it alone.

"Hell. He chose what he was gonna do, now he better get on and do it. You letting him think he can slack off ain't helping matters. I know what'll learn him good. I can guarantee you'll be thanking me for helping him see straight."

Ballard remained unaffected, flipping pages on his tally book while speaking in a calm voice. "I said I'll handle it."

Crow's words kept a fear in her. Her day off was the following, a Sunday, and while she knew she ought to rest, she found herself cleaning the inside of the shanty while worrying over how to work faster. She swept and swept, scrubbed with a bit of turpentine and water, moved things around, and though she made improvements, her mood hadn't. She eventually went to the creek to wash out the spare shirt. She reveled in the quiet of the woods without the usual shouts. From somewhere in the camp, hymns were being sung, accompanied by the thumping of feet against floorboards in time to the music. She sat on a rock nearby, closed her eyes, and before she knew it, she woke to the day almost gone.

She stood, brushed off her overalls, and grabbed the clean, almost dried shirt off the branch where she'd hung it. She made her way back to her shack, where the thin, reedy trill of the harmonica floated through the air from her neighbor's porch. She allowed herself a brief glance, and he sat with his back propped against the wall, intent only on making music. She went inside and stared at the inside of the shanty. It hit her again, like it always did. *Warren is gone.* Those three words always came with an unsettling jolt, and always in the quiet moments. As soon as she let them in, what happened back home in North Carolina assaulted her senses once again. Later on in bed, she hugged herself inside her husband's shirt, hoped to dream of him so she could see him smiling, and so she could remember how it used to be.

Morning came bringing Clyde and his wagon. She hopped into the back, not meeting anyone's eye.

Clyde said, "Hep, hep, Jackson!" to the mule, and the wagon lurched on to the worksite.

She felt their stares boring in, knew she was being judged because talk got around and they knew she couldn't keep up. She sat where she could, meaning she sat with her back to them, feet dangling off the back end. The ways of men were still foreign to her, but as luck would have it, their silence and hers lasted until they approached the hang-up ground.

When she jumped off the back end, she overheard someone say, "He ain't got it in him."

Someone else said, "Why we breaking our backs when he ain't?"

She moved away quick, found a lower limb to hang her bucket. Overhead, it was as if someone had tacked a metal sheet to the heavens, the gray clouds smooth and even. Despite the early morning, moisture trickled down her face, and the gnats and biting flies started in and swarmed around their heads. She stood in the heavy air, breathing deep, readying herself for what was to come.

Ballard called out to them all. "Git your pullers, we're working some older drifts today."

Rae Lynn winced at those words. Was he trying to make it impossible for her?

He said, "You look like you could fall over, kid. You gonna keep up today?"

She nodded while watching several work hands milling about, a few still hanging dinner buckets, then grabbing pullers, while some took the time to have a smoke.

He shouted again. "Come on! Let's get going!"

Have mercy, she was sure to have a harder time. Anyone would, but her height didn't help matters none, and neither did half a finger. Using a puller was tough going, even for the best of them. She had to show she could do it, because she couldn't appear any less able than she already had. There was nothing to do but get back on the wagon and hope for the best.

After she was dropped off, Rae Lynn stared at the catfaces, which began near her knees and stretched to a point above her head. These faces and these trees were almost at the end of their use. Someone had moved the cups and gutters, and it tested her ability to reach above the last strip and angle the puller to chip away a strip of bark. As she worried over mak-

ing quota, Crow's threats rang in her head. Someone started
singing and the call names came one after the other, adding
pressure.

"Bluesy!"

"Whisky Time!"

"Sally's Man!"

They were starting all over again before she finally was able
to add hers. "Tar Heel!"

She'd worried about using the name, afraid it might create questions. She could give any manner of reasons for using
it if she was ever asked, like the story about the Confederate
soldiers standing their ground under heavy fire, or something,
but, so far, nobody had except Del Reese. She reached up,
struck the bark, and pulled the tool across. She swung the
puller one way, then the other, figuring how to leverage it so
the blade went deep, but not too deep. Finally, she stepped
back, satisfied.

"Tar Heel!"

She kept on, scraping the angled strips. It was about finding
a rhythm and keeping on until it was as comfortable as walking. After several trees, and after switching the puller around,
testing what worked best, it came. Over and over, chip, chip,
pull, chip, chip, pull, until she was calling out "Tar Heel" a
bit more regular, or at least she hoped so. The tin gutters followed the slant on the scarified bark, and the clay cups sat at
the point of the chevron so resin ran into them. This was the
Herty system Warren had refused to take on. He should've
done it this way instead of using the old box method. The
gum went a shorter distance with the cup system, which
meant less dried on the catface, so less needed to be scraped
off. It was actually called "scrape" and could be used, though
it was a lower grade of gum.

She swiped her forehead with her sleeve and swatted at
the mosquitoes landing everywhere, and then there were

the gnats trying to fly into her mouth, up her nose, and into
her eyes. Battling the insects wasted time. She noticed a few
workers carrying buckets working in the distance. They were
dippers and had to scoop gum from the cups and into buckets,
which were then emptied into barrels and hauled off by the
wagons back to the distillery. Their numbers were high too,
with daily totals anywhere from eighteen hundred to three
thousand cups a day. Thinking about the numbers made her
move quicker between each tree. The overcast sky gave relief
from the sun, yet the humidity continued to climb, and before
long sweat was stinging her eyes, as well as any part of her that
had a scratch. She didn't stop, though. Every second counted.

At noon dinner, with aching and burning muscles, she
made her way to the hang-up ground. In a way, she wished
she could've kept on; she needed the time, but Ballard wasn't
taking counts, and she needed the rest, even if she wasn't
hungry.

Ballard came by and spoke to her. "You're off by four hundred trees, but if we go till dark, you might make it, but
you're gonna have to hustle this afternoon."

She said, "Yes, sir."

Four hundred. If she could do one more tree every minute,
she might make her numbers.

She unhooked her pail and moved to a quiet spot to eat
alone, sitting on a stump, while facing the woods. She bit into
the biscuit and chewed, willing herself to eat. After the men
finished, most laid down and closed their eyes. Some went
right to sleep, some smoked, some talked, eyes drooping, their
voices like a crooning lullaby, quiet and soft. Rae Lynn moved
to stretch out on the pine straw, crossed her feet, put her arms
under her head, and stared at the trees above her. She noticed
how when Crow came around, anybody who'd been smiling
quit, while eyes fell to study gum-stained feet or scrappy shoe
tips, looking near about as wilted as flowers without water.

Their uneasy feeling put her in the same mood. Meanwhile, Ballard carried an air of patience, and the men who worked for him didn't cower like stray dogs.

Altogether she was uncomfortable being among men in general. For one, they were like a bunch of overgrown schoolboys sometimes with their cutting up and expressive body functions. And it seemed to her no one ever went too long in any conversation before it eventually turned to the opposite sex. Right now there was talk going on she couldn't help but overhear.

One man said, "How y'all doing now? She forgive you yet?"

The other said, "She ain't speaking to me. She ain't over what went on over to the juke joint."

"You mean that fun with Lucinda who works in back?"

"Man's got needs."

"What you got is a whole heap a trouble you thinking Alice gone tolerate you being a fool."

Snickering and sneaky glances went left and right, shifty and nervous-like. She worried someone would try to bring her into one of these conversations, and if they did, would she be able to hold her own with that sort of talk. At least she wasn't the only one who didn't join in. Del Reese never talked about anybody special. He sat some distance away, tooting on his mouth harp. Sometimes the talk grew serious, expressing worry over being abused for some small thing. They talked of that contraption, the sweatbox, of the people they knew who went in and came out really bad off, or who'd died. Some said a little prayer as soon as it was mentioned, so great was their fear of it.

Crow and Ballard appeared and yelled out to their men. "Get back to it! Hurry it up! Get a move on!"

Rae Lynn jumped to her feet. As she passed by Crow he gave her a cockeyed grin. The workers spread out like ants, lines of them filtering through the trees, the long, hot after-

noon before them, the only thing pleasant, the spicy smell of
pine all around. Crow followed his men and disappeared. Rae
Lynn was quick getting to her drift, pulling at her overalls
and shirt, which were still damp from the morning's work.
Each time she finished a tree, she said a little prayer as she
moved on.

An hour later, Crow showed up, winding his horse through
the trees, mouth twisted like he'd bitten into a sour apple.
Rae Lynn focused on a song a distant worker sang, faint, but
she caught the tune and hummed along. She struggled with a
particularly high catface, aware he could see her having trouble. After the scene at the commissary, she was certain he'd
been biding his time, waiting for her to mess up, but she refused to acknowledge him. He wasn't her boss man, he wasn't
in charge.

"Best pick it up!"

She gritted her teeth, yelled, "Tar Heel!" and moved on to
the next tree.

Under his scrutiny, she fumbled with the puller and a piece
of bark fell in her right eye. She immediately dropped the
puller to the ground, bent over, and began blinking rapidly.
Her sweat mixed in with her tears and made the eye burn.

She delicately moved the eyelid around, and said, "Dammitall."

Crow's voice was closer now, and he said, "Tick tock.
Times a-wasting."

Rae Lynn shifted away from him and gently rubbed at her
eye, blinked several more times, but whatever was in there
hurt, so she quit. Her nose began to run.

Crow said, "Ain't gonna make your count, again. Ain't no
time for stalling."

Tears streamed down her cheek like she was crying. She
did her best to ignore the scratching pain and faced the tree

trunk, puller held aloft, but looking up made her eyes run more.

Crow said, "Crying. I'll be damned."

Rae Lynn muttered, "Ain't crying."

Ballard's voice came from behind her. "What's going on here?"

Crow said, "All he's done for several minutes is worry over a speck a dust in his eye."

Ballard got off his horse, came around to look at her, then said, "Here, use some a this."

She angled her head, saw with the one good eye he held out a canteen. She went over to him and took it.

He said, "Try rinsing it out."

Rae Lynn leaned her head back, attempting to do as he suggested, but most of the water ran down her cheek. She sneezed. Ballard approached her.

"Tilt your head back again," and she did as he said.

He slowly poured a thin stream into the corner of her eye while grabbing her chin to hold her head steady. His hand felt hot, and dry.

She rubbed at her eye, and he said, "Naw, don't, let the water wash it out."

He stopped, and Rae Lynn blinked and blinked. The water made her eye feel sticky and rough. She sneezed again. Crow mumbled something under his breath. Ballard ignored him, and Rae Lynn flapped her hand at him to pour more water. It felt like a piece of metal in there. Tilting her head back, he did so while Crow snickered.

Ballard said, "What the hell's so funny?"

"You playing nursemaid. That's what's funny. You ain't a pansy, are you, Ballard? I don't know which I can't stand the most. A pansy, a shirker, or a nigra lover. What's the world coming to?"

Rae Lynn blinked again. The piece of wood or whatever it was, was still there, but she pulled her chin out of Ballard's hand.

Speaking in a low tone, she said, "It's fine. I'm fine."

Ballard ignored Crow's taunt and said, "Good. You can work?"

In response, Rae Lynn went back to the tree, raised the puller, and began scraping while her eye continued to stream. Despite the discomfort, she only wanted them to leave her be. She didn't want to cause no trouble, or bring any more attention to herself.

She finished making her scrapes and said, "Tar Heel."

Ballard said, "See, only took a few seconds and good as new."

Crow said, "He won't make quota."

"It ain't the end of the day yet."

"Yeah, we'll see."

Ballard dug a dirty rag out of his pocket and wiped his forehead.

He said, "Maybe you ought to tend to your own while I tend to mine."

Rae Lynn began chipping at the next tree. God bless Ballard. She really needed to make a showing, especially since he kept defending her.

He was back on his horse and called out to her. "Good?"

She nodded.

"All right, then."

They left, and she could hear Crow arguing, his voice rising above Ballard's, and that soon faded. Glad for the peace, now there was nothing to hear but the scrape of her tool and the distant shouts mingled in with her own.

Despite her best effort, she didn't make her numbers. Her eye gave her a fit, burning and running nonstop the rest of the afternoon, and she couldn't hardly see what she'd done. It felt like it was on fire, and so she ended up short by two hundred trees. Her not meeting her count caused another stir between Ballard and Crow at quitting time, with both men arguing until Peewee was brought into the discussion as soon as they arrived back in camp.

Crow pointed at her and said, "He needs to know what happens when he can't get the work done."

Ballard said, "He's got good reason to miss trees. Look at it. That eye a his looks like a damn tomato."

Crow turned to Peewee. "He ain't made quota since he got here."

Ballard threw his hand out toward Rae Lynn, and said, "He would've today if not for that."

Peewee sucked on a cigar, eyes darting between the two woods riders. Rae Lynn stood by the wagon. She crossed her arms, then dropped them. Finally, she shoved her hands into her pockets.

He pulled the cigar out of his mouth, and said, "I know what all's going on here."

Peewee gestured at her in a way she didn't like while swirling his tongue around his teeth to dislodge a piece of tobacco.

He spit on the ground. "He ain't who he says he is."

Ballard said, "What's that?"

Peewee said, "He ain't no man."

Rae Lynn's heart rate skyrocketed. *By God, he knows.* Del Reese and the other men who worked for Crow were listening too, and every head turned toward her.

Peewee started nodding, as if he was growing more confident. "Naw. A man could make his numbers, if'n he's fit and all."

Should she confess? What would happen if she did? She hadn't thought about how she would explain herself if she was found out.

Peewee said, "Hell, he can't be more'n fifteen, maybe sixteen. Ain't it right, boy? I 'spected it when you first showed up. Come on now. How old is you?"

Rae Lynn's muscles went slack with relief. It was a question of age versus her sex. This she could handle.

Crow said, "I always said there won't something right about him."

Rae Lynn spoke in a deliberately gruff, snide tone.

"I ain't fifteen. I'm . . . sixteen. So what?"

Crow sauntered up. "It don't mean you don't have to do the work, that's what."

Rae Lynn stepped back. His fingers tapped on the "leather snake" looped from his belt. Ballard put himself in front of her.

He said, "He's *my* worker."

Peewee said, "We got rules, Ballard, as you well know, so this is his last chance. Crow, I need to speak to you."

Ballard said, "He'll make count," while Crow glowered at her with his midnight eyes.

He followed after Peewee, and Rae Lynn exhaled as she watched them go. She turned to thank Ballard and saw how he kept his hand on his gut, as if in pain. It reminded her of Warren, the way he held himself.

He leaned toward her and said, "Don't keep letting me down, kid. You're here now, and you got to do the work or it's gonna be outta my hands, sixteen years old or whatever."

Both his eyes were bloodshot, glassy looking.

She said, "Yes, sir. Thank you."

He walked away, hunched over, while the colored workers from both crews stared at her, and while most appeared detached, a few looked angry. There was a low-level muttering from them she couldn't help but hear.

"He gone mess it up for all a us."

"Watch. Somebody's gone have to do his dirty work."

"How about Bones, what they done to him for less."

"Ain't fair."

"Naw, it ain't."

"Shoot, Big Dubya, he got whipped *and* the box."

Del Reese had stayed too, and stood nearby, hands shoved into his pockets, his expression so bland she couldn't decipher it. Exhausted, her head pounding, she headed toward her shack. When she got there she made her way around to the outhouse to relieve herself. During the day, she had a fear of being caught, and her personal needs had surfaced as yet another problem she hadn't thought about. She didn't want to chance squatting in the woods. This meant she didn't drink as much, and had to be part of the reason she felt so worn-out. After she was done, she went around front, intending to wash off the dust and grime of the day, eat, and go to bed, but there stood Cornelia at the fence, holding something covered with a delicate tea towel.

The other woman kept her eyes on the ground and spoke quietly. "I didn't get to thank you proper for what you done. I was rude too. You shouldn't a stepped in on my behalf, though, and you surely shouldn't have paid for that cloth. I aim to pay you back, but 'til then, I brung you this."

She held out what she had, and Rae Lynn took what she offered. It was still warm and smelled like vanilla.

Cornelia said, "It ain't much. Jes' water pie."

Rae Lynn said, "Why, thank you. Ain't had me one a these in a while."

"I wished it could've been some kind a fruit one, but what I dried and put up last year got et up by critters. Don't nothing last for long round here it seems."

She finally met Rae Lynn's gaze and put her hand to her mouth. "What on earth you done to your eye?"

Rae Lynn said, "It ain't nothing. Piece a bark fell in it."

Cornelia said, "I reckon you ain't got you no rose water."

"No."

"Use tea, then. Soak some tea leaves in a cloth, put it over your eye, keep it there a few minutes."

"All right."

Rae Lynn brought the pie to her nose to sniff at it while Cornelia stared at her like she was deciding something before letting her eyes move to some distant spot beyond Rae Lynn's shoulder.

Rae Lynn said, "You didn't need to do this. You don't owe me nothing."

Cornelia said, "Sure I do. Like I said, I don't like being indebted to nobody."

She crossed her arms and rolled a rock around with the tip of her worn-out shoe. Rae Lynn thought she might say something about Otis, but after a few more seconds of silence, she turned to leave.

"Well. You enjoy the pie, Mr. Cobb."

Rae Lynn said, "I'm sure I will."

Cornelia nervously brushed back a lock of hair before hurrying away, holding herself tight like she didn't want anything or anyone touching her. Rae Lynn watched her go, wished she could say, *Straighten up, look the world in the eye.*

Her stomach rumbled, and as she turned to go inside, she spotted Del Reese on his porch. He leaned against the rail, staring after Cornelia. She could draw the eye of any man even if her manner was timid, so it didn't surprise her that Cornelia had caught the attention of her neighbor.

He tossed a comment her way, "Wonder why she wants to stay with someone mean as Otis. She sure is a real looker, ain't she?"

Rae Lynn made like she didn't hear him, went inside, and shut her door.

Chapter 13

Del

It was something about Ray Cobb. He couldn't figure it exactly, despite knowing he wasn't as old as he claimed. So, he was trying to pass as grown-up, but lots a boys did that, wanting to be men early. One of Del's careful observations had to do with his hands. Sure, they were reddened across the knuckles, a few scrapes and dirt under the nails, common for the kind a work they did. And, there was that missing section of his finger. Still, none of that made up for the fact they looked small. When he was Cobb's age, about to become a man, his own hands had not only been loaded with calluses, they'd been made thick and strong from working alongside Pap for years.

Cobb had other ways about him too. Like how his eyes grew big and round when one of the other men farted, belched, or cussed more than was necessary. How he put his hand over his mouth the way some gal might for that sort a behavior. Maybe he'd been raised in a real strict family with refined manners. Maybe he was a pantywaist. One way or the other, he wasn't cut out for camp lifestyle. Hell, if he had half what Cobb had, the truck and a fistful a paper money, he'd live up to Nolan's call name and be "long gone."

Del stepped onto his porch. His neighbor's was dark still, and he leaned against his rail to have a smoke, listening for the work wagon. When he heard it coming, he went back inside to grab his dinner bucket and rinse out his cup. He met it at the fence as it pulled up, and as he had every morning since coming to Swallow Hill, he hopped into the back, but instead of acknowledging Nolan, Earl, and Leroy, or any of the other coloreds like he had before, he was quiet. This was out of respect for what Nolan had said to him at the juke joint. Of course, it hadn't taken long for Crow to notice Del no longer engaged in small talk.

Not long after, Crow had said, "See? Thought y'all was friends, didn't you? White man mixing with nigras. Shoot. Like a dog being with a cat. You reckon God intended that, Butler? Them nigras, they know where they stand. They know 'cause a what'll happen. Ain't it right, Long Gone?"

"Yessuh. We sure do. Always been knowing it."

Crow said, "How about that, Butler? How come he's smarter'n you?"

On this warm morning, with the sun sending golden rays through the trees and across the dewy ground, Del brought Melody out. He played a soft tune as they rode to work, and his music joined in with the creaking wagon wheels, tired sighs, and pain-filled groans from the others. All of them showed the effects of camp living and work. Covered in mosquito bites, sores from abscessed wounds, rashes, cuts, bruises, and scrapes, the men roamed through the pine forests like a pack of mangy dogs. None, including himself, were any better off for all the work they did, not from what he could tell.

The wagon ride was short, and before long, they'd arrived at the day's hang-up ground. Del spotted Cobb running for the woods, bark hack held like a weapon, like he expected to fight the trees. He wished the kid well, and while he knew Ballard watched out for him, he could only make excuses for so long. Crow constantly brought it to Ballard's attention, yapping about Cobb's counts and how it was sending the wrong message to his crew. Said some thought they could do less work too. He put a pall over the work hands, filling them with worry over what he might do. They'd been working like this all their lives, and with their worn-out bodies, they wouldn't last much longer than a baby bird without its mama if they were punished in the manner Crow liked.

Everyone unloaded, eyes lifted to a steel-blue sky while the sun stared down at them, not a blink of a cloud anywhere to be seen. Del swatted about his head, neck, and arms, where armies of mosquitoes swirled, landing on any patch of exposed skin. Fires burned nearby using damp wood to increase the smoke, an attempt at keeping the biting insects away. Mostly, it contributed to the hacking cough they'd all developed. Del felt sorry for the mules, their tails twitching nonstop, skin rippled and lumpy with bites. He'd heard tell of a mule stung so bad during the night in the Florida Everglades, it died.

On this morning, as the air hung heavy, Ballard appeared to cough more than usual. He rode bent forward, as if he was having trouble staying upright on his horse. He drew a rag from his pocket, wiped his forehead, and Dell noted the man's complexion was a gray, sickly color. Maybe he was purely worn-out, like they all were. Del entered the woods, grateful for the solace among the pines. There was a slight breeze out of the west, and it was as if the trees whispered a soft greeting. With the soothing sound filling his head, he began his work. The morning went along nice and quiet, and before he knew it, the dinner break bell rang. He didn't see hide nor hair of Cobb among those who ate, and rested under the trees. Soon Del was back at it, chipping his catfaces at a steady pace, occasionally hearing the other men call out, his own voice chiming in quick and sure. Crow wandered by more than once, for no good reason other than to make some snide comment.

"Y'alls lower'n low. You and Cobb. Worser'n their kind. The both of you go against what's intended. Hell. Least they stick to their own. Damn shame is what it is. Downright common, you ask me."

Del had become adept at tuning him out, and eventually Crow moved on. At one point, the baying of hounds owned by a woods rider named Woodall rose above the men shouting their call names. It had to be some poor soul who decided to try their luck escaping. Close to quitting time, more shouts filtered through the woods. Taking a final swipe at the face of his last tree, Del stuck the tool in his waistband and headed toward the yelling, expecting to see one of the runners about to be whipped. Instead, a group of men stood around Ballard, who had collapsed and was stretched out on the ground. Cobb was nearby, his hand over the eye that still bothered him. Crow stared at the fallen man and believed he was dead, but then Ballard quivered like he was having a fit. He tried sitting up, only to collapse on his back again.

Del approached one of the workers. "What's the matter with him?"

"Got the fever, I betcha."

Crow said, "Dewdrop, get Gus, tell him to bring the wagon round and to hurry it up."

Dewdrop took off running down the path, while Crow reflected further on Ballard. "Thought he seemed a mite puny these past couple of weeks."

Ballard's eyelids fluttered, his chest rose, sank, and didn't rise again. Crow dropped to his knees, put his hand over the man's mouth. Next, he laid his head on his chest. He straightened up, lifted Ballard's arm, and let it drop. It hit the dirt with a dull thud.

He bent over, shouted in Ballard's ear. "Hey! Ballard!"

He sat back on his haunches, elbows propped on his knees, gazing with a puzzled look at the body in front of him.

With a hint of wonderment, Crow said, "The son of a gun's done died on us."

Del had seen enough dead people to know what a body looked like after the soul fled, and Ballard was good as gone. Those who worked for the fallen woods rider spoke in low voices, clearly worried over what would happen. The kid appeared upset. He'd dropped the hand covering his eye, and Del winced at the sight. Gus Strickland arrived with the wagon, and the men grew quiet as he pulled alongside Ballard.

Somehow word had got to Peewee, who arrived right after Gus and he said, "I'll be damned. He's dead?"

Crow said, "He's a goner."

Peewee said, "Got a missus, them young'uns too. It's a shame. Got to have me another woods rider. Somebody's got to take over his work hands."

Crow said, "Put'em under me. I'll work'em better'n anybody else."

Peewee said, "You can't handle twice the men. Too much area to ride, too many to keep up with. Naw. Woodall, he done lost two today. They didn't never find'em, and I can't be having no more opportunities for'em to run."

The work hands shuffled about, hearing the big boss man discuss men escaping. Del had heard of Woodall only a couple times. He had a pack a coon hounds used to hunt the ones who took off. Aside from the thick woods, there were areas of cypress waters a few miles to the east of the camp, and some had been led to believe they had a chance of escaping through them. Nobody ever heard back from those who made the attempt. This was either good news or bad. Del dropped his eyes to where Ballard lay and didn't dare spare a glance at Peewee.

The silence grew, then Peewee said, "Butler. Why'nt you take Ballard's job? You said you'd done it all when I hired you on."

Crow made a derisive noise. "He'll go softer on'em than Ballard did. He'll hold'em by the hand, pat'em on the ass, let'em do as much or as little as they want."

Peewee waved at Del to step away from the others. Crow paced, clearly agitated as they went out of earshot.

Under the shade of a tall pine, Peewee said, "Here's the truth. I got to have someone keeping Sweeney in check. Every single one of them workers needs to do what we expect'em to do. Everyone liked Ballard. He could get these hands going and he did it without damaging the goods, if you get my meaning. Now, I know the new kid ain't keeping up. I expect he'll get better as time goes on. Sweeney, he's heavy-handed, but I always hold out hope he'll see it can be done different. Will you do it? I'll up your pay. How's a dollar a day?"

That was twenty-five cents more than what he was making. Del contemplated everything taking the job meant. He'd be in charge of workers all good at making their quota except Cobb, and he could worry about him when he had to. While he loved working the trees, being a woods rider won't so bad, either. He would be equal to Crow. He studied his worn-out boots, the Hoover leather having been replaced many times over. A bit more money might allow him to buy some things he was needing. Pay off his commissary debt. The thing was, he remembered telling Crow he'd be better at it. If he took it, Crow was sure to remember, and he was the sort who'd make it his job to prove him wrong.

Peewee said, "A dollar twenty-five."

He'd be a fool not to take it.

Del said, "All right."

Peewee clapped his hand on Del's shoulder, "Something tells me you'll do real good."

Del stuck his thumb over his shoulder at Crow. "Don't let him know you think so."

Peewee dipped in closer to Del. "Yeah, he can be tough

to deal with. Him and Otis, they's tight. Like to stir things up. Mean sons a bitches is what they are. It worries me sometimes when I see the two of'em together; they're the conniving sort."

Peewee had his hands full with such a big operation and probably needed help in more ways than one. They went back to where Ballard's workers hovered around his body.

Peewee waved a hand toward Del. "This here's your new boss man."

The men under Ballard appeared both relieved and nervous. They didn't know Del. He half expected Crow to run his mouth, but his only reaction was to snort and spit a stream of tobacco juice on the ground.

Peewee said, "Go on and get Ballard's horse, there. You might have to work something out with the missus. I got to break the news to'em anyhow, tell'em they can't stay, not unless they can work. I can't see it happening, not with them kids and all. Why don't you come on with me and we'll see what she'll take for this ole nag."

Del went over to the mare. The horse stood close to her previous owner, head down, and near Ballard's shoulder. Del led her away and ran a hand over the white streak on her nose. He hadn't been on a horse in a while, but was familiar enough with them, and liked them. He continued rubbing her while those who'd worked for Ballard watched him with wary eyes. Del gathered the reins from where they hung, and faced his crew. He felt he ought to say something to them.

He said, "It's gonna take some time to get to know you, and vice versa. I don't expect nothing from any one of you more than an honest day's work. I'm fair-minded, and you'll come to see that in short order. Long as you do the work, we'll be all right. Any questions?"

Crow said, "I got one."

Del said, "I ain't directing that to you."

Crow ignored him. "Wonder what you'll find in Ballard's tally log? Reckon there's a problem noted anywhere?"

The man was like a dog with a bone, once he got ahold of something, he didn't want to let it go.

Del said, "I know what you're getting at, Sweeney."

"Do you?"

Del faced his workers again, refusing to let Crow get under his skin. He made eye contact with Cobb deliberately, an attempt to reassure him. The kid remained wide-eyed and uncertain. Del left the men, leading the mare, and he and Peewee went along the path back toward the camp.

Peewee said, "Crow's bound to test you."

"It'll be over the kid and his counts."

Peewee grunted. "I been thinking of telling young Cobb he's got to move on 'fore something happens to him."

Del said, "I feel kind a bad for him. Got to be here for a reason."

"Could be, but he'd be better off doing something else."

One solitary yell came from behind them, almost like a scream, and Peewee said, "Now what."

They stopped to listen, but nothing else was heard except the rapid fire tapping of a distant woodpecker.

Del said, "Reckon we ought to go back and see?"

Peewee didn't seem concerned. "Probably someone shouting at the mule."

Ballard's place, which was next door to Crow, was whitewashed with flowers planted and chickens clucking and pecking quietly in the yard. There were a couple well-fed hogs and a milk cow penned in the back area. Mrs. Ballard was hanging out the wash, but her eyes quickly flitted to Peewee and then Del, a stranger leading her husband's horse, and her face crumpled like she'd already heard the bad news. Del waited while Peewee spoke quietly, confirming what she'd already guessed. Del noticed Ballard's children, a gangly boy of about twelve and two girls, twins, about four years if he was to guess. The girls huddled together, solemn-faced, while the boy stood by his mother's side.

Mrs. Ballard hugged him and said, "Lord, help us. You got to be man of the house now, Jimmy."

Jimmy pulled away from his mama and turned to Del, his face red with anger, his grief spilling out with it.

He said, "Give me them reins. That's my Daddy's horse."

Del felt bad for the boy and carefully said, "I come to buy her. What'll you take?"

Jimmy squared his shoulders, defiant.

He said, "She ain't for sale."

Peewee spoke to Mrs. Ballard. "Best not be too hasty about any decisions. I'd recommend you consider taking what you can for the horse, to tide you over. It'll give you enough 'til you find you a new place."

Jimmy looked at his mama. She gave him a single nod, and he faced Del again.

The boy glared at him, and with a tremble in his voice, he said, "Fifteen dollars."

Peewee said, "Seems fair. I'll pay'em and add it to what you owe at the commissary."

Del said, "Fine."

What else could he do but accept? He wanted the extra pay, and he needed the horse in order to get it. The slow clop of hooves came above the soft crying of Mrs. Ballard as the wagon approached, bringing her husband to his family. Del and Peewee removed their hats as Gus brought the wagon close to the house. Mrs. Ballard put her hand to her mouth as she went to the wagon, reaching out to touch Ballard's head, her voice quavering with emotion.

"I knew something was wrong with him. It was the fever. He got it and it didn't never let up."

Del said, "I'm sorry."

Peewee said, "He was a good man."

They helped get Ballard off the wagon and inside. They took him to the small bedroom and laid him on the bed.

She said, "I'll sit with him tonight. Bury him tomorrow."

Peewee said, "I'll be sure to send a couple men by to dig the grave at first light."

"Thankee kindly."

They stayed a bit longer, letting Mrs. Ballard talk about "her Jim" long as she wanted.

When they finally left, they made their way back through the camp, and Peewee said, "It's gonna be rough trying to raise them young'uns alone."

Del said, "It's a damn shame. Ballard was a good man."

Peewee said, "True that." He pointed back the way they'd come. "Once she figures out where she's going, that's where the woods riders stay. I'm afraid the Ballard place is the only one available. It's beside you know who."

Del said, "She can take her time. I ain't in no hurry to be his neighbor."

They walked a bit farther and saw Crow coming their way, his expression sly, like he knew something they didn't. It was how he stared down his nose as he swaggered by, staring at them with a little snarl of a smile curling one side of his mouth.

After they were by him, Peewee said, "I seen that look before."

Del said, "Yeah, me too."

Del glanced over his shoulder only to find Crow watching him. Crow tipped his hat, and Del had the distinct feeling he'd been up to no good.

Chapter 14
Rae Lynn

Rae Lynn and the rest of the work hands watched as the fallen woods rider was trundled away, his boots rocking back and forth as the wagon rolled along the path, giving the illusion of life still within. Crow waited until the wagon was out of sight, and then he turned to the men who stood in a semicircle. They had been talking low amongst themselves and hushed at the look on his face.

"Those who worked for Ballard, stand over there."

Rae Lynn and a few men moved to where he pointed, hands holding hats or hands shoved in pockets. Most seemed to have trouble standing still, shuffling their feet, looking at one another or at the ground. Rae Lynn felt vulnerable, exposed without the protection of the kindly Ballard. Crow's work hands stood nearby, waiting to see what was going to happen. Crow paced back and forth in front of Ballard's little group, glancing at each of them, except he ignored her. Forgotten were the sweltering days of work, the insects, the hunger she'd felt only moments ago. Her heart bumped unevenly, and her mouth turned the kind of dry no amount of water would cure.

The man who went by the name of Preacher because he was always spouting off Bible phrases as he worked, leaned over and said, "Best get to praying."

From someone else behind them came, "He got something up his sleeve."

Crow stopped in front of Rae Lynn but didn't face her. He spoke, randomly commenting in a thoughtful tone.

"I reckon y'all made your numbers today."

Heads bobbed with a murmur of assent, "Oh, yessuh, sure did. Always do."

Rae Lynn could hardly think. Her stomach rolled. This was about her. He whipped about, the move so sudden, she stumbled back a step. She quickly righted herself and crossed her arms. She made herself look him in the face.

"How about you, Cobb?"

She hadn't, and he knew she hadn't.

He said, "Did you make count?"

She didn't move. Didn't answer.

He turned to Ballard's men. "Now, it don't seem fair, him slacking off when the rest of you do what's expected, day in and out. Sure don't seem right to me." He spread his arms, like he was giving a sermon. "Say what you want about your boss man, Ballard, but way I see it, he played favorites. Way I see it, whites, nigras, you choose to be out here, you do the work. Fair's fair. Maybe he had him a thing for this one. Now, wouldn't that be unseemly?"

She felt all of them staring at her now. She dared a glance at the group, saw a mix of distress or indifference. She tried to think of something, anything to help herself. Crow pointed at one of his own men, the one called Pickle who'd seen his share of trouble at the camp, thereby acquiring his name honestly.

"Pickle, what you reckon?"

Pickle raised his shoulders and said, "Can't say it'd be right."

Crow zeroed in on one of Ballard's other men, Big'Un.

Crow pointed at Rae Lynn and said, "What you think?"

Big'Un had been one of the ones who'd let it be known what he thought on those early-morning and late-evening wagon rides. Under other circumstances, it could've gotten him into trouble because she was a white "man." To speak against one was risky. For such an offense, one could end up dead. Rae Lynn watched him struggle for the answer he thought Crow might want.

His voice a whisper, he said, "I reckon we all got to do what we's supposed to. Got to learn right if we don't."

"Why, ain't you smart."

Big'Un hung his head as if in an apology of sorts. Rae Lynn felt faint, and her fear over what was happening made her hot, then cold.

Crow yelled out. "Anybody else got something to say about this? Come on! We're having us a trial here. What's the verdict gonna be? I know for a fact your new boss man ain't gonna do a damn thing about it."

The men shifted as one, uncomfortable with the direction they were being taken in. All their lives they'd been schooled about the whites. *Keep your head down. Don't speak unless they talk to you. Hope and pray nobody thinks you done something you shouldn't.*

Crow was having none of it. "Come on. You don't start talking, I'm gonna pick one of you."

He uncoiled the whip from his belt, letting the length of it lie on the ground. They started off soft at first, until everyone was eagerly yelling something.

"He ain't made his numbers since he been here!"

"Naw, it ain't fair!"

"Everybody's s'posed to do what they's s'posed to!"

"He about grown now. Got to do a man's work!"

Crow nodded with approval. "There you go. That's right."

He raised a hand, and they all hushed. Rae Lynn stood

alone because Ballard's men had quietly sidled over to stand
with Crow's group.

He tilted his head and said to her, "Only seems fair, don't it?"

He wiggled the whip, and panic shot through Rae Lynn.
She tried to speak, and couldn't.

Crow pointed at her and said over his shoulder, "Cat got his
tongue. Or is it catface got his tongue?"

He laughed at his little play on words before snapping the
whip at her. It struck her right shoulder, barely grazing it,
and she couldn't help but let out a little yelp. She understood
immediately how she sounded. *Not like a man.* Crow looked
at the others in surprise, and when he turned back to her, he
moved his arm back, readying it to strike again. The workers
appeared as stunned as she was.

I ain't a man! I'm a woman! The truth almost flew out of
her mouth, only there was something about the fact she was
alone. With all these men. Could she trust any one of them?
She could Ballard, but he was dead. Del Reese and Peewee
might be fine, but they weren't here. Crow raised his eyebrows, whip poised, waiting on her to speak. Something ran
down the shoulder he'd struck, whether sweat or blood, she
didn't know, but she knew she didn't want to be whipped.

Careful with her tone, she said to no one in particular, "I
been doing the best I can."

A few men behind Crow shook their heads as Crow guf-
fawed, slapping a hand on his thigh. He pointed at her with
the handle of the whip.

"He says he's doing his best. What y'all think?"

Discomfited, they fell silent.

Crow said, "Aw, come on. We done discussed how y'all go
out in the woods every day, make your numbers, and here's
this young whippersnapper coming along, thinking he can do
like he wants. He needs a taste of this, or the box."

Rae Lynn said, "It ain't true. I . . ."

Crow said, "What? You what?"

"I'll take the box."

Crow narrowed his eyes. He turned to the work hands and pointed at her.

"What y'all reckon? Is that fair?"

They mumbled, but it was hard to tell what they said. This was all new territory, and they were unused to having much say about anything, particularly when it came to the business of white men. It was usually taboo for them to speak out against one. Crow looked disgusted.

"Let me clarify it for y'all. What we got here is a shirker. Something else I can't abide. Come on, now's your chance. Speak up!"

Finally, someone from the back said, "Three days is what we get."

Crow grinned big at Rae Lynn.

"Walk," he said.

Rae Lynn did as she was told and made her way toward the camp while Crow whistled a tune, like this trouble made him happy. She contemplated running. She looked to the left, and to the right. Nothing but trees, and more trees. There was swampland to the east, filled with patches of tea-colored water and cypress trees. What lay to the west was probably more of the same. She plodded along, going slow, hoping Del Reese and Peewee would come back, but delivering such news to a family couldn't be done quick. Behind her Crow carried on like he had not a care in the world. She was developing an intense dislike for the man, but her fear was even bigger. She'd gone and got herself into a real mess here. No one else she knew of could stop what was happening. She heard hammering from the cooper's shed, and this was met with the distinct odor of wood smoke from the distillery. Meanwhile, a mockingbird sang from a nearby tree, and cicadas worked themselves into a frenzy, their buzzing ending on a pulsing drone, only to begin again.

The heavy air was laden with the sharp scents of pitch, tar, turpentine, and the sweat of men as they went along the path. Soon enough, she saw it, appearing as inoffensive as any other wooden structure unless you understood the use. Some ways away, a handful of colored women went about the business of ending the day. She focused on them and slowed down more, until Crow prodded her in the back.

"Keep moving, kid."

The sight of it, the knowledge of no food or water, or any way to take care of the most basic needs, was enough to make her consider trying to run again, or tell him she'd changed her mind, to whip her instead.

"Kin I have some water before I get in?"

It came out rough with emotion, and she figured at this point she had nothing to lose.

Crow mocked her.

"A drink of water?" And then with more incredulity, "A drink of water?" He turned to his workers, "Does anybody ever get a drink of water?"

There was no answer, only the scuffling of feet, like they were uncomfortable facing what they all feared. Like they wished they could get on home, get to their suppers, forget what was happening.

Crow said, "It ain't only about them numbers, boy. It's about getting out of line with nature, same as I told your buddy, Del Reese. Now, why don't you hop on in and get comfortable."

As she faced the moment of truth, she spoke her mind. "He ain't gonna take kindly to you telling one a his men what to do. It ain't your job."

Crow hooted. "Hell, he ain't gonna know. He's gonna think you run off. Ain't that the way of it, men? Let me hear you say it, 'cause if I catch any one of you nigras telling any-body about this, you won't last long. I'll see to it."

The work hands stood in a semicircle around the box, and other than the insects zipping around them, nothing moved. Each man was as still as a stone on the ground, the stark fear evident on their faces, whether for her, for themselves, maybe both. There wasn't any choice here. She could do nothing but get in. A tornado of bottle flies flew out. She swatted them away, sat, and tried not to stare at the stains of unknown origin, tried not to think about what they were, why they were there. She took her hat off and placed it where her head would rest.

Once she was within the confines, she wanted to gag, and stopped herself. She stared off to her left, away from them all, her attention on the tops of the trees as they moved in the wind. She captured them in her mind's eye, and when she heard the creak of the lid, she shut her eyes along with it, refusing to watch the top come down. The light against her lids disappeared. She pressed her hand into her mouth to keep from crying as she heard it being secured. She shouldn't waste tears. She somehow knew this. There was a double thump delivered to the top, a few mumbled words, and then silence.

She began praying. She prayed for time to go fast while knowing it would feel like a lifetime. Maybe, somehow, someone would tell Del Reese, or Peewee. Report Crow for stepping out of line. Rae Lynn concentrated on what she could hear. She carefully tested how far she could move her legs, her arms. She was smaller than most men, but the fact she felt cramped meant it must've been horrible for anyone even an inch taller. A tear slipped out of the corner of her eye, and she wiggled her arm up and wiped it away. She schooled herself to think about the good times with Warren. The house in Harnett County with its cheerful kitchen and the garden out back. The flowers planted in the yard. Sitting out on the porch in the cool of the day, watching sunrises and sunsets, the waving limbs of trees, that bold blue sky. She wished herself there in her mind.

Time passed and she did her best to not think of her thirst, her hunger, how the hard boards pressed into her shoulder and hip bones. She ruminated on the idea to come to Swallow Hill, at what had seemed like a good plan. It had been her only choice—or was it? She dwelled on what had taken place and her decision to disappear. Butch Crandall hadn't given her time to get her head on straight after what happened with Warren, and with what he proposed, what he'd threatened to do if she didn't, she couldn't have stayed. Nobody would've understood what happened, even if she'd tried to explain. Nobody but Warren. She was certain Eugene would've had her arrested, put on trial, locked up. And here she was, locked up anyway. Maybe this was God's way of punishing her.

Her mind went over and over this, until she must've drifted off. Sometime later a stabbing pain in her lower abdomen roused her, and disoriented, she lifted her hand to press on her belly, and it knocked against the hard surface of the lid. It took her a few seconds and then she realized where she was, and she had to control the urge to bang on the top, to scream for help. The pain came again, sharp and deep, persistent now, as it had for the past fourteen years, once a month like clockwork. She'd not accounted for this, least not when she was in a situation where she couldn't manage it. Her throat was terribly dry, like she'd been breathing with her mouth open for days. She coughed, and as she did, a warm, wet sensation spread from between her legs. Why now?

Her eyes adjusted to the interior, and through a small gap in the lid, a tiny sputtering star appeared in the night sky, and she stared at it until her eyes closed again, and she slept.

Chapter 15

Del

Cobb was an early riser like Del, yet no sound came from his little shack. The two shanties were fairly close together and poorly made, so normally Del would hear him as he stamped his feet into his boots every morning, then, like clockwork, came the rattling of his coffeepot. Once, he even thought he'd heard something like crying, but had doubted his hearing. This morning as he stood outside, there was nothing but silence. He wanted to let the kid know he needn't worry about his counts too much. He'd be sure to keep an eye on how he was doing, maybe cut him some slack if he was only off by a couple hundred trees or so. Although, he'd not tell him that. The way he saw it, him not making his numbers sure didn't come from lack of trying. After another minute or two, he went back inside.

For the first time since he'd hung it above the door, he reached for his shotgun. His plan was to kill small game and give whatever he shot to his work hands. They weren't allowed weapons, and while they were skilled at setting traps, getting fresh game was hit or miss given the work hours. As he went out, he looked once more to see if Cobb was up. The tiny shack remained dark and still. It was at least thirty minutes or so before the work wagon would start rounding everyone up, and it could be Cobb was only catching him some extra shut-eye.

On the way to the barn, Del saw the camp coming to life with some men washing and shaving their faces on their porches. Women pumped fresh water into buckets while calling out to one another. Others were already in their gardens picking tomatoes or beans, or sitting on stumps and shucking corn for supper that night. A few gathered eggs from their hens. He made his way to the barn, sniffing the deep, rich scent of horse, hay, and manure. The smells conjured thoughts of the two horses his pap had used for pulling their wagon. He led Ruby out of her stall and gave her some feed and water while he cleaned it out. After he finished, a slim edge of molten red edged the land. It was time. He saddled her and lifted himself onto her back.

Patting her neck, he said, "It's me and you now, old girl."

At the hang-up ground designated for the day, the men who'd worked for Ballard unloaded from the wagon and moved to stand in a cluster, talking amongst themselves. They quieted as he approached, more nervous seeming than the day before. He took it in stride. They had to get used to him, how he was, though he'd said he was fair like Ballard, they'd have to see it to believe it. He dismounted and immediately noticed who was missing.

"Where's Cobb?"

He looked at each of them. He couldn't read their faces, he didn't know them well enough, and besides, most coloreds were used to hiding their thoughts and feelings. Their faces were like staring at an empty glass.

He asked another way. "Won't he picked up by Clyde?"

Ah, there, a barely noticeable twitch from the one called Birdie.

He homed in on him and said, "Can't nobody tell me if he got picked up or not?"

Birdie rubbed his face and said, "He won't waiting for a ride this morning."

"Where's Clyde?" Del asked.

"He gone to haul the gum."

Del began to think Cobb was either sick or he'd run off. He scanned over the work hands once more. No one offered more. No one would meet his eyes. He decided to go on and let them get to their work.

"Y'all be sure to start small fires near to where you're working. Anybody need'n anything 'fore we get started?"

A collective, "No suh!" rang out.

"All right. Let's get to work, then."

As the men left, Del called out, "Where's the water boy, Georgie, at?"

The small boy came from behind one of the trees and eased up to Del like he was afraid.

"How old are you, Georgie?"

Trembling a little and big-eyed, the boy said, "Nine, suh."

He remembered this kid, or at least his scars. Georgie was the one who'd seen a taste of the whip.

"Georgie, will you go check on Mr. Cobb for me?"

"Yessuh."

"Go to number forty-four. Knock on the door good and hard. If he answers, ask if he's sick, and come right back and tell me."

"Yessuh."

Georgie didn't move.

Del said, "Go on, be quick."

He still didn't move.

Del said, "What's wrong?"

The boy twisted the hem of his torn burlap shirt and focused on some spot to Del's right.

He mumbled, "I ain't knowin' what a forty-four looks like."

Del said, "Hang on."

He reached into his pocket for his tally book, ripped a piece of paper out of the back, and on it he wrote in big numbers, *44*.

He showed it to Georgie. "See this?"

Georgie nodded.

Del said, "This here is what number forty-four looks like. Here. Take this paper with you. Go back into camp and go by the cooper's shed. You know where that is?" Georgie took the piece of paper, nodded again, and Del continued. "Stay straight and keep going to the back end of camp. Know where I mean?"

Georgie said, "Yessuh."

"The second well you come to, start looking for this number over the doors. Got it?"

"Yessuh."

"Be quick as you can."

Georgie took off, scarred legs pumping. Del watched until he disappeared around the curve in the path, small dust clouds puffing up under the pink soles of his churning feet. After Georgie was gone, Del realized he hadn't thought to check if Cobb's truck was still by the shed, although somebody was bound to have heard him start it up and seen him drive off with all the main buildings right there together. He'd see about that later. He got back up on Ruby and began his first day as a woods rider.

Del was busy making marks by call names when he felt a tap on his boot and looked down to see Georgie.

He smiled at him and said, "What'd you find out for me, Georgie?"

"Won't nobody there, Mr. Boss Man."

"You sure?"

"Yessuh. I banged on the door like you said. The missus who works in the store? She come by too."

"What'd she say?"

"She say, 'What you think you doing, boy!'"

"I said I'se looking Mr. Cobb. So she banged on the door herself, then she opened it. Said ain't nobody there. Said he working. I didn't say nothing else, only, yessum, and I run back quick, like you said."

It was puzzling, but right now, he had to keep up with his men, and on his first day, he couldn't afford to miss counts and make it look bad on himself, or all of them.

He said, "Thank you, Georgie. Here you go."

Del reached into his pocket and gave him a piece of peppermint. Georgie's eyes lit up as he took it. Del had the idea he'd never had a peppermint candy before.

Del said, "These men need a drink. Will you get them some water?"

"Yessuh!"

After Georgie started water rounds, Del got busier, as the calls came in fast and furious. It was going good by his calculations, and if it hadn't been for Cobb's disappearance nagging at him, he'd have felt like he was having one of his best days since coming here. Part of it had to do with the fact he hadn't seen hide nor hair of Crow. He'd been sure the man would come and run his mouth about something asinine, as usual. Dinner break came and Del's workers, despite doing well all morning, were subdued. There was none of the usual carrying on and storytelling.

Del ate amongst them, and when he was done, he said, "Rest another thirty. We start again at one o'clock sharp."

They stretched out on the ground or sat on old stumps, heads hanging, scratching at bites, swatting at insects, still quiet. He mounted Ruby and cantered toward Cobb's shanty. It took him only minutes, and once he was there, he dismounted and went up onto the porch. It was possible Cobb had been in the privy out back when Cornelia and Georgie came by, so he banged on the door again and waited. All he heard was the shouting of children in another section of the camp. Del shoved the door open and stood on the threshold. A small green lizard sitting on the windowsill, its throat billowing into a quick red bubble before collapsing, pegged him with tiny golden eyes, then disappeared into a crevice.

Inside, the first thing he noticed was a clean shirt hanging on the nail near the bed. His gaze fell to the mattress and he gaped for a split second. He went closer and squatted down. Why, look at them fancy sheets. Cobb's mother must have sewn them decorations. They had a woman's touch, edged in yellow and blue, like his own mother used to stitch. Damn. Sheets like this were much too nice for the likes of this place. Cobb sure did have him some finer things in life. Del stood and glanced around the room. Maybe he *had* left, and only taken what mattered. What money he still had, his pistol, the truck. Didn't need much else. Either way, Del needed to get back to his work hands. He felt somewhat annoyed by the kid leaving without a word, while also realizing he was pretty young, still wet behind the ears. He'd done good to stay long as he had, he reckoned. Maybe Ballard's death scared him off. Del went out and shut the door tight. By the time he made it back to the men, they were stirring around, ready to begin. Everyone made their numbers that morning, some even going over a bit. This was good, considering it was going to be a blistering afternoon.

"All right, we got us a long, hot afternoon. Sooner we make the numbers, the sooner we quit."

Preacher said, "We always work 'til dark, no matter if counts is done early."

Del said, "It ain't like that now. You do what you s'posed to, and we quit."

The men glanced at one another before spreading out to begin again, and the afternoon was quickly underway. Still, they didn't sing, and when he rode among them, they didn't stop, they only worked harder as if avoiding conversation, other than hopeful talk of rain or catching a little breeze. It grew as hot as it had ever been, not a breath of air to be spared. He had Georgie bringing water often, and gave the boy a peppermint each time he did. The day wore on, and the air grew thicker, not only from smoke from the fires, but humidity. The sun baked them from overhead, and he felt as if they all might suffocate. He gave poor Ruby a break when he saw her coat lathered white with salt. He took his shotgun and left her to idle under the shade of the trees, grazing on small patches of grass. He had Georgie fill one of the water pails full and give it to her. She was still slurping as he walked away, following his workers. Of all the days he'd been here, this one beat all, an out-and-out scorcher.

It was midafternoon when someone went to yelling, a fear-some howling and hollering like nothing he'd heard before. It grew louder, words coming out like gibberish, before it stopped as abrupt as it had begun.

Del called out, "Who's in trouble? What's going on?"

Preacher was nearby, and said, "Could a been Birdie. I ain't sure, though."

Del said, "Let's go see."

They went deeper into the woods, and after going a hundred yards or so, sure enough there the worker stood, his back to them. He gave them a quick glance over his shoulder and then immediately faced forward again, to whatever had drawn his attention.

Del said, "Hey, man. What is it?"

Birdie didn't answer, didn't move again, except to shake his head.

Preacher said, "Boss man here, he talking to you."

Birdie's shoulders rose, and they heard him mumbling, "Can't move. It gone get me. Red'n yeller, hurt a feller."

Preacher said, "Got to be a coral snake."

He and Del walked over to Birdie, but Birdie yelled at them, "It right *there!*"

Preacher shouted, "Whoa, lookout now! Damn! Damn!"

The snake, its telltale bright bands of color gleaming in the wiregrass inches from Birdie's bare foot, felt threatened with three men surrounding it. Without warning, it struck and attached its mouth to the top of Birdie's foot. Birdie screamed, all movement now, shaking his leg and swiping uselessly at the snake stuck to him like a burr.

Birdie cried out, "Help me, Jesus . . . !"

Del slung his shotgun off his shoulder.

Preacher said, "He still on'em! How you gonna shoot?"

Del said, "I got to do something!"

Birdie quit flinging his foot about and whimpered a prayer. Del couldn't get over the behavior of the snake. It made a chewing movement on Birdie's foot, like it wanted to eat it.

Del gripped the barrel of his shotgun and smacked the stock over the lower end of the snake. It released Birdie's foot and Birdie stumbled backward, bumping into Preacher as Del flipped the gun around, aimed, and pulled the trigger. Where the head had been disappeared. The body rippled and curled as if still alive. Birdie pointed a shaky finger at his foot. Both Del and Preacher bent down, studying two tiny puncture wounds with twin spots of blood not much bigger than a pinprick.

Del said, "Don't move."

Birdie was too scared anyway and could only nod. Del removed his belt and used it like a tourniquet, cinching it just above Birdie's knee.

When he was done, he said "Kin you walk?"

Birdie had calmed down some, his fear turning to wonder as he said, "I can't tell I been bit. Ain't no pain. Don't feel nuthin'."

Preacher said, "Maybe it didn't get you too bad."

Del said, "Damndest thing I ever seen, how it chewed on him."

They returned to the work area and Birdie, who apparently had recovered from his initial fright, described to some of the other workers how he'd come upon it. Del listened to him tell his story, and he seemed all right, but a snake bite was a snake bite.

"He was hanging on me like a Christmas ornament on a tree not five minutes ago."

Big'Un bent over and examined Birdie's foot.

He said, "Can't see nothing."

Birdie said, "He done got me all right. I ain't feeling so bad, though."

Del said, "Look, if you can't work . . ."

Birdie was quick to say, "Oh, I gone work. I ain't wantin' no whip."

Del said, "It ain't what I mean. Hell, I don't even own a whip. What I meant was, you been snake bit, might want to take it easy."

Birdie frowned as if Del spoke to him in another language.

He bent down, undid the belt, and handed it to Del. "Naw suh, I got to work."

"All right. It's up to you, but take it easy."

"Yessuh."

Del walked to the designated drifts to see what the other workers had done, and as the afternoon progressed, he kept thinking one of two things would happen. Somebody would come and tell him Birdie was sick, or Crow would make an appearance to run his mouth. Neither happened, but still, it was midafternoon before Del's shoulder muscles eased. The day came to a searing end and as they gathered back in the hang-up area to grab their dinner buckets and load into the wagon, Del spotted Birdie, moving a bit slow, but otherwise the man appeared unfazed by his earlier encounter. As he drew closer,

Del noticed his dark skin had turned ashen, and his eyelids drooped. Still, he'd worked all day and was probably just tired.

Del said, "You done all right today?"

Birdie said, "Yeshuh."

Del frowned. When Birdie worked through the afternoon, he'd seemed fine, but now he sounded like he'd been drinking. Del reckoned any of them could sneak a little juke'n juice, but it wasn't something he wanted them doing. He didn't need a bunch a drunk workers getting hurt because they couldn't see straight.

He said, "You been drinking?"

"Naw shuh."

Del couldn't be sure if he was lying or if it was something else. Birdie weaved about.

"You sure? 'Cause if I catch you lyin', I'm gonna have to dock your pay."

He'd learned from his pap it hurt a man the most when you hit him in his pockets.

Birdie held both his hands up. "I ain't. I shwear." And he stumbled and weaved some more as he talked.

Del was hardly convinced.

Preacher said, "He ain't never touched a drop I know of. It's what killed his daddy. He ain't about to touch it."

Right before Del's eyes Birdie slowly crumpled to the ground. Del rushed to his side and the man's body convulsed. The workers circled around him, muttering amongst themselves, unsure of what was happening.

Del said, "I ain't ever known nobody bit by a coral snake. Anyone of you here know anything about it?"

There were a few mumbled no's, then Big'Un said, "Mrs. Riddle, she do."

Del said, "Let's get him back to the camp."

Preacher and another worker helped put Birdie in the bed of the work wagon and climbed in beside him. Preacher held

Birdie's head on his lap. Del retrieved Ruby from where he'd left her and rode behind the wagon. When he saw Birdie having trouble breathing, Del skirted around the wagon and put Ruby at a fast trot toward the commissary to give Cornelia Riddle a heads-up. He rushed inside, the bell on the door jingling. She was the only one behind the counter, stocking can goods. Otis was nowhere to be seen.

Before she could speak, he said, "You know anything about coral snakes?"

She frowned at him and said, "Who?"

"One of my men. Birdie."

She reached under the counter, grabbed a bottle of turpentine, and followed Del outside.

Del said, "He didn't act like he'd even been bit right after it happened. He worked all afternoon, but now he sounds like he's been drinking."

Cornelia said, "With them kind a snakes, it hits'em later."

As they went back to the wagon, Del noticed a woman with dark hair shot through with gray. She talked with lots a hand gestures to Crow, who stood, arms folded, eyes on the ground. Del didn't have time to dwell on them, but it appeared like Mama Sweeney had arrived for a visit, and neither of them looked happy about it.

Chapter 16

Rae Lynn

She lay soaked with sweat, yet shivering. The crack above her, the one she couldn't look away from, told her all she could take in about the outside world through the half-inch-wide space. Her fear for what was to come rose with the sun. It had been so hot the day before, when Ballard died. She didn't know what to expect of today, and while she was used to the heat of summers, it wasn't while cramped inside something the size of a pig trough with a lid on it. Without food. More important, without water. She'd have to do like she done at the orphanage when she'd been forced to work in the laundry all them ungodly hours the summer. Try to think positive, and not about how much time she had left inside.

She hadn't been at Swallow Hill long enough to know if anyone in her predicament ever made it out alive. She hadn't wanted to ask. Right now, she was already so thirsty her tongue stuck to the roof of her mouth, and her throat was just as dry. Her stomach had cramped off and on all night. She found she could roll a little, side to side, and in the desire for movement she did this until her muscles spasmed, so she stopped. She was losing the internal argument about the need to urinate. Why hold it when she'd have to go at some point, but she couldn't bring herself to do so. Not yet.

Somehow she fell asleep again, and the next time she woke, the inside had become an oven. Sweat ran off of her, little rivulets of distress along with her ever-increasing thirst. She attempted to lick her arms, the salty perspiration drying on her tongue. She laid her palms against the lid. It was hot to the touch. Each time she swallowed, she coughed. What was odd was her sense of urgency to urinate was gone, but now her head hurt, and though she hadn't moved, she was dizzy. A distant rhythmic banging matched the heartbeat she heard in her head. Voices ran out in song occasionally somewhere in the belly of the camp. She strained to hear the tune until it stopped and was replaced by yelling. She rolled her head to the left, to the right, twisted each foot the same, left then right. A cramp seized the calf muscle of her left leg, and the pain made her grit her teeth.

Be still. Go back to sleep. Get through this. Get through it.

The next time she woke up, her ability to breathe was like sucking on a clogged straw while a peculiar pressure had developed in her chest, as if a heavy weight had been set on top of her. She made herself calm down and slowly took in the stifling air through her nose and let it go slowly out of her mouth. She smelled blood. The tinny, metallic odor was more obvious along with other unpleasant smells as the heat built in her little prison. The narrow crack above her revealed a sky that was hazy. She tipped her chin down to her chest, and a wave of nausea made her stomach roll. She shut her eyes until it passed, and when it had, she opened them. Here and there, other cracks in the wood allowed the sun to decorate her body with golden stripes over her legs and stomach. Dazed, half awake, *lovely*, she thought. If only some sort of breeze would slip in, it might give a bit of relief, but it was only wishful thinking. Since coming to the camp, most days had been as still as a corpse.

She shut her eyes again and hummed. Behind her lids, colors spun and shimmered. It was probably midafternoon and only the first full day. She didn't want to get too far ahead of herself, but if she made it (and she didn't like to think like that), she had to decide what she could do to stay on. Her confidence at making numbers was shaken, but maybe Peewee would let her try dipping gum. There were a few colored women doing it, and after their bucket was filled, one of the men would usually empty it into a barrel in the back of the wagon. Thing was, Peewee might refuse. She'd not given him the best impression thus far. If that happened, she had no idea where she'd go. With the country deep into the Depression and jobs scarce, now wasn't the time to be without a way to eat unless she wanted to resort to what some women did, prostituting themselves out. She couldn't begin to consider such a thing.

She wished she'd not been so quick to part with that three dollars on behalf of Cornelia, because now, she might need it. Her physical discomfort brought her back to the present. Strangely, her hunger and thirst were disappearing. Through the hole, she caught a bit of a cloud slipping by. The patch of blue returned. As she laid there, one image flickered over and over in her mind, and she held on to it because it stood out above all the rest. As the lid was raised, she saw herself stand, and with defiance, she looked Crow in the eye.

Chapter 17

Del

Cornelia administered turpentine to Birdie's bite by pouring it over the puncture marks. Birdie's breathing had become more labored, his chest sinking inward as he took in air and creating a strained, whistling noise as he expelled it. He didn't seem to know where he was or who they were.

Del turned to Preacher. "He married?"

"Naw suh. He stay by hisself. I can bring him with me. My missus'll look after him."

Cornelia handed the bottle of turpentine to Preacher and a bag of Epsom salts. "Soak his foot in this for at least fifteen minutes, then put more turpentine on it."

He said, "Ma'am, please put all this under my name in that book you keep."

Cornelia raised a hand and waved away his words.

"It ain't necessary."

"Sure do 'preciate it, ma'am."

Del said, "Let me know how he's doing."

"Yessuh."

As the wagon pulled away, Del realized he didn't know

anything about the injured man except he couldn't be more than twenty or so. He didn't know what his real name was or where he was from. Matter a fact, he didn't know a thing about any of his work hands. He'd been put into this situation so quick and unexpected, he'd not had time to find out. He made a mental note he'd get to know each one of them.

He turned to Cornelia and said, "Thank you."

Cornelia waved a dismissive hand as she stared after the wagon.

She said, "He won't make it the night. I didn't want to say it where he'd hear me."

Del tugged on his beard.

He said, "It's a damn shame."

She said, "Ain't it, though?"

Shaking her head, she went back into the commissary. Del picked up Ruby's reins and started for Peewee's office to tell him about Birdie. After everything that had gone on, he'd forgot about Cobb's truck. There it sat, still parked neatly under the lean-to, adding to the mystery. He was still studying it when Peewee came out and locked his door.

He came over to Del and said, "Good day?"

"It was 'til Birdie got hisself bit by a coral snake. Cornelia tried tending to him, but she said he won't make it the night."

Peewee put his hands on his hips and stared at the ground.

He said, "We done lost two hands as it is." He looked around. "Won't Crow here a second ago?"

Del said, "He was. He's got a visitor."

Peewee wrinkled his nose. "Woman?"

"Yeah."

"Damn. Whenever she shows up, he gets even meaner, if you can believe it. It's getting to be some tough times. Lost a couple hands, one's sick, the other 'cause of that damn fool Crow. Now Ballard's gone and Birdie's been snake bit."

Del hated to have to share more troubles, but it was only right to let Peewee in on Cobb.

He said, "I reckon now's as good a time as any to tell you, but we got one more gone."

Peewee's shoulders drooped. "Who else?"

"Cobb. I'm thinking he's done run off. Course, Crow went on and on about him not making his numbers. He might of got scared after Ballard died, thinking there'd be some changes with boss men. Who knows? Either way, he didn't meet the work wagon this morning. I sent Georgie to his place once I got my men going to see if he was sick. Then I checked myself at dinner time. He won't there, but he didn't take none of his things. I don't reckon he came with much, 'cept that truck of his and there it sits. Seems odd he didn't take it."

"Maybe not. He said it had radiator problems. Plus, if he took off in the middle of the night, he wouldn't want to make a bunch a noise starting it up."

Del said, "True. Still, I can't hardly believe he'd leave it behind."

"Well, if he owes Swallow Hill, I'm gonna have to have him hauled back here by the sheriff. I'll have to put the word out so deputies can keep a lookout on the main roads."

"What'll happen if he's caught?"

Peewee rubbed his head. "Anyone leaves owing money generally gets a few lashes."

"You'd have him whipped?"

Peewee raised his shoulders. "Can't be helped. He done wrong by leaving, he has to answer for it."

"Couldn't you take the truck as payment?"

"Company ain't gonna like it."

"What if he don't owe?"

"That would make a difference. He's a free man to come and go, then."

Del said, "Let's check the commissary."

They headed over to the building. Del had always known this to be standard practice at most camps. Runaways got treated as criminals, and he hoped for Cobb's sake his debt was free and clear. Cornelia was behind the counter, and so was Otis.

Peewee said, "Hey, you up to date in your ledger, Otis?"

"Always."

"Great. What's on Cobb's account? What's he owe?"

Otis said, "I ain't even got to look. He don't owe nothing. He don't buy much, and when he does, he pays cash. Been paying that a way since he got here."

Del relaxed, but this only puzzled him more. What would make the kid come to a camp and do this sort of work if he had money?

Otis, always nosy, said, "Why?"

Peewee said, "He took off. Must've decided life at Swallow Hill won't to his liking."

Cornelia looked troubled, and Del thought he saw a hint of sad too.

He said, "By the way, how about the others who work for me?"

Otis flipped the pages with irritation, like it irked him to have to provide Del the information, but he read through the list one by one, and all of them owed at least five dollars or more. By the time they got their pay for a week and bought what they needed for the next week, it might fluctuate a few cents here and there, but they'd always owe. It was a vicious cycle, one his pap had worked hard to avoid, but still had, at one point or another, been indebted to some camp.

Del said, "Thanks," and he and Peewee made their way back outside. The sun was down, and Del was drained. It had been a hard first day.

Peewee said, "Mrs. Ballard and them kids left this morning. She's going to her sister's. The place is yours if you want it. Can't say it's completely varmint free, but it's definitely a step up from what you're in now." Peewee clapped him on the shoulder. "Glad you decided on being one of the boss men. We need more like Ballard. He knew how to get along and didn't get worked up over things. I asked Ballard once how he got his men to do as good as them what got beat regular-like. He said, 'They're willing to work. They have to eat and provide for their families, no different than any other man. They's God's creatures too.' I ain't ever forgot that."

Del was encouraged and began to believe he could possibly count on Peewee as an ally.

Peewee went on. "It don't surprise me, not with Ballard, not considering his background 'fore he come here."

"What was that?"

Peewee said, "He was a preacher who liked his liquor a bit too much, 'til one of his young'uns drowned in a river. Lost a bit of his religion afterward. He come here needing work, another chance. I said fine, gave him that chance."

Del wished Ballard had lived and that he'd got to know him better. He might've told him about what he'd experienced in the grain bin. Maybe he could've made some sense out of it.

Peewee said, "Well, I'm calling it a day."

He waved his hand, and Del went to where he'd left Ruby.

He tugged the reins gently and said, "Come on, old girl. Time for us to call it a day too."

He took her to the barn, gave her plenty of water and feed, fastened the stall gate, and went out. It was a twilit evening with the first stars flickering, tiny pinpoints against a deep purple sky. Once he was at number forty-two, he considered Cobb's little cabin, sitting silent and dark. The thought of the kid gone made him a bit glum. Though they hadn't got to know each other well, he'd liked him just fine. The kid had standards, so to speak, and stood by them, an admirable trait. He'd shown no fear toward Otis, a much bigger man, and older. He wished he'd stuck around. He could've helped him with a couple techniques, maybe showed him a way to improve his tally.

Del had been thinking about that, and it's what made him decide he wasn't going to let someone like Crow keep him from improving conditions for himself. He gathered his few things and made his way back across the camp to the woods riders' section. Crow was sitting on his steps as he was wont to do, dragging the tip of his knife under his nails. The sight brought back when Del first set eyes on him, only weeks ago, eating an apple, with that same wily look. Del had got used to the perpetual mockery that shaped the man's features, but tonight, he believed there was a touch of scheming.

Crow said, "Hell. Ain't this a hoot? Neighbors now."

The stuffy little shack with its nightly scurrying, slithering visitors had suddenly grown more appealing, but if he changed his mind now, Crow wouldn't never let him forget it.

Del said, "Appears so."

Crow kept scraping at his nails.

Del said, "Word gets round in this camp, so I've learned, and I 'spect you've heard about Cobb."

Del watched him carefully. Crow paused in his nail cleaning and stared off into the distance.

"What about him?"

"You ain't heard?"

Crow returned his gaze to his knife, applied it to his nails again.

"I been a little busy."

"He's not around. Ain't no one seen him all day."

"That right?"

His lack of reaction was peculiar. Matter of fact, his attitude was downright dull, and what Del had expected him to do, he didn't. No talk of Woodall and his pack a hounds. No cussing, or comments about whippings, or the box. Nothing. Crow's front door opened and the woman Del had seen earlier glanced at him, barely. She didn't speak to either of them, and Crow remained as still as she was, as if one waited on the other to do something.

Del said, "Well. Good night."

He shoved the front door open, went inside, and shut it. You couldn't never tell with some. He'd met a lot of different kinds of people in his life, but he'd never met anyone like Crow. Maybe he'd come by his ways honestly, because his mama sure was a strange one. He moved about in the murky interior, feeling his way until his fingertips encountered the edge of a table and a lantern in the middle of it. He brushed his hands over the surface and found a small box of matches. He struck the match, lit the wick, and adjusted it. He then walked around the main room, pleased to see he had a small bedroom with a bed off to the right. How about that, a real bed, nothing like what he'd been sleeping on. It almost brought a smile to his face.

Back in the main room against one wall was a crudely built frame holding a wash pan like what he carried his things in. There was a wooden cabinet beside it for keeping flour, sugar, and such. He had two window openings at the front, and one on each side too. He went to the one at the front, pushed it from the bottom, and propped the stick left on the sill against the edge to hold it open. There was no breeze, but letting the night air in gave him the notion of it being cooler. He untied his belongings, such as they were.

As he was settling in, a barely discernible thumping came to him, and at first he paid it no mind, but then he did. It came from Crow's house. He went over and stood by the side window, listening, and began to question what he was hearing. If it was what it sounded like, it didn't make no sense. Del eased the shutter open. He should mind his own business, but he couldn't hardly believe his ears. He glanced over to Crow's, where the side window was open as well. The lantern's glow cast a torrid scene before him, and Del backed away from the window, accidentally stumbling over one of the chairs set at the little table.

"Damn," he said.

Suddenly, the window next door slammed shut and was so loud it echoed through the woods. Del stood in the middle of the room, replaying the snippet of what he'd witnessed over and over in his head. Crow and his mama? It was then he began to understand, perhaps a bit, what made the man the way he was.

Chapter 18

Rae Lynn

She wanted to call out for help, only she didn't have it in her, and if she had, who would hear? She'd overheard the work hands say the box held nothing but sorrow, and all the tears and sweat of the suffering, as well as a bit of each soul who'd fled from it to the Great Beyond. If they did have to go by it, and they certainly had when the crop they were working happened to be beyond it, they'd turned their eyes away, some believing by looking at it, the sorrow it held would jump on to them.

Time no longer made sense. Whether it was light or dark, it all melted into one and the same. She'd gone deep inside herself, where she could escape the sticky, hot, suffocating interior. Once, she'd woke to what she thought was rain. She instinctively moved her head, opened her mouth, and caught a tiny stream of water, cool and sweet, falling through the thin crack, her only eye to the world. She wasn't sure it was rain, though, because it stopped as quickly as it started. And there was the sun, high in the sky, creating a streaked pattern across the top of her. A miracle had happened, she determined. The water had been a miracle.

Another time, Warren appeared to her, but what a strange place for him to be, near her feet, staring at her from that impossible spot. Where was the rest of him? Was he coming up through the ground? He appeared different, too pale, his hair and eyes too black, and when his arm stretched up, up, and up, his fingers, extra long and narrow, she didn't want him to touch her, not this Warren of the other side. Cold fingertips brushed her brow, and there was nothing she could do. Was he saying something to her? His words came like a hiss, unintelligible. She didn't like this Warren. She wanted him to go away, and as she rose from the depths of her delirium, she jolted awake, aware the hissing was her, straining to breathe.

The nightmare Warren gone, she quickly descended to where she was most comfortable now, a serene area of soft dreams where no pain, thirst, or hunger were allowed. There she could take in long, cool drinks of water. She could rest under shade trees. She barely moved, if at all, and the only part of her that did was her heart rate, which grew more erratic and rapid. She was well into her second day and no longer fully conscious. She hovered between the here and there, her mind delivering only one persistent, yet clear message to the rest of her body: *I am dying.*

Chapter 19

Del

As the man came along, he kept his eyes on the ground and Del waited for him to speak, but he already had a bad feeling Birdie hadn't made it through the night.

Del said, "No?" once Preacher was close enough to hear him.

"The missus, she say he went to meet our Maker about three this morning."

Del sighed. His other men were already disappearing into their sections of the woods, and now with Cobb and Birdie both gone, he needed more workers, that was all there was to it. He'd have to speak to Peewee about it.

"Has he got family back home?"

"Think his momma's still alive. Know he had him a little gal back home he was wantin' to marry."

"I got to see Peewee about hiring on some more workers. I'll ask him if he has an address."

After Preacher went to work, the day fell into a curiously quiet pattern. Del rode Ruby in and out of the woods, making marks in his tally book as call names were shouted. He pondered on what disturbed him most, the irregular seriousness of his workers, or what he'd witnessed the night before at Crow's. Both gave the day the sense of feeling abnormal, like the world had gone off-kilter. He'd not seen Crow since yesterday, but then again, he'd not wasted any time leaving this morning, wanting to avoid any chance encounter. He was going to have to face him, no doubt about it, but he needed more time before that happened.

Dinner break came, and the men trickled into the hang-up ground either on foot or by wagon if they were far enough out. The quiet was as unnatural as it had been. They'd not been right since Cobb disappeared. And come to think of it, Crow's absence was irregular too. He'd always seen fit to be somewhere around where he could spout off nonsense or try to stir up trouble. Del ate what he had, then sat with his back against a pine, watching them. Despite his concern, his eyes grew heavy, his consternation slipping away as he rested. Before long, the break was over, and they were back at it, working until the sun started setting. This was the hottest part of the day and Del was checking his counts, happy because he could let the men know they could stop. They'd done good. Made their numbers. He was going to show'em he was good on his word.

He rode Ruby in and out of the drifts, calling out, "Quitting time! Quitting time!" to the surprise and happiness of the men.

Clyde came with the wagon, and Del said, "We're done, go on and round'em up."

Even Clyde smiled as he steered Jackson into the woods. Del rode toward the camp when he spotted movement by a large pine. Georgie had two water buckets filled up, but stayed by the tree staring at Del intently, not speaking, yet clearly wanting to say something.

"What is it, Georgie? You bringing water? We're quitting, but you can come on and give Ruby some."

Georgie lifted one of the buckets and came forward. He set it down in front of the horse. She lowered her head immediately and slurped in long draughts. Georgie glanced over his shoulder. The wagon was approaching, though still some distance away, but it appeared to make him uneasy. He edged a bit closer.

He stared up at Del, wide-eyed and serious. "I got sumpin' to tell you, but I'm scared to."

Del climbed off Ruby and reached into his pocket

He got out a piece of peppermint. "Here, this might help."

Georgie's eyes didn't shine like they usually did at the sight of the candy, but he took it and popped it in his mouth. He scooted back a few feet, watching the approaching wagon with nervousness, as if unsure what to do. Del watched how it all played out on the boy's face, mostly in his eyes. It was evident little Georgie had already seen way too much. He was only a kid, but he'd been beat, and Del didn't know what else he'd experienced, but it had made him appear wiser than his years. He was an old soul in a nine-year-old's body.

Finally, Georgie said, "Somebody's in trouble."

Del went still. "Oh, yeah? Who?"

"Mr. Cobb."

Del immediately squatted eye level with the boy.

He grabbed hold of Georgie's arms, and he said, "Cobb? What do you mean, Georgie?"

Georgie was afraid now. Tears formed as he squirmed to get loose, but Del held on to him. The wagon was within fifty feet of them and Georgie's mouth clamped shut.

Del's voice rose. "What do you know about Mr. Cobb?"

Georgie's eyes darted from Del to the wagon. "He . . ."

Del half shouted, *"He what?"*

His raised voice drew anxious stares from the work hands.

Del heard them mumbling, "What's going on," and "What's that Georgie sayin'," and "He best be quiet."

Del let go of Georgie and pointed at him. "He said Cobb's in trouble. What's he mean?"

Georgie took off and hid behind the nearest pine. Frightened, he leaned out only enough to keep an eye on his elders. They climbed down from the wagon, frowning and shaking their heads as they switched from one foot to the other. Because they suffered from swollen, cracked, and bleeding soles, it was possible their work-worn feet made them do that, but Del was sure it wasn't so much the question, but the way he asked it. The state of their clothes, nothing but rags hanging off bone-thin frames, the lack of decent food, what they went through day to day, the brutal conditions, the workload, the danger, none of it mattered as much as the person they had to answer to. A boss man was the one who held their life in his hands, and they didn't know, not yet, that he wasn't like Crow. There was hand wringing, and the fear he brought by yelling. Del's gaze wandered over their faces, one by one. Clyde leaned against the wagon, looking on with interest.

Del calmed his voice and said, "Listen now. You ain't got to worry about me. I ain't like most. I sure as hell ain't like him. You know who I mean. Won't someone tell me what's happened? Won't someone help me?"

They sure were a suspicious and doubtful lot. All he got was coughing as someone in the back went to hacking. He heard them spit.

Heard, "Whew. Had to get rid a dat fling."

His frustration growing, Del held his expression neutral. He homed in on Preacher.

Del said, "I'll put my very hand on that Bible I know you carry in that back pocket a yours and swear on my own mama's grave I ain't meaning not one a you no harm. Take my word, and if it ain't good enough, then I ought to go on and quit, 'cause that means ain't none a y'all ever gonna trust me. And if you don't trust me, I can't be trusting you."

Preacher looked at the others before he slowly stepped forward.

He took his hat off and said, "After y'all took Mr. Ballard to his missus, Crow gathered his men, and all us who worked under Mr. Ballard, had us tell him what he wanted to hear. Said we was having a trial about how that kid didn't never make his numbers. Said it was time he learned, and if we was to say a word, he'd see to it we'd never talk agin. He done put him in the box."

As Preacher spoke, Del could see it happening.

His stomach dropped, and with his voice tense, he said, "Three days ago?"

Preacher nodded. "Yessuh."

Del spun on his heels and ran to Ruby, his quick movements so unlike him, he spooked her and he had to grab her reins before she skirted out of his reach. He got his foot in the stirrup by some miracle as she turned sideways, and heaved himself into the saddle. As he tore down the path, he heard a noise behind him and turned to see Clyde coming at a good pace, with the men and Georgie hanging on in the back of the wagon. Del rode Ruby as fast as he dared, and as he tore through the camp, he spotted Crow near the cooper's shed. It was the first time he'd laid eyes on him since the night he'd seen what he wished he could forget.

"Damn you!" he shouted as he flew by.

He was now on the other side of the camp and the wooden structure lay straight ahead. Was it his imagination, or did it seem like the rays of the sun only touched it, making it appear as if caught by a blistering sunbeam? He jumped off Ruby, and she trotted over to stand in the shade, her sides heaving. Del ran to the box as the wagon arrived and the men spilled out of the back.

Del knelt by it and hollered, "Cobb! Cobb! Hang on! We're getting you out! Somebody get me something to get this lock off!"

The men pulled out their bark hacks, and he grabbed one

and began pounding on the lock, but it was big, thick, and he succeeded only in nicking the steel. He ruined one hack and grabbed for another. Clyde and the work hands gathered around him. Preacher began praying, and the men joined in. As their voices rose and fell with fervor and passion, off in the distance came pounding of horse hooves. Del knew who was coming.

Clyde said, "There's Crow. He'll have the key."

Del's insides burned with a rage as furious as the sun scorching his back. Crow thundered into the area, scattering a few men at the back, got off of his horse, and sauntered over. Del continued pounding on the lock.

Crow said, "I was coming to see if he was done baking."

It was all Del could do not to jump on the man. The men around him continued chanting Scripture, and their voices echoed throughout the woods. Crow stared at them in disgust.

"Ain't this something. The lot of you praying and carrying on like saints. Shut up with that racket."

Del stood and, with gritted teeth, said, "Get him out. Now."

Crow grinned and sauntered back over to his horse to rummage around in the saddlebag.

"Now, I know it's got to be in here somewheres."

Del said, "Hurry it up, for God's sake!"

Crow stopped his hunt through the saddlebag. He patted his shirt pockets and pulled out the key.

"Aha! Now, that's what I call a miracle, ain't it? Looks like them prayers worked after all."

Del held himself in check. It took all he had to control himself and not jerk it from his fingers. Crow moseyed over to the box and dropped to his knees. He knocked on the lid.

"Hello?"

He raised his hands up as if to say, *Oh well.*

Del said, "Get on with it!" and stepped closer.

Crow stuck the key in the lock and grinned over his shoulder at the group of men who dared to still whisper prayers, while Del paced, clenching and unclenching his fists. Finally came a tiny click, and Crow raised the lid. There was a collective drawing in of a breath as he peered inside. He stood up quick, stumbled backward, tripped over a root, and fell on his rear. His reaction disturbed the stillness holding the group in check. They broke loose, some yelling and running for the large pines, eager to put something between them and what the dreadful box held. Anybody who'd left the Earth in such an awful way was likely to have suffered mightily and might now be a haint who could come back to haunt them.

Crow lurched to his feet, backed away, his hand rubbing his chin like he couldn't quite figure what he'd seen. For once, he was tongue-tied, no words, no smart remarks. Del peeked in at the form. Everything had gone still, even the birds in the trees. Preacher raised his voice, as if yelling at the heavens, lending an eerie tone to what they were experiencing.

"'Do not fear, for I have redeemed you; I have called you by name, you are mine. When you pass through the waters, I will be with you; and through the rivers, they shall not overwhelm you; when you walk through fire you shall not be burned, and the flame shall not consume you!'"

Del stared at this person called Ray Cobb and felt like someone had dumped a bucket of water over his head. He squatted down, reached inside to touch him, and the men, all of them, those behind the trees and those who'd not moved, waited and whispered in fear. Del's thoughts were hectic as he dealt with the truth. This was no man. This was some poor young woman, no mistaking it. What in the hell had she been thinking? Why would she do such a thing?

Del turned and nailed Crow with an unforgiving look. "This here's a young gal."

Voices started into a low hum that rose as everyone mulled over the information.

"He ain't no man?"

"A woman?"

Del rose to his feet, angry as he'd ever been. Crow adjusted his horse's halter, brushed his hands down his pants, looked at a tree as if there was something interesting about it. Acted dumb.

Del said, "You're a damn fool."

Crow spat out an answer. "How the hell was I supposed to know? Didn't nobody. Not even you."

Del said, "Man, woman. Colored, white. You go too far. You always go too far."

"Yeah. Like you been around all that long. Hell. It ain't up to you, now is it?"

"We'll see about that. We'll see what Peewee's got to say. I hope he throws you outta here. Better yet. Maybe you ought to spend some time in there yourself. You done killed an innocent young woman."

Del jabbed his finger at the box and in that instant, a horrible croupy noise rose from within. The workers heard it and this time, they all fled, certain that Cobb, who wasn't Cobb, but a woman, had, by some strange happening, been raised from the dead. They scattered through the trees helter-skelter.

Crow came to life, jumped on his horse, yelling, "Git back here! Don't think you're gonna run off! I'll whip the black off'n your hides! Damn!"

Del couldn't worry about the men right now. He held his breath against the stench as he put one arm under the woman's shoulders and under her knees before lifting her out. She didn't weigh much more than a sack of potatoes. Her coloring was awful, somewhere between ghastly white and splotchy, as if her blood was having trouble circulating. Her breathing was sporadic, and when it came, it rattled loudly in an alarming fashion. To those who'd stayed, Clyde and Preacher, it was obvious how Del had made his determination of her gender. A large, dark burgundy stain in the crotch of her overalls clearly signified she was someone other than who they thought. They averted their eyes as Del went to the back of the wagon and laid her down. He climbed into it and pulled her up so her head rested on his lap.

He said, "Preacher, will you take Ruby to the barn, feed her good, and give her plenty a water."

Preacher said, "Yessuh, ain't no problem."

Clyde waited, sitting in the front, and Del said, "Let's get her to the Riddles, see what Miss Cornelia can do, if anything."

Clyde clucked at the mule to get him going.

Del said, "Hurry."

On his way he watched as the men who'd scattered came out of the woods and started for home.

They raised their voices to shout, "She gone make it!" "She be all right!" as they made their way back into Swallow Hill.

Del studied the woman. It all made sense to him now. The oddities he'd noticed, like her hands, the flowers on the table, the girlie sheets. Ways she'd acted. He should've seen through it, but he hadn't. Maybe he'd have sensed her femaleness before the grain bin robbed him. Why she'd come here pretending to be a man to begin with was peculiar, but in listening to her periodic, noisy gasping, he doubted he'd ever find out why. Like Birdie, it was likely she was a goner and wouldn't make it through the night. Funny, how the name he knew her by still suited her. He didn't know how else to think of her. Ray Cobb was who she still was, least to him.

Pillowing her head on his lap to make the ride into camp less jarring, she was so far gone, it was possible him fussing over her comfort didn't matter nohow. She only moved as the wagon did, her feet splayed out to each side in the new boots that didn't look so new anymore. They arrived at the Riddle house, and Del eased her head off his lap and placed it on the hat like it had been in the box. He climbed out of the back, and the odd harsh breathing came again. Damn Crow. If Peewee didn't chase him off after this, he wouldn't know what to think. The noise of their arrival brought Cornelia out onto the porch, along with the smell of whatever she'd been cooking for supper. Otis came too, a napkin tucked into the top of his grimy shirt.

She said, "What is this? The commissary's closed."

Del pointed into the back of the wagon. "Cobb? He ain't doing so good. And he ain't a he. He's a she."

Cornelia's mouth dropped, and she came off the porch and stared into the back of the wagon. Eyebrows raised high, she took in the form, the issue of blood, where it was, as well as the lack of response.

Del said, "Can you help her? She's been cooking in that damn box for three days."

Cornelia said, "Oh, my dear Lord. Well, I don't know. I'll surely try. Hurry, bring her on in."

Del climbed back into the wagon and scooped up what was left of Ray Cobb. Her body felt like it was made of nothing but the overalls, shirt, and bones and only held together by parched skin and the cloth wrapped around it. Cornelia stood by the front door, holding it open for him. He went inside and followed her into a tiny backroom off the kitchen. It had a bed with a lacy bedspread, a chair, and a small night table with a Bible and a lantern on it. A small window sat at the opposite end of the room, and if a person was propped in the bed, they could see out of it. Del thought it an odd thing, this little extra room. Otis followed on their heels, disgruntled at his supper being interrupted.

Del laid Cobb on the bed, while Cornelia asked questions. "What on earth happened? How did he, I mean *she*, end up there?

He straightened up and said, "Crow."

Cornelia said, "Oh."

Otis said, "We ain't no hotel here, and ain't you already got plenty to do? Hell, she looks about dead already."

Cornelia twisted her hands and said, "It's the Christian thing to do."

Otis stepped over, pushing Cornelia aside. "Hmph. He don't look like he's gone make it another hour."

Del said, "She. It's a she."

Otis stared at Ray Cobb. "That ain't normal what *she* done. It ain't natural."

Del ignored him and spoke to Cornelia. "She was hot seeming. She ain't sweating none, neither. She's been breathing real hard."

Cornelia laid a hand on Cobb's brow. She took it away, glanced at the men jammed into the small space.

She said, "If I'm gonna try and help her, y'all got to get out."

Otis said, "I need my supper!"

Cornelia said, "I put your plate on the table, Otis. Go on and eat, now."

Del said, "If something happens, let me know. You need anything, let me know. Otherwise I'll be back at first light."

He left with Clyde knowing he might never get any answers as to the secrets of a woman named Ray Cobb.

Chapter 20

Rae Lynn

She quit fighting long before she got to Heaven. She stopped begging herself to hang on. She quit praying, quit wishing someone would find her. None of it mattered, and now she was here, and Heaven was *everything*. Whenever some remote tiny part of her brain awakened, if only enough to register something good happening, she savored it, then slipped away, diving deep into the dark. The landscape of her body carried the signs of war. Damaged. Weakened. Wasted.

All manner of good, if strange, things happened in Heaven. Her arms and legs, light as the wind, moved and lifted one by one, and she was touched by a soft coolness across her forehead, over her face, her breasts, belly, and thighs. She'd been in hell, burned by the brimstone, forced to breathe sulfur spewed by evil. No longer. Heaven held only freshness, gentleness, and soothing, slow movements. Her reward.

She didn't know who in Heaven talked to her, but the voice came now and again, light and soothing, speaking like a mother to a child.

It said, "Safe."

Sometimes, "Miracle."

Other times, "Stay."

Mostly, it only quietly hummed. An angel.

When there were words, she couldn't understand if they were meant for her, or if the voice was only soothing the feverishness of her mind, as would be natural for such a fine, orderly place. She didn't want to leave this sanctuary, but there were moments when it seemed the perfect thing to do. It would come on her like the sensation of falling, and by falling she understood deep within herself that if she gave in, if she allowed it, this fragile fragment of existence, such as it was, would be no more. She contemplated this choice many times over, stepped closer to some unknown edge more than once.

Only the light, cool touch would come again, and she'd turn into it, let it lead her back to Heaven and the tender, soothing state of rest.

Chapter 21

Del

He showed up to the little house beside the commissary before the sun was up, having spent the evening worrying, half expecting someone to come with the bad news. If the woman didn't live, he would tell Peewee to call in the sheriff. If she did live, he wanted Peewee to kick Crow out of the camp. Hat in hand, he knocked on the door. Cornelia opened it and almost immediately started giving him an update.

"She ain't changed much since yesterday. She's hanging on, but barely. I was sure she was a goner a time or two," Cornelia said.

Del said, "It's hard to believe she ain't."

Cornelia said, "You want to see her?"

Del said, "If your husband don't mind. It's early yet."

Cornelia waved a hand in dismissal. "Shoot. He ain't even up."

She took him to the backroom, where the wick was set low in the lantern, throwing his shadow tall and thin against the wall. Cobb lay there covered with only a thin sheet, her shoulders bare above it. She looked . . . well, she looked like hell. Her skin was pale, the color of flour, and her cheeks and eyes created hollow, dark areas that gave her the look of the dead. Her mouth was the brightest thing about her because her lips were reddened, swollen, and cracked.

Cornelia said, "I swiped some lard on her lips to help, but they still look painful."

Del murmured, "You're doing all you can," as he approached the bed.

He couldn't tell she was breathing, but there, there it was, a slow rise and sinking of the sheet. It hadn't been quite as hot for him as it had been for her. He'd been trapped for a day. She'd lasted three. He stared down at her, curious about the story that went along with her reasons for disguising herself. If she made it, and right now that was still seeming a little sketchy, he was sure she was, had been, someone he'd have found admirable.

Cornelia whispered to him. "Had to burn them clothes a hers. I've been wiping her down with cool cloths. Been able to get a tiny bit of water in her. She swallered a time or two, then got choked, but I'm doing it often as I can, though she can't take in but a small amount. I been putting a bit a sugar in it. She's got a fever, but for now, it's all I know to do."

Del said, "You know more'n me. Thank you."

Cornelia folded her arms and shook her head in amazement. "If she makes it, it'll be a wonder, as much as I hate to say it."

Del said, "If there's anything she needs, I'll pay for it."

"Ain't no need of that."

Otis appeared like magic in the doorway, his hair stuck up on one side.

"Dammitall, Cornelia! How stupid can you be?" To Del, he said, "Hell yeah, if something costs, you're gonna pay. It ain't like we running some free-for-all here."

Del said, "I ain't got no problem with that."

"Damn right, you ain't."

Del held back. There was no need to get into a competition of last words with Otis. What a pair him and Crow were. Del couldn't imagine what made people like them so hateful.

Del said, "I'll come back by around dinnertime and check on her."

Cornelia said, "You're welcome to eat with us if you want."

Del wouldn't have minded a good home-cooked meal, but not while sitting at the same table with Otis, who was as congenial as a snarling bear. "We barely got enough for our-selves."

Cornelia said, "Oh, Otis . . . we have plenty. We always have leftovers."

Otis opened his mouth, and Del was quick to politely decline and start making his way out.

"I 'preciate it, but I won't have the time nohow."

Otis said, "Oh, sure, sure. He's a big boss man now. Real important and all. Ain't got time to eat with us common folk."

Otis reminded him of the bad smells he'd tried to get rid of, unsuccessfully, back at number forty-two. No matter how hard he tried, they remained, steadfast and annoying. He couldn't imagine how an attractive woman like Cornelia got tangled up with the likes of him. It wasn't that he was ugly, only his ways. Maybe he'd charmed her, until she'd married him, and then changed. It happened. He gave Cornelia an understanding look, while Otis demanded his breakfast. Del backed out of the room, and took his leave. He wanted to catch Peewee anyway, if he could, and his timing couldn't have been better. Peewee was in the process of unlocking the office door and turned around in surprise at the sight of Del.

"Thought you'd be in the woods about now."

Del said, "Do you know what Crow did? He tell you?"

He said, "What now?"

Del unloaded. "Let's just say I found out where Cobb went.

To add to the problem, Cobb's a woman. That bastard put her in the sweatbox for three days, and we all know why. He thinks he's running this place. You got to do something about him."

"Wait, whoa, wait. Cobb's . . . he ain't a he?"

"No."

"I *knew* something won't right about that situation. How'd you find out?"

Del said, "It don't matter. Back to Crow, he can't keep getting away doing this to them workers, leaving'em to die, or come close to it. You need to tell him he's done here."

Peewee said, "Is she alive?"

"Barely. Since I been here, he's put three people in that sweatbox, including me. If it hadn't been for Ballard, he'd have left me there till I was done for."

"I didn't know about that. He gets carried away, granted. But he's a knowledgeable woods rider, despite his shortcomings."

"Shortcomings."

"Look. I can't be losing no more men. We're already short. I got one crew down by three. Birdie, Ballard, and now Cobb. You takin' Ballard's job makes Crow short, 'cause he lost a man a while back. Woodall's lost a couple too."

"If Crow's got anything to do with what goes on around here, you can expect to lose more."

Peewee narrowed his eyes against the glare of the sun and mumbled about what was ahead.

"I expect the rest of this summer's gonna be hell. I got to send word we need'n to hire more men. Got to be somebody wanting work in these tough times."

"You ain't gonna get any if they know what goes on."

"Hell, this place ain't no different than any other."

"I been in'em before, and it won't nothing like what's going on here."

"Wait just a dang minute. You saying I ain't a good operator?"

Del was angry, and now Peewee was too. They quit talking and stood there, neither one looking at the other, at odds. After a few seconds of silence, Del walked to his horse.

He said, "Mark my words. It ain't gonna get any better if you don't take care of it."

He mounted and rode off. He had to get his day started. He was late, and as soon as he got into the woods, and the men saw him, the call names started coming fast, and he spent the rest of the morning it seemed trying to catch up. Right before the dinner break, Nolan Brown came into their work area, bark hack in hand.

Del said, "Hey there, Nolan, what's going on? What're you doing?"

Nolan said, "Boss man, he told me to come give y'all a hand. Said you was short."

Del said, "We are, but ain't he needing you?"

"I reckon, but he sent me on anyhow."

What was Crow up to?

Del said, "Come on, I'll show you where you can start."

He went into the woods with Nolan. After a few minutes they came to the drift Cobb had been working.

Del said, "This is partly worked. Start here, keep going that way."

"Sure thing, boss man."

Del said, "You ain't got to call me that. Call me Del. Or Butler."

"Naw suh, can't do it."

Del said, "You don't give in, do you?"

Nolan exhaled and said, "It's jes how things is. Why you got to question it?"

Del shrugged, pulled out his tally book, and added "Long Gone" to the list of call names, which consisted of Preacher,

Big'Un, Sweet Thang, and Juke-n-Juice. Long Gone disappeared into the woods, and within seconds, Del had made a couple marks for him. He sure was fast. He'd catch up Cobb's drift and be ready to start a new one before day's end. While Del weaved in and out of the work areas, he thought it a curious turn of events for Crow to send on a worker, but who could figure what went through his head? Nolan had said when his mama showed up, he got real different, and he'd sure proven it.

By five o'clock the men had done the day's work. They still had a few hours of daylight, but he called quitting time. They acted like they still couldn't believe this could happen, and some kept working until Del made them stop. Nolan tossed him the same dubious look he'd given him when Del said he didn't drink. After the woods had cleared out, he heard a couple squirrels in the trees above his head. He eased his shotgun out of the holder and aimed. He got them both because the second one got confused by the noise and the disappearance of his buddy. He gathered them up and trotted Ruby to the hang-up ground where the men were crawling into the back of the wagon. He gave one to Preacher and the other to Big'Un.

Del said, "Ain't nothing better'n stewed squirrel."

Preacher agreed. "Don't you know it. This here's a fine one."

Big'Un held his up by its tail, admiring it while Nolan gave Del a look like he was trying too hard. Nolan sure wasn't an easy one to win over.

Del followed the wagon out of the woods, wondering how Ray Cobb had fared, and hoped since nobody came to get him, that meant good news. Once he arrived at the Riddles, Cornelia must have been on the lookout because she opened their door right away, looking relieved.

"You ain't gonna believe this. She woke up."

Surprised by this outcome, he said, "She did?"

"Um-hmm. Opened them big green eyes of hers a couple hours ago. I ain't been able to talk to her much 'cause she went right back to sleep afterward, but she's awake again."

She motioned for him to follow her into the room, and there sat Cobb, as she still was to him. She laid propped against some pillows, looking like death still hovered, but Cornelia was seeing to things, and one was a tempting glass of fresh lemonade on the table beside the bed.

Cornelia bent over her and said, "Here now, shug, you have some more a this."

Cornelia put the glass to Cobb's mouth, and she sipped a little. Cornelia set it back on the table while Del stood with his hat in his hands, not knowing what to say. Had it been Cobb, the kid, he would've figured it out.

But when she cast her eyes in his direction, all he could think to say was, "Hidy."

She went to smile, but it must have hurt her mouth because she winced. She still sounded like the kid, her voice raspy, but lighter.

"Hidy."

He dipped his head, twirled his hat.

"How you feeling?"

She raised her shoulders, then coughed. She was still so weak, and Del figured he shouldn't stay. She was going to make it, and this eased his mind.

He said, "Cornelia here, she's gonna take good care of you."

Cobb nodded once.

Del went to the door, stopped, and faced her. "What's your real name?"

She picked at the edge of the sheet covering her, like she wasn't sure of what she ought to say.

Finally, she spoke, her voice weak. "Rae Cobb. Rae with an *e*."

Surprised, he repeated the name. "Rae Cobb."

She nodded again.

He said, "How about that. Still Rae Cobb."

He smiled at Cornelia, put his hat back on his head, and left the room. Outside he found himself adjusting his frame of mind around the idea of the feller he'd come to know as the kid actually being a woman. An attractive young woman at that, even with crooked, cropped hair. There was something about her. Despite what she'd been through, it wasn't hard for him to see her now, in a true sense, and he found her appealing, very much so. All the same questions he'd had flooded back in over who she really was and where she'd been, what her past was. It must be complicated. Life shouldn't be that way, but it often was.

He rubbed Ruby, giving her his thoughts. "Old girl, sometimes I wish I were in your shoes, without a worry in the world except when my next meal and watering was coming."

Chapter 22

Rae Lynn

Right after she was brought to the Riddles, Rae Lynn lingered near the here and there. Cornelia stayed close, fussed around the room, and though Rae Lynn didn't open her eyes, she could hear her, and felt at peace. Before Cornelia left the room, she always put her hand to Rae Lynn's forehead. Her touch was cool. Calming. *Heaven.* She took care of Rae Lynn as if she were a family member. She argued with Otis on her behalf, who looked at her like he didn't know what to make of her. He insisted she was more trouble than Cornelia or he had time for.

"Otis, she ain't no trouble to you."

"She sure as hell better not be."

"You still get all your meals and on time. Ain't nothing no different. She only needs rest."

He stomped out onto the porch, puffing and mumbling until finally it was only her and Cornelia. Poor Cornelia. She hadn't chosen good husband material.

Cornelia mumbled sometimes as if she were alone. "The mess I have to put up with. Acts like a spoiled child!"

Under Cornelia's fine care, her body healed, and when she became alert enough, she agonized over what she ought to say about herself, what she ought to do. More questions would surely come. It was doubtful Peewee would allow her to stay, not unless she could work. She could tell them she'd lost her husband unexpected like and needed somewhere to go. While it was God's honest truth, they might wonder why she hadn't remained where she and her husband lived, with people she knew. Surely that made more sense? Her lack of family was easily explained away because of the girls' home, but after years of marriage, what about her husband's own family, and if not them, people she'd known? Them who could help her so she didn't have to go traipsing round the countryside as a man? Didn't she have nobody close to her she could've counted on? Why not find work in the town she'd come from?

All these questions.

On top of it all, she had to work to avoid the deepest, darkest corners of her head, where her worst secret was kept. She picked apart the final moments with Warren. What he'd said. What she'd said. The split second she'd pulled the trigger and immediately changed her mind, wishing the bullet back in the gun. She didn't want to spend one second on Butch, or his cockamamy idea. She hadn't had any time to grieve, much less think on how she ought to move forward. No time at all. She'd only reacted, done what she thought best.

Tormented, she also couldn't stop reliving her time in the box. The memory of it caused her breath to catch, in spite of being able to look over and see the sticky summer day right outside the tiny window of her room. She recollected the relentless heat and threw the thin sheet off. While she had started drinking lots of water, her terrible thirst wasn't close to being quenched. Above it all was the horror of how she'd quit fighting, had given in to whatever would happen. It hadn't scared her like it did now.

God help her.

Del Reese came often. She'd seen him a couple times, standing in the doorway in the early-morning hours, staring in at her. She kept her eyes closed, cracked her lids just enough so she could watch him watching her. He'd go away and the murmur of his voice and Cornelia's would last a few seconds until the screen door at the front of their house would squeak, and he'd be gone. After he left, Cornelia would arrive with a pan of warm, soapy water and would go about the business of cleaning her while Rae Lynn stared anywhere but at her. Cornelia's care was matter-of-fact, get done what needed doing. After a couple more days, Rae Lynn was able to stand with Cornelia's arm around her waist. Cornelia would sit her in the chair as she straightened up the sheets, cleaned the chamber pot, and talked the whole time about nothing much. Busy chatter about the heat of summer, the song of a particular bird, what she'd bring her to eat next. Rae Lynn sat quiet, did as she was told. She didn't want to make no trouble for her.

On her fourth morning at the Riddles, Rae Lynn offered her first words on her own. It felt good to use her natural voice.

"Kin you smell that?" she asked Cornelia.

Even to her ears, her tone sounded soft, not bearing the odd gruffness that was Ray Cobb.

Cornelia turned her head, sniffing the air. She immediately dragged the chamber pot out from under the bed to look at it. It was empty.

"I thought I forgot to empty it. It ain't got nothing in it."

"It's . . . not that. It's . . . different. Like what I smelled in the . . ."

Cornelia's expression was bewildered. "I only smell them sausage biscuits we had for breakfast. Which you didn't eat much of."

Rae Lynn dropped her eyes, feeling her face grow warm. "I reckon it's here."

She pointed at her head.

Cornelia spoke with a soft voice. "Well, now. You don't worry none. With all the bad you been through? It ain't no wonder. You just wait. You gonna get better and all of that will be gone one of these days."

She went out, and within minutes she was back with a couple vases filled with pale-yellow flowers clustered among shiny green leaves. She set one by the bed and the other on the windowsill, which stayed open, allowing in any breeze that might come.

"Smell that?"

Rae Lynn could.

"Honeysuckle's one of my favorites."

Cornelia said, "Mine too."

Rae Lynn didn't tell her the sweet aroma mingled with that other odor that seemed very real to her. She didn't understand why it lingered so strong in her mind. The box held on to those who'd been there before her, the bits and pieces of them, their distress, their frantic will to live. She understood it, had felt it too. She was sure she'd left some part of herself there as well. Not just the blood from in between her legs, or the sweat that had poured off of her. Not just them physical things. Some other part of her had broke off and got left behind, even as she was lifted from out of it, saved by a man named Del Reese. This was punishment for what she'd done.

The fifth morning, Cornelia came in smiling, ready to start the day, but this time, she had him with her. Rae Lynn immediately pulled the sheet to her chin and stared toward the foot of the bed.

He said, "Morning."

She felt at a disadvantage, still in bed and all. She dipped her head in greeting, barely.

He said, "I come up with this idea. Won't take but a second."

He went to work, fashioning a pull cord using some twine. He tied it first to her bedpost, and with him being so close made her lean the other way. He dropped the ball of twine out the window and went out. Rae Lynn next saw him holding the twine spool on his thumb letting it run out as he walked toward the commissary, where he set it on the window, a distance of about fifty feet. She leaned forward to watch, and in a few seconds he was inside the commissary and at the window, picking it up. He waved, and she sat back quick. She watched the string move, tighten a bit, and a minute later, Cornelia came into the room smiling.

She said, "He looped the other end over a hook and it's got a bell hung off it. I'm going back over there, and when I wave to you out the window yonder, you pull on your end here."

Rae Lynn said, "Okay."

When Cornelia was at the window of the commissary waving like Del Reese had done, Rae Lynn reached up and gave the string a light tug. In the quiet of the morning, she could hear a faint tinny *ding, ding.* She watched Cornelia hurry back across the yard, and Otis stomping along right after her. Rae Lynn thought, *Uh-oh.*

Cornelia rushed into the room and said, "It worked perfect."

Otis came barreling in seconds later.

He said, "What the hell's that for?"

He pointed at the twine looped around the bedpost.

She said, "It's in case she needs me."

Otis said, "Woman. Is you crazy? You can't be at her beck and call, answering to a damn bell while you're working. You got to get your priorities straight."

"Otis honey, it's only if something urgent comes up."

"Like what?"

Cornelia glanced at Rae Lynn, her face going pink.

"*Woman* things, Otis."

"Aw, hell. I ain't needin' to hear about that."

He went back out, but not before yelling at them. "Ain't nothing more urgent than her getting out of bed and earning her keep. I'm keeping tabs on what she's costing me."

"She ain't hardly had a chance to yet!"

"I don't wanna hear no back talk!"

"Yes, honey."

"She better get right, or she can get out."

"Yes, honey."

He went out, slamming the door behind him. Cornelia faced Rae Lynn, who sat in the bed looking like a child about to cry, rubbing on the little nub of finger, over and over. Cornelia sat with her and leaned forward, patting her hand.

"Aw, now, shug. Don't you let him upset you. His bark's always been worser'n his bite. He got it from his own daddy, who acted like a tetchy old mule most days."

Rae Lynn reached out and lightly touched Cornelia's arm, where three round, puckered scars were visible.

"That bite a his seems right ferocious to me."

Cornelia in turn stared at Rae Lynn's hand on her arm. She touched the stub where her finger was missing.

"What happened here?"

Rae Lynn pulled her hand away. Tucked it under the sheet.

"It was an accident. Happened years ago."

Cornelia sighed and said, "It don't matter nohow. They's only the marks of life, showing what we been through." She leaned back to study Rae Lynn, tipping her head to the left. "And, here I was thinking you was a man! After I brung you the pie, I thought, he sure is sweet looking compared to most."

Rae Lynn gave her a little smile. "Well, I should've known it won't the smartest thing to do, maybe. They'll probably want me to leave here, and soon."

"We ain't gonna worry about that right now. Peewee's a reasonable man. Now, Crow? He's the one to worry over. Thinks he's running things."

Rae Lynn flinched at the thought of Crow, of facing him again. Maybe he'd be different, but she somehow doubted it.

She said, "Peewee might say it's my own fault. You know, lying to him and all."

Cornelia turned a sage eye to her and said, "I bet you had your reasons. We always do what we have to do, what's necessary, don't we?"

Women folk, is who Cornelia meant. They were most often the ones to bend, sometimes until they broke. Or got broken. She believed with all her heart in that moment, she and Cornelia would get along just fine. Rae Lynn felt an instant kinship. She ought to tell her who she was at least. She was real understanding. Seemed real trustworthy, and already a friend.

Rae Lynn said, "My name?"

Cornelia smiled and said, "What, don't tell me. It ain't Rae Cobb?"

Rae Lynn shifted in the bed. "Well, it is, but it's actually Rae Lynn. Rae Lynn Cobb."

Cornelia smiled big. "Ain't that something," she said.

"Call me Rae Lynn."

"Well, all right."

She got up and went to stand by the door. "Now you need anything, you use the pull cord. I'll be back at dinnertime to fix you something to eat."

"Okay."

They established a rhythm over the next few days and Cornelia didn't pry her with any more questions. Bit by bit, Rae

Lynn was up and moving about, Cornelia's nightgown hanging off her and reaching to her toes. The other woman was a bit taller and a few pounds heavier. She went from the bed to the chair and back to the bed for a while, until one day, she sat in the chair by the window for most of a morning watching the comings and goings of the camp. She was taking care of herself once again and felt almost normal. She wished she had her clothes, but couldn't seem to find them anywhere. She went and checked around to the backside of the house, where she found the laundry pan and a washboard. A couple of Otis's shirts hung drying on a line; the dress Cornelia had made from the material Otis burned a hole in, it hung there too. She wanted to take it and put it on, so she'd be decent, except it seemed rude to assume such was all right. Cornelia might think it had to do with the fact she'd paid for it, so she stayed in the gown for now.

In the late afternoon Cornelia came in from the commissary and found her in the kitchen, apron tied around her waist over the nightgown, cooking supper. Cornelia always came home a bit early to cook while Otis stayed at the commissary finishing up. She stood in the doorway, arms filled with a sack of flour, sugar, and beans for the pantry.

Surprised, she said, "My, oh my. Look at this. You ain't supposed to be doing such, you ain't well enough!"

Rae Lynn carried a platter full of fried cured ham over to the table and set it down. She wiped off her forehead and stood by the set table with her hands on her hips.

She said, "I'm feeling fine."

Cornelia said, "I declare. You done fried ham, made rice and red-eye gravy, and field peas. Look at them biscuits, high and fluffy as a cloud. This sure looks mighty fine."

Rae Lynn said, "I was about to go stir-crazy laying around. It feels good to cook again. I used to . . ."

She stopped and put a hand to her mouth. All of a sudden

she felt the heavy sadness come over her again as she remembered her and Warren's suppers together. She'd not allowed herself the luxury of those memories. Cornelia watched Rae Lynn, a question on her face.

She said, "Used to . . . what?"

Rae Lynn swallowed hard. "Cook."

Cornelia's focus on her sharpened. "You all right? You look upset. Maybe you done too much."

"It's . . . I was just thinking about how much I liked to cook for someone other than myself."

"Well, I can see you're a mighty fine one too."

"Cornelia?"

Cornelia had gone over to the table with the food, looking as pleased as could be. "Um-hmm?"

"Where's my clothes? I'd feel so much better if I could get dressed."

Cornelia said, "I'd have got you something if I'd known you was going to be getting around so soon. I had to burn them things a yours. I couldn't get the, you know, your monthly had come on. I couldn't get the stain out. It got on the backside of the shirt too. I'm real sorry."

"Do y'all have anything over to the commissary that might fit?"

Without a word Cornelia went to the back of the house, and out to the line, and right to the dress she'd sewn herself. She took it down. It was like she'd read Rae Lynn's earlier thoughts.

"You can have it. You paid for it anyway."

Rae Lynn held both hands up. "No! I can't take this."

Cornelia was busy holding it against Rae Lynn's shoulders and talking to herself. "It might need a bit of a tuck here and there. You're a mite smaller'n me."

"Cornelia, did you happen to check the pockets of my overalls before you burned them?"

Cornelia was still busy checking on the fit and stopped at how strained Rae Lynn's voice sounded.

"I didn't. Why?"

Rae Lynn's head dropped. There went the last of her paper money.

She said, "It's nothing. I thought I might have left something in them, but I remember now, it's probably back over to number forty-four. I reckon I got to figure out what I'm doing, go and see Peewee. I can't be staying in the single men's quarters, not now."

Cornelia said, "Shoot, you can't leave! I been thinking. You can help here, like you done today. I'd be awfully grateful for it. Least until you know what you might want to do."

Had it only been Cornelia, she wouldn't think twice, but what about Otis, and how he treated Cornelia. Could she ignore him, how he was? It would certainly solve her immediate problem. Cornelia looked disappointed at her lack of reaction, and Rae Lynn quickly explained her hesitancy.

"I ain't so sure everyone would agree it's such a good idea."

"Oh. Otis."

Rae Lynn gave her an apologetic look.

Cornelia said, "Let's see what he says after he eats what you fixed here. One of the best ways to a man's heart is good cooking. My own mama said so."

Well, that right there was a problem. You had to have a heart to begin with, but Rae Lynn kept that thought to herself.

Chapter 23

Del

It had been ten days since he'd lifted her out of that hell, doubting she'd see another sunrise. After the first few days, she'd come around quick, and once he knew she'd be all right, his focus turned back to the work in the woods. Day by day he was getting used to the ways of his men, and they were becoming more used to him. After a while, they set about doing their jobs with more energy. He'd learned their given names, their wives' names and wrote them in his tally book. Preacher: Beaufort Pindell; wife, Howardena. Big'Un: Harold Fuller; wife, Minnie. Sweet Thang: Horace Parks; wife, Lorna. Juke-n-Juice: Roger Robison; wife, Faith. They eyed him curiously when he asked. He liked knowing their Christian name, felt it was only proper, and right. When they weren't working, that's how he addressed them.

He'd shot several squirrels, a couple of possum and gave them out. After one long, hot day, he caught a mess of bream from out of one of the many ponds surrounding the camp. He couldn't eat them all, so he went by Sweet Thang's shack. The structure, from the tar-papered roof with sections that flapped about as soon as the wind came, to the wooded slats for the walls, all of it looked as if it was about to fall in. There were large cracks between the wood stuffed with paper and what-not, and Del was certain it would be near about as cold inside as outside come winter. Sweet Thang sat on a stump under a pine, smoking a cigarette.

He called out to him. "Hey, Horace, got a mess a fish here. Y'all want'em?"

Horace stood up and said, "Lorna was just saying I ought to go catch us some fish."

Lorna came out, wiping her hands on a towel.

"Hey, Mr. Del."

Del held up the fish.

"I brung y'all some bream, here, fresh caught just now."

She came down the steps and said, "Sho do 'preciate this now. Won't you stay to eat? I got some dooby too."

Del smiled and said, "Why, I ain't had me none a that since I was a young'un. I believe I will."

Del sat on another stump beside Horace and they started cleaning the fish. Nolan passed by, and without a word, he rolled a stump over from the woodpile, sat down, and joined them. All three men worked quietly, while Lorna tossed chunks of lard into a black kettle pot and built a fire underneath it. When they were done, she dredged the pieces in cornmeal and began frying them, all while dropping in cornmeal batter. While Del, Nolan, and Horace waited, they talked about the weather and the work under the pines. Lorna started serving fish, two at a time on tin plates, and the talking stopped as they went to eating as fast as she brought them. She'd also set out the dooby, which was meat, onions and cornbread, and some sweet pickles on the small wooden crate near them. For each bite of fish, Del took a bite of pickle and corn bread, and then a forkful of dooby.

After a while, Del put his plate down and said, "I think that's some of the best eating I've done since I come here."

Horace said, "Lorna knows how to cook now."

Nolan said, "Sure was good."

Lorna said to Del, "We 'preciate you thinking a us."

Nolan reared his head back. "You caught them fish?"

Del said, "Yep."

Nolan didn't say anything more, and the conversation moved on to each telling a story about fishing. Lorna had the best one.

"My daddy, he caught a catfish big as me when I won't but five years old. Our whole entire family, and that's saying something 'cause momma had ten other kids, ate off that one fish that day."

After they'd shared a few more stories, Del put his hat on and stood to leave.

He said, "I'd like to stay longer, but I need to get some sleep. Thankee kindly for supper."

He left them still chatting, and as he walked home, his thoughts turned to Rae Cobb, who was never far from his mind anyway. He thought about her more than was warranted, and in a way, it made him feel odd because he was still trying to get past who he'd thought she was initially. He thought maybe he ought to go see her. Maybe it would help in getting her set right in his head. Around midweek during dinner break, he rode Ruby over to the Riddles'. Cornelia was outside hanging laundry, and when she saw him, she stopped working and came over to speak to him.

She said, "She's been doing purty good."

He said, "That's good to hear."

Cornelia didn't need to say more because Rae Cobb appeared from around back of the house where the Riddles had their kitchen garden. It was easy to see she was getting past what had happened to her, and was feeling better. He noticed a couple little things right off. Her hair, washed now, held a high shine, and from where it fell midway on her ears, the style reminded him of them flapper gals he'd seen in girlie magazine pictures. She glanced at him, and he was struck by the green of her eyes, while noticing her mouth had healed too. It was still pink. Pink as the petals of the wild rose bush his mama had grown outside one of the front windows at the house back in Bladen County. He rubbed at his face, wondering why he'd think in such terms about her mouth.

She carried a basket of beans she'd picked, and dipped her head at him as she walked over to the porch, saying, "Hidy," easy as you please.

He tipped his hat, his mouth spreading in a ridiculous-size grin. She began sorting through the beans while humming a little tune and after a few seconds, he found himself still grinning, and when he realized it, he forced himself to stop and cleared his throat to speak.

"How you doing, Rae Cobb?"

Cornelia giggled and said, "You gonna tell him?"

Rae Cobb stopped sorting and said, "Tell him what?"

"Your name."

Del was puzzled. "It ain't Rae Cobb?"

She went back to sorting the beans, picking out a bad one here and there and tossing them off the side of the porch. She was frowning slightly as she worked, the borrowed dress loose around her and gathered in folds.

She finally said, "It's actually Rae Lynn Cobb. Call me Rae Lynn, if'n it pleases you."

His grin came back, and he said, "It sure does. Suits you to a tee."

She was quite the looker now she wasn't wearing that hat too big for her head and them ill-fitting overalls. He found himself grinning stupidly again, but she didn't return it. Her eyes flicked over him, then off to something distant, as if distracted by her thoughts.

He'd been thinking about her situation, and he said, "You know, it ain't gonna work out, that job in the woods."

Her mouth pressed tight like she didn't care for his input. "I'm aware of that."

Cornelia quietly interceded and said, "I told her she can stay here, help out at the house."

Rae Lynn's hands went still, and she said, "It ain't enough to pay for your kindness, for all you done."

Cornelia said, "I can always use help in the commissary too, if you can handle working with Otis."

Del caught the smile she gave Cornelia before she ducked her head. "After all is considered, don't you reckon I can handle about anything?"

He realized it was the very first time he'd seen her do that.

Cornelia grinned back, then grew serious. "Ain't a doubt in my mind. For now, though, you need rest."

Del wanted to stay longer, but he had men waiting on him.

He said, "I gotta get back to work. Gonna be a long, hot afternoon."

Cornelia said, "It's coming on late summer and that's always the worst."

Ruby stood patiently under a pine, flicking her tail at the flies on her back, and after Del swung into the saddle, he glanced back. Rae Lynn was busy snapping beans, as if he'd never been there. He had to admit he was bothered by this. He'd never had trouble with women paying him attention, or anything that followed such attention. Except now he had that *issue*. There'd been a time or two after coming to the camp when he tried to help himself do what was supposed to come naturally, and both times ended in failure, just like after he'd tried to spend a little time with that gal at the store. He didn't want to think about it. He didn't want to get ahead of himself either when it came to this new situation with Rae Lynn Cobb.

Yet, after that visit, he found ways to go to the commissary more than normal, hoping for glimpses of her. The day after he'd seen her, he went back with the excuse he needed some side meat, hoping she'd be on the porch or somewhere in the yard where he could strike up a conversation. She was nowhere to be found, and only Otis was behind the counter inside the store. Otis sliced the meat, added it to his tab, and then there was no reason for Del to stick around. He wanted to ask about her, but Otis was more ornery than usual, so he left. The next day, he decided he needed some canned mackerel.

"Fresh out," Otis growled.

He went back the following day under the pretense of wanting some canned peaches, and Otis acted put out as he bagged a couple cans, like Del was starting to annoy him. These attempts to see her were setting him back financially, but he didn't much care. He took a chance on asking, since he was there and all.

"Where's Miss Cobb at?"

Before Otis could answer, a door slammed near the back of the commissary, and seconds later Rae Lynn appeared with Cornelia on her heels. Both were carrying boxes of potatoes, and both were a bit grimy.

Otis said, "What took y'all so damn long? It don't take no time to go to the root cellar to gather a few taters. Cornelia! I said put 'em over *there*."

Cornelia said, "I heard you, Otis, no need to shout. Hey, Mr. Reese, how're you?"

Otis gave her a disgusted look and turned to Del. "Damn women. Ain't got the sense God give a turnip."

Del could've sworn he heard Rae Lynn say something like, "How would you know," but he couldn't be sure.

She didn't look exactly happy and she didn't speak to him. The women left again, carrying the now-empty wooden crates.

Otis yelled after them. "And get them sweet taters! We need'n some of them put out too!"

He gestured at Rae Lynn's back as she went out of the room.

He said, "That one's gonna owe right much if this keeps on, what with me putting her up, and her eating at my table."

Del lifted his eyebrows and said, "How's that?"

"'Cause it's costing her two dollars a week for the room and fifteen cent a meal, that's how. I mean, it ain't no little ole shack over there like she what she had before. She's getting to stay in a nice house, with a sitting area and all."

"Now that don't seem fair."

Otis said, "Fair? Like I said, we ain't running no boarding-house. It's an inconvenience."

Del couldn't figure out how Otis was inconvenienced with two women tap dancing to his demands.

He did the figures in his head quick, and said, "Comes out to over five dollars a week. What're you paying her for doing all this work?"

"Fifty cent a day."

It was less than what she got for chipping, but even if she were making that, Otis had arranged it so she'd owe him, no matter what. He was being unreasonable, but what could Del say? They were all in over their heads, that's how it was in these camps. The women came back and immediately began unloading sweet potatoes. He wished he could catch Rae Lynn alone, ask her what she thought of this arrangement. By the way she acted, not much, but Cornelia sure did seem happier. She stayed close to Rae Lynn's side, and Del watched how they communicated without any words. A gesture. A look. A nod or shake of the head. Women sure could be mysterious creatures. He took his leave before Otis got it in his head to show off his authority some more and embarrass the lot of them.

On his way out he said, "Y'all ladies have a good evening."

Cornelia spoke for them both, "You too, now."

Disappointed, and out of sorts for reasons he couldn't land on, he slowly made his way home. There he spotted Crow's mother sitting on the porch. Wishing he could go inside, mind his own business, he felt obliged to speak since he'd always been taught to respect his elders. She was the man's mother after all.

"Evening, ma'am."

She didn't bother with the likes of him. He could have been dead. Crow came out of the house, and it was the first time he'd seen him since right after finding Rae Lynn Cobb. That was unfinished business. Crow made sure he reminded Del of his favor, as inconsequential as it was.

"How's that worker I sent doing?"

"Fine. Quick."

Del waited, expecting he'd mention something about the woman he almost killed. Maybe ask how she was. The awkward silence built for a few seconds.

Del, disbelief tinging his voice, said, "Ain't you even gonna ask?"

"Ask what?"

"About her, you know, the woman you stuck in that box?"

"Heard she's over there working at the commissary. What's to ask?"

"You almost killed her, doing what you done."

"Maybe she ought to have thought of the consequences 'fore she come here in that getup. Seems to me she asked for it."

Crow shifted his attention to the taciturn woman next to him. If Del thought Crow's eyes were dark, hers were like looking at a black skillet, same kind of black, same kind of hard. Ready to end this odd little visit with the Sweeneys, he opened his door. He didn't thank Crow for sending Long Gone to work with him. To hell with manners.

Crow called out to him. "What you reckon makes a woman do like that? Dressing and acting like a man? It don't seem natural."

Del paused. All he wanted to do was eat and maybe sit out back so he wouldn't have to deal with them, enjoy a bit of time unwinding before he went to bed.

He said, "What's it matter?"

"Got to be a reason for it. Gonna have to keep an eye on her."

"She's more than paid, don't you think?"

"Could be she's one of them funny ones. Queer as a two-headed goat."

Del raised his voice and said, "You need to leave her alone, now. She almost died. Ain't that enough?"

Crow hooted. "Hoohoohoo! Well, now. Lookie who's getting himself all in a dither. What's that, Butler? You liking her, or something? Is she looking good to you? Hell, maybe I ought to go have me a second look."

Crow's mama stood so abruptly her chair fell over, hitting the porch floor with a bang. She went inside and slammed the door. Crow rubbed his neck, and emitted an odd little laugh. Inside his own place, Del pulled out some side meat, potatoes, and some of the corn bread he'd made the other night. He cooked the food, heated up what was left of his morning's coffee, and as he was about to sit and have a proper meal, a knock came at his door. He dropped his head and sighed. He hoped it wasn't Crow. He was in no mood to hear more stupid talk. He waited, hoping he'd go away. The knock came again. Frustrated, he got up and looked out the window. When he saw who stood there, he quickly opened the door. Rae Lynn Cobb and Cornelia Riddle smiled big at him, and each carried something. Cornelia had two jars of stewed okra and two jars of beans.

She said, "I put these up not too long ago. It's a little thank-you for helping."

Rae Lynn said, "And this is for you too, but I owe you so much more than this little ole cake. You saved my life."

Del said, "Y'all didn't need to bring me nothing. It's not called for. I done what anybody would."

Rae Lynn rolled her eyes at Cornelia and said, "Not anybody."

Cornelia said, "That's right."

Del said, "Come in, come in. I was about to have a bite to eat."

They went in and set what they brought on the table. Del was a bit embarrassed at his meagre little spread but felt he should at least offer them something to drink.

He pointed at the coffee pot and said, "Would y'all care for some? I could make some right quick."

Cornelia shook her head and said, "It would be nice, but we got to get back before Otis notices us gone. He still had to close the commissary, so we came straightaway."

Del said, "Well, thankee kindly. I know I'll enjoy all this."

Cornelia said, "It was Rae Lynn's idea."

This pleased him, but when he turned to Rae Lynn, she appeared struck by the tops of her boots. She wore them with the borrowed dress, and Del liked how she looked.

Cornelia said, "We best be getting back."

The women went out, and he watched them link arms as they hurried away in the twilight, heads together, whispering to one another. As he started to go back inside, he noticed Crow back out on his porch. Crow was staring after the women like he'd seen something he didn't like.

He gestured toward the women. "That's what I'm talking about. That right there."

Del said, "What?"

"Something's off with them two."

Del mumbled, "You're one to talk."

He went inside and shut his door, bothered by the man's need to find trouble where there was none.

Chapter 24

Rae Lynn

Rae Lynn knew when to count her blessings. She could be driving a broken-down truck and needing to find work again. Instead, she still had a roof over her head and food to eat. It was early on a Thursday morning, and Cornelia had come along to help carry the few things she had from number forty-four. Cornelia stepped inside and looked around.

"I bet you had to turn it inside out to make it the least bit agreeable."

Rae Lynn was pulling her sheets off the squalid mattress.

She said, "You have no idea."

Cornelia peered closely at the stitching.

She said, "Woowee, that Ray Cobb, he sure can turn a fine stitch."

They snickered a little at that, and later on, back at the Riddles, Cornelia went by her with an armful of laundry and said, "I'm real glad you chose to stay."

Rae Lynn smiled a little as she prepared their noon dinner.

She said, "I'm grateful to you."

"Honestly. You're the best thing to come into this household since Mama sent me money to buy a bus ticket a few months after me and Otis was married."

Rae Lynn held an empty can she'd been using to cut biscuits, her hands coated in flour. At Cornelia's comment she went still and gazed out the window, a dreamy look on her face.

She said, "Law, I ain't never rode on a bus. Was it fun?"

"I don't know. I didn't never go."

"Why not?"

Cornelia raised her shoulders. "I wrote Mama to tell her when I was coming. I also told her how he was and said I didn't only want to visit. I wanted to come home, you know, to stay. She wrote me back and said, in more or less words, don't. She told me to use the money to buy me some pretties. Said my place was with my husband now. Shoot, Rae Lynn. How can a man be so different one day and then like somebody you never met the next? He won't always like this, least not right away. He changed once I found out some things about him."

"Oh? Like what?"

Cornelia shifted the laundry and didn't answer. Rae Lynn let it go and went back to cutting the biscuits.

She said, "Well, I reckon you ain't the first woman in such circumstances. And you surely won't be the last."

Cornelia sighed. "You're right about that. Hey, Rae Lynn?"

"Um-hmm?"

"What made you come here trying to act like a man? I mean, where'd you come from? What happened?"

Rae Lynn answered carefully. "I needed work, and somewhere to stay."

Cornelia gave her an assessing look, while Rae Lynn acted like it was the most commonplace thing to do.

Cornelia said, "But you could a done all kinds a work as a woman. Seems complicated to me, even more so to try and do turpentine work."

Rae Lynn feigned a casualness she didn't feel. "Oh, I'll tell you about it someday."

Cornelia waited a second longer, then went onto the back porch with the wash. Rae Lynn heard her pumping water. She looked outside and saw her sorting her and Otis's sheets near the big black kettle. Here it was, a Thursday, and they'd just done the wash on Monday.

Cornelia came back in and said, "I'll let'em soak a bit."

"Is it your . . . ?"

Cornelia went red. "No."

She began washing dirty breakfast dishes while Rae Lynn put the last biscuit on the pan. She slid them in the oven, before going to stand by Cornelia to dry the plates. Rae Lynn had her suspicions about what was going on with them sheets, but if Cornelia didn't want to talk about it, she ought to respect her.

She said, "Like I mentioned, I'm sure grateful to you, Nellie. Can I call you Nellie? It worries me how I'm gonna be so far in over my head I won't never be able to pay y'all back."

Cornelia glanced at Rae Lynn, her eyes gone watery.

She said, "Only Mama ever called me that."

She'd skipped right over what Rae Lynn said about paying them. Otis reminded her enough as it was, practically lording it over her. He'd not done anything hurtful to Cornelia as of late. He still yelled at her, at the both of them actually, but for now, no new burn marks or bruises showed on her friend's arms. She wished Cornelia would be more careful about getting too bold. It was as if Rae Lynn's presence had given her a bit more gumption. She'd got to where she mimicked Otis behind his back while he bragged about something he'd done. Recently he told Rae Lynn how he'd once killed a twenty-foot gator with his bare hands. Cornelia rolled her eyes and held her hands about two feet apart to show the actual size.

Rae Lynn said, "Oh my," while she fought to keep a straight face and not give Cornelia away.

Otis could barely contain himself over the idea she was interested in what he had to say and it spurred him on. "Yeah, and then I . . ."

He loved to hear himself. He'd go on and on about his daring accomplishments until Rae Lynn had a headache, and Cornelia dared to speak up.

"Otis, honey, it's getting on late. Save some stories for another time."

He went deep red, and started sulking. Rae Lynn worried Cornelia would be made to pay. Sure enough, she wore her dress with the long sleeves the next day, even as the temperatures rose close to a hundred.

Rae Lynn pointed and said, "Nellie, did he . . ."

Cornelia cut her right off and said, "I meant to tell you yesterday, we got to get some canned goods out on the shelves over to the commissary."

Rae Lynn let it go. That evening Otis had made a snide comment about Cornelia's appearance.

"Damn, woman. You looking about as wore-out as a old flat tire."

He slammed a palm on the table and belted out a laugh that was more like a bark. Rae Lynn actually saw Cornelia's shoulders sag as if the very weight of him sat entirely on her.

She said, "Yes, honey."

Otis mimicked her. "Yes, honey. You're pathetic."

He went back to shoveling his food in, while Rae Lynn wanted to slap him. She didn't know how Cornelia stood it.

The next morning when Cornelia came from their room, walking with difficulty and wearing a blue bracelet of bruises on her wrists, anger shot through Rae Lynn, but she stayed calm.

Her voice troubled, she said, "Nellie."

Cornelia said, "It ain't nothing. Don't you say a word, now, Rae Lynn!"

Rae Lynn raised her hands in the air, concerned. "But, he shouldn't treat you like he does."

Minutes later, Otis came into the kitchen hiking up his pants with a self-satisfied, smug look. The fear on Cornelia's face kept Rae Lynn quiet. All day, Cornelia was subdued. Midday she dropped into a chair and rested her head on her arms.

"I'm so tired, but I got to do them sheets."

Rae Lynn's mouth dropped. "Again?"

Cornelia didn't look at her.

Rae Lynn said, "I can help if you want. It ain't no problem atall. I got most everything else done for right now."

Cornelia kept her head on her arms. "It's all right. I just need a minute."

Rae Lynn was worried for her. Cornelia had always been careful about her looks, but she hadn't washed her hair in some time, and the dark curls capping her head, typically glossy, lay lackluster over her arm as if they too were too exhausted to shine.

Rae Lynn touched her again, on the arm, and said, "Why're you having to wash them so many times in a week? Are you okay? Are you not well?"

Cornelia raised her head. She stared toward the bedroom first, then turned to the window where the commissary building could be seen. She got up and went to the front of the house and stood half inside the doorway, half out, staring toward where Otis ought to be busy working. Experience had shown, like a summer storm, he might appear unexpectedly and bring thunderous yelling along with lightning flashes of temper. Rae Lynn observed how cautious she was, and understood. Living with Otis Riddle meant always being watchful for his storms.

Cornelia came back to the kitchen and said, "I'll show you why I wash them sheets all the time, but we got to hurry. He'll be here any minute looking something to eat."

Rae Lynn followed as Cornelia led her to the main bedroom, where she pointed at the bed, her arm trembling, whether with weariness or anger, Rae Lynn wasn't sure. The window was open, but an odor hung in the room like Cornelia hadn't emptied the chamber pot.

"Look a there. This is why I'm always washing them sheets."

The bed sat against a wall, hidden in the shadows. She could see the sheets were rumpled, but not much else.

Cornelia pulled her closer to the bed and said, "There. Right there."

Rae Lynn could now see the large wet spot, yellowed at the edges where it was starting to dry.

"Oh. I'm sorry, Nellie. I imagine something could be done if you was to see a doctor."

Cornelia put a hand over her mouth, smothering her amusement. "No, no, it ain't me. It's Otis. He's the one wets the bed. First time it happened, he tried to say it was me who done it. I pointed out it was his drawers that was wet, not mine. That was the first time he hit me. Now, when it happens, he goes on a tirade, takes it out on me like it's my fault. It's getting to where I dread going to bed. I can't sleep, waiting for it to happen, knowing how he's gonna get the next day."

Rae Lynn said, "Gosh, Nellie. No wonder you're bone tired."

The screen door gave a rusty screech, and Otis yelled, "Where you at?"

It was as if the air got sucked right out of the room. There they both were, and him already in the house and no way to get back to the kitchen without being seen. There'd be hell to pay, and the fear blooming on Cornelia's face once again reminded Rae Lynn of the kind a man Otis Riddle was. She gripped Rae Lynn's arms, her fingernails digging in.

She whispered, "Wait here, behind the door. Don't make a sound. Let me fix him his dinner and while I'm doing that, see if you can't sneak out somehow."

Cornelia's distress at being caught set Rae Lynn's own stomach to churning. It was senseless to be so afraid of one's own husband. Cornelia had certainly drawn the short straw marrying him.

They heard splashing at the kitchen sink, then Otis bellowed, "Cornelia! Where you at!"

Cornelia rushed from the room using a light singsong tone as she replied, "Right here, honey. I was just straightening the bedroom."

"Where's my dinner? Why ain't it on the table? It's twelve o'clock!"

"It's coming. I got it all ready."

Rae Lynn peeked and had to draw back quickly. He sat facing the bedroom door. There was no way she'd be able to sneak out without him seeing her. Without another thought, she stuck one leg through the open window and straddled the edge. Holding on to the raised window sash, she brought her other leg through and dropped to the ground. The garden was right there, and she picked a couple of ripe tomatoes. As she went in the back screen door she let it slam good and hard. Cornelia was at the stove, spooning black-eyed peas onto Otis's plate, and she jumped.

Rae Lynn said, "Here you go," as if she'd been asked to pick the tomatoes.

The terror in Cornelia's eyes melted away to relief. "Oh, thank you. Nothing better'n fresh tomatoes with peas. Otis, honey, would you want some?"

Otis, none the wiser, waved his fork in a grand manner.

The women's eyes met over his head, and Cornelia mouthed, *Thank you.*

Over the next couple of days things went on like they normally did in the Riddle household, with her and Cornelia working sunup to sundown at the commissary, keeping meals on the table, cleaning, and canning what they were getting out of the kitchen garden, their bit of funning forgotten under the harsh glare of Otis's watchful eyes. Saturday afternoon they were in the kitchen, and despite the fact the day was sweltering, they were busy canning tomatoes and beans, while enjoying a rare moment of peace because Otis had gone to get supplies to restock the store. They'd talked this and that, but mostly, they worked in the quiet, side by side, until someone knocked on the front door.

Cornelia glanced at Rae Lynn, frowning, and said, "Wonder who it could be? Might be Del Reese. He ain't been around lately."

Rae Lynn said, "Want me to get it?"

Cornelia was about to lift some jars from the pot of boiling water and said, "Would you?"

Rae Lynn wiped her hands on the front of her apron, smoothed her hair back off her forehead before going to the door. She stopped short, immediately crossed her arms at the sight of Crow staring at her through the screen. In the heat of the day came an uncommon chill, as if he'd blocked the sun.

He said, "I come to see what the real Cobb looks like."

Rae Lynn managed to keep her voice steady. "Well, you seen me. What do you want?"

Cornelia had come to stand behind her, and she felt better with her there.

Cornelia said, "Mr. Sweeney, what can we do for you?"

"Considering what I recollect, I don't see much difference than the scrawny boy you was playing, if you ask me."

Cornelia said, "I don't recall nobody asking."

Crow said, "Your husband must not be around for you to be acting so smart."

His eyes swiveled back to Rae Lynn, and the heaviness she used to get each morning when she had to worry about making numbers returned. She had to remind herself he couldn't do nothing to her anymore, and she owed him nothing. Let him say what he wanted. She fought against showing any reaction. Why couldn't he go on and leave them alone?

His eyes bored into hers. "I got a question's been bothering me. Was what you done pretend, or real? Acting like a man?"

What he was implying went in a whole other direction, and she found herself flummoxed by the question.

Cornelia nudged her aside. "I don't see as how it's any of your business."

"Ain't you the mama hen? Can't she speak for herself?"

Rae Lynn touched the back of Cornelia's arm.

"Come on, Nellie. We got work to do." But Cornelia continued staring him down.

Crow said, "It don't matter. I seen enough to make up my own mind as to how things is. Sure, I can see it real clear. Y'all have a nice day."

He went down the steps whistling off tune and meandered off toward the distillery.

Rae Lynn mumbled, "He scares me."

Cornelia said, "He scares everybody. Even Otis, though Otis says they's friends. If you can call sitting around agreeing to whatever the man says being friends. Come on. Let's not let him ruin the day."

They went back to the kitchen and resumed work, but Crow's sudden appearance and comments left Rae Lynn unnerved. She stopped wiping out a jar and turned away from Cornelia.

Cornelia said, "Rae Lynn, you all right?"

Rae Lynn stared at her shortened finger, thought how it wasn't so long ago she'd lived in a little shotgun house under the whispery pines in North Carolina alongside a loving husband who'd provided for her, took care of her. They'd loved each other the best they knew how, and were certainly devoted, without a doubt. Since coming to Swallow Hill, she'd made an effort at keeping her thoughts on the present, not the past. She didn't want to dwell on what happened, it made her too sad, and she'd hoped the worst part of her memories would fade eventually. She'd never figured much beyond getting here and making do. She'd not counted on someone like Crow making it harder than it already was.

Rae Lynn sorted her thoughts while her friend stayed quiet. If she told Cornelia the real reasons she was here, what would she think? For a split second she considered it. How she and Warren met, got married, what they'd accomplished, or tried to, and how it had ended. As was habit, she rubbed her half finger, worrying the stub over and over until Cornelia grabbed her hands and held them still.

She said, "Aw, honey. It's gonna take time for you to get over what all you been through. It'll get better. Main thing is, don't worry about him. He can't do nothing."

Rae Lynn let Cornelia think that's all it was.

"I reckon you're right."

"About this, I am."

The women stood quiet, both caught up in their thoughts when the slow creaking of a wagon drawing near came to them, and they raised their heads simultaneously and looked toward the window at the front of the house. There went Otis, trundling down the main path, his shape like a giant tree perched in the seat. Cornelia dropped Rae Lynn's hands and without another word, hurried to the stove and began dragging out cooking pots. Rae Lynn could hear her mumbling something. She looked out the window again, at Otis heaving himself down off the wagon. The sight made her gut clench almost as bad as when Crow appeared at the door. Rae Lynn could only imagine what it did to Cornelia.

Chapter 25

Del

Rae Lynn stayed on his mind most days. He couldn't quite figure why or what it was about her that made him want things he'd never had. Her and him together back home in North Carolina, or anywhere, for that matter, would be all right. He got to pining for them sons he'd thought of a time or two, only now the idea came often, like his thoughts about what life might be like with her. Or daughters. Hell, if they were scrappy and brave like her, he'd want lots of girls too. There was only one problem with all this dreaming: she appeared about as interested in him as yonder bird sitting in a tree, and what good did them dreams do him nohow, with a compass that no longer faced north?

He sat easy on Ruby, listening to the men give their final calls of the day, their voices ringing out from all directions, his pencil softly scratching as he kept count. When the last one came, he marked it and closed his tally book. Right on time Clyde brought the wagon. Clyde had gotten used to him and his work hands getting done about five o'clock. The mule's head swung left and right, pulling the wagon along the narrow path while Clyde leaned against the back of the seat letting him determine the best way as usual. Right behind him came Peewee, Crow, and Woodall. Peewee threw up a hand, and Del responded, while Crow and Woodall didn't bother.

Peewee hollered out, "How's it going?"

Del said, "We're done."

Crow said, "Hell. Got an hour or so a daylight yet."

Peewee said, "Well, that works out good. We got to talk about where we going next and about how we gonna manage these men from here on out." He turned to Del and said, "Your hands been getting them crops done quick. Working faster than most in this camp, turning in high numbers to boot." He faced Crow and Woodall. "Reckon y'all can learn something from him," and he tipped his head toward Del.

Crow and Woodall glanced at each other.

Crow said, "My men make their counts."

Woodall said, "Mine too."

Peewee stared at Crow. "The other day, a couple of yours didn't make'em, Sweeney."

"I took care of the problem too."

Peewee said, "Now, you think about that. They didn't make numbers 'cause you already whipped on'em over something else entirely different. Ain't you noticed they can't work proper when they all tore up, or if you stick'em in the box? Don't think I don't know what goes on around here. I'll tell you this. If you'd a killed that gal, you'd be outta here. See'n as how you didn't, you're still here, but that could change."

Crow's voice was tight. "Oh. I see. We're gonna go soft on'em now. Let'em do what they want."

Peewee said, "Ain't nobody saying that. There's gonna be some changes, though. From here on out, ain't nobody going in that sweatbox lessen I say so. Ain't nobody getting whipped lessen I say so. We're trying a different way. His way." He pointed at Del, and asked him, "What do you do if someone ain't getting their numbers?"

"Dock their pay."

"It works?"

"Ain't had to do it but once."

Peewee said to Crow and Woodall, "That's the new way round here."

Crow said, "Hell, you hog-tying us. You think telling'em they ain't getting their money's gonna make'm work harder; you watch and see they don't turn even more lazy. He's a damn fool he thinks his way's gonna last. I know how they are. They gonna turn into no-account shirkers, you wait and see."

Peewee's voice went sharp. "I'm telling you how it is, and if you can't abide by it, you can leave. That's how it's gonna be."

Crow looked away, his expression lifeless, while Woodall spit out a stream of tobacco juice and shrugged. This decision by Peewee caught Del off guard. Peewee seemed reluctant to say anything when he'd come to him, pointing out that Rae Lynn had lived, and how Crow was a good woods rider, how he couldn't afford to lose him. Maybe he'd only been biding his time for the right opportunity.

Peewee eyed all of them as if daring anyone to argue some more, then continued. "Now. As to the next crops. We'll be working the areas due east, starting tomorrow morning."

Crow came back to life. "Woodall, you best be sure them coon hounds is fed good and rested up. Looks like we might get us a chance to go hunting."

Woodall said, "Hell, they was born ready. They sure do like that two-legged variety the best."

Peewee wagged a finger. "Ain't nobody running. Ain't nobody gonna need no hounds."

Crow and Woodall exchanged a shrewd look, but Peewee ignored them and finished up.

"Wagons will show up earlier tomorrow at five o'clock since it's a little farther out from camp. And y'all be sure and get them fires going soon as possible since we'll be right next to the swamp."

He turned his horse around and trotted off down the path. Meanwhile, Clyde, who'd been quiet the entire time, clucked his tongue at Jackson. Del tugged on Ruby's rein to follow Clyde when Crow called out to him.

"Hey!"

Del pulled up, waiting to hear what dumb thing he had to say. Woodall wore a little grin while he slouched in his saddle, sucking on his teeth.

Crow came close to Del, and said, "You think you know it all, don't you? First day you showed up, telling me what you was hired to do, I said it to myself, now there's a nigra lover." Crow pointed at Del and spoke to Woodall. "I'm telling you, I can spot one a mile away. Can't you, Woodall?"

Woodall said, "Why sure. I seen it too. Ain't no doubt."

Crow said, "Tell you what else I know. I know somebody's been hanging around the commissary a lot, acting interested in that Cobb character. I can't hardly imagine why a woman would go and do something like'at, can you, Woodall?"

"Naw, sure can't. Real curious, ain't it?"

Crow leaned his head back so his eyes were slits. "You interested in her, him, whatever it is?"

Coincidentally, a crow flew overhead, emitting a raucous cawing, and received a distant response from another perched at the top of a tall longleaf pine, and meanwhile, Del considered what he was about to say. He figured he ought to keep his mouth shut, but he chose to speak.

He said, "I'd say it's better'n being mama's little boy, I know that much."

Woodall made a choking sound, and Crow flushed a deep

red. Even as Del lit the fire he was sure burned in Crow's belly for revenge, he didn't much care.

Crow said, "What in hell are you talking about?"

"I seen you the other night. The both of you. You and . . ."

Del couldn't resist clapping his hands together, mimicking the sound he'd heard. He never thought he'd see Crow speechless. Crow yanked his horse around, kicked its sides, and rode off.

Woodall watched his departure, and said, "Reckon you done it now. If I was you, I'd sleep with that shotgun real handy."

Woodall clucked at his horse and followed Crow. Del was only vaguely worried, and more than a bit smug. He'd finally one-upped the son of a gun, and he rode back to camp enjoying that fact. After he situated Ruby in her stall, he left the barn and made his way to his house. There was no sign of movement over to Crow's and for that he was grateful. Inside, he grabbed a pair of scissors Mrs. Ballard must have left behind, his razor, and after pumping water into a pan, he stood on the back porch, facing a mirror hung on a post. He began snipping off his beard. It was long overdue. He'd been letting it grow ever since he'd wandered the South Georgia woods and it was too hot, plus his face itched. As he trimmed, he wondered about Rae Lynn's hair, how it looked longer. She'd not done such a bad job cutting it, if that's how it got so short. He got to thinking about her cutting his, and this led him to ruminating on her being close, her skin colored like golden syrup, her green eyes like newly sprung grass, her soft breasts within inches of his face as she bent down to run her fingers through. . . .

Out of nowhere, something started happening that hadn't in a long while. He went absolutely still, hands midair, staring back at himself in surprise. He looked down. It was *happening*, and his thoughts tumbled one over the other at what seemed like a miracle. They became as tangled as his beard, and then what was happening, reversed. *No. No. No.* Gone. But, still. This was a good sign. Maybe all he needed was the right woman. Maybe all he needed was *her.* He finished shaving and rubbed his fingers along his clean jawline. Better. Much better. She might notice.

Early the next morning, he guided Ruby onto the new trail. It was just before five o'clock and the eastern sky lay before him, plum colored with the last dwindling stars scattered in the west. He followed the double-rutted path, most parts overgrown with wiregrass, but here and there cream-colored sandy soil stretched before him in two distinct parallel rows where wagons had gone before. He reflected on how long it might have been since this section of the camp had been worked. After a while he came to a fork and he nudged Ruby to go right. A barred owl took off from a turkey oak; wings stretched wide and with a flap or two, it sailed into the depths of the woods and disappeared. He spotted Clyde's wagon in the distance. It had grown lighter by now, and the early-morning sun washed the land in warm, honey-colored tones. He urged Ruby to go a little faster, and when he was close to the wagon, he called out to Clyde and the men.

"Morning, y'all."

"Morning," came as a subdued chorus.

Preacher did a double take and said, "Ain't he fancy now!"

Nolan said, "Smooth as butter."

Clyde said, "Hell, I almost didn't recognize you. Peewee and Woodall's somewhere ahead of us. Crow is too, and in a foul mood."

Del said, "I ain't ever known him to be otherwise."

The men chuckled in agreement. He went ahead of the wagon, taking in the area near to the swamp. The palmettos and wiregrass waved with his passing, and he envisioned the wildlife watching secretly as he made his way. Ruby spooked a time or two, her nostrils flaring. He guessed some sort of snake, and he let her go around whatever it was in the way she wanted, and she calmed down. Eventually he caught up to Peewee, Woodall, and Crow, who stood by their horses waiting on the men to hang their dinner buckets.

Woodall did like Preacher and said, "Reese?"

"Woodall."

Crow looked down the trail and said, "Where's your workers?"

"On their way."

"I'm getting my man back."

Del shrugged. "Up to you."

As soon as Del's men arrived, Crow strode over to Nolan before he'd had a chance to put a foot on the ground.

His voice rose above the low din of the work hands talking amongst themselves.

"You're with me."

Nolan made the mistake of looking over to Del, and Crow said, "What're you looking at him for?"

Nolan clutched his hat in his hands, worrying it. "No reason, boss man. Happy to come back."

"Reckon I'm gonna have to train you all over again."

Del frowned, while Peewee wagged a warning finger at Crow. Crow leaned into toward Nolan and spoke quietly. It looked to Del like Nolan visibly shivered, before busying himself by sticking his bark hack in his waistband and hurrying to hang his bucket on a branch. He then joined Crow's men, a ragtag clump of workers as slump-shouldered and downtrodden as any Del had ever seen. Nolan blended in, adopting the same defeated look. As bad as Del hated it for him, the man had been working for Crow a long time and knew how to handle himself.

He turned to his own men and said, "Let's go see what this

new spot's all about. Preacher, didn't you say you worked this section before?"

"Yessuh, been about a year ago."

"What'd you think?"

"Got stung, bit, and ate up by more damn bugs out here than anywheres else. Even with them fires going."

"Let's do the best we can."

Del motioned for Georgie to bring Ruby some water.

As the boy set the bucket down, Del said, "Hey, Georgie, be sure and bring us extra today, okay?"

"Yessuh, I will."

He smiled and handed Georgie a peppermint candy. It was a routine now, and he made sure he always carried some in his pocket. As he gathered the reins, ready to mount and follow his men, he spotted Nolan hanging back from the others, eyes on Del. Nolan mouthed a word. Del, unable to make it out, didn't react, not wanting to draw attention to the man. He nudged Ruby forward and missed the moment Nolan broke out of the group, sprinting for the tree line.

Crow yelled, "Hey! Son of a bitch! Stop!"

Nolan didn't look back, didn't look left or right. He ran for his life. Del couldn't have been more astonished than if he'd jumped Crow and started beating him up. Crow jerked his shotgun out of its holder, aimed, and pulled the trigger. Nolan was in the woods by then, and he zigged, then zagged.

Crow shot again, lowered the gun, and pointed at Del.

He was so outraged, he was wheezing as he yelled at Peewee, "What'd I tell you?"

Del said, "I'd warrant he didn't care for his revised work arrangement."

Crow swung the gun back to his shoulder and aimed it at him.

Peewee grabbed his pistol off his hip and hollered, "Sweeney!"

Crow's voice dropped so low, Del almost couldn't hear him.

"You mark my words. Before long, every damn nigra's gonna think he can do the same thing if you let'em think they can get away with it."

Del said, "Funny. Ain't nobody under me took off yet. I reckon if you hadn't told him he had to come work for you again, he'd still be here. I'd bet on it."

Everyone looked to Peewee. He stared at the spot where Nolan had disappeared. After a minute or two, he let out a heavy sigh, apparently having come to a decision.

He said, "Woodall?"

"Yeah, boss."

"Got your hounds?"

"I do."

"Go on and turn'em loose."

Del turned away, wishing he'd never come here.

Chapter 26

Rae Lynn

Though no one said a word about it, the distant baying of the hounds in the swamp told the camp someone was being hunted. General activities could typically be heard throughout any given day, but all sounds of living had stopped as the echoes of yelping from enthusiastic hounds hung in the air. There wasn't one note of singing while women hung out the wash, no chatting over fences, no children shouting in play, not one chant of the alphabet from the schoolroom; silent were the swishing of brooms in yards and absent were the fragrant smells from cook pots. Chickens clucked and pigs rooted, but otherwise, the camp had quietly died, its lifeblood withdrawing, the same way blood withdraws to the center of the body when dying.

Rae Lynn and Cornelia heard from Otis, who heard from Weasel at the distillery, who heard from somebody in the camp it was Nolan Brown, or Long Gone, as his call name went. The dogs continued to bay, and random, periodic shouts of encouragement to them from Woodall or Crow could be heard throughout the morning and on into the sultry afternoon. Rae Lynn and Cornelia worked at putting the dry goods onto shelves Otis brought back the day before, then set about canning peaches, their faces reddened and damp as they hovered over steaming pots of water. They remained occupied, but not much was said between them. Every once in a while Cornelia went to the small window at the front of the house to look out and listen.

She would return to the kitchen and say, "They're still after him," or "Them dogs is louder, must be closer this a way."

Otis whistled and seemed almost cheery, while the sky reflected Rae Lynn's mood. For the first time in a while, heavy clouds hung over them, draped low, and dark and more ominous to the west. Occasionally she searched for any sign of the woods riders and the dogs to come into sight. She didn't know why she felt such dread in the pit of her stomach, but it likely had everything to do with what Cornelia had told her.

"If they catch him, it's gonna be almost like sport what they'll do. To set an example, is what they get told, if they can hear anybody by that point."

Rae Lynn's concern deepened. She reckoned she'd been sheltered somewhat against this difference between people, what with immediately marrying Warren straight out of the orphanage before she'd seen the true ways of the world. She reckoned she was naïve. She was certain she was about to witness something that would stay with her all the rest of her born days. Cornelia bent close so Otis couldn't hear her.

She said, "If he's caught, they'll bring him in with a rope tied from his neck to his hands. I seen'em drag one in behind a horse once. He was already dead before they got here, but it didn't stop them from pulling him on in so everybody could see him. They strung him up in a tupelo tree, let him hang there a day 'fore they let his family take him down. We need to stay out of the way till it's over. Try not to think about it. Try not to hear it, if it can be helped. I know this. When it happened before, it sure was a long time 'fore I could bear to look at any of them colored folks straight in the eyes. Like to have tore me all to pieces, and I didn't hardly know the feller. Way I see it, Rae Lynn. A life is a life, you know?"

Rae Lynn couldn't speak. Her stomach was trying to crawl up her throat. The howls and yelps faded in and out and told them the hunt was still on. How long could someone stay on the run in this heat without water, or food? Toward suppertime, Rae Lynn noticed the long, drawn-out howls coon hounds are known for had gone silent. She paused, rag in hand and suspended midair where she'd been wiping off shelves. Her mouth went dry in the way a drink of water couldn't fix, and she was filled with a sense of dread. Otis drummed his fingers on the counter, then started pacing back and forth at the front of the store. Several times he went outside onto the stoop only to come back in with a grumpy expression.

He said, "Ain't no sign a them coming back yet. Can't hear no wagons, no nothing. Damn. What's taking so long?"

Cornelia said, "Well."

Otis said, "They either got him, or he got away. They should a been back to the camp by now. Them dogs is quiet. I wished they'd hurry it up." He rubbed his hands together, like he was excited, and said, "I wanna see what they gonna do. Hell, we might have us a bona fide lynching! I ain't seen one of them in a while!"

Rae Lynn stopped her work. What talk! Like he was eager for something like this to happen!

She swung around, her palms instantly going sweaty as she spoke up. "What is *wrong* with you?"

"Huh? What do you mean?"

Otis acted like he'd half forgot she was there, or could speak.

Without giving thought to what she was doing, she repeated herself. "I asked you, 'What is wrong with you?'"

Cornelia gave her a warning look, but Rae Lynn, while aware she was in dangerous territory, couldn't stay quiet.

Otis blustered. "What kind a question is that?"

"You act like you *want* to see a man get lynched."

Cornelia tried to distract them from one another. "Rae Lynn, would you hand me the plate there?"

Otis inhaled, his chest expanding like a male grackle as he approached Rae Lynn, and still, she refused to budge.

He scowled at her and said, "Justice got to be served. He's indebted to this camp, and we got call to do what's necessary to make sure don't nobody else get no dumb ideas. Why in the hell am I explaining it to you, nohow? You a damn woman. Oh, wait. Come to think of it, we ain't so sure what you might be."

The hairs on her scalp prickled with apprehension as he stood in front of her. She clenched her hands into fists. Unexpectedly, he shoved his hand in her crotch, prodding her with his fingers to prove to himself what she was.

Cornelia screamed, "Otis, I see somebody!"

Otis lost interest in her and hastened toward the door, shoving Cornelia out of his way.

"Move!"

He barreled down the steps, his eagerness to see such a spectacle furthering Rae Lynn's disgust of him. She was still gasping with outrage at his offensive handling of her while Cornelia pleaded.

"Rae Lynn, please. Watch what you say. Not just for your sake."

Rae Lynn put a hand over her heart. "I'm sorry. He brought it out in me."

Cornelia said, "It ain't hard. Best we go see what's happening."

Rae Lynn started to refuse but was so worried about Nolan Brown, she followed Cornelia outside, her hopes on Del Reese preventing anything terrible from happening. They stayed behind Otis so as to not draw his attention, and Rae Lynn watched as the work wagons came into camp first, shrouded in a cloud of dust. They needed rain, but the gloomy clouds refused. In the back of the wagons sat mute, brooding workers, every head down, so they resembled swaying stumps. Behind them came Crow and Woodall, and Rae Lynn dismissed them, on the lookout for Del Reese. When she saw him, she almost didn't recognize him. He'd apparently shaved his beard off.

Dread filled her chest as Rae Lynn searched for the one who'd taken a chance. There was no sign of him and while Rae Lynn couldn't tell how Del Reese felt, she could have sworn he gave her a little nod and wink. The dogs, the supposed stars of the show, walked alongside the wagons, tails drooping. For all appearances, their behavior told a story of failure, of a hunt without reward. She let her breath out. They didn't have him. Thank the good Lord, he'd got away. Better to take a chance on what the swamp doled out than what some of these men would've done. Peewee came out of the office building, hands on his hips.

"Well? Where is he?"

Crow threw his arms wide, clearly annoyed. "Them dogs, they was on his scent most of the day, then lost it at some point this afternoon."

"Damn. It would have to be him who took off. He owes me more'n anyone here."

Del said, "How long's he been here?"

Peewee said, "Since he was about Georgie's age. Ain't never been nowheres else. Him and his missus got married right over yonder."

Del said, "It ain't like he took real money, I mean, hell, you don't pay in real money."

Crow tipped his head toward Del and said, "See? His way ain't gonna work here."

As the men argued, Rae Lynn nudged Cornelia, who chewed on her thumbnail.

She said, "Least somebody's got some sense."

Cornelia mumbled back. "Peewee's fair minded, too, but he don't like nobody running. He has to report it. He also don't like nobody telling him how things ought to be."

Otis said, "What're you whispering about?"

Cornelia straightened up and said, "Just telling Rae Lynn here since she's new to all this what might happen."

Otis said, "You two don't need to worry about that. You need to get on to the house and fix my supper. This here's men's business." He watched the other men, mumbling, "Only thing matters is they keep searching for the bastard. I warrant they'll go back out after supper."

Rae Lynn didn't want or need to see more, nohow. She went across the yard, avoiding looking at anyone directly. There was a pause, her movement momentarily distracting the men, and she hurried to get out of sight.

Cornelia came behind her, and when they got to the house, she said, "Could you feel all them eyes on you?"

Rae Lynn squirmed and said, "Kind a hard not to." She got out the lard and flour to make the biscuits. "What should we fix for supper tonight?"

Cornelia didn't answer the question, instead she said, "You're a wonder to'em. Some can't get over the fact you lived."

Rae Lynn sniffed. "You mean Crow."

Cornelia huffed. "Him. Who cares about him?" She came close, bumped Rae Lynn's shoulder with her own, and said, "You don't find him handsome?"

Rae Lynn wasn't in the mood, but she went along with Cornelia's playfulness. "I have no idea who you mean."

"Sure you do."

"Del Reese?"

"Gosh, Rae Lynn. You got blood in them veins, ain't you? I think you might consider him, is all. I think he's interested."

Rae Lynn was quiet as she dumped a measure of flour into a bowl. She cut in the lard and began blending it in with her fingers. Cornelia stoked the fire in the stove and moved some pots around, all the while sneaking peeks at Rae Lynn.

Finally, Rae Lynn said, "Nellie, there's things you don't understand."

"What? You married already, or something? You got a husband trying to find you? Is that why you played like you was someone else?"

Rae Lynn faced Cornelia with the weight of what she knew, her past corralled within the fence of her mind. All she had to do was open the gate, let it flow from out of her, let it go, and maybe, just maybe, she could quiet her mind. Out of anyone, it ought to be Cornelia she should tell, the one who'd taken care of her, the one who'd whisked her from Death's very hands. She owed her that much, didn't she?

She tried a bit of the truth. "I was married. Once. We lived in North Carolina, in Harnett County."

Cornelia puffed up, almost preening.

She said, "Ha. I knew it. You're too pretty not to have been attached to somebody. Harnett County?"

The compliment made Rae Lynn blush.

She said yeah to Cornelia's question, then focused on making a pit in the bowl of flour with her fist.

She reached for the clay pitcher of milk, and before she poured, she met Cornelia's eyes, soft brown as a wren's feathers, gazing at her in a manner not unlike the way Warren had sometimes when he was of a mood. It was disconcerting, and she dumped the milk too fast, adding more than she should have.

"Shoot!" She set the pitcher on the table. "I got to add more flour and lard."

"Rae Lynn?"

Rae Lynn wiped her hands off and reached for the flour, disturbed by the uncanny look.

"What?"

"You said, 'once.'"

Rae Lynn hesitated, then finally said, "He's gone on to his Reward."

"Oh, honey. I'm real sorry."

Rae Lynn kept working, adding what she needed to her bowl. She supposed she could say a bit more that wouldn't point to anything of consequence.

"He fell off our roof trying to fix it and got hurt."

"How awful!"

Rae Lynn said, "It was the most awful thing I ever been through. He got hurt bad."

"What you reckon was wrong with him?"

"Some internal injury, though I don't really know. He wouldn't let me get no doctor. He was stubborn as the day is long. Set in his ways. He was older'n me. He had him a son from a first marriage, named Eugene. I reckon he was probably closer to my age, though I never met him. He's a lawyer, and didn't seem to care much about nothing his daddy had, not 'til he was gone."

The more she talked, the easier her words came, but also memories she didn't like. The ones that forced her to relive the moment she'd taken up Warren's pistol. The tragedy played out in her head, and she struggled with it, her breath coming faster as she concentrated on controlling her emotions. She pressed her fingers to her lips, as if physically preventing the rest of her story from spilling out. Cornelia grabbed her hand away from her face.

"Rae Lynn? You all right? What happened? Won't you tell me?"

Rae Lynn wished she could convey the agony of it all without having to say it out loud. She couldn't imagine what Cornelia might say, or what she might think. She pulled her hand away and went back to fixing the biscuit dough. She tried not to shake.

"I can't. You'll think I'm the most awful person you've ever known."

Cornelia was vehement. "No, no, no. I couldn't never think that. I couldn't. Not even if you killed somebody. I'd say to anyone who asked, they must've had it coming."

How surprising her choice of words.

Rae Lynn said, "I got to get these biscuits done."

She began working the dough again; then she stopped and the words came, slipping from her as if they would choke her.

"That's what happened."

Cornelia stared. "What do you mean that's what happened?"

"It's hard to talk about, Nellie. Real hard."

She spread flour over the tabletop, dumped the dough out while her heartbeat sounded like a hammer in her head. She was about to cry, and if she did, she didn't think she'd be able to stop. She'd lose that careful control she'd kept hold of so well.

Cornelia said, "You can tell me. I won't breathe a word. I can see how it causes you such pain."

Rae Lynn sank into a chair. She buried her face into her arms, her hands still coated with flour. She heard Cornelia move away, but in seconds she was back, pressing a cool rag to the back of Rae Lynn's neck. Bless Nellie. She was an awful good friend. They'd grown close in a short amount of time, and Rae Lynn had grown to depend on her calm manner, her ability to put her at ease, but she'd held on to this thing she'd done for so long, the thought of telling someone made her sick.

She mumbled into her arm. "I can't never take back what I done."

"What you done?" As she spoke, Cornelia flipped the cloth over, and the cool came down on Rae Lynn's neck again, and Cornelia said, "It can't be all that bad."

Rae Lynn sat up and the cloth fell to the floor. She stared at the whorls in the wood of the tabletop and her voice trance-like, empty, she began telling Cornelia.

"After he fell, whatever was wrong, it was like he was dying from the inside out. Spitting up blood, black as that tar made out yonder in the distillery. Like I said, he wouldn't let me fetch a doctor. He couldn't get out of the bed. He was trapped in a living hell, and begged me for his gun. Said he wanted to kill himself. Then he asked me to do it, like he'd done for his old dog. I refused, so he quit eating and drinking. Nellie, he looked dead already, but still, he breathed. It was unnatural seeming, and I couldn't stand seeing him suffer after days of this. I finally give him his pistol like he wanted, and I ran. I didn't want to stay, only, I changed my mind. I thought I was horrible for leaving him in such a moment. I went back, heard the gun before I got in the house. I thought I would die my-self, right there. Lordy, what he'd done to his self. He messed up bad. Gut shot. I reckon it's where his pain was greatest. Worse, he was still alive. I don't know how. Laying there, bleeding something awful. It was only a matter a time, but his agony was so great, I done like he asked. Like he was begging me to do. I . . . I . . . took that gun, and I held it here."

She put the stub of her finger against her temple and stopped talking. She waited for judgment to come, for Cornelia to condemn her actions, for Cornelia to tell her she had to leave. She couldn't look at her, didn't want to see her friend's horror. While she believed she had no choice, did it matter? Wasn't she still a murderer? They should've let her die in that box. Cornelia's silence was enough. Rae Lynn sighed, prepared to hear the disgust. She heard a rustle, felt the tip of a finger come under her chin.

Cornelia said, "Look at me."

Rae Lynn did, eyes spilling over, her nose starting to run. She held herself in check, not wanting to sob.

"Now listen. You had call to do what you done. It was an act of compassion. Why, I could a killed Otis more than once, for no good reason other than he's just plain mean. What you done couldn't be helped."

Rae Lynn felt a knot rise up in her throat. She couldn't speak she was so grateful for the kindness of her friend. Cornelia's face was close to hers and Rae Lynn clung to the hope she'd tell her more, tell her she'd have done that very same thing. Instead, Cornelia leaned in and pressed her mouth to Rae Lynn's, an awkward move that lasted only a second because Rae Lynn jerked her head back and jumped up.

She yelled, "Nellie! What're you doing?"

Cornelia put her hand over her mouth, her eyes as wide as they could go.

She said, "I don't know! I . . ."

A thump came from behind them. Rae Lynn spun around and saw the broad back of Otis scurrying through the house, hands clenching his head like he thought it might come off. He ran outside. Alarmed, Cornelia gave Rae Lynn a terrified look before she ran after him.

"Otis!"

He'd seen Cornelia kiss her. He would kill her. That's what he'd do. He'd kill her.

Otis was in the front yard, arms thrown wide, shouting at the sky. "I can't believe it! What's this world a coming to?"

He charged one way, then the other, hands back on his head, while Cornelia followed him as he stormed about the front yard. She tried to grab his arm, but he shoved her backward, and she barely caught herself from falling. A few coloreds stopped what they were doing and began to watch the commotion.

Otis paused in his tirade long enough to point at Rae Lynn, who was in the doorway of his house. His entire body shook as if afflicted with some illness.

"You ain't right! You got to get the hell outta my house!"

Cornelia said, "Otis, calm down. Listen to me."

He ignored her, his attention solely on Rae Lynn. "You . . . you . . ."

Meanwhile, more coloreds crowded doorways, while others stood in their yards, watching from afar. To make matters worse, Crow, the one person she never cared to see again, came toward them. Rae Lynn hurried over to stand with Cornelia, who'd given up trying to talk to Otis. When Rae Lynn approached her, Otis was like a bear and shoved her so hard, she fell to the ground. He stood over her, one beefy hand pressing down on the top of her head. She twisted to get away, but he gripped her hair, making her eyes water.

Wheezing, his color gone ruddy, he yelled at Crow, "Do you know what I caught her doing? Kissing my wife! I seen it with my own eyes."

Saying it brought a renewed anger, and Rae Lynn heard her roots tearing as he clenched her hair. She put her hands over his in a futile attempt to loosen his grip.

She tried reasoning with him. "She didn't mean nothing by it. It ain't what you think."

Otis yelled. "*She!* You're the one come here dressed like a man, going round trying to act like one. Everything was fine till you got here."

Rae Lynn let out a small scream.

Cornelia's pleading voice broke through her pain. "Otis. Please. Don't."

Crow acted nonchalant about what was going on.

In a calm tone, he said, "Hell, it don't surprise me none. I had that one pegged from the start. I knew she won't right. Goes the other way, if you know what I mean."

Cornelia tugged on Otis's hand, trying to pry it off of Rae Lynn's head, but he only yanked harder, making Rae Lynn cry out. Her scalp was on fire. Cornelia collapsed by her side, and Rae Lynn put her arm around her. At that, Otis let go of Rae Lynn's hair and tried dragging Cornelia away. To his surprise, she bit him. He yelped and then struck her in the face, but he let them alone.

Crow said, "They have no shame. You gonna stand for such?" He goaded Otis. "Your wife, damn, she's got to learn respect."

Rae Lynn said, "Leave her alone. It's my fault."

Crow said, "Now, ain't that a twist. She admits it. Hell, I got just the thing for this situation."

Crow walked away and Rae Lynn bowed her head, shut her eyes, while Cornelia continued to try reasoning with Otis.

"Otis. Listen to me. He ain't the boss of you, is he? You're your *own* man."

Otis ignored her, then he chuckled and said, "Hey, now, look a there."

Rae Lynn opened her eyes. Crow came toward them carrying a bucket where tiny puffs of smoke rose from the top. She began trembling, felt like she was going to be sick. Dread filled her, and her hand tightened on Cornelia's.

She whispered, "Cornelia."

Otis said, "Don't you talk to her!"

She tried to get up, but Otis slapped his hands on her shoulders and held her down. Rae Lynn shut her eyes.

Otis yelled at Crow, "Hurry it up!" then at Cornelia, "Move away from her!"

Cornelia gripped Rae Lynn's hand tighter. "No!"

Several things happened at once. To Rae Lynn's left the blast of a shotgun rang and the hot spatter of tar, like black raindrops, fell, stinging the arm she'd put around Cornelia. Above them, Crow yelled, "Sonofabitch!" and Cornelia's sudden cry of pain made Rae Lynn believe she'd been shot. Instead, half of Cornelia's head and face were slathered in the hot tar, and it ran in slow motion over her beautiful dark hair, her cheeks, and her neck. A glob of it fell into Rae Lynn's lap. Mouth open, soundless, Cornelia lurched to her feet, flapping both hands like a bird trying to take flight.

Rae Lynn shouted at Otis and Crow, "What has she ever done to you?"

Otis appeared filled with confusion, while Crow stared stupidly at his bleeding hand. Rae Lynn rushed to Cornelia's side.

Otis, fury filling his voice, yelled at Crow, "Look at what you done, you idiot! Not my wife! Her!"

Beyond the chaos, and through a glaze of tears, Rae Lynn saw Del Reese running toward them, shotgun still raised to his shoulder. *Too late*, she thought. *Too late, too late.*

Chapter 27

Del

Del ran to the women huddled together on the ground and assessed the horrible deed done to them.

"I tried to get him before this happened."

In the periphery of his thoughts came *gorgeous* when Rae Lynn raised her eyes to him, but that thought evaporated like mist under a hot sun when she spoke. Her voice had a hitch in it.

"Too late."

It was true. If he'd been a second sooner, Crow would be the only one nursing an injury. Peewee, his hair dripping, his face covered with soap, came running, still in the process of pulling his suspenders over his shoulders. It was apparent he'd been washing up. His eyes grew big and round as he stared at the women and then at Crow.

Crow immediately yelled, "That sonofabitch shot me!" while Del offered nothing.

Peewee was flummoxed.

He said, "What in the hell's going on. What happened to Cornelia?"

Crow pulled a handkerchief out of his pocket and wrapped it around what amounted to nothing more than a nick.

He said, "I'm gonna tell you what's going on, and any questions you might've had about a certain somebody's gonna be answered."

Otis was in a dither, trying to get ahold of Cornelia's hand, only she kept batting him away.

Crow pointed at Rae Lynn. "Otis caught her kissing his wife."

Otis exclaimed, "S'truth! I seen it with my own eyes."

Rae Lynn gave an imperceptible shake of her head, and Del was willing to bet cold, hard cash it hadn't happened that way.

Bewildered, Peewee said, "And so you dumped hot tar on Cornelia?"

Crow pointed with his bandaged hand at Del. "If he hadn't shot my hand it would've gone where it was intended!"

Otis circled them like a buzzard.

"He was gonna dump it on her!"

His flailed his arms wildly at Rae Lynn, who helped Cornelia to her feet. The women started for the house and Otis fell in behind them, blabbering and making a nuisance of himself. If the situation hadn't been so tragic, Del would've laughed at how each time he got within a foot of his wife, she swatted him away. The women went inside with Otis trailing after them dejectedly.

Peewee said, "Sweeney. First thing, you're fired. Second, you ain't leaving before you pay for what you done here today. You know, since you're always talking about what's fair."

Del sure did appreciate this side of Peewee.

He snapped his fingers like he'd just had a thought, but in reality, he'd been knowing all along if he had a chance, what he'd do.

"I got just the remedy."

Peewee spread his arms wide, indicating he didn't much care what Del decided.

He said, "Just don't kill him 'cause I have to answer to that."

Del gestured at Crow with the shotgun. "Git moving."

Crow's jaw jutted out. "I ain't going no damn where."

Del said, "Sure you are."

He aimed at Crow's boots. "Sure would be easier walking if you ain't got your foot shot too."

Peewee said, "Be a man about it and do as he says."

With a furious look at them both, Crow started walking, but he taunted them as they went.

"What're y'all gonna do? Take me out to the woods and shoot me like an old dog?"

The men said nothing, so he tried another avenue.

"Tell you what. Y'all let me take my chances in that swamp, and you won't see hide nor hair of me again. Might be a good way to get out from under the old lady too. Heh, heh."

Del wished he'd shut up. He cut his eyes toward Peewee, who rolled his at Del. Minutes later, they stood under the silver-coated sky, air thick as syrup and reminding them they still had a lot of summer to get through.

Del said, "Step on in."

Crow stared down into the box and didn't move. As Del watched him hesitate, he became thoughtful.

"I reckon you're scared. You got good reason to be. Lots a men didn't make it out 'cause of what you done to'em beforehand. If you're the praying sort, I'd pray if I was you. That wood is soaked with them you left to rot. They'll come for you, when you least expect it."

Crow was stone-faced, and Del couldn't resist a small dig.

"Get in, and get comfy."

Crow's eyes scanned the area like he might try to escape. The woods and the swamp beyond offered him no more reassurance than what sat on the ground before him. He finally did as he'd been asked; he stepped in, and he sat. He turned a little pale, and Del imagined he was catching a whiff of the special essence it held.

Del said, "Oh, come on. You told them it won't so bad."

Crow shot him dead with a look. Del reached for the lid, and Crow was forced to lie down. He remained uncharacteristically quiet until it was almost shut.

Then, he said, "You best keep eyes in the back of your head, the both of you. When I get outta here, first thing I'm gonna do is—"

Del slammed it shut and secured the padlock. From inside came a deathly silence, and he sensed Crow glaring in his direction. Neither man spared another glance at the wooden container as they walked back into Swallow Hill.

"Maybe that'll learn him good," said Peewee.

Del said, "Maybe. He might get hell-bent on retaliation."

Peewee said, "Wished I'd known how he was. What I need is more men like you and Ballard, less like him 'cause he won't nothing but trouble. I'm gonna put Woodall on notice too. To tell the truth, I don't know if I want to stick around and manage this place much longer. I might want someone to run this joint and deal with all there is to deal with."

Del thought Peewee was hinting, but he had his own plan about his future.

When Del didn't respond, Peewee said, "How long you reckon I ought to keep him in there?"

Del said, "Good question. You got a key?"

Peewee stopped. "Ain't nobody ever had it that I know of, but him."

They looked at each other and at the same time said, "Uh-oh."

Peewee waved a hand. "Ain't a problem. I'll get somebody to bust it open when I think he's had enough. I reckon I best let his wife know he won't be home for a couple days."

Del gave Peewee a surprised look. "Whose wife?"

Peewee pointed over his shoulder to where they'd been. "His."

Incredulous, Del said, "She's his *wife?*"

"Who you think's over at his place? His mama?"

"Well. Yeah."

Peewee grunted. "That's been the joke round here. She's got land here in Georgia. Wants her a son, 'cording to him. He'd get a good chunk of acreage if that happened. His dream come true, so he said. I guess the idea turned sour on him, her pestering him about a baby. He come here so he wouldn't have to perform his conjugal duties, if you get my meaning."

Del thought again about what he'd seen.

"Yeah, I get it."

"I didn't know who she was at first. Thought it was his mama too. She's been coming regular-like, stays a couple weeks and leaves. Two months goes by, and here she comes again, probably when she knows she ain't got no baby in her belly. Either way, I ain't got to worry about them no more. He's fired. Listen, why don't you stay on? You could run things good as me, probly better."

Del said, "Actually, I don't think I'm staying either. Soon as I can get my debt paid, I think it's time I went home."

Peewee looked surprised, then disappointed.

"Where's home?"

"North Carolina."

Peewee nodded. "Now there's a purty area."

The thought had come out of the blue when Peewee started talking about leaving Swallow Hill. What was holding him here? Nothing, except what he owed, really. He'd like to think Rae Lynn could be in his future, but she'd given him little, if any, hope. If she was interested, she'd have let him know by now. He might not have his full capabilities as a man, but he could still read women, and she'd indicated zero interest. The more he thought about it, the more anxious he was to be on his way.

He said, "I got a sister, and she's got a husband. As time goes on, this Depression don't seem to be getting any better. I'm gonna go and see if I can't help them out in some way."

Peewee said, "Times like this is when we need to be near family."

When they were back in the camp, Del said, "I reckon we ought to go check on how the women are."

Peewee nodded, and they made their way onto the Riddles' porch.

He peered through the screen door and shouted, "Hello?"

Otis came stomping into view, pointed at him, and yelled, "That damn woman you hired! Or man! Whatever she is!"

Peewee ignored that and said, "We came to check on them. How is Cornelia?"

"My wife's ruint!"

The men entered the house and followed Otis to the kitchen. Cornelia sat at the table, a basin of water nearby, a jar of Vaseline, and a mirror. She cried softly while trying to delicately pick at the tar on her right cheekbone. At the sight of the men, she stopped and sat with her head bent, hands in her lap, like she was ashamed. Her dark hair blended with the black goo on her head. Half her scalp was covered, the other half fairly clean with only a few small clumps of tar here and there.

Del glanced about, and Otis said, "I know who you're lookin' for and she ain't here. I told her to get the hell out."

Cornelia said, "You had no call! She ain't done nothing."

"Nothing! You call what I seen her doing to you nothing? Shameful!"

Del said, "Where'd she go?"

Otis jutted out his jaw and said, "I don't give a damn where she goes, long as she ain't in my house."

Cornelia said, "Well, I do."

"Only thing you need to care about is acting right, behaving proper."

Peewee said, "Now, now. That ain't called for."

Del spoke to Cornelia. "Did she say where she was going?"

After Otis's comment, Cornelia's spirited moment passed, yet she managed to give Del a look that made him think she knew. Otis scowled at her, as if he was replaying in his mind what he'd seen between her and Rae Lynn. Del shifted his attention to Cornelia.

"I came to see how you were, and to wish you the best."

Cornelia sat up. "You leaving?"

Del said, "Soon as I can."

Otis said, "You can't leave. Not when you owe money."

Peewee said, "He owes nothing. My company's gonna take care of it. Matter a fact, if Miss Cobb owes anything, we're gonna take care of that too."

Astounded, Del said, "You ain't got to do that, it ain't necessary," but Peewee waved him off.

Otis's mouth opened and shut several times, speechless, while Cornelia looked like a woman who'd lost everything. Del couldn't fathom why she'd stay with a man like him, and without thinking of the consequences, he made a suggestion.

"You could leave too, you know."

Cornelia regarded him carefully, like she'd never had the thought before.

Otis sputtered, outraged. "What the hell? She ain't going no damn where!"

Del squatted by her chair.

"All you got to do is go into Valdosta, catch the train. I'd help see to it you got on it. Seeing as how my obligation here has been met, thanks to Peewee's generosity, I'm leaving as soon as possible."

He could see the temptation was there. She was thinking

about it. Otis maneuvered himself between her and Del, his hands clenched, like he would hit him, and Del stood up.

Otis said, "Her place is here, with me!"

Del ignored him and stared at Cornelia. Her life with Otis was captured in her eyes, a cesspool of turmoil, and submission, but mostly fear. Voice flat, without hope, she repeated what Otis said.

"I belong here with my husband. Besides, I ain't got nowhere else to go."

Once she said that, Otis was smug and self-righteous.

"She knows she's lucky. Especially now."

She stood and said, "Let me get you a few things to take."

Del had to let it go. If she wouldn't leave, he couldn't make her. She couldn't say much nohow, or she'd pay for it later.

Otis said, "Huh? You ain't giving him nothing!"

Del said, "Ma'am, I ain't wanting to cause you any more trouble."

Cornelia ignored Otis, and said to Del, "It ain't no trouble atall."

Del was of a mind Cornelia was perhaps the strongest of them all, living as long as she had with a cruel, pigheaded man like Otis Riddle. He went outside to wait, and not too soon after, Peewee came out too.

He looked back at the house and said, "It was a mighty fine thing for you to offer to help her. She's too scared, though."

Del said, "Yeah, damn shame, is what it is."

"Who knows, maybe you've given her something to think about."

A minute later, Cornelia opened the door and came down the steps, a paper package in her hand. Otis was right on her heels. When she handed the package to Del, she quickly flicked four fingers at him, twice, while staring at him intently, clearly wanting to convey a message.

Otis said, "Cornelia!"

Del frowned, looked askance, but she could offer nothing more with Otis watching her every move. She hurried back into the house. He looked at her retreating back until Otis slammed the door behind them.

Peewee said, "I got a feeling she ain't gonna tolerate him so easy from here on out."

Del said, "I sure hope not, not for her own sake," still perplexed over what she'd tried to signal to him.

Peewee said, "Listen, I'd like to buy that horse back off of you, if you're innerested."

Del didn't like being indebted and Peewee had already cleared what he owed at the commissary.

He said, "Only if you'll let me send you money once I get back home."

Peewee raised a hand and said, "Ain't no need. You done enough around here. We're flush."

Del had pictured riding Ruby home, but he needed folding money worse. He didn't mind walking, and if need be, he'd hitch a ride here and here.

Del said, "I'll take you up on that."

They went to his office, where Peewee opened a drawer and counted out the money into his hand. Then he scribbled something on a piece of paper and handed that to Del too.

"Here's my address, back home. It'd be great to stay in touch."

Del took it and said, "Thank you. It sure would."

Peewee grabbed hold of his hand and shook it good and hard.

He said, "Safe travels."

Del said, "I hope you get to leave soon too."

Peewee said, "Can't be quick enough. When're you heading out?"

Del was undecided. Knowing Rae Lynn had been kicked out of the Riddle house, he felt he should try and find her, make sure she had somewhere to go. Would she even want his help? She'd never shown more than a mild interest in what he might have to say, and not a thing more.

He said, "I don't know," and he scuffed his boot across the ground. "I wonder if the Cobb woman is all right."

Peewee said, "Something tells me she'll be fine, no matter where she goes."

Del said, "Probably," resigning himself to the realization he would likely never see her again.

Chapter 28

Rae Lynn

Meanwhile, Otis was preoccupied in the outhouse, declaring without any sense of decorum that what had happened had upset his bowels, shouting at Rae Lynn that when he came out, by God she better be gone. She had quickly gathered the few things she had, with Cornelia trying to help, despite the pain and discomfort she must have felt. The hardening tar turned part of her face into a grotesque mask while her eyes begged, *Stay.* That same plea, once spoken in a soft voice as Rae Lynn hovered near death, silent now, filled the room.

Rae Lynn put her hand on Cornelia's arm and said, "Nellie, he saw. Let him think what he wants. Let him blame who he wants. Dear Lord, look what's happened to you over it. It ain't worth you getting hurt more. Let it be."

If it hadn't been for Otis, no one would have been the wiser over the incident between her and Cornelia. While it perplexed Rae Lynn, it changed nothing. Whatever it was that had compelled Cornelia to kiss her, the most important thing was Cornelia cared about her. And, no one had, not since Warren.

She was glad Otis had kicked her out, only because she didn't think she could bear to stay under the same roof after what he'd caused, yet she worried at what would become of her friend, who at this very minute was fussing about food. She'd wrapped ham biscuits, two jars of tea, and a couple peach tarts. Rae Lynn dropped the pistol in her dress pocket last, and she shuddered before she could stop herself.

Cornelia said, "What's wrong?"

"That."

Rae Lynn gestured toward her pocket.

"The pistol?"

"It's the one . . ."

Knowledge dawned. "Oh. Warren."

Rae Lynn nodded. Cornelia brushed her fingertips lightly down Rae Lynn's shoulder, while shaking her head. "It"— and she pointed at the gun—"set him free from his pain."

This was what Rae Lynn loved about her, and part of what she would miss. Cornelia's ability to take her worries and make sense of them. What she didn't like was how Cornelia looked in the general area of the pistol, as if it held an answer she'd not considered. Rae Lynn patted Cornelia's arm, but, couldn't delay any longer. She had to leave or risk running into Otis.

They left the small room, and Cornelia said, "It'll be dark in a couple hours. You ain't leaving now, are you?"

"No, I'll go to where I was staying before. Just for tonight. After that, I ain't sure."

The women hugged, their manner furtive and nervous, and Cornelia's face crumpled, the hardened tar pulling and distorting the skin, giving her features an even more tragic appearance.

She grabbed Rae Lynn's hand and said, "I don't know what come over me. I'm sorry. Now I've gone an' ruined things. I'll be worried sick about you."

Rae Lynn squeezed her hand and said with a confidence she didn't feel, "Please don't worry. We'll always be friends."

"But, I ain't never gonna see you again."

Rae Lynn knew this was true, and Cornelia put her other hand to her mouth while her shoulders shook with distress. Rae Lynn hugged her tight, released her, and cradling her belongings, she left. She passed the trail to the colored quarters, where it was quiet, and she imagined everyone inside, most likely eating supper. Finally, she was back at number forty-four and being extra careful, she tapped on the door and waited. She could sense it was empty, but she was taking no chances. After a few seconds, she glanced around furtively and shoved the door open. The same fusty air greeted her, quickly reminding her of the weeks she'd spent here. Inside, she flopped into one of the chairs at the small table, despondent.

She had to think about what she might do, where she might go. She pondered the idea of going back to the house in North Carolina for all of a few seconds. There was no telling what had happened since she left, no telling what Butch had said, and for all she knew, Eugene could have the law looking out for her. She could wait tables. Cook. Wash dishes. Work in a store. Take on washing and ironing. Whatever anyone had. First, she had to see where she was going to end up. She pulled the small bundle across the table toward her, undid the string Cornelia used to tie everything together, and at the sight of carefully wrapped food she grew teary-eyed. She thought about how they worked together in Cornelia's kitchen, at the commissary, in the garden, and how, despite Otis, she'd enjoyed being there. It seemed like a dream now.

She had no appetite, so she wrapped everything back up and drifted dismally around the room, and when she rubbed her arms, the tiny dots of tar spotting her skin drew her attention. She believed a small piece of soap might have been left behind on the shelf. At the wash basin, she felt along the rough wood of the shelf, and it was still there. Carefully, she cracked open the door, making sure no one was around. She quickly pumped a bit of water, hurried back inside, and began scrubbing at the black speckles. When she was done, the soap was gone, but so was most of the tar.

She went over to the god-awful mattress, and a plume of dust rose up when she sat. She'd been so dog-tired after working the trees, the discomfort and stink hadn't bothered her much. After sleeping at the Riddles in a decent bed, on clean sheets, she might as well have been wallowing in a hog pen. She laid down anyway, closed her eyes. She thought it was only minutes later when a noise aroused her, but as she sat up, she noted how the inside of the shanty was now dark. *Tap, tap, tap* came on the door. Rae Lynn reached for the pistol, glad to have it now, despite its history. She made her way carefully, quietly, to the door. *Tap, tap, tap* came again. She cocked the gun and winced at how loud it seemed to her.

She spoke loudly. "Whoever it is, there's a gun aiming at you through this door."

A low, but familiar voice said, "Rae Lynn, it's me."

"Nellie?"

She pulled the door open, and Cornelia rushed inside.

"Hurry. Shut it."

Rae Lynn did as she asked and said at the same time, "What're you doing here?"

Cornelia appeared overcome and held her hand to her chest, breathing hard. Rae Lynn went to the table, struck a match, and held it to the wick of the lantern, adjusting it so the flame stayed low, but enough to light the room in a warm glow. The burns covering Cornelia's face glistened, like tiny bodies of water across the landscape of her skin. While the tar was removed from her face, her hair was still covered on the one side. Cornelia set a similar bundle to what she'd given

Rae Lynn on the table. She pulled on a glob of tar in her hair, winced, and let it go.

She said, "We got to hurry."

"*We?*"

"I'm going with you."

Rae Lynn tried to understand what Cornelia said.

"Leaving? You're leaving Otis?" she repeated.

Cornelia said, "I can't stay another minute with Otis. I can't take him no more, not without you there to help me get through the days! He fell asleep and I took a chance."

"Oh, my word."

"We got to go 'fore he wakes up and finds me gone!" She pulled a pair of scissors out of one of her pockets. "Will you help cut this mess out of my hair? I couldn't do all of it. It won't take long. Get this part here and here. It's what hurts the most."

Rae Lynn didn't know what to make of all this, or what to do other than take hold of the scissors Cornelia held out to her. Cornelia plopped down into a chair, her back to her. Rae Lynn began to carefully separate chunks of tar-covered hair, and as she started cutting, she made Cornelia tell her everything. Cornelia was still breathless but spoke slower now.

"First of all, after you left, Peewee and Del showed up. Crow's done for in this camp. Peewee fired him, but even better. Guess where he is."

Mystified, Rae Lynn said, "Where?"

"Del Reese put him in that sweatbox. He's also leaving, Rae Lynn. He said to me, 'You can leave too.' Said he'd see to it I got on a train. Except, as you know, I can't go to Mama's. She'd tell me to go back to my husband. She says it's a woman's fault if a marriage turns bad."

Rae Lynn quit snipping off pieces of Cornelia's hair. "Nellie, I ain't got no plan, no place to go."

"It don't matter! I'd rather go round the countryside empty-handed, no roof over my head than spend one more minute with him. I shouldn't've ever married him. I mean, he was all right for a while, till I found out his problem. He always thought I was gonna tell. I would threaten to, as you know, but it only made him worse."

Rae Lynn did know, and opened her mouth to say so, but Cornelia couldn't seem to stop as she went on telling Rae Lynn everything.

"I took money Otis had squirreled away. He's not only gonna have a fit when he finds out I'm gone, he might even try and have me arrested for stealing, knowing him. My mind was in such a tizzy over what I was doing, I couldn't hardly think straight, but that's what I done. Oh, my word, I done stole from my own husband!"

She seemed astounded at her own audacity as she stuck her hand in a dress pocket and withdrew a wad of paper money. She held it up for Rae Lynn to see. Rae Lynn moved around the chair to face her, and Cornelia's eyes begged her to understand. Rae Lynn remembered how hard it had been when she'd chose to leave the little house under the pines, to not know exactly what might happen along the way, to feel so alone.

"It ain't going to be easy with nowhere to go."

Cornelia lifted her shoulders. "There's different kinds a hard, and being with someone like him, waiting on when he's gonna get mad when I don't do something to his liking, that's the kind a hard that can make you think on thoughts you ought not be thinking. Please, Rae Lynn. It's my only chance."

Rae Lynn was filled with worry, but leaving Otis was likely the bravest thing Cornelia had ever done in her whole life, and to tell her no would be heartless. It *was* her only chance, otherwise she might as well tell her to go back home and deal with Otis the best she knew how. That look on Cornelia's face when she'd told Rae Lynn the pistol was what had set

Warren free was worrisome. Cornelia had lost hope. Cornelia had helped save her. She owed her this much, and likely much more.

Rae Lynn said, "We can figure it out."

Cornelia clapped her hands together and held them tight, like she was in prayer. "Oh, thank you. Thank you. Thank you."

Rae Lynn's voice was dry. "Ain't much to be thankful for, not just yet."

"Just getting away from him is enough. The rest don't matter."

Rae Lynn stood back and examined what she'd done to Cornelia's hair. It was really short. A lot shorter than hers when she was Ray Cobb.

She said, "You can wear my hat."

She grabbed the mirror off the shelf and handed it to Cornelia, who stared at herself. The tar was gone and there were only a few scalded areas, while in other spots, it had to be cut almost to the skin.

Cornelia said, "I sure don't make a handsome man."

Rae Lynn sniffed. "Neither did I."

In ordinary times, they'd have laughed at their attempt to joke. Now, they were only able to smile a little. Rae Lynn got her boots from beside the bed where she'd dropped them and tugged them on. Cornelia wore strappy shoes with heels, and Rae Lynn wished for a pair like them instead of what she was wearing, but shoes like that wouldn't be practical if they ended up having to walk a long distance—or run. She explained to Cornelia what she'd planned.

"We'll take the truck. It's got a radiator problem, but we can fill that jug with water and take it with us, just in case."

"Maybe we ought to leave it. It's so close to commissary, and the house. Otis might see us."

Rae Lynn said, "We got to try. You'll wish we had," and she looked pointedly at Cornelia's shoes.

Cornelia said, "I suppose you're right," her voice trembling.
Rae Lynn said, "Now?"

"Might as well. Best to go while it's dark."

They went outside, and as they walked by the unoccupied
number forty-two, Rae Lynn wished once more she could
thank Del Reese for saving her. She wondered where he
would go, what he would do from here on out. She'd likely
never know. A glorious, full moon rose over the trees and allowed them to see the path, a milky-white trail of soft, sandy
soil. After a few minutes they came to the section for the coloreds. In the distance, music flowed and rippled on the night
air like a river. From the depths of the juke joint, a woman's
laugh rang out, and somewhere overhead in a nearby tree, a
whippoorwill sang its high-pitched warbling night song. The
air was still warm, still fragrant with the things of summer,
honeysuckle, wild grapes, and the fishy odor of nearby creek
water. Rae Lynn thought they were safe as long as they stayed
tucked into the shadows after entering the main section of the
camp. They walked quickly until the sight of Cornelia's home
glowing like a jack-o'-lantern, light pouring from every window, made them stop. Rae Lynn heard her gasp.

She grabbed Cornelia's hand and tugged, whispering,
"Hurry."

They ran in a hunched-over fashion to the truck. They
eased the doors open and jumped in, shutting them as quiet as
they could. Cornelia flapped her hands anxiously, while Rae
Lynn tried to sort through the steps in her head about how to
crank it.

Cornelia squeaked, "Hurry, Rae Lynn! Oh, my God, he's
done figured out I'm gone!"

"I'm trying, I got to do it right. Can't afford to stall or flood
it. It don't help none it's pitch-dark."

She sat in the seat and tried to recall where she'd put the
key. She fumbled around searching on the floorboard until

fingers brushed across it near her left foot. She jammed it into the ignition, while remembering she had to adjust the fuel cutoff. She pulled the choke out and turned the knob as Warren had shown her to allow a certain mixture of gas. His voice was in her head, directing her. They'd done it time and again, and as she moved through the steps, all he'd taught her started to come back. She put the truck in neutral, made a couple adjustments to the throttle. Finally, she turned on the ignition, one foot on the clutch and the other on the starter button. She adjusted the choke again, and unbelievably, it started. It wasn't noisy. It only made a soft *putt-putt-putt*, but to Rae Lynn, it might as well have been a jackhammer. Cornelia bounced on the seat, hand over her mouth, as she stared over her shoulder at her house.

Cornelia said, "We got to go! He might hear this thing!"

Rae Lynn glanced over at Cornelia and said, "I need to let it warm a bit before I—" She froze, her wide-eyed gaze on Cornelia's front porch. Cornelia looked, then grabbed Rae Lynn's arm so tight it hurt.

"Go, go!"

Rae Lynn fumbled with the gear stick, while Cornelia squeaked out, "Oh, dear Lord. He's coming down the steps!"

Rae Lynn moved the gear into reverse, pressed the clutch, once, twice, and they backed up. She prayed she'd find first, and second . . . and the truck acted like it wanted to stall, coughing and spewing smoke when she forgot to double clutch as she managed to get it into first.

She mumbled to herself, "Come on, remember what you been taught! Pay attention!"

The truck jolted forward and rolled along, cooperating under her clumsy adjustments, but a man with good legs could still outrun them. Rae Lynn didn't know if Otis had good legs or not and when she dared to look again, he was closer, the angle of his head and his posture telling her he was trying to make them out. She saw the moment recognition struck, his mouth a gaping maw, before he started running for the vehicle. She managed to slip the gear from first into second and as they whizzed by, he grabbed at Cornelia. She squealed and leaned to the left against Rae Lynn, while Otis's fingernails left long scratches along her forearm. He slapped his hand on the back end of the truck as they picked up speed.

He bellowed, "Cornelia! What the hell you doing!"

Rae Lynn dared to look over her shoulder, and he was still running. Meanwhile, Cornelia was bent forward, head down, hands braced on the dash.

She screamed, "Faster, faster, don't let him catch us!"

Rae Lynn looked back again and saw not only Otis but another figure running right behind him. She thought it was Del Reese, but she wasn't sure, and she had to drive. She adjusted the advance, increased her speed, while Cornelia, scared to death Otis had somehow hitched onto the back, couldn't, wouldn't dare look. The headlamps shone on the wiregrass, pines, and scrub brush as they sped away.

They rounded a bend, and she said, "Nellie. We're going too fast for him. You can sit up. Can't even see him no more."

Cornelia lifted her head, appearing dazed as she stared out the windshield. Then, she turned in the seat and stared over her shoulder. When she faced forward, she smacked her hand on the dash.

She shouted, "We done it! We done it, Rae Lynn!"

Rae Lynn smiled at her. "We sure did."

She pressed on the gas and they left Swallow Hill behind.

Chapter 29

Del

It dawned on him what Cornelia had signaled in that heartbeat-like double pulse of her four fingers as he was gathering his things to leave. He quickly threw some food together and left the woods rider's house, not looking back. He was headed for the single men's quarters when a faint voice came from out of nowhere, and he was forced to stop.

"Have you seen him?"

Crow's wife. She stood in his way, holding a flickering lantern, waiting for him to speak. The light did nothing to soften her features.

He lied, of course. "Naw, I ain't seen him."

Impatient, he waited to see what else she'd say. She dropped the lantern so it lit their feet instead of their faces.

She said, "He does this. Disappears sometimes. He didn't show up for supper."

Del made helpful noises, for no other reason than to escape. "If I happen to see him, I'll let him know you're looking."

"Ain't hardly worth the trouble. If he ain't here by morning, I'm leaving. I'm fed up."

She appeared to be in despair, though he couldn't really tell. She moved on, swinging the lantern left and right, searching, as if Crow might jump out of the weeds. Del went on his way, putting Crow and his wife out of his mind. He'd already concluded he had nothing to lose. He was going to tell Rae Lynn he was of a mind they had a future together, of some sort. If she rejected him, at least he'd tried. The rumble of an engine turning over caught his attention. Only one person in the camp had a truck. He reversed course and ran, and was just in time to see the truck take a sharp turn and Otis trying to grab—Cornelia? Rae Lynn looked over her shoulder right at him. Then they were gone, the truck fading around the bend. Del's heart sank. Otis, fit to be tied, plowed a furious path, back and forth.

"Hey!" Otis yelled when he saw Del.

He stomped his way over to him and wildly waved his arms about as if Del couldn't see him.

His voice carried across the night air. "See that? They done took off together! By God, I knew it! I knew she was bad news!"

Otis yelled at Del like it was his fault. He only wished he'd resolved Cornelia's secret message sooner. He'd have stood a chance at catching the both of them. He played dumb with regard to Otis's declarations.

"Who?"

Otis quivered in agitation and tossed his hands up.

"Who! Who you think? That damn Cobb woman and my wife, that's who!"

"Are you sure?"

"Am I sure? What the hell! You damn dumb, blind, or both?"

Everything out of Otis's mouth was a shout.

"My wife ain't been right since she stepped foot in my house! She got to mouthing off with her around. The both of'em carrying on behind my back all the time! Acting like I was stupid!"

Del stood quiet while Otis panted, his distress so great he had to slow his tirade, or pass out.

He wagged his finger at Del and muttered, "I tell you what you ought to have done. You ought to have left her ass in that damn box. Should a let her rot right where she lay. She won't worth saving. Damn dyke is what she is."

Without really thinking about it, Del clenched his hand and popped Otis right in the mouth. Otis's head snapped back, and his eyes flew open, stunned. The blow had been meaty, solid, and the movement so unlike Del, he'd stunned himself. Otis bent over, covering the lower half of his face with both hands.

He mumbled through his fingers, twisting his head so he could glare at Del. "Why'd you go and hit me!"

Del said, "'Cause you're running your mouth about the woman who could be my future wife, that's why."

Otis eyes went a little buggy. "Your future wife! Good luck."

Del had said it, and now he wanted it to be true. He pointed at Otis.

"Not another word about her."

Otis spit, then said, "I only want my own wife back. What am I gonna do without her?"

His voice rose on the last word in a childlike wail.

Del said, "Maybe you should've thought of that while you were sticking cigarettes on her arm, shoving her around, yelling at her. Maybe she wouldn't have left your sorry ass."

Otis twisted his hands in distress.

"Who's gonna cook for me? Wash my clothes? Keep my house?"

His lower lip had swelled and made him appear like he was

pouting. It was fitting, considering. Del stared in the direction the truck had gone. She was gone. He had no idea where, no idea if he'd ever see her again. This hadn't turned out like he wanted. Del gave Otis a disgusted look, grabbed his pack, and figured now was as good a time to leave as any. There was nothing left for him here. Otis was left standing outside, a solitary figure staring at his empty house like he had no idea what to do with it. Del didn't speak to him again. He hurried along, passing the path to the box, and from a distance, he heard faint yelling, noticed a lantern bobbing, and stopped for a second. That had to be Crow hollering, and the glowing orb fluttering about like a firefly had to be his wife. How she'd found him, he didn't know, didn't care. Before too long, he was far enough he could no longer hear anything but his own footsteps.

When he came to a small clearing in the trees, he stopped and looked at the isolated encampment under the moonlight. It appeared such an innocuous-seeming spot, a soft, ghostly evening mist swirling in and around the shanties and the pines surrounding it. He couldn't hardly believe he was getting to leave. He'd expected to remain stuck there for some time, his debts mounting. Instead, thanks to Peewee, he was free to go. A little smile relaxed his features as he strode through the grassy savanna, the sense of his liberation flowing through every muscle and bone in his body, like being released from the grip of the corn. The moon rose higher, and he absorbed the furtive noises he heard to his left and right, night creatures out like him.

He walked for hours, until the skyline began to turn pink. It would be another hot day, but it wouldn't be the kind of hot brought on by toil, or the rush to make numbers, or from hustling along under the pines in order to tally calls. Once again, he answered to no one and he could stop when he wanted, only he had no wish to do so. He was eager to keep moving. He tried not to think about Rae Lynn. Tried not to have any regrets. He was only fooling himself, but he tried.

Around midday, as the sun rose above the trees, he found a quiet spot with a small running stream nearby. He believed he'd made good progress. He was in his element, the area remote, with nary a soul in sight. He sat under a pine, eating his usual travel fare of cheese, crackers, and Vienna sausages and while doing so, he pulled out the piece of paper Peewee had given him. He unfolded it and read Peewee's hectic scrawl: *Come see me sometime. No work involved. We'll go fishing. Best, Pritchard Taylor, Rt. 2, Woodbine, Georgia.*

Del folded the piece of paper and tucked it back into his pocket. He'd write to him once he was back home. At the creek, he dipped his tin cup in, drank his fill, and when he was done, he started off again, walking down the middle of the wide dirt road, the main thoroughfare from west to east. Over the next hour, he passed needy souls working dry, crumbly fields filled with poorly growing beans or tobacco. He encountered only one vehicle, unfortunately going the opposite direction or he'd have stuck his thumb out. A ramshackle house or two came into view here and there, adding a bit of interest to the flat countryside. At one such house, a young boy sat under a pecan tree, a fat puppy lolling nearby. The kid waved and the puppy jumped up and barked. Del waved back. Red dust settled on the tops of his boots, while the peace and quiet settled his mind.

If only . . .

Before he could think her name, he pushed the thought away.

The afternoon was soon gone, and now the sun sat behind him, skimming the treetops. It was time to finally stop, and it wasn't too soon; he could tell he needed the rest. He kept on while searching for something that suited him for the night.

He'd hoped to first pass a small store where he could buy a cold drink as a nice end to a hot day. About the time he'd decided he was going to have to make some sort of decision about where to sleep, a squat, square building with a sign cropped up in the distance. That just might be the store he'd been looking out for. He pressed on, and as he came closer, as luck would have it, it turned out to be a Conoco filling station. A Pepsi was going to be possible after all.

As he approached, he noticed a truck parked in front. It looked awfully familiar. No matter where Rae Lynn and Cornelia chose to go, they'd have come this way as it was the only main highway. Still, what an extraordinary coincidence if it was hers, because while he'd come some thirty miles or so, they should've crossed into South Carolina a long time ago. He walked around it and noticed a gaping hole in the radiator. Hadn't Peewee said her truck had a radiator problem? The bell on the door jingled as it opened, and out came Rae Lynn and Cornelia. The surprise on their faces matched his own. He touched a finger to the brim of his hat.

"Ladies."

Cornelia was the first to speak. "I can't hardly get over this. Why, if it ain't Del Reese! Look, Rae Lynn, it's Del Reese! Ain't we glad to see you!"

Del grinned and said, "Likewise."

Rae Lynn smiled back, at least.

She pointed at the hole in the radiator and said, "It didn't take no time for it to overheat. We brung along some extra water that got used up quick. We only just made it here and been sitting here most of the night and day."

It was the most Del had ever heard her say.

He said, "Can't they fix it?"

"Ain't got the part. He'd have to order it," and she indicated with a tilt of her head, the store behind them.

"Where were y'all headed?"

Neither answered, and Del felt bad for them because it was obvious neither one knew. The owner came out, an old man with white hair, his face the color of a pecan from years in the sun. His hands were jammed in the pockets of his overalls, and his lower lip was packed with snuff.

He said, "Shame I ain't got what they need. It would take days to get that part here. We ain't got much in the way a nothing round here, as you can see. Takes a while to get things, don't cha know."

Del said, "I imagine so."

He squatted by the front of the truck and poked at the radiator.

"There's some waxy sort of stuff on this grill."

Rae Lynn said, "It was a chunk of soap. I reckon it dried up sitting under that shed in the heat and fell out."

Del said, "I have soap."

The station owner said, "Now ain't that a stroke a luck? They asked fer that too, but it ain't something I carry."

Rae Lynn's face lit up. "You do?"

Cornelia chimed in. "Thank the heavens."

Del slung his pack off his shoulder and untied it. He withdrew a bar of Fels-Naptha, brand-new, still wrapped in paper.

"This'll fix it right up."

Rae Lynn followed him to the front of the truck. "Thank you."

He pulled out his pocketknife and cut out a chunk, then crammed it into the hole. He stepped back to eyeball his handiwork.

"That ought to do it for a bit."

Rae Lynn turned to the station owner. "Can we get some water?"

"Sure thing."

He took their jug and went out back. He returned with it

full, and after the water was added, Rae Lynn slid into the driver's seat and went through the steps to crank the engine. It started, no problem. She turned to Del and gave him a brilliant smile. His heart keeled right over, and didn't get up. It lay inside his chest panting in the manner of a dog trying to cool off. She sure got to him in a way no other woman had. He made himself break eye contact, thinking, *Lord, but she's pretty.*

Facing Cornelia, he said, "It sounds fine."

She grabbed his hand and pumped it up and down. "Thank you so, so much."

He said, "You're welcome."

She let his hand go, then no one moved.

"Reckon you might ought to top her off?" the owner asked.

Del said, "Y'all got money?"

The women looked at each other and at the same time said, "Yes."

The owner motioned for Rae Lynn to move the truck over to the pump. Del waited while the pumping went on, worried about them driving out of his life for a second time. The owner pocketed the money handed over by Cornelia, and it gave Del an idea.

The owner said, "If nobody cares, I'll be closing up now. Lessen y'all need something else?"

Del could have stood that cold drink, but he didn't want to miss the opportunity to somehow stick together. The women shook their heads. The owner gave a little wave, went inside, pulled the shade, and flipped his OPEN sign to CLOSED.

Rae Lynn got out to stand with Cornelia, who said, "Where you headed?

Both stared at him curiously.

He took his chances and said, "Home to see my sister. Listen, if you'd consider giving me a ride, I'd be glad to pay for the gas from here on out. I know she'd welcome y'all to stay until you know what you want to do."

Cornelia said, "Why, that's mighty generous of you. Rae Lynn, what do you think?"

Rae Lynn paused, then said, "Where's your sister's?"

"North Carolina."

Her eyes widened, and she shook her head vigorously.

"Thank you, but no."

Cornelia said, "Oh. Oh my."

He frowned. The call name Rae Lynn had used was Tar Heel.

"Where'd you say you were from again?"

She avoided looking at him and didn't answer. He could've sworn she'd said South Carolina back at Swallow Hill, but he'd had a suspicion it wasn't the truth. Del backed off, held his hands up, palms out.

"Never mind. It was just an idea."

Cornelia said, "It was real kind of you to offer. I think it's a good idea, seeing as we have no other options."

Rae Lynn spoke again.

"No, it ain't," she declared.

If Del was a betting man, there was fear in those three little words.

Chapter 30

Rae Lynn

Rae Lynn immediately got back in the truck and watched them in the side-view mirror. Cornelia raised her shoulders in a shrug as if she didn't know what bothered her. It irritated Rae Lynn more when Del made a similar gesture. Their reactions made her feel like a fool, like she was being hardheaded without good reason. Well, they hadn't been through what she'd been through either. She averted her gaze while she twisted her hands like she was wringing out a dish rag. Cornelia approached the driver's side window.

"Can't we give him a ride for a little ways, Rae Lynn?"

"First it's just a ride a little ways, and next thing I know, we're in North Carolina."

"No, we won't go that far. Just a few miles. A little thank-you for helping us."

Rae Lynn thought about it. How would doing that hurt? No telling how long it would take him if he had to walk the entire way.

She didn't want to seem unreasonable, but then Cornelia went on to say, "North Carolina's a pretty big state. In my opinion, we could at least find out where his sister lives. Could be it's all the way to the other end from your house."

Now they were back to that idea.

Rae Lynn's voice went sharp. "I said I won't never going back there, and you know why, Cornelia."

Del had shouldered his pack as if he knew he'd caused a problem. He was already making his way down the road again. Rae Lynn stared after him, torn between guilt and what she felt was self-preservation.

Cornelia stared after his dwindling figure and said, "I'm sorry. I know you got your reasons."

She walked around to the passenger side and got in. When they passed him, Cornelia turned around in the seat and gave a sad little wave. If Del responded, Rae Lynn didn't know. She reckoned she was hardhearted, and pigheaded to boot, and neither would allow her to look at him again. No one talked, and the farther she went, the more Rae Lynn got to feeling like a fool. Grim-faced, she pressed on the gas and created a swirling mass of dust behind them. She checked the side-view mirror. Del Reese was no bigger than a speck. She checked again seconds later, and he was gone from sight. They went for several more minutes before Cornelia ventured to speak.

"Rae Lynn?"

"Don't say nothing."

Rae Lynn clenched the wheel, both hands in a white-knuckled grip of tension. Cornelia stared out her window. The only noise was the engine and the wind in their ears. The mood had shifted in the small truck. The farther they went the worse she felt. What she must seem like to him. Ungrateful. Unreasonable. Selfish. Minutes later, Cornelia tried again, persistent.

"Rae Lynn."

Rae Lynn let off the gas some. "Yeah."

"He's helped a lot, you know."

Rae Lynn huffed and said, "Yeah, I know."

"He saved you from that torture chamber. Checked on you to make sure you was all right. Stood up to Crow and Otis for the both of us. Gave that nasty Crow a lesson he won't soon forget. A little ole ride seems like a real small thing to do, considering."

Rae Lynn slowed some more. She hated how reasonable Cornelia sounded.

"Maybe."

"We got to think about our own situation here too."

"I guess."

"Like you said, you ain't got a plan, and since we ain't got nowhere to go . . . I mean, what if it rains? What if we can't find jobs? What about—"

Rae Lynn cut her off. "*I know.* I told you when we left it would be hard."

Cornelia, arms crossed, quit talking and for the first time since knowing her, Rae Lynn thought she might be mad. She stopped the truck. They sat in the middle of the road, engine puttering, staring through the grimy, bug-spattered windshield.

Cornelia turned to Rae Lynn and said, "Why're you so afraid of going back to North Carolina? What happened to your husband and all, ain't your fault. You done what you had to, and if no one knows, what does it matter?"

Rae Lynn rubbed her hand across her forehead. Her head was starting to hurt.

She said, "Because someone does know. He saw me right after and has his own ideas about what happened. There I was, holding the pistol. And there was Warren. Twice shot. It didn't look good."

She ventured a peek at Cornelia, whose mouth hung open, speechless.

Cornelia said, "Oh."

Rae Lynn looked away, her voice soft.

"His name's Butch Crandall. He was a friend of Warren's. He tried to blackmail me. Said unless I, you know . . . be with him . . ."

Cornelia gasped. "He wanted you to . . . ?"

"Yes."

Incredulous, Cornelia said, "Why, what kind a friend asks such a thing?"

"He said he'd always cared about me. Sure was a funny way of showing it. He threatened to tell Warren's son, Eugene, unless I did what he wanted. I was afraid I'd end up in jail. It would've been my word against his. It's why I pretended to be a man, in case they put the law on me. And, well, these camps had places for workers to stay. It seemed like the perfect solution at the time."

"But, how did you come to know about Swallow Hill?"

"It won't nothing but chance when I think back on it. Butch told Warren about the turpentine work going on here in Georgia back when we were trying to get our small operation going. With it being so far away, I thought it could be a new start."

Cornelia said, "It's a shame he drove you away from your own home. What happened to it, you reckon?"

"I guess it's Eugene's. Warren never got around to changing his will after we married."

Cornelia said, "I declare. Men like that Butch, and believe me, I ought to know, they ain't nothing but trouble. Still, I'd bet not a soul's been looking for you like you think."

Rae Lynn said, "I ain't taking no chances."

"I reckon I wouldn't neither. But now, take Del Reese. He's different. We *owe* him. Just take him a little ways."

Rae Lynn sat thinking and drumming her fingers on the steering wheel. Without a word, she turned the truck around and headed back the way they'd just come. Eventually a figure appeared.

She pointed and said, "Reckon that's him?"

"Got to be."

"Don't say nothing about what I told you."

Cornelia looked offended. "Of course not. I wouldn't do that."

Rae Lynn slowed down as she came close, then stopped. She tried to smile when she asked him, "Wanna ride?"

He appeared surprised, but he didn't hesitate. He quickly tossed his things in the back, before he came and stood by her window. He gazed down the road, where waves of heat made the horizon shimmer and dance.

He said, "Awful warm today."

Rae Lynn said, "Sure is."

"I 'preciate this."

She said, "It's fine."

At least he didn't ask why she'd changed her mind.

She said, "Where's your family's home?"

"Bladen County."

Rae Lynn contemplated on what she knew. First, her house in Harnett County was a good hour away from there. Second, they didn't have any other plans like Cornelia kept reminding her. It was true, if she were on her own, she wouldn't have come nowhere near North Carolina. She'd have bought newspapers as she came to small towns in Georgia or South Carolina (to her mind, the closest she ought to get), search for jobs, rooms for let. That would have been what she would do, but who was to say she'd have found a thing. Not with the country still deep into this Depression. Well, they didn't have to stay long, they could leave at any time, and it did solve their immediate problem. She felt their eyes on her, waiting.

"You said your sister would have room?"

Out of the corner of her eye, Rae Lynn detected movement. Cornelia, probably thanking the Lord she'd come to her senses.

Del said, "It's a big ole farmhouse, got lots a room."

"Thankee kindly for the offer. We'll take you up on it."

He smiled openly at her. "Sudie May will be more than obliging, I'm sure of it."

His shadow cast long and lean against the ground in the twilight.

She gestured toward the front of the truck and said, "Them headlamps work all right, but I ain't much for night driving."

He said, "I don't mind driving. We can keep going until we find a suitable spot to rest."

Rae Lynn said, "Okay."

She slid to the middle. It was cramped in the cab, but the work they'd done at Swallow Hill, along with the camp diet, meant all three of them were as stringy as backyard chickens. He turned the truck around, and they headed northeast once again, each minding their own thoughts. Rae Lynn tried to ignore the fact her hip and shoulder touched his, but each time the truck went over a bump, she felt him against her. Occasionally, Cornelia would point out something she thought interesting. People still fighting to save their cotton crops infested with boll weevil. A store selling watermelons out front, where Del, without a word, pulled in and bought one. He hefted it into the back, and as they continued on, they saw a man pushing a child in a homemade wooden cart. The child, a girl, rang a bell, and the cart had a sign attached to the front that said, JESUS IS COMING! ARE YOU READY? Next in sight were two boys, standing at the edge of a narrow bridge, fishing a creek with cane poles and a can a worms, while a man sat nearby directing them and drinking hooch out of a bottle.

Cornelia said, "Ain't no end to the entertaining things one might see right before dark."

Rae Lynn and Del murmured in agreement. Del drove about another half hour before stopping. No one said much, they were all too tired, and eager to get out and stretch their legs. Del got the watermelon and used his pocketknife to cut it up. They dug into the red flesh and declared it was the sweetest, juiciest they'd ever had. They ate the whole thing between the three of them, enjoying it enough to let pink juice run off their chins. Rae Lynn felt carefree for the first time in months.

When they were done, he said, "Whyn't y'all sleep in the back, and I'll stretch out here in front?"

Rae Lynn was exhausted and had no argument against what he suggested.

"That's fine by me."

He said, "Mind if I play a little song or two on Melody here?"

He held up the harmonica.

Both women said no at the same time.

Rae Lynn said, "I used to listen when we was neighbors, so to speak, at Swallow Hill. You call your mouth harp Melody?"

"Yeah, kind a dumb, I reckon. I hope I didn't bother you none."

Rae Lynn said, "Not at all. I always enjoyed it."

They climbed into the truck bed and propped their heads on the bundles with their meager possessions. Rae Lynn moved around once to get into a more comfortable position and saw Del had pulled off his boots, had his feet stuck out the passenger window and his head against the driver's side door as he played. She laid back down and looked toward the heavens. It was a perfect summer night, warm with a slight breeze, and above them, a black canvas, where stars winked and pirouetted. In between the notes coming from the harmonica, she heard the howling of coyotes and a screech owl, until she heard and saw no more.

At dawn, the truck rocked a little, and Rae Lynn lifted herself onto her elbows. Del was at the front, where he bent down to check the radiator. She watched him surreptitiously, wondered why he wasn't married and what his life had been like. He straightened up and walked into the woods. Rae Lynn eased out of the back of the truck, not wanting to disturb Cornelia, who slept on, emitting soft little snores. After a couple minutes, he was back. She stood on the passenger side of the truck waiting until he saw her.

He looked a bit startled, then said, "Mornin'. What I wouldn't give for a cup a coffee."

She smiled and said, "Mornin'. Me too."

Their voices woke Cornelia.

She sat up. "Oh, gosh, is it morning already?"

Rae Lynn thought how different Cornelia was, now she wasn't with Otis. She was so relaxed, smiled a lot more, seemed fun-loving.

She flopped back down and said, "I could sleep forever."

Rae Lynn went into the woods to relieve herself. When she returned, Cornelia wobbled that way, still half asleep.

Once everyone was done, Cornelia announced, "I'm staying in the back."

They pulled out onto the road, and an odd feeling came over Rae Lynn. The last time she'd rode in this spot, Warren had been driving them somewhere. Feeling nostalgic, she pretended it *was* Warren, and that the past months hadn't happened. If Del thought her behavior standoffish, so be it. She couldn't help how she felt, although he was just as quiet, as if he too were preoccupied. He stopped at a store advertising, WE SERVE HOT HAM BISCUITS! He bought for all three of them, and the owner somehow had real coffee too, served in paper cups. They stopped for gas around dinnertime in Dillon, South Carolina. Under a small tent beside the station, a man was boiling peanuts in a kettle pot hung over a fire under a big oak tree. They got bags of these along with cold Pepsis. They leaned against the truck where it was parked in the shade of the building and began eating. Side by side, with Rae Lynn in the middle, they talked quiet, mostly about the subtle changes to the landscape since they'd left Georgia. The level grassy savannas had turned a bit hillier as they traveled farther north and east, but the air held the same sticky feeling. A slight breeze came every so often and made the small, multicolored flags the owner placed around the station flutter in the breeze.

Rae Lynn watched Del take a peanut, put the whole thing in his mouth, suck the juice from the shell, then hold it longways and use his front teeth to pop it open. He tossed the soft beans in his mouth, took a swig of Pepsi, and did it again. She was mesmerized because Warren used to eat boiled peanuts the same exact way.

Cornelia was careful to check that no one was around before taking the hat off her head and rubbing her hand over the stubs of hair left on her scalp.

"I could get used to this. You men are lucky. This is much cooler, and easier than long hair."

Rae Lynn said, "Sure is. Makes me want to cut mine again, only shorter. Like yours."

Del was quick with his reaction. He said, "No, don't."

Rae Lynn couldn't imagine feeling any hotter, but the way he looked at her right then was like the time she'd caught a fever, like she was baking from the inside out. She glanced down at her bag of peanuts. He fumbled for the right words and finally assembled a coherent sentence.

"I mean, I kinda like how it is now. Growing out and all."

She felt Cornelia's elbow nudge her in the ribs. She nudged back, harder. It didn't matter what he liked. Any talk of longer hair brought to mind cutting hers off and how she'd scattered the strands over Warren's grave. The boiled peanuts lost their appeal as Rae Lynn was once again thrown backward, thinking how only a few months before, her daily routine had been pondering what she might fix for supper, washing clothes, tending the garden, and any one of the other many things that consumed her and Warren's days. She would cut her hair again if she wanted, no matter what Del Reese liked. They finished the peanuts and drinks, wadded up the bags, and threw them in a barrel intended for trash.

Rae Lynn changed the subject and said, "How much farther, you reckon?"

Del said, "We're almost there."

Cornelia waved a hand in front of her face in an attempt to stir the air.

She said, "It's too hot to ride squished together. I'm gonna ride in the back again the rest of the way."

Rae Lynn wished she wouldn't. It left her alone with Del, and while he'd not asked her anything this morning, she was aware he'd looked her way more times than she'd care for, as if he was on the verge of saying something. Small talk with him wasn't what she wanted. She could imagine the questions that might come, what had she done before Swallow Hill, what was her childhood like, what about her parents, why had she done what she'd done . . .

She grabbed Cornelia's arm. "Let me ride in the back. I need to stretch out. My back hurts."

It didn't, but she had to think of something.

Cornelia said, "Are you sure?"

Rae Lynn tried to joke. "Yes, I'm sure my back's hurting."

Of course Del wanted to help her, and she had to let him, or appear as if she wasn't telling the truth by being nimble enough to climb up on her own. When he took hold of her upper arm to give her assistance, she thought he held it a second too long, but she didn't want to seem rude by pulling away. She sat sideways against a wheel hub, so she could see where they were going, and where they'd been. She observed how Del and Cornelia got along, laughing much of the time and pointing things out to each other. She wondered what they talked about. Del slowed down at a crossroads, stopped, and got out.

He said, "Want to ride in front? We're about there."

She slid toward the tailgate and said, "All right."

Of course he helped her off the back of the truck because of her supposed back problem. And, Cornelia hopped out so she'd have to sit in the middle, and gave her a look that she ignored. No one talked much those last few miles. When they turned onto a dirt path, Rae Lynn detected nervousness coming off of Del in the way he tapped his fingers on the steering wheel. They bumped and rolled along the dirt drive leading to the house, and his head swiveled left and right. Rae Lynn was certain they could walk faster.

She said, "How long since you been home?"

"Too, too long."

Acre upon acre of longleaf on either side of the land caught Rae Lynn's eye. Del pointed out they'd been planted some time ago by his granddaddy and his pap. Next were corn and bean fields, and last, a split rail fence. The opening led to a white clapboard, two-story farmhouse with a slate roof situated beneath a few large elms and white oaks. Rae Lynn watched Del, who sat smiling a little, hands resting on the steering wheel. After a minute, he got out and stood by the driver's door, still looking around. A woman came out onto the porch, along with a tall, rawboned man. Two children, a boy and a girl, stood on either side of him, and he rested his hands on their shoulders. The woman held a hand to her brow and eyed the truck with suspicion. She wore a pale-yellow dress, and over it, a pastel-flowered apron. She reminded Rae Lynn of a garden filled with the soft blooms of spring.

Del called out, "Don't you recognize me, Sudie May?"

The woman's hand dropped from her brow and she brought

both to her cheeks, and her voice raised the question in her mind. "Del?"

He held his arms out like he was leading a choir.

"Del! It *is* you! Oh, my word!"

She came down the steps, ran across the yard, and launched herself at him with enough force to make him stumble backward, laughing. He caught her up and spun her around in a circle. Rae Lynn watched, wishing for such a connection. The man and children stepped off the porch as she and Cornelia got out and stood by truck. Cornelia self-consciously pulled the hat lower on her head, while Rae Lynn worried about being a bother to this family. Del, his arm still slung across his sister's shoulder, shook his brother-in-law's hand. Next, Sudie May introduced the children. Rae Lynn caught their names, Norma and Joey. Del squatted in front of the children and started talking to them, and when he did, the red muscle beating in the center of Rae Lynn's chest quickened ever so slightly. Del stood, pointed toward her and Cornelia. He leaned over to speak to his sister and her husband. Rae Lynn tensed, and Cornelia gripped her hand so tight her knuckles cracked. Rae Lynn had never felt so aimless, so without a purpose and disconnected, until Sudie May came toward them, arms outstretched, like a mother welcoming home two long-lost children.

Part III

Nest

Chapter 31

Del

The sun struck his face in the same spot as it had back when he was a kid sleeping in this very room. The moment he opened his eyes, and realized where he was, he was filled with comfort and a sense of well-being. He sat up in his childhood bed, his feet bumping against the footboard. Two windows, positioned side by side, had the very same curtains, yellowed with age, and through them, the warm beam slanted across his pillow. Outside those windows was a familiar scene, one he didn't need to get up to see. Elms, oaks, acorn trees surrounded the house, and then there were the fields everywhere else, up to the beginning of the longleaf woods.

He rose, poured water in the wash bowl, rinsed his face, ran his fingers through his hair, and put on his clothes. As he went down the stairs, his fingers trailed along the dark wood banister. On the bottom step, he stopped, encountering the spot where he'd carved his initials on the underside of the curved post back when he was about nine years old. He leaned over to look at the rough, etched out D.R. The house was wallpapered, the same pattern throughout, a cream background with bouquets of flowers. His mother used to say it was her inside garden. The only room different was the kitchen painted in light yellow.

Voices came from there now, and when he went through the door, everyone sat at a long table, drinking chicory coffee with Norma and Joey on each side of their mother, quietly eating fried eggs, tomato slices, and biscuits with molasses.

Sudie May said, "Morning," and the others did too.

Del nodded. "Morning."

Sudie May got up and poured him a cup as he sat down, staring around the table and thinking it was like being in another world. Two days ago, he'd been in Swallow Hill, and now, he was here with his sister, her family, Cornelia, and Rae Lynn. What a twist in events he'd never considered coming to pass. He sat back listening while the women resumed talking about the news. Sudie May was reading from a recent newspaper about the WWI Bonus Army camping out in Washington, D.C., awaiting news on their payout, and from an older paper about Roosevelt winning the Democratic nomination. Next, she read about the stock market. It was the lowest it had been since the Crash, and the paper said there'd been an eighty-six percent loss overall.

Amos said, "Read to us about the corn prices."

Sudie May shuffled a page or two and found it.

She said, "It's still down about seventy-five percent. Ain't worth the cost or the trouble."

Cornelia said, "What a mess."

Sudie May said, "Can't see no end in sight."

Del watched Rae Lynn as she listened, head down, hands folded in her lap.

She said, "We don't want to be no bother to you. Extra mouths to feed and all."

His sister, as he knew she would, said, "Oh, now, I told y'all, we got a garden. We're doing fine. We ain't gone hungry, and there's more than enough. 'Sides, y'all will be good company. A couple pairs of extra hands is always needed, 'specially with them two. Don't let the quiet fool you."

The kids kept eating, bright eyes fastened on the newcomers. Del figured if they were anything like he and Sudie May had been, those blameless faces and peacefulness wouldn't last. He gazed across the table at Rae Lynn and found her staring back. She shifted her attention elsewhere, turning red as the tomato on her plate. She sure was twitchy. She could say what she wanted to about where she was from, but he'd bet it wasn't South Carolina. Something had happened she didn't want to talk about. Something that sent her all the way to Swallow Hill in that getup. She was a real mystery.

Sudie May leaned forward on her elbows, like Mother would when she wanted to give her undivided attention.

She said, "What will you want do today?"

Del said, "What do y'all think about getting a small turpentine farm going as a way to bring in a little money?"

Sudie May said, "Ain't nobody around here doing it much no more. Ain't hardly any of them trees left except what we got, far's I know. You'd not have any problem selling the gum, I wouldn't think."

Del said, "I'd like to try. It's true. Them trees are near about gone everywhere. I'm glad we got what we got. I thought I'd check on what Granddaddy and Pap planted."

Rae Lynn was pouring hot coffee in her saucer, and he had a thought that she could come along. He could ask her about herself, maybe find out what it was about North Carolina that put her in such a mood. Sudie May perched on the edge of her chair, birdlike, eyeballing him, and giving him the same look she used to give him when she knew something. Her attention flitted between him and Rae Lynn, and she wisely tilted her chin up. He could hear her in his head, *Ah. I see how it is.* There was time. No need to seem too eager. He sipped from his cup and burned his mouth. Ignoring his sister, he poured some in his own saucer to let it cool.

Amos said, "If you think them trees is ready, I know somebody who makes barrels. He's got plenty and can make more. Plus, there's the steamboat that comes upriver, and it could take your gum to Wilmington."

Del said, "Where's the closest landing?"

Amos said, "There's one down to Rockfish."

He said, "It'd not be too bad getting it there. I could haul it in a day. I'd like to do some burning first, clear out the underbrush. I reckon I could go back and use the old box method, but I'd rather do like what they done down in the camp we was working at."

Amos said, "I seen it. Them newfangled clay cups and tin gutters. Ingenious idea."

Del said, "Sure was. This feller, a troublemaker really, he suggested it at the camp we was at down in Georgia. I swear he loved them trees more'n himself maybe."

Amos said, "I knew a feller like'at. Hey, use my truck today if you want."

Del said, "Thankee kindly, but I think I'll walk, see how it all looks from on foot."

He rose from his chair, and hugged his sister like they used to do their mother each morning.

Sudie May squeezed him in return and said, "I ain't gonna cry, but I am gonna tell you every chance I get how happy I am you come home."

He tugged her hair, and with a nod to the rest of them, he went out the backdoor and stared at the land of his boyhood for a good long minute. God, how he'd missed being here, and hadn't even known how bad till now. It set his heart on fire, and made him want to run across the yard like he used to when he was a kid, ready to explore the countryside. He went to the wild roses growing along the fence, picked a few, and noticed how the woods beyond appeared more dense and overgrown than he remembered. There was the old barn, and off in the distance, the tobacco barns. Eager to see how the land had changed since he'd last been here, he set off, entering the woods by way of a familiar, yet overgrown trail, almost hidden from his view. Nostalgic, he got to thinking about the times he'd gone with his granddaddy and his pap to check on the longleaf, how they'd dreamed their dreams of what might be one day.

Their long-ago voices accompanied him as he came to familiar bends and turns, and he recalled how they'd said these trees would outlast them all. He stared up, and up, until he got a crick in his neck. They'd done well. They stood tall and graceful, with a beautiful evergreen plume at their tops. They bent and swayed in the wind, and as the breeze brushed over the needles, they produced a murmuring sound as if whispering a welcome home. Next, he came to the creek where he and Sudie May used to plunge their bare feet into the cool water on a hot summer day. Finally, after some time, and when he'd seen all he wanted, he retraced his steps and made his way toward the family graveyard. Through the trees, he could see the roof of the house. His parents had been buried side by side, no different from how they'd lived their lives together. He laid the blooms across the top of the gravestone, took off his hat, and bowed his head. He expressed his sorrow for not having been there for them at the end, told them he loved them and hoped they'd known that.

When he was done, he thought back on how they'd been with each other. Pap hadn't been the easiest man to love because Mother said he was hardheaded. Funny, 'cause Pap said the same of her. He reckoned he'd come by some of it himself. What they'd had was what he wanted. Someone by his side, who loved him despite himself. He wanted stability, to know how each day would end, and to share it with one person. He hadn't been sure of this until Rae Lynn Cobb. The biggest question about his future rested on her, and she didn't even know it.

Back at the house, he spotted the women in the garden, along with Norma and Joey, doing their share of picking. The area of the garden they worked had tomatoes, squash, and okra. The chickens strutted along the edge, following where they went, waiting on someone to toss them a scrap. Here and there, the ground was littered with the vegetables unfit to eat, and when someone would lob a tomato or squash, they'd flap their wings enthusiastically, making a run for it.

Sudie May waved and called out to him. "We're about to finish up."

Cornelia waved too, and bent back down to her work. Rae Lynn was a row apart from everyone. She hadn't bothered looking up, even when Sudie May spoke. His sister approached, wiping off her face with the back of her hand, and it struck him how much she resembled their mother, having matured and changed since the last time he'd seen her. Her face, arms, and lower legs were tanned brown. She had the same light-colored blue eyes he did, a trait of Pap's, but she had their mother's hair, dark brown with red highlights. She still had a sprinkling of freckles across her nose same as when she'd been a girl.

Some part of his earlier daydreams about the future went a little haywire when she said, "Who *is* this Rae Lynn Cobb?"

His attention turned back to the two women working in the garden, and he admitted, "I ain't real sure."

"You can't hardly get two to three words outta her. I asked her about her family; she said she was raised in an orphanage. I asked her how she'd come to work at the camp, and she got this real peculiar look on her face. Then Cornelia cut in and asked me some silly question, and it was obvious she was trying to change the subject. Rae Lynn's been working off by herself ever since."

Del said, "She's got a hell of a story, least the parts I know. She come to Swallow Hill pretending to be a man."

Sudie May said, "She did?"

"Yep, that's why her hair is short, though it was a lot shorter'n at when I first met her. She wore men's clothes. Said her name was Ray Cobb. Everyone there could tell something won't right, and for a while, we thought she was some runaway boy."

"Well, I'll be."

"Yep, she worked alongside the men, stayed in the single men's quarters. It won't until this hateful son of a bitch, feller by the name of Crow, put her in the sweat box when she couldn't make count that we found out she was a woman. She was in the thing for three days. Liked to have died. Cornelia nursed her back to health. They's close. I suspect Cornelia probably knows her story. Anyway, we left the camp after the bastard, Crow, tried to dump tar on her. He missed and got Cornelia instead. That's why her hair's cut off like it is."

"What on earth for?"

"Cornelia's husband, Otis, said Rae Lynn kissed her. Said he caught'em."

Sudie May shot a surprised look at Rae Lynn, then her eyes came back to him. "Do you believe him?"

"I believe he saw kissing, but as to who instigated it?" He shrugged.

Sudie May said, "I reckon she's got her reasons for doing what she done, the disguise and all. A woman doing such sounds desperate."

Rae Lynn and Cornelia were now working side by side, each in a separate row still, but close enough to talk, and he could tell they were.

Sudie May said, "Them camps can be horrible. I reckon we was lucky."

"We were 'cause this place won't like any of the ones we

was at with Pap and Granddaddy. There were some good people, but Cornelia's husband, Otis, and Crow, they were the worst kind of trouble."

"How'd you end up there? Last we heard, you were working on some big farm in Clinch County."

Del rubbed his neck. "I was. Part of what happened was my own fault, I reckon. I done something I shouldn't've done."

Sudie May narrowed her eyes, and again, he was reminded of his mother, with the same sternness that saw a different meaning behind his words.

She said, "It must've been something serious."

Del crossed his arms, felt his face flush like he was a schoolboy again. "Well."

"So, what happened?"

"The man who owned the farm tried to make it so I'd have an accident, if you want to call it that. He had me go inside a grain bin to walk down the corn."

Alarmed, Sudie Mae exclaimed, "You're lucky you didn't die in there. People do all the time."

"Something peculiar happened."

Sudie May said, "What?"

Del shuffled his feet and didn't answer.

Sudie May said, "Why're you looking like that?"

"Like what?"

"Like when we used to try to scare one another telling ghost stories."

Del nudged her and joked. "You could be talking to a ghost right now."

Sudie May's eyes went big and round.

"What're you talking about?"

"The corn collapsed on me."

She gasped and said, "Oh, my Lord."

"It gets more interesting. I guess that's how I could put it."

She gave him a curious look. Del stared at his boots while he explained.

"I blacked out, and all of a sudden, I could see everything happening. I'd been working with two other men, saw them shoveling the corn out, trying to get me free. Then, a third man come who'd been working somewhere else. He started shoveling too. Next thing I knew, I was on the grass, choking on dust. When I could talk, I asked where the third man was. They wanted to know how I knew about him since he showed up after I was already buried. When I come to, he'd already gone back to work. Can't nothing explain that."

He'd not talked about it for so long, it sounded foolish. Like a dream. He lifted his shoulders and looked away. He was inclined toward thinking it had been intended as some sort a lesson.

Sudie May took it in stride and said, "It must not have been your time."

"I reckon not."

She raised an eyebrow toward Rae Lynn. "And . . . ?"

Rae Lynn and Cornelia had separated again, and Rae Lynn was working on a different row.

Del rubbed his chin and shrugged. "And what?"

"What do you reckon she's running from?"

"Beats me."

"She's real pretty."

"I guess."

"Have mercy, you blind?"

"I can see perfectly fine. She don't see me is the problem."

Sudie May smiled and said, "Ain't but one reason I can think of makes a woman ignore a man."

Del tried one of his old jokes. "I'm ugly?"

She laughed and said, "That, or another man."

He'd wondered about that. Maybe she was married already

and, like Cornelia, escaping some jackass who didn't know what he had. If that was it, he must not have cared much about her, not in the way he would if he had a chance.

Sudie May continued to ponder. "I mean, why else is she acting like she's hiding from something?"

Del didn't know what to say. He had no idea. Sudie May watched Rae Lynn, who happened to look their way, as if she sensed their attention on her. From across the way, Del pictured what she might see, the house in the background, the garden filled with good food, the children, a pastureland dotted with cows, the beloved pines. They could have so much together, her and him. He wanted to convey this to her, but just like at Swallow Hill, when the moment came over him, and it was all he could do to keep it to himself, she simply went back to work, and whatever she thought of this place, or of him, was as obvious to her as the air he breathed.

Chapter 32

Rae Lynn

Eventually the hard knot of fear centered within her turned soft, yielding to the ease of life at the farmhouse. What never changed were her memories of Warren. As persistent as the heat, as constant as time, her thoughts, the good and the bad, were always there. Her final moment with him was still so vivid, she expected anyone who happened by to suddenly look at her in horror, as if she'd somehow projected an image for them to see. She felt bad for not handling Sudie May's questions very well in the garden the week before, and she was pretty sure she appeared like she was hiding something. While she realized how her behavior might seem, she couldn't very well blurt out the truth. Aside from Cornelia, only she herself understood the story from beginning to end. No matter how often she justified to herself what she'd done, to her mind, it would portray her in a different light. They would think the worst of her. She already struggled with it, herself.

She'd seen Del and his sister having a long conversation that day, turning their heads her way every so often. Maybe they were thinking, given her lack of answers to the questions, she was trouble and would bring trouble to them. What was starting to complicate matters was she really liked it here, enjoyed Del's family and the spacious house. She loved the stained hardwood floors, the wood darkened to the color of molasses with different styled scatter rugs placed here and there. She and Cornelia each had a room with a soft bed. Rae Lynn admired the furnishings in hers: a night table with a lantern by the bed; a soft, lovely tufted chair by one of the windows; a chest of drawers; and another smaller table with a little upholstered stool. That table held a wash bowl, a pitcher, always filled with cool spring water, a hair brush, and a handheld mirror. She liked the print wallpaper running throughout the house, and Del had told her one day in passing his mother had chosen it and had called it her "inside garden." It wasn't that they had money, or the house was all that refined. Matter of fact, it was dilapidated in some areas, needed a new porch rail and a good paint job.

None of this mattered when it came right down to it. What mattered was it held the sense of a real home, the graciousness of those living here, their generosity and good will. Rae Lynn had taken to sitting in the chair at one of the windows first thing in the mornings, a slight breeze coming through, the white sheers hung on each side waving about. Such peace, she thought, as she sat with her arms folded on the sill, gazing out, listening to birdsong. Their days were filled with good, hard work, and after supper in the evenings, everyone went out on the large wraparound porch, sat in the rockers, fanning themselves, while Norma and Joey played in the yard. She felt guilty for enjoying these moments. She didn't really want to leave now she was here, and did she dare admit, a tiny bit happy at times? A deal was a deal, however. She and Cornelia said it was only for a short time, and for all they knew, Del, his sister, and Amos were too polite to ask them to move on.

One morning, soon after she'd come to the conclusion they

needed to think about what they were going to do, she went to find Cornelia to talk about how they might be overstaying their welcome. She found her hanging clothes on the clothesline at the backside of the house. Norma was with her, handing her clothespins as she needed them and chattering a mile a minute. Rae Lyn leaned against one of the wooden posts. Norma grinned at her, revealing the gap from her two front teeth missing, freckles like her mother's dusting her nose and cheeks. Cornelia reached for a wet shirt and smiled at her too.

"Hey, Rae Lynn."

"Hey."

Cornelia had shaved off the rest of her hair after they'd been there for a couple days. There was no more tar left, and the burns on her face were healing. She wore bright kerchiefs around her head, sometimes along with the hat Rae Lynn let her use. Her cheeks were pink from the heat, but her eyes were clear and shiny with happiness. She no longer held herself like she was expecting to be yelled at or hit. She moved about the house and yard relaxed and easygoing. Rae Lynn could see being here was as good for Cornelia as it had been for her, but the simple fact of the matter was, they couldn't take advantage of this family's kindness.

Rae Lynn said, "Norma, would you mind checking with your mama to see if she needs anything out of the garden?"

Norma said, "Yes ma'am."

She took off running toward the house, yelling, "Mama!" while Rae Lynn took over handing out the clothespins. It was the time of year when the buzz of the cicadas began to dwindle, their summertime symphony coming to an end. The surroundings were quieter without the vibrant hum of their song. Cornelia finished hanging the clothes and stood with her arms folded against her waist, face lifted to the sun, the burn scars patches of pink against tanned skin.

Rae Lynn said, "I reckon you ain't missing Otis none."

"How awful is it to say not one bit?"

"It ain't awful. The truth ain't always easy, is it?"

Cornelia faced her, and her expression changed ever so slightly to reveal a hint of the forbidden peering through.

"No, it ain't."

While Rae Lynn loved being around Cornelia, whatever went on in her head in these odd moments unsettled her. She broke off the gaze and plunged into why she'd come out there to begin with.

She said, "You know, we been here for over a week now."

"Has it been that long?"

"It has. We got to start thinking about what we're doing, where we're going."

Cornelia's shoulders slumped.

Rae Lynn persisted. "It's what we told Del."

"I know."

"Maybe Sudie May knows somebody needing help. She takes supper to the preacher at First Baptist Church every Wednesday night. Maybe someone at the church needs help. Knows of rooms for let."

"Yeah."

Cornelia sounded glum, and Rae Lynn couldn't blame her. It felt safe here, and the both of them had said off and on to each other it had been a good decision.

Cornelia said, "Do you want to leave?"

Rae Lynn didn't answer the question directly.

"They've been kind to give us what they have, and ain't said a word about how long we been here, nothing. But we can't expect them to let us stay on forever."

Sigh. "No."

"I'm gonna bring it up, and soon, okay?"

Cornelia exhaled again and said, "Okay."

Rae Lynn waited a couple of days, a Wednesday, and went

to Sudie May and said, "Let me help you with the preacher's supper. I got something I wanted to talk to you about as well."

Sudie May said, "Oh, gosh, that would be wonderful, thank you."

This was part of what Rae Lynn liked about Sudie May. She always showed appreciation, no matter how small the things they did to help out. They headed for the brooder house chatting about the relentless heat. There wasn't a hint of a breeze, and even the leaves on the trees hung limp and forlorn. The chickens appeared to sense one of them was doomed for the supper table because they didn't gather at the fence like usual. As soon as Sudie May entered the fenced area, they set off running and clucking. Sudie May eased toward the hens, but they were wily and smart. They dashed one way and the other. She stopped after a few decent attempts, panting. She and the birds eyed one another. Rae Lynn thought she seemed a little peaked.

She said, "You okay?"

Sudie May blocked the glare of the sun with her hand and said, "Feels extra hot today. This humidity is awful."

Rae Lynn said, "You come on out. Let me do it."

Sudie May didn't argue, and stepped out while wiping her neck with a handkerchief and then fanning the air with it right after. Rae Lynn scooted by her and, seconds later, nabbed a hen. She held it cushioned under her arm, and by the time she was out of the gate, she'd wrung its neck. It barely had time to emit a final squawk. Sudie May led the way back to the house, and Rae Lynn followed, the chicken dangling from her fingers. When they came into the yard, she tossed it in the scalding pot Sudie May set to heat earlier. Rae Lynn poked at the fire, watching as she dunked the bird a few times.

When she brought it out of the water the final time, Rae Lynn said, "Here, let me."

She started plucking rapidly. It was half cleaned in a matter of a minute.

Sudie May put her hand up to her head and said, "Law, I sure am grateful for all the help y'all give me here."

It was the perfect opening.

"We want to thank you for letting us stay as long as you have, but it's time we moved on."

Her eyes wide, Sudie May said, "What on earth for?"

Rae Lynn worked fast, yanking on the feathers, grateful for something to focus on so she only had to glance at her now and again.

She said, "We told Del it was only 'til we found work and somewhere to stay."

Sudie May said, "But"—and she swept her arm around— "you did."

Rae Lynn said, "Well, I know, but this isn't what we meant. It ain't right to overstay our welcome."

"You ain't overstayed nothing."

Rae Lynn said, "We don't want to take—"

Sudie May suddenly waved her hand. "Del!"

He was with Amos over by the barn, and if Rae Lynn had noticed this, she'd have waited. It was already difficult to do.

He walked over and had no more than acknowledged Rae Lynn with a little wave when Sudie May pointed at her and said, "They're wanting to leave."

Rae Lynn lifted a hand coated with feathers and said, "That ain't exactly right . . . it's not that we—"

Del cut her off as if she hadn't said a word. He looked confounded and said, "Want to leave?"

Rae Lynn was furiously plucking feathers and paused long enough to reply.

"I didn't say that. We said we'd only . . ."

Del turned to Sudie May and said, "You ain't told her yet."

"Not yet, but I guess I ought to right now."

Rae Lynn stopped yanking feathers and looked from one to the other.

"Ain't told me what?"

Sudie May said, "Norma and Joey are going to be a big sister and brother, probably in early spring. I guess I thought I was done with babies with Joey being five, but here I am. Pregnant."

Rae Lynn said, "Oh."

Sudie May took hold of her hand, and a few feathers drifted to the ground.

She said, "Joey's was a hard birth. It'll do me good not to have so much on me around here. I need to rest as much as I can. I can't if y'all ain't here to help. At least till after the baby comes. Please?"

Del and Sudie May waited, both eyeing her expectantly. Sudie May looked like she might cry, depending on the answer. Del was motionless, watchful. He didn't even blink. Rae Lynn finished plucking the feathers and dunked the bird again. They'd already been here well beyond what was proper. It didn't seem right, showing up out of the blue and staying on and on. No one had pried her with questions, but she felt her lack of background only complicated matters. Sudie May dropped her chin to her chest. Rae Lynn thought she saw a tear fall, while Del's extraordinary blue eyes remained on her in a way that made her squirm. It was as if he wanted her to stay as bad as his sister. Maybe more.

She lifted the plucked chicken from the pot and said, "Well. All right. Until then."

Sudie May pressed her hands together over her chest, and Rae Lynn saw she *had* been crying.

"Oh, thank you, thank you."

"It ain't nothing. We should be thanking y'all."

Del did something surprising to Rae Lynn. He reached out, rested his hand on her shoulder, and gave it a light squeeze.

He said, "I'm grateful to you."

He dropped his hand and walked away while Rae Lynn stared after him.

Sudie May said, "This truly is the answer to my prayers."

Rae Lynn had to admit she was relieved too. She had no idea where she and Cornelia would have gone.

She smiled at Sudie May and said, "Let me tell Cornelia; then I'll come back and help you finish this supper."

Rae Lynn found Cornelia in her room, sitting on her bed, doing nothing, like a child waiting on punishment from a parent. She tapped on the doorframe, but Cornelia didn't turn around.

She spoke to the wall and said, "When?" her voice subdued.

Rae Lynn said, "Ohhh, probably not till early spring."

Cornelia spun around on the bed.

"What?"

"Sudie May's having her another baby. She needs us to stay. She said it was hard birthing Joey and needs to rest as much as she can."

Cornelia jumped up, grabbed Rae Lynn's hands, and spun them around and around the room. Rae Lynn giggled at the playful, unexpected reaction, and when Cornelia let her go and swirled away in a circle dance of her own, Rae Lynn was overcome by a sense of peace and the thought, *We get to stay, we get to stay.*

Summer gave one last belch of hot air in early October, the gift of an "Indian summer." Fall crept in almost quiet-like until Rae Lynn noticed how they awoke some mornings with a nip in the air. Before long, the leaves adorning oaks, acorn, and sweet gum showed off their vivid reds, oranges, and yellows. With time, the events at Swallow Hill took on a dreamlike quality, some of the details becoming as faded as their sun-dried clothes. Not the ones of Warren, though.

They remained sharp and clear in her mind, as prominent as Sudie May's growing belly. In spite of it all, Rae Lynn became more like herself. Much of this had to do with Del's sister. She was a rhythmic sort in spite of her pregnancy, up at the same time each morning and doing what tasks Rae Lynn or Cornelia allowed. Most of the time they made her sit, and worked around her. Rae Lynn loved the routine of running a household, the day-to-day steady schedule, no surprises, rarely any change with given days of the week set aside for certain chores, including certain meals.

She and Cornelia earned their keep, having turned the garden over to fall plantings, the final summer vegetables canned and shelved. They gathered eggs, while Sudie May mended everyone's shirts, pants, and dresses. They cooked meals, did the laundry, while Sudie May helped Norma and Joey with schoolwork in the afternoons. She and Cornelia worked together like they had in Swallow Hill, and before too long, it was as if they'd always been there, both having adapted to life at the big farmhouse. Sudie May read to them from the newspapers, mostly about the prices of staples they might need and if there were specials. The news with regard to the economy was still dire, and the country appeared to want Hoover to lose to Roosevelt.

In the evenings, Rae Lynn withdrew to her room at the top of the stairs and next to Cornelia's. On the opposite side were Amos and Sudie May's, then the children, who shared a room for now, and Del's room was last, centered in the long hall. She still couldn't quite get used to being in such close proximity to him, and they often ran into each other in the hallway on the way to bed. He kept mostly to himself, and whatever had been in his eyes the day she'd decided they would stay must have had to do with what his sister wanted. Rae Lynn was aware he spent his days in the woods raking and clearing out around the longleaf in preparation for the next year. Sometimes she caught the smell of smoke where he was burning off scrub and underbrush, a way of controlling any unnecessary growth that might take from the pines. It reminded her of working with Warren, and there was a longing in her to be under the shelter of those trees again, to smell their sharp, crisp scent.

One Sunday evening, she was on the porch with Sudie May and Cornelia, and she spotted Del weaving his way through the woods. When there was no work going on, he would do this, going the same way each time.

Sudie May watched him thoughtfully and said, "I reckon he's trying to make up for lost time. Mother and Pap, they sure did want him to come home something fierce."

Rae Lynn said, "Where does he go?"

"To their graves. He gets flowers from out of the yard for the headstones each week."

Rae Lynn watched Del until he disappeared, before nudging her chair back into motion again. She'd abandoned Warren, stuck him in the ground like he meant nothing to her. The spot was likely neglected, pitiful looking, overgrown with weeds. Warren didn't even have a headstone to mark where he lay. Time had calmed her fears. She thought maybe she ought to go see about his grave. But, *if* she went, she might get caught . . . no. She wouldn't get caught. She would be careful. Besides, she didn't know what had happened to the place since she'd left. For all she knew, it was abandoned. Eugene certainly wouldn't live there. He'd have sold it, if anything, and gone back to South Carolina. She rocked faster. The more she thought on it, the more she believed no one would be the wiser. It was the only way to put her mind at ease.

The day before she planned to go, she worked all afternoon on a chocolate pie using one of Sudie May's recipes. After she put it in the oven to bake, she busied herself cleaning the kitchen, then went outside to sweep off the porch. Lost in thought, she pictured herself seeing the little shotgun house under the pines for the first time in months. She replayed the moment in her head over and over, how it would make her feel, how she'd handle it. She sat in a rocker, shut her eyes, and went from room to room in her head. She completely forgot about the pie until she smelled it and by then, dark smoke was coming out kitchen window. She ran back inside, pulled it from the oven, and went about throwing open more windows. Sudie May came from some other part of the house and started flapping a dish towel, trying to clear the air. Cornelia ran in from the field where she'd been digging up new potatoes, a scared look on her face.

She rushed in breathless, declaring, "Law, I thought the house was burning down."

They stood in the hazy kitchen, and Cornelia scrutinized the blackened edges of the crust, the smoldering chocolate pudding, and finally, Rae Lynn.

"You all right?"

"I'm fine."

"You been kind of quiet lately."

Rae Lynn coughed, the burned stinky smell getting to her. She said, "I have?"

Sudie May chimed in. "Um-hmm. Preoccupied."

Rae Lynn flopped down in a chair and rubbed the palms of her hands on her thighs. There was no way she'd tell Cornelia what she was thinking, much less Sudie May, who still knew nothing about Warren or where she'd lived. She needed to say something to satisfy them, though.

She said, "Sorry. I reckon I been thinking on how it feels to be pregnant."

Where that came from she had no idea, but who cared, it worked.

Cornelia gaped at her, mouth open, while Sudie May said, "Well, I can sure talk about that."

And for the next hour she did, first how it was with Norma, next Joey, and now this one. She said it was different for each and told them how. If Rae Lynn hadn't known better, it was like she tried to hint a time or two about Del, how she thought he was ready to settle down, how he'd been such a ladies' man, and how he'd changed a lot since she'd last been around him. Each time she brought him up, she directed her comments to Rae Lynn, as if she'd asked about him. Rae Lynn leaned her head one way and the other, listening, but also thinking about how she was going to get out of the house in the morning without anyone knowing.

Sudie May ended with, "Do you want to have children?"

It was a question Rae Lynn didn't expect, but she was honest in her answer.

"One day."

After supper, she helped clean up, then excused herself.

She said, "I'm a bit tired. I'm going to bed."

Everyone said good night, and from Del, "Hope you can get some rest. You been working hard around here."

She acknowledged his remark with a nod and went upstairs. To her mind, it got too quiet, as if they were making sure she was out of sight before they discussed her. She readied herself for bed, and once she was in it, she turned one way, then the other, unable to sleep, playing out every what-if scenario she could come up with. It was no surprise she was up before the sun rose, and dressed. She carried her boots in one hand, a piece of paper and a pencil in the other. She carefully navigated the staircase step by step. She wasn't perfectly quiet, but she was quiet enough. In the kitchen, she scribbled a note.

Be back by noon. Rae Lynn

She propped it on the table, against the little pitcher for cream. Whoever was up first to make coffee, usually Sudie

May, would see it. She eased the back door open, stepped outside, and turned the handle to shut it. It was cold enough her breath came in small clouds in front of her face while the moon, a soft golden color, hung low in the sky, like a ripened piece of fruit. She sat on the back steps and pulled on her boots, thinking she'd not dressed warm enough for an hour ride in a less-than-airtight cab. She wore one of the dresses Sudie May said was too small for her. It was long sleeved, and she had on a sweater and now her boots, but she shivered still. It would simply have to do. She moved quickly across the yard, knowing it would be hard to get the truck started without waking the entire household. Plus, they were all early risers.

The truck's door gave an uncustomary squeal when she opened it. She got in, sat for a second gathering the steps in her head, and began adjusting the gas mixture, the throttle, and luck was with her again as the engine coughed, and caught. She let her foot off the brake enough to allow it to roll backward and clear the tree it was parked under. She gave a quick glance toward the house, checking for any sign of movement. She saw nothing. Soon she was rolling by the now-fallow cornfield, and it was then she flipped on the headlamps. They illuminated the dirt drive and the landscape. It wasn't until this second that dread began building in her for what she might find.

Chapter 33

Del

He'd had trouble sleeping lately, which meant he was awake and heard someone up just as early as him. He got out of bed, cracked open his door in time to see Rae Lynn, boots in hand, descend the staircase, slow and easy. There was that one squeaky step, and watching her reminded him of how he used to sneak out on Saturday mornings when he was a boy so he could meet his friend, Buddy Blalock. Buddy had lived on the next farm over, and their early morning rendezvouses were usually about fishing or hunting. This could only happen when Pap didn't need him for turpentining—which wasn't often.

Del shut his door and hurried to get dressed. He and Rae Lynn could enjoy a cup of coffee together. He hadn't been around the house much, too busy working to prepare the pines for the next season. It would be nice to talk, just the two of them. She'd been acting quiet the past day or so, like something was on her mind, and he couldn't help but think of what his sister said. There was another man. He hoped not, but if there was, he needed to know so he could quit thinking like he'd been thinking. He was buttoning his shirt, when he heard a truck starting. He pulled back the curtains and saw her backing up. Grabbing his shoes, he hurried down the stairs. He was about to go out the door when Cornelia appeared in the kitchen, still in her nightgown, yawning. She shuffled over to the stove, while asking him a question.

"Where're you heading so early?"

He stood at the back door, feeling a bit foolish.

He shoved his hand in his pockets and said, "Did Rae Lynn happen to say she was going anywhere today?"

Cornelia gave him a confused look.

"No. Why?"

"She just left."

She frowned and said, "Huh. She ain't said a word. Least not to me."

"I heard her come downstairs, and thought maybe she and I could have some coffee and talk."

Cornelia's mouth bent in a crooked smile, and she said, "Talk? She ain't much on talking case you hadn't noticed."

Del hadn't shared his thoughts with anyone about Rae Lynn, and fact of the matter was, Cornelia would make a good ally. She might know something that would help him understand Rae Lynn's caginess about her past.

He said, "I noticed. That's why I thought it might be good to try. Sudie May thinks the reason she doesn't appear to know I exist is to do with another man."

Cornelia raised her chin in a knowing manner and said, "Ah. So you care about her. And?"

"And what?"

"You care about her, but how much? Do you mean as in *no matter what*?"

He tried to make light of it. "That sounds like a 'for better or for worse' sort of question."

Cornelia said, "Well?"

"What difference does it make how I feel if she's got some-one already? You got any ideas where she'd be going?"

Cornelia went to the table and sat down. She hugged her-self, but was quiet.

Del persisted and said, "Whatever is going on, I'd like to know, so I ain't got my hopes up for nothing."

"It ain't up to me to say. It's her business." She spotted the note and picked it up. "She left a note. Here, it says, *'Be back before noon. Rae Lynn.'*"

Del saw his future disintegrating. All of his planning, how he'd been thinking for some time now began to collapse, holding up no better than the scrub brush he'd been burning off for weeks now.

"Is it another man?"

"You could say that, but it ain't like you think."

"How is it, then?"

Cornelia said, "All I'll say is, if where she's going has any-thing to do with what she's told me, you might ought to hurry."

"Is she in trouble?"

"I ain't sure, but I'm going with you. I reckon I ain't got time to dress."

"Not if we want to catch her."

Cornelia grabbed the pencil Rae Lynn left next to her note and added her and Del's names below Rae Lynn's. She gath-ered her nightgown and housecoat around herself, and they left the house.

They climbed into Amos's truck, and Del said, "Where would she be going, exactly?"

"Harnett County is all I know."

On the trip home, he'd noticed Rae Lynn's driving was se-date. His was not. Cornelia clung to the dash and the door as he pushed Amos's truck, which vibrated and rattled loud due to the speed, so much so, conversation was impossible. The road was good in spots, bad in others, and the only other traffic they saw was a mule-drawn wagon heading in the other direction. The sun had just broke over the horizon when they spotted another truck just in front of them, maybe a half mile away.

Cornelia said, "That's her."

They hung back, and as the sun rose higher, it drenched them in warmth. They went slow, kept their distance. They passed a tiny sign that said HARNETT COUNTY, and the truck in front of them crept along even slower.

Del said, "We might have to pull over and let her get ahead some. Her driving like this, it's bound to start looking suspicious if we stay behind her and don't pass."

Cornelia said, "She's slowed down 'cause she's scared, I'd imagine."

She immediately smacked her hand over her mouth, then lowered it. "I shouldn't've said that, but it's God's honest truth."

"Why would she be scared?"

"I can't say, but I think we're gonna find out."

Maybe Rae Lynn had made a poor choice in a husband like Cornelia. He didn't want it to be true, to think of someone treating her the way Otis treated his wife. It made him grit his teeth, but worse would be if she *was* married. After all the women he'd been with, none affected him the way she had. He pulled off on the side of the road, and they sat watching the truck shrink, and shrink, until it was barely a dot.

Cornelia said, "Better go again before we can't see her no more. She might turn off somewheres, and we wouldn't know."

Del got back on the road and drove fast until the truck reappeared as a dot again. He wondered how much longer this would go on and his answer came a few minutes later, when the dot disappeared. He floored it.

"Damn, where'd she go?"

Cornelia was gripping the dash once more and said, "She must've turned."

He hunched over the steering wheel, speeding along, trying to avoid potholes. They came to a dirt road, and ahead, there was nothing, not even a small cloud of dust. She had to have turned here, so he did too, and pressed on the gas again. The road was nothing like what they'd been on. While many were getting better, most were in the shape of the one they were on now, and Amos's truck shuddered, and bumped, and lurched until Del finally had to let up on the gas before he risked damage to the underside. Cornelia had turned a little green as it was. She leaned forward, hand to her mouth.

He said, "You all right?"

"Don't pay me no mind. Keep going, don't lose her."

I'm trying not to.

Out loud, he said, "I hope this is the right way."

"Me too."

There was a curve here and there, and he slowed to a crawl, afraid he'd come around one and there she'd be. The road was lined with pines, and he pointed them out.

"Mostly loblolly and a few pond pines. Ain't seen not one longleaf."

Cornelia barely grunted. He looked left and right, and suddenly braked.

"There's a barn over yonder."

Cornelia said, "I wonder if we're on the right track."

He crept forward and spotted another shape among the tree trunks and brush. He nudged Cornelia's arm and pointed.

"A house."

"Sure enough is."

He stopped and cut the engine off.

"Let's walk the rest of the way."

Cornelia nodded, and they got out, leaving the doors open. She cinched the belt on her housecoat tighter.

She grumbled, "Ain't I a pure d fool traipsing about the countryside in my nightgown and housecoat. No matter at this point, lead the way."

Del kept close to the edge of the woods, and Cornelia tucked in behind him. After a minute, he stopped and pointed out Rae Lynn's truck. Where it was parked told him she'd been to this house before. It wasn't in the drive like she was visiting, it was parked under a pine, near an old chicken coop, and beside the coop was a shed. The cab of the truck was empty. He stared at the narrow house, which to him looked abandoned. There was the front door and on either side of the door, a window. It was a long, narrow house, one Del was familiar with. Shotgun style. There was a wooden planter off to one side where flowers grew, although most had been taken over by weeds. In the quiet, he could hear the pines above his head, a slight wind creating the soft whisper he loved so much.

Suddenly, Rae Lynn came from some area off to the side of the house, beyond where the planter set. She was crying. Not soft crying, but heaving sobs that reached their ears. Both moved forward, wanting to go to her, except a man came out of the house, and Del threw out an arm out to stop Cornelia.

He said, "Damn. Sudie May was right."

Rae Lynn appeared shocked, as if she hadn't expected to see him. From his vantage point, Del weighed his adversary while his heart splintered like old wood.

The man called out, "I knew you'd be back."

Rae Lynn wiped her eyes and said, "What're you doing here?"

"Waiting on you."

Del whispered, "Who's he?" and Cornelia whispered back, "Ain't sure."

The man said, "You're back on account of me, ain't you?"

Rae Lynn gestured in the direction where'd she'd come from and said, "I come to make proper arrangements."

The man came down off the porch, thumbs hooked in his pant pockets. Del didn't like how he stared at Rae Lynn. It told him they had a past. This man knew her well enough to be acting like he was. He was a fool for having followed her, but he'd wanted to know, and now he did. He and Cornelia should leave, if possible. He glanced around. The woods were thick, and as long as they stayed off the path until they were around the curve, no one would ever know. He pointed back the way they'd come, and Cornelia gave him a questioning look.

He mumbled. "Let's go," but she shook her head and held up a finger.

The man came close to Rae Lynn, and Del couldn't bear to watch. Here it was, the grand homecoming. She'd returned to her life, and to whoever this man was. Whatever their differences, whatever had set her on the run down to Georgia was over now. He had to let her and his dreams go. She was back home, where she belonged.

Rae Lynn yelled, "Butch!"

Cornelia nudged Del's shoulder. "Law, it's Butch!"

Del didn't know who this Butch was, he only saw how he held Rae Lynn, his arms all the way around her, hugging her tight. But, she wasn't returning his hug. Instead, she struggled, only she might as well have been trying to push a building over for all the good it did her. Del didn't like that, not one bit. He rushed forward, Cornelia right behind him.

Del called out, "Hey, Rae Lynn!"

The man called Butch immediately released her. She

backed away from him and glanced over her shoulder at Del and Cornelia in surprise, and relief. They went to stand by her side. This man was as stunned as she was at their sudden appearance.

He said, "Who the hell are you?"

Del asked Rae Lynn, "You all right?"

Breathless, she said, "I'm fine."

Butch directed his attention back to Rae Lynn. "Oh. I see how it is. You with him now, is that it?"

Cornelia put a protective arm around her and said, "That's right."

Butch tilted his head.

"I wonder when this all come about?"

Del followed Cornelia's thinking and said, "Does it matter?"

"I bet you ten to one she ain't told you what happened to her first husband, now has she? Wonder what you'd think about that?"

Cornelia said, "She told me. She told me about you too, and you ought to be ashamed of yourself."

Butch had the grace to flush red.

Rae Lynn said, "I done explained to you what happened."

"You should a gone for a doctor. It didn't never make sense to me why you didn't."

"I tried. More than once. He wouldn't have it. You said so yourself."

Butch's eyes roved from her to Del, back to her.

"It's like this, is it? Poor old Warren's already forgotten."

"If that were true, why am I here now?"

Butch ignored that and said, "You living a new life now, with him?"

He jerked his thumb at Del.

Butch didn't wait on her to answer. "Eugene allowed I could buy the place. Told him I wanted it. When he asked me where you were, I said I didn't know, and that was the truth. I went and sold everything I had. My house. My land. My hogs. All on account of you. I was gonna give you a way to stay here, in your home. With me. Now don't this beat all? Here I done give up all I had, been waiting, praying, all this time. And for what? For nuthin 'pears like."

Rae Lynn said, "That ain't my fault. I ain't ever give you reason to think such a thing could happen."

Butch said, "I could hope, though, couldn't I? I weren't gonna say nuthin,' Rae Lynn. I believed what you told me. I only wanted you to think I didn't." He tipped his head at Del. "Does he know? You tell him?"

Rae Lynn said, "Ain't nothing to tell him."

He said to Del, "Go on, ask her. Ask her what happened here in this very house."

Del stared at Rae Lynn, and if he'd never been sure of anything before, he was with what he was about to say.

He said, "Far as I'm concerned, ain't nothing this woman could ever do that would make me think any different of her than I already do. I seen her in the worst of circumstances. Seen everything I need to see. Know everything I need to know."

His gaze and voice were steady as he spoke, and he saw she considered him in a way she'd never done before. She didn't stare through him. Not this time. She didn't look away, neither. All he'd ever wanted was for her to see him as he was, imperfect, but a man who loved her no matter what.

Butch, his voice a lament, replied, "I know exactly what you mean."

Chapter 34

Rae Lynn

The sharp bite of winter was upon them, but she still went ahead and bought a small marble headstone and arranged to have it shipped to the little house under the pines. When she made the trip back to Harnett County again, this time she took Cornelia along, and in a strange twist, Butch helped them to place it, proper and all.

After it was done, he said, "You can come back, if you want. You know. Tend to it, and whatnot."

She gave him a distrusting look. The house no longer held the same meaning for her as it had when Warren was alive, but she thought maybe this would help her in some way.

She said, "I'd only come every now and then, maybe leave some flowers, if that's all right."

Butch said, "Sure, sure. No problem."

Rae Lynn pondered this while he returned her gaze with a bland one of his own. She chose to trust him.

Later on, in the truck, Cornelia said, "Maybe he's changed?"

Rae Lynn said, "Wonders never cease."

Through long winter days, she and Cornelia did the outdoor work quickly and came back in to cook hearty meals in the kitchen. It was in mid-February they had an unexpected week of warmer weather, and the daffodils and forsythia went into an early bloom. Rae Lynn hadn't been to Warren's grave in months, so she cut some of the forsythia branches and daffodils and snipped off a lock of her hair, which had grown past her shoulders again.

She stuck her head in the back door and said, "I'm going to the old place!" as she'd come to call her previous home.

Sudie May was in the kitchen, "Okay."

Cornelia was washing dishes and said, "Want me to come?"

Rae Lynn said, "Nah, I won't be gone long. I'm only going to put some flowers out there."

As she drove, she'd hoped for solitude and was dismayed to see Butch at the door as she pulled up. He disappeared back into the depths of the house, and relieved, she got out and went around the side of the house, toward the headstone. She stood a moment looking. Ida Neill Cobb's stone and Warren's were situated in the shade of the trees. She was about to set the flowers on Warren's when Butch spoke from behind her. He was close. Too close.

"Ain't nothing ever gonna be different for me, Rae Lynn."

His proximity made her draw up.

"I ain't gonna be here but a minute or so, and then I'm gone. Leave me be."

"Like before. Just gone. I don't think so. You owe me. Even more so now, after what I done for you."

He grabbed her the way he had before, his arms like a vise while professing his love for her all over again. She reacted violently, struggling to break free, and somehow, in the chaos of the moment, she freed her arm and when she did, her elbow hit his nose. He let go of her so fast, she fell back, stumbled, and twisted her ankle.

"Damn it, Rae Lynn!" he hollered.

She felt stupid for trusting him. He'd only been pretending, biding his time till she was alone.

She said, "I don't feel the same about you, Butch. I ain't ever *going* to feel like that. I mean, is this what you want? Trying to force me to feel something for you I don't?"

"It's 'cause a him, ain't it. That new feller."

"He ain't got nothing to do with it."

"But . . . I bought this place on account a you."

"Like I said before. I ain't never given you one reason to do none of this."

"I could change my mind, tell Eugene my version, you know."

Furious, she said, "Go on ahead, but I think he'd find it mighty peculiar you bringing it up after all this time. Maybe he'd think *you* shot Warren. Matter a fact, maybe that's what I'd tell him, and say you wanted this place all along."

They glared at each other, his eyes glassy with pain and anger, hers unwavering, determined. After a few tense minutes, his body sagged, the fight seeping out of him like the blood dripping from his nose.

He pointed at her with a shaking, bloody hand and said, "It's best you don't never come back here."

It was true. She thought it could have worked, this little arrangement, but she could see it wouldn't. Facing the gravestone, her eyes traced Warren's name, the dates. She took in the sunny yellow of the flowers against the white marble and committed it to memory.

She said, "I agree."

As she hobbled off toward the truck, Butch yelled, "Not never again!"

She didn't let on she'd heard him.

Back at the farmhouse, she was careful to walk as normal as she could into the kitchen, except she couldn't get anything past Cornelia.

She said, "Were you just now limping?"

Rae Lynn waved a hand through the air in a dismissive gesture, reminiscent of Warren, and said, "I'm all right. I stumbled, turned my ankle."

Del said, "They said you went to the old place this morning?"

She nodded, squirmed a bit, and Del opened his mouth, then closed it.

Then he said, "Was Butch Crandall around?"

"Yes."

"Did he bother you?"

It was such a direct question, it caught Rae Lynn off guard. She first focused on the scene out the window, the pastures dotted with cows, the sky with not a cloud in it. She remembered how Butch acted, and it made her face go hot. She didn't want to lie about it, she wanted to forget it.

Del gave Amos a look, while Sudie May pointed to a chair and said, "Sit."

Rae Lynn said, "I'm fine, I'm fine!"

Cornelia said, "Um-hmm. You can't hardly walk worth a lick."

Del said, "Amos, want to go for a ride with me? I got to go into town and get something."

Amos said, "Sure."

The men left while Cornelia filled a tub with water, pouring in Epsom salts.

She said, "Stick your foot in that."

Rae Lynn did as she was told, and a bit later, Cornelia rubbed turpentine on it and wrapped her ankle in strips of old sheets.

She said, "See now if you can't walk a bit."

Rae Lynn stood and took a step. "Better. Thank you."

Del and Amos came back later on in the afternoon and

when Del got out, he held a wood crate. In the back of the truck she thought she heard clucking. He brought the small crate to her as she sat on the porch, her foot propped on a stool.

He said, "I picked up some things for you."

Puzzled, she pulled aside newspaper to find Ida Neill Cobb's milk glass dinnerware. Shocked, she lifted her eyes to Del's, and he winked.

Amos plopped into the chair beside her and said, "Funny how some find they can be reasonable with only a little persuasion, ain't it right, Del?"

Del said, "Works every time. I got your laying hens too. I'm going back with the trailer to get the mule, while we're cleaning house, so to speak."

Rae Lynn hid her smile as she pressed a plate close to her chest, her chin touching the edge. It was like hugging an old friend. She rose from the chair and hobbled over to the truck to look at her hens.

She turned to the men and murmured, "Thank you, the both of you."

In mid-spring that year, 1933, Del began working the longleaf on the back acreage behind the farmhouse. He'd told her how his granddaddy and his pap always wanted a turpentine farm. She had finally started talking to him some about Warren. Not much, but when certain things came up, she offered a little bit of information.

One evening in the kitchen as she was getting supper on the table, she said, "Me and Warren tried to run a small operation too."

Del said, "Is that how you learned how about turpentining?"

"Yes. We couldn't never seem to get it going like Warren wanted, though. I could help you," she offered.

Del tilted his head, surprised. "Well. All right."

Rae Lynn would never admit she'd been paying attention to Del Reese. She'd observed how he was careful, methodical, and particular in how he went about his work. He was always watchful and had snatched Joey out of the way of the corn picker when Amos missed seeing him one row over, playing at hiding from Norma. Over time, like a pond that's been frozen all winter, the spot gone numb in her after Warren died started to thaw. She began to want to spend more time with him, and Cornelia eyed her knowingly while Del washed his hands at the kitchen sink. Rae Lynn ignored the look and dumped buttery new potatoes into a bowl.

He said, "Amos is bringing in some workers. We could get you a horse. You'd be one of the first female woods riders I ever heard of. You care about doing that?"

Rae Lynn sprinkled salt and pepper and said, "I think that would be great."

"When Peewee comes next week, we might take us a little ride to Rockfish to see about getting the gum into Wilmington. You want to come along?"

Sudie May made a noise as she sat crocheting a small blanket, her belly full term, the baby due any day.

Then she said, "Oh my," and Rae Lynn assumed she was reacting to what Del had asked, like Cornelia was always doing.

She went to the stove, smiling to herself, and stirred the gravy.

Sudie May said, "Oh. Oh. Oh," in such a way, it was clear what was happening.

Cornelia said, "How about that? It's time. Rae Lynn, can you put some water on? Be sure to put them scissors in when it starts to boil. I'll get a few old sheets out of the closet."

Rae Lynn hurried to do what Cornelia asked, and then remembered what Del had asked her.

She turned to him and said, "Yes, I'd like to go."

Norma and Joey started arguing over who wanted what, girl or boy.

Sudie May said, "Oh, gosh, the pains are coming quick. Hurry!"

The children, hearing the different tone in their mother's voice, quit fussing. Cornelia put her arm around Sudie May's waist and helped her up the stairs. Amos and Del took Joey outside with them and disappeared into the barn. After the water boiled, Rae Lynn carried it upstairs, and Norma followed with the rest of the items on a tray. Cornelia had drawn the curtains to keep the evening sun from heating the room too much.

She took what Rae Lynn brought and said, "It's her third, so hopefully it ought to be quick. Considering how she's doing, I'd say before midnight, we're gonna have us another little Whitaker."

Rae Lynn couldn't hardly believe it. In a few hours a new human being would become part of this family. She felt a pang. Any child who benefited from having a family was the luckiest child in the world to her mind. The evening wore on with the occasional cry of pain and distress from the upstairs room. Rae Lynn was in and out often, bringing cold sweet tea and anything else she could think of to help. She thought Sudie May's color was quite good considering, but Cornelia looked tired.

She said, "You all right?"

Cornelia nodded and said, "It won't be long now."

They watched as the miracle of birth unfolded before them. Cornelia was skilled, and a few minutes later, the baby was laid on Sudie May's chest. Cornelia went to cut the cord, but her hands shook.

Rae Lynn said, "You want me to do it?"

Cornelia stepped aside and said, "I'm feeling light-headed. I didn't eat much supper."

Rae Lynn said, "Tell me what to do."

Cornelia directed her where to cut and how to tie it off with some string.

When Rae Lynn was finished, Cornelia said, "She's got to deliver the afterbirth yet."

Rae Lynn said, "Oh."

Cornelia swiped at her forehead, then said, "Law, it's been a while since I helped with a delivery. It ain't no easy thing, is it, Sudie May?"

"It sure ain't."

Rae Lynn said, "Congratulations. He's a fine baby boy."

"Amos said if it was a boy, we ought to name him after his great-granddaddy, Darren. Darren Boyd Whitaker."

Rae Lynn said, "It's a fine name. I'll send Amos up."

As she went downstairs she ran a hand down her flat belly. Could she ever have a baby? She and Warren had tried, but it never happened. Naming it after a relative must feel real special, like honoring family history. This brought another twinge of longing. Warren's death had given her a sense of detachment, as if she was isolated and alone. She now had Cornelia's friendship she cherished, but she had no blood relatives, and being among this family had left an impression. She entered the kitchen and found Amos and Del sitting at the table, expectant faces turned to her.

Rae Lynn smiled at Amos and said, "Congratulations, it's a boy."

Del said, "How about that!"

Amos said, "She's all right? Sudie May?

"She's tired, but perfectly fine."

Amos jumped up from his chair, grabbed Rae Lynn in a big bear hug, and spun her around the room. When he set her back on her feet, it was so quick, she had to catch hold of a chair for balance. He rushed from the room, and she started to tidy the kitchen while Del wandered about, as if he had something to say. Rae Lynn stole glances at him and wondered what he was thinking. Norma appeared, rubbing sleep out of her eyes.

When she heard she had a baby brother, she said, "Shoot. Now him and Joey's gonna gang up on me."

Rae Lynn said, "Well, you'll just have to show them they can't."

"Yeah."

Norma grabbed Rae Lynn's hand and held on to it. She stared at the little girl's hand in hers and raised her eyes to find Del watching them before he turned away abruptly.

The following day, right after supper, and after most everyone had gone to bed, Rae Lynn stepped out onto the porch and sat in a rocker. She pushed it into motion and gazed at the stars sprinkled like salt across the sky. The air was cool yet, but before long the heat of summer would be back. She heard the screen door open, and Cornelia came over and sat in the rocker beside her.

She said, "It's a nice evening."

"It sure is."

"You know, I couldn't have children."

Rae Lynn stopped rocking. "You couldn't?"

"No. Something else Otis didn't let me forget."

"Is it hard delivering someone else's baby?"

Cornelia sighed. "It don't bother me too much."

Rae Lynn said, "Me and Warren tried, but it didn't never happen. He was older, but he'd had Eugene, so I figured it must be me."

"Maybe not. Only one way to know."

Rae Lynn laughed and said, "Now, don't you start."

They rocked for a bit, and after a while, Cornelia reached over and held Rae Lynn's hand. At first, Rae Lynn thought nothing of it. It was only a grateful, shared moment passing between the two of them for how things had turned out. But

Cornelia didn't let go and when her thumb began to lightly stroke the back of Rae Lynn's hand, she grew uncomfortable. She wanted to pull away, but didn't want to hurt Cornelia's feelings. A tiny noise, like a hiccup, broke the silence.

Rae Lynn said, "Nellie?"

"I'm fine. I'm fine."

Rae Lynn didn't push, but she knew good and well Cornelia was crying.

She pulled her hand from Cornelia's and said, "Ain't you happy? At least happier here than before?"

Cornelia wiped her eyes.

"Some days, I'm the happiest I've ever been. I get these moments, though, when I get to thinking too hard on things."

"What things?"

Cornelia wouldn't meet Rae Lynn's eyes when she said, "You ever think back on what happened at Swallow Hill?"

"Every day. Why I thought I could pull off that harebrained idea. The only good thing to come out of it was meeting you and Del."

"I'm talking about a particular thing."

"The sweat box?"

"No, though I think a lot about that too, how you almost didn't make it. I'm talking about what happened in the kitchen, why Otis went nuts."

"Oh."

In the dim light of the evening, Rae Lynn saw how well Cornelia hid within herself, but she wasn't hiding now. The same look she'd got before radiated from her without restraint.

Cornelia said, "I know it ain't the same for you. It's all right. Truth is, I can't help myself, how *I* feel. I can't. I thought if I tell you my own secret, like you told me about Warren, maybe I can try to accept my lot in life, such as it is."

Rae Lynn didn't know what to say, other than, "All right."

"I liked someone once, back when I was sixteen. Her name

was Rebecca. We started spending time together. She liked coming to my house because her daddy was so strict, and she was afraid of him. She came to the house one afternoon, and Mama was busy working in the garden. We weren't paying attention. We got wrapped up in a moment, and Mama caught us. She told my daddy. He was friends with Otis's daddy, and Otis had always had his eye on me. That's how I come to marry him. I was an abomination to them, and they wanted nothing more to do with me unless I did what they wanted. So, I did. As you might've guessed, it changed nothing. They don't want to see me, especially if I've left Otis. This is the real reason why I couldn't go home."

Rae Lynn grabbed Cornelia's hand again and held on to it tight.

She said, "Nellie. I can't lie to you. It's true, I don't feel the same as you, but I do care about you. As a friend. I hope you can accept that."

Cornelia gave her a sad little smile. "Of course. It's the best gift you can give me."

The melancholy little smile Cornelia gave her was heartbreaking and honest. They sat for a long while, quiet and peaceful, both women pondering what the future might hold for them.

A week later, Rae Lynn followed Del to the barn, where he was cleaning and organizing the turpentine tools. He'd laid out an assortment including tin gutters, Herty cups and aprons, bark hacks, pullers, hanging boxes filled with nails and gutters that would be carried from tree to tree to tack tin, and in another corner she saw all the implements needed for dipping, from buckets, to dip barrels, and to dip irons. He was organized, methodical, and careful. It didn't seem right to compare him to Warren, but she couldn't help it. She rubbed at her half-missing finger. She felt confident she wouldn't have to worry about carelessness or accidents.

She said, "You got most everything you need."

He said, "I do. Only waiting on the work hands, and they'll be coming next week. And a horse for you. We ought to go look at one I saw over to Rockfish. How's the baby and mama doing this morning?"

"Sudie May said he ate twice last night. She said it's all he wants to do. And sleep."

Del started sharpening the bark hacks, his movements rhythmic and efficient.

He said, "Them Whitaker boys are gonna be tall like their daddy." He pushed the hair off of his forehead, and Rae Lynn thought he'd gone from relaxed to a little nervous. She had this effect on him lately, like he'd get to thinking on something, look at her, and just as quick, turn away.

He continued talking and said, "Hard to believe we been gone from Swallow Hill eight months now."

Rae Lynn said, "I know. It don't seem like I was ever there, sometimes."

Del studied his boots, then lifted his head.

"You want to go into town with me later on today?"

Rae Lynn picked up a bark hack, hefting it in her hand, remembering the work she'd done at the camp, the aching muscles, along with the gratification of being able to labor in such a way. The way he asked her sounded different, like there was meaning behind the question.

"Sure. I don't think Sudie May needs me."

Del said, "She might not, but I do."

Rae Lynn wasn't sure she'd heard him right.

"What did you say?"

He didn't answer.

Instead, he held out a hand and said, "Come with me."

All of a sudden nervous, she slipped her hand in his, and he gripped it tight. They left the barn, and he led her across the yard, toward the woods. She caught movement out of the corner of her eye and when she stole a glance, Cornelia was waving at her madly and making gestures in the area of her heart. Rae Lynn suppressed a smile, paid attention to Del as he started pointing here and there, talked about the work, the vision he had of the land, of a family, and of her by his side.

He turned to her, and he said, "Can you see it?"

Rae Lynn said, "Yes, I can."

Chapter 35

Del

Bladen County, 1940

He'd made some mistakes in his life, no doubt. Too many, if he was being truthful, but marrying Rae Lynn hadn't been one of them. He sat in one of the rockers on the porch, watching her tease Peewee. Cornelia, Amos, and Sudie May were shucking corn, listening too, and laughing now and then. Peewee had kept in touch with Del and visited at least twice a year. Del turned his attention to his children, Delwood, six, and Jeremiah, four, and baby daughter, Belinda. His thoughts went deep. He had to make them mistakes, go through all he'd been through to fully appreciate what he had and he was grateful. He'd already started teaching the boys about the longleaf, the skills of a woods rider, as well as how a cooper worked and what happened in a distillery. He wanted all his children to understand the entire way of life in turpentining, end to end. For him, it was important because in that understanding, they would appreciate it; that appreciation would make his vision, his love for the pines everlasting.

To that end, he and Amos had joined up with the American Turpentine Farmers Association (ATFA) and planned to take their boys to a few of the local meetings. They'd heard about the "Olustee process" through the ATFA, a new way of distilling pine gum with steam, and he thought it would be interesting to let them see the plant down in Hoboken, Georgia.

The women went into the house to finish cleaning the corn, and the men followed, talking about how the longleaf was becoming a tree of the past and the same would eventually happen for the work of turpentiners; their trade would disappear like the trees. All of them were aware of the one area in North Carolina that still had "round timber," the name for "old growth" trees. They were located in Moore County, purchased about three decades before by James Boyd, father of nature-loving Helen Boyd Dull. The story goes after an impromptu delay of their train in Southern Pines, James Boyd and his daughter took a carriage up to a ridge, where, when they looked down at the surrounding area, they saw lumberjacks taking the majestic pines down. She pleaded with her father to save the remaining trees.

Peewee said, "Shoot. Ain't gonna be long 'fore nobody even knows what a longleaf pine looks like, much less about turpentining."

Del said, "Not if I can help it. That's why I wanted to get something going here. We can work the trees and then let them be. Let them stand as evidence of that work."

Peewee said, "The name is perfect. Memorable. Tar Heel Turpentine. Wonder how you come up with that."

Rae Lynn and Del looked at each other, smiling.

Peewee said, "By the way, I got some news on old Crow right before I came. Slim Smith called me the other day, said he'd finally met his match."

Rae Lynn stopped pulling the yellow threads off the kernels. "Somebody beat him up?"

Cornelia snorted. "That would be too good for him."

Peewee rubbed his head and then shook it as if he still couldn't believe what he'd heard.

"Naw. Sounds like he got more'n he bargained for by about fifteen feet worth. Some old gator out there in the Okefenokee."

Incredulous, Del said, "It got him?"

"Apparently he was doing the usual, chasing some poor colored feller through the swamp. They heard it more'n saw it. Said he went to screaming, carrying on, and he stopped sudden-like. By the time they got there, all that was left was that hat a his floating in the water, crow feather still in it. Nothing else."

Del said, "I sure didn't care none for him, but what a helluva way to go."

They sat quiet for a while until Del pulled out his harmonica. He played several slow, melancholy tunes, and everyone, the children included, sat quietly, reflecting on the lonesome notes. He finally stopped and stared around the table at the faces of the people he cared about most in this world, and knew if he were to die in his sleep this very night, he would go a contented man.

Chapter 36

Rae Lynn

Rae Lynn drove her old truck down the dirt road and pulled it under a large pecan tree by the farmhouse to keep it in the shade. The men had taken the boys to Rockfish to unload barrels of gum into the warehouse, and Rae Lynn expected them back anytime, hungry as a pack of wolves.

She hurried into the house, calling out to Sudie May, "Yoo-hoo!"

She dropped her purse and keys on the table by the door, kicked off her shoes, and walked barefoot across the worn floorboards and into the kitchen.

Baby Belinda, who everyone had taken to calling Beebee, was in the high chair, and Norma was attempting to help her teach herself to eat. Beebee had chicken-n-dumplings on her face and on the floor. She waved a chicken leg happily at her mother and gave her a newly sprouted toothy grin.

Norma said, "I tried to help her get it in her, not on her."

Rae Lynn smiled.

She said, "You should've seen her when I tried to feed her

beets," and to Beebee, "Look at you! I need to put you in the bath."

Sudie May came in from the pantry off the kitchen and said, "Despite what's on the floor and in her hair, she still ate a lot. I saw what was in the bowl before she started."

"She takes after her daddy. Well, me too, 'cause I feel like I could eat that whole pot of dumplings right about now. I can't seem to eat enough lately."

Sudie May set the jars she'd retrieved on the table, and said, "Huh. Sounds a lot like last time you were pregnant."

Rae Lynn gave her a sage look, a hand on her belly.

"That's because I am."

Sudie May's eyes flew open, and she rushed over to Rae Lynn and hugged her.

"Oh my. I'm so happy for you."

Rae Lynn said, "Funny, Del only mentioned the other day he was going to start building the extension onto the house. We're gonna need it. It seems a peculiar thing to say. When we first come here, there was so many rooms I'd get lost."

Beebee hiccupped, and the women turned to her as she hurled the chicken leg on the floor.

Rae Lynn said, "I reckon you're done."

She wiped off the baby's face and carried her outside. The men and boys were back from town, and she watched from the porch as Delwood and Jeremiah jumped out of the back of the truck, along with Joey and Darren. Del blew her a kiss, before going to help Amos unload the new barrels they'd picked up. Rae Lynn's heart trembled at the sight of them. Her husband, and sons. Del showed the boys different ways to roll the barrels so they'd be easier to maneuver while standing behind them, helping guide small hands. He was an excellent father, patient and loving. She squeezed Beebee to her, sniffed at the soft hair on the top of her head, her baby smell coming through despite the fact she'd practically bathed in her dinner. She and Del had agreed they wanted a big family, and they were well on their way, though Del had his doubts in the beginning.

Right before they married, he said, "I need to tell you something." He acted in a way he never had. Nervous, preoccupied.

He sat her down, took hold of her hands, and said, "There's things about me you need to know."

He told her about his past, how he'd been, what he'd done. He told her what happened to him in the grain bin, and how it had affected him.

He said, "I tried to be with anything in a skirt. All kinds a women. Other men's wives. I didn't care. That is, until this farmer I worked for, named Moe Sutton, caught me with his. Had me work in his grain bin, and I think . . ."

He stopped talking.

She said, "You think what?"

He went through the events of what he saw, and what happened after.

Rae Lynn had taken his hand and said, "You think you might've died?"

He raised his shoulders, then expanded a little more on his inability to, as he put it, aim high for the sky.

She said, "You can't . . . ?"

He gave her such a forlorn look right then and said, "I ain't sure."

Rae Lynn emitted a soft, "Oh."

"Yeah."

She said, "We'll just take it one day at a time. I was married seven years and never got pregnant. I don't know what to think about that. Warren had Eugene and all. I got something I need to tell you too, speaking of Warren."

He said, "You ain't got to if you don't want to."

She said, "No, I need to."

And so she did, observing his face, his eyes mostly, looking for his reaction to what happened. There was none, only quiet listening, and a nod here and there as she poured out all of the pain and distress of what it had entailed. What it had taken out of her. When she was finished, his grip tightened on her hand.

He said, "It's terrible, but what you done was merciful at that point, not murder." And the most important thing he could say was what he said next. "I'd have done the same thing. It's a hurt near about impossible to get over, but I'm hoping when I tell you you're the first woman I've ever truly loved, Rae Lynn, it'll help, if only a little."

Her heart soared from out of the darkness that day, and here they were now. Three children later, another one on the way, a small but flush turpentine farm, and most important of all, each other. Rae Lynn couldn't get enough of looking at their children, watching them when they didn't know it. She found herself thinking on how her and Del's blood ran in their veins. They were an indelible symbol of what they'd accomplished; like the catfaces on the trunks of the longleaf pines, they were the imprint of their love, their existence proof of what they'd been, who they were, even long after they'd left this Earth. For now, all she needed was to hold them close, and so she went to them and did just that.

Chapter 37

Delwood and Jeremiah

Bladen County, 1942

Dark haired like their mother, they had their father's startling blue eyes. Eight-year-old Delwood, born in May of '34, was quiet and thoughtful, while almost six-year-old Jeremiah (as he liked to remind everyone), born in August of '36, chattered endlessly and couldn't sit still. On this early summer day, they followed their older cousins, Joey and Darren, as they ran through the woods to where their parents waited. With the Reese boys ran their coonhound, Rabbit, named so because of his long, floppy ears and twitchy nose. Delwood and Jeremiah were excited. Today, their father was going to show them how to make the funny catfaces on the special pine trees he called the longleaf. The Reese boys each carried a small tool made by their father. He told them it was a bark hack.

Since they were old enough to walk, they'd spent a good deal of time in the woods with their parents, and like their older cousins, the Reese boys already knew the names of all the different pines, the hardwoods, plus many other plants and flowers. They knew about scrape, pine gum, pitch, tar, and that smelly stuff called turpentine, which their mother used for most anything that ailed them. They knew about crops of trees, the small sections the work hands called drifts, but most of all, they knew the work their family did was hard, but meaningful. The special trees, the longleaf, their father said, used to be all over, but now, most were gone.

The boys spotted their mother and their little sister, Bee-bee, walking around smacking her hands and singing. Their mother was by their father, and both were talking with Aunt Sudie May, Uncle Amos, and their adopted relative, Uncle Peewee, along with several work hands near a drift of trees. Cousin Norma held their baby brother, Joshua.

As they ran up, their father squatted down eye level to talk to them.

He said, "It's gonna take time before your work looks like this," and he pointed to the odd markings on a tree that made the catface. The face was almost as tall as Jeremiah from top to bottom. He said, "You got to be patient."

Their mother came close, listening, while their father spoke. To the boys, she was the prettiest lady they'd ever seen and they loved her with all their might. They spent hours look-ing for and bringing her flowers and colorful rocks from the river. What she gave them in return they craved. Like when it was nighttime, she'd slip quiet into their room, kiss them on the cheek, and sit in a rocking chair by an open window, the curtains shifting and swirling on a warm, summer wind. She'd hum softly until they fell asleep.

Young Delwood pointed at a tree trunk and said, "Mother, show us how you done it."

She had a bark hack hanging from the waistband of her trousers, and she took it in hand.

Uncle Peewee, who the boys understood really wasn't their uncle and who came to the farmhouse at least twice a year, said, "She was as good as any of them men I used to hire."

They watched close as their mother took the tool and walked over to one of the longleaf pines yet to be worked. She ran her hand down the tree trunk, the one missing part of a finger an endless fascination to the boys. She'd not yet told them how it happened. She studied the surface of the tree for a second, then lifted the tool and struck against the bark. She struck again and made a swipe to the right. She cleaned the streak to the pale-yellow wood with a few shorter swipes. She did the same to the opposite side, until she had another mark that slanted the opposite way. The marks were like a V.

Father said, "Ain't lost your touch atall. By my calculations, you'd make your daily counts. You're hired."

It was this little joke they had between them. She wrinkled her nose at him and pointed at what she'd done as Delwood and Jeremiah looked on.

She said, "See? Now what happens next with this fresh new streak we cut above this gutter, Delwood?"

Delwood glanced at her, then using his forefinger, he carefully pointed at each item as he recited what he'd been taught.

"This tin gutter here guides the gum so it runs into the cup. When the cup is full, it gets dipped out and put into a bucket. The bucket gets dumped into a big barrel, and all the barrels get took to Rockfish. They go down the river to Wilmington to be dis-dis-distaled."

Mother beamed. "Distilled. Very good. And what's it called, what I just done?"

Both boys yelled, "Chipping!"

"What's it called when we put up the gutters?"

They hollered, "Tacking tin!"

"When we get the gum from the cups?"

They shouted, "Dipping!"

Their father and mother said, "Very, very good."

Young Delwood smiled, his chest puffed out. Sometimes their parents would talk about another time, back when they first met at this place they'd worked along with Aunt Nellie, who had also been adopted as family, like Uncle Peewee. That place was called Swallow Hill. The boys didn't know what to make of these stories. Swallow Hill sounded scary, especially when their parents talked about the box thing they'd been put into by a bad man. They didn't like him, the one named Crow. They'd overheard one night when they were supposed to be asleep how he'd almost killed their mother, and how he'd poured tar on her and Aunt Nellie. They were relieved they wouldn't never have to meet him, or the other bad man who'd been married to Aunt Nellie. They were like the bogeyman to them.

If the boys were sad at all, it was over Aunt Nellie. They missed her a lot, but they tried not to let their mother know how much. After she got sick, their mother did everything she could to help her get better. They knew this because sometimes they would listen outside the door of Aunt Nellie's room, where she was always resting. Their mother urged her to drink and to eat. Aunt Nellie's sickness started right after Christmas the year before. They were at the supper table and she'd picked at her food and acted like she was having trouble swallowing. Their mother had asked if she felt okay.

Aunt Nellie had said, "It's the oddest thing," and she pointed at her throat.

Mother said, "You have a sore throat?"

Aunt Nellie said, "No, it feels like a lump there I can't get rid of, like when you got to cry and you hold back."

Their mother brought her water, tea, Cokes, and soups. Aunt Nellie got to choking, even over those things. The doctor came to see what he could do for her, and the boys steered clear of him because he'd given them a shot a time or two in his previous visits.

He disappeared into Aunt Nellie's room, and when he and their mother came out, she started crying after the doctor said, "Six months."

Aunt Nellie passed in the late spring of '41 and their mother, who had called her "Sister," stayed sad for a good while. The boys picked her violets and wild roses off the fence and brought them to her by the fistfuls. They dove in the river, searching for their special rocks, and set them about her room. They only wanted to see her smile again. Their father stayed close by, took her on small trips. Eventually their mother was her old self again, but every week, right after church, and without fail, she tended Aunt Nellie's grave. She'd been buried next to their grandparents. They'd see her sit, and talk, and wondered what she said. Sometimes their father went too. When they came back, they would go out on the porch, rock in the rocking chairs, hold hands, and not say much. The boys watched all this, mildly troubled their parents were sometimes sad, but they were too. They'd loved Aunt Nellie.

One day their mother received a letter and her reaction disturbed them immensely. After she read it, she sank into a chair and stared a long time out the kitchen door without speaking, not even when they asked her a question. Their father came in, and she waved the piece of paper in the air. They went to their room, and the boys waited in the hall after the door clicked shut. They heard the murmur of their voices, and their mother crying. A bit later, they all went to this house in Harnett County. She said she used to live there, but now a man named Butch Crandall lived there, alone. Another man came that day too and introduced himself as Mr. Eugene Cobb. He gave the boys such a piercing look, they grew uncomfortable.

They didn't know who Mr. Cobb or Mr. Crandall were exactly, but Mr. Cobb acted real important, so they figured he must be. Mr. Crandall focused only on their mother.

Mr. Cobb didn't say a word to them, and the only thing he said to their mother was, "Good to meet you. Sign here."

Then, he gave her an envelope. After, he finally turned to the boys and they locked eyes with him. He reached into his pocket and pulled out two pieces of hard candy, their favorite, butterscotch.

He said to their mother and father, "Fine-looking boys. I wish you all well," before he walked away.

Their mother looked relieved.

Mr. Crandall said, "I reckon it's settled."

Their mother didn't say much, only, "Yes."

Before they left, she visited a grave. Their father stood beside her quietly while she got out a hankie and wiped her eyes.

Delwood took her hand, worked the candy to the side of his mouth, pointed at the headstone, and said, "Mother, who is Warren Cobb?"

She said, "Someone I used to know. I'll tell you and Jeremiah about him one day." She handed the envelope to their father and said, "We can put it aside for the boys' schooling."

They said their goodbyes to Mr. Crandall and Mr. Cobb and went back to the big farmhouse on the Cape Fear River, where the boys immediately ran upstairs to put on their swim trunks. Back outside they dashed along the embankment, racing to their rope swing. Young Delwood reached it first, grabbed on, and swung out over the water, and for a few seconds, he was suspended in the heavens. He dropped into the river and bobbed up like a cork. Jeremiah came next, and they did this over and over, each time looking toward the edge of sloping hillside to see their mother and father watching over them. Beebee zipped in and out between them on the grass, and their father ran after her, grabbed her, and swung her around, mirroring their soaring play. Their mother held Joshua, the one everyone said resembled her most.

The family stayed on the river bank all afternoon, and the boys laughed as they played with a joy that was untroubled and carefree. They were contented, happy. Time and again, they were told how much they were loved, but they already knew this implicitly in their hearts. A while back, their father had taught them about longleaf pine roots. He'd said the main one, called the tap root, was as wide as the tree and went underground a long way, up to fifteen feet. He'd told them the trees could live five hundred years, and to them, that was forever. They paused in their play now and again to watch their parents, and what they saw were two people whose love was as deep and as solid as the tap root of their beloved longleaf, and the boys were certain their love was forever.

Author's Note

I was plundering the Internet looking for my next story idea when I ran across the term *naval stores*. If it sounds strange to you, you're not alone. These two seemingly mismatched words are like pairing a tennis shoe with a dress shoe, and I got my share of quizzical looks when I first mentioned them. I knew nothing of this industry that existed hundreds of years ago, when ships were wooden and powered by wind through tall sails. From Colonial times into the last quarter of the twentieth century, naval stores were an integral and necessary part of the South's economy, and the region was renowned worldwide for the products. Today, there remain a few spots in the southeastern United States that still rely on these goods as a main part of their livelihood. So what the heck is it? Naval stores make perfect sense once you understand it's rosin, tar, pitch, and turpentine, which are produced from oleoresin, or pine gum. Tar and pitch were used to waterproof wooden ships, sails, masts, and rope. As use of these vessels declined, the trade kept going strong because rosin and turpentine remained in high demand. These are used in common household products like soap, paper, paint, and varnish.

Next came my understanding a particular pine tree, the longleaf, was most desirable for its high production of gum. A slash pine comes in a close second. Here I was, thinking the longleaf was just another type of pine tree like the loblolly, pond, Eastern white, and others located throughout the South. Sadly, millions of acres of longleaf have been greatly diminished given the process of harvesting gum for naval stores. Long ago, from Virginia to Texas, ninety million acres of forests were filled with these trees. Today, only three million acres of what is called "virgin" or "old growth" timber exists. Conservation efforts are in place, and this includes the special periodic burning of the area around the trees to encourage seedlings to root and grow. That's right, fire encourages longleaf growth and restores the unique grassland ecosystem known as a pine forest savanna. About an hour from my home (and elsewhere) exist patches of old growth timber, a rarity. The one near me is in an aptly named location, Southern Pines. There is mention of this area toward the end of the book and a bit of the history of how it came to be.

Who extracted the pine gum? Small landowners hired a few laborers to do the work, while labor camps were often used by large landowners. In the early twentieth century, the famous writer Zora Neale Hurston spent time in Florida documenting what it was like to work in such a camp. Her interviews became part of the anthropological work *Mules and Men*. Camps used a debt peonage system, ensuring workers were always at a financial disadvantage. Add in the woods riders (camp bosses specific to turpentine) and the forms of punishment to address issues, and many compared the camps to a form of slavery. Still, workers enjoyed an uncommon peace and solitude in the forests, and came to labor in them for that very reason.

North Carolina was at one time the top producer of naval stores in the world. Those from here who did this work came to be known as "tar heels," because pine gum stuck to the soles of their bare feet. The name used to be an insult, but, as history tells it, it was flipped into an accolade during the Civil War when soldiers from North Carolina were said to have stayed in the battle, as if they had tar on their heels. Today it is a well-known nickname for the sports teams associated with the University of North Carolina at Chapel Hill, and of course we're known as the Tar Heel State.

The discovery of this bygone history was one of those lightning strike moments authors sometimes have. For me as a writer, it was time for something a little bit different, and this book is the result of that effort. Even while applying a fictional narrative, I hope I have in some small way honored the Southern states that were part of this history and, more important, offered a tribute to the original tar heels who lived and toiled in the deep piney woods of the South.

THE SAINTS OF SWALLOW HILL

Donna Everhart

ABOUT THIS GUIDE

The suggested questions are included to enhance your group's reading of Donna Everhart's *The Saints of Swallow Hill*!

DISCUSSION QUESTIONS

1. What did you make of what happened to Del in the grain bin?

2. What is your view of Rae Lynn and Warren's marriage? Do you think it was a little bit of convenience for them both at first that ultimately turned to love?

3. Del is immediately on guard after meeting Elijah Sweeney, a.k.a. Crow, sensing the man is trouble. Have you ever met anyone who gave you the same sense? Did your instincts prove you right?

4. Swallow Hill was filled with dangers, not only from an environmental perspective, but with regard to some of the practices. How did the setting of the labor camp impact the story for you?

5. Keeping in mind the time frame, and the need for people to be very self-sufficient, especially in remote areas, would/could you have done what Rae Lynn did for Warren after his accident?

6. A method of solitary confinement, known as a sweat box, is used in this story. How did it make you feel reading about the experiences of individuals placed inside them?

7. Crow shares his appreciation for the trees and doesn't want to see them ruined unnecessarily. Del admires this. Did Crow's view of nature in this way give you a bit of a different perspective of him? How did you feel when you learned what happened to him?

8. Before reading this story, were you familiar with the naval store industry and the distinctive terminology and tools used?

9. Rae Lynn and Cornelia are both strong and brave women in their own way. What was Rae Lynn's strongest, bravest act? What about Cornelia's?

10. Both Del and Rae Lynn must confront their past in order to move forward. Are you aware of something from your own past that has held you back?

11. Did you have a favorite character/s? Which one/s, and why?

12. What does the title mean to you?